G A Y   E   A

WITH THE RISE OF GAY CONSCIOUSNESS and pride has come a growing recognition and increasingly open appreciation of gay erotic literature. This exciting anthology, by acclaimed editor and author John Preston, brings together the outstanding examples of a genre no longer consigned to a literary netherworld of private printings. Including such major mainstream writers as Edmund White and Anne Rice, as well as other masters of sexually arousing fiction, this is a collection that will arrest the attention of both gay and straight readers, as it brings to life the full spectrum of gay sexuality.

FLESH AND THE WORD

JOHN PRESTON is the editor of *Hometowns,* the author of *The Big Gay Book,* and the former editor-in-chief of *The Advocate.* He is a renowned erotic writer, with novels that include the celebrated Master series and *Mr. Benson.* He lives in Portland, Maine.

EDITED AND WITH AN
INTRODUCTION BY
JOHN PRESTON

F L E S H

AND THE

W O R D

AN ANTHOLOGY OF
EROTIC WRITING

A PLUME BOOK

PLUME

Published by the Penguin Group
Penguin Books USA Inc., 375 Hudson Street, New York, New York 10014, U.S.A.
Penguin Books Ltd, 27 Wrights Lane, London W8 5TZ, England
Penguin Books Australia Ltd, Ringwood, Victoria, Australia
Penguin Books Canada Ltd, 10 Alcorn Avenue Toronto, Ontario, Canada M4V 3B2
Penguin Books (N.Z.) Ltd, 182–190 Wairau Road, Auckland 10, New Zealand

Penguin Books Ltd, Registered Offices:
Harmondsworth, Middlesex, England

First published by Plume, an imprint of New American Library,
a division of Penguin Books USA Inc.

Simultaneously published in Dutton hardcover edition.

First Printing, March, 1992
9 10 8

Ⓟ REGISTERED TRADEMARK—MARCA REGISTRADA

Pages 331–334 constitute an extenion of this copyright page.

LIBRARY OF CONGRESS CATALOGING-IN-DATA:

Flesh and the word: an anthology of erotic writing / edited and with an
introduction by John Preston.
p.   cm.
ISBN 0-452-26775-7
1. Gay men—Literary collections.   2. Erotic literature, American.   3. Gays'
writings, American.   I. Preston. John.
PS509.H57F57   1992
813'.01083538—dc20
91-31910
CIP

Printed in the United States of America
Set in Garamond No. 3

Designed by Steven N. Stathakis

For Anne Rice,
who always said
it was worth doing.

If a writer uses literary craft to provoke sexual delight, he is doing an artist's job.

—KENNETH TYNAN

CONTENTS

ACKNOWLEDGMENTS

PAT CALIFIA, LEIGH RUTLEDGE, SCOTT O'HARA, STEven Saylor, William Schwalbe, Mark Thompson, and T. R. Witomski were among those who recommended stories and essays to me. Thanks to them and all the others who made suggestions.

Celeste DeRoche and Gail Geisenhainer typed much of the manuscript. It was a great help to me and kept them in dinner conversation for many months in their home in far northern Maine, a warming influence on their friends, no doubt.

My able and stalwart assistant, Tom Hagerty, found reservoirs of enthusiasm for researching, proofreading, and filing the material for this book that were much deeper than those he's tapped for any other project. It's been inspiring to see the ardor of youth in full force.

More seriously, the publication of gay male erotica is not one of the most popular undertakings in our society at this time. I am deeply appreciative that my agent, Peter Ginsberg, my editor, Matt Sartwell, his assistant, Peter Borland, and the officers of NAL/Dutton, especially Arnold Dolin and Elaine Koster, were all willing to take this project seriously and to support it fully.

Robert Riger is another person who once again performed a vital supportive role while I worked on this book. It was no less costly to him than his assistance on other projects, but I'm sure it provided unique entertainment. (May all your boyfriends be pornographers!)

Finally, I'm grateful to all the writers and all the editors who worked for so long to make gay magazine publishing a reality, often without any financial reward. They join me in the belief that sex is something to be taken seriously.

INTRODUCTION

MY LIFE

WITH

PORNOGRAPHY

WHEN I WAS A TEENAGER IN THE SIXTIES I USED TO find every excuse possible to travel, alone, through Harvard Square. There for sale at a kiosk that specialized in foreign and exotic publications were small, digest-sized, black-and-white photo magazines, many of them from Britain, that featured pages of nearly naked men. The magazines were almost hidden in a corner of the booth with their titles—names like *Physique Pictorial*—hardly visible. Their existence took my breath away. Getting from the stand to the cash register with an obliquely titled, pocket-sized magazine took all my adolescent courage, and then I could never look the clerk in the eye. I most often wouldn't dare take the books home after I bought them—something might be discovered there—but I'd find some private place to sit (usually a library) and study the images, a young boy's erection painful in my pants. I would memorize the faces and the bodies and keep them in my mind, my private reserve of sensual delight.

It wasn't that there weren't other images that I could make

sexual. Harlan Green writes about a common teenage experience in his novel, *What the Dead Remember* (New York: Dutton, 1991):

> . . . I picked up *The Saturday Evening Post*. . . . I turned the page and stopped. They were already complete, requiring no imagination; as full-blown as images on television. I breathed out, transfixed at what I saw, but it was more like a space within me, really. I saw a picture of men and boys in black-and-white advertising Hanes or BVDs.

I had those same experiences with such seemingly innocent media as the Sears Roebuck mail-order catalog, with its pages and pages of underwear models.

What made *Physique Pictorial* and its peers so devastatingly powerful was their sexual purpose. Their models were not merely male mannequins on whom clothes were hung, their crotches airbrushed into a soft, sexless mound. These were nearly naked men whose photographers obviously knew they were creating erotic images as they emphasized the lines of barely draped genitals with lighting and pose.

The newsstand still stocks newspapers from around the globe, esoteric journals, and a plethora of specialized publications. Today, there are dozens of magazines published in a large format on glossy paper with art-directed covers aimed at attracting gay men. Their names boldly announce their interest: *Honcho, Jock, Inches*. They aren't so unique anymore. They are, in fact, publications that I can buy in my current hometown of Portland, Maine.

Three decades ago, their forebears were only sold in New England in that kiosk in Harvard Square, at least so far as I knew. Today, I pick up my copy of *Mandate* with its muscular model nearly nude on the cover (totally nude in the centerfold), and talk to Joe, the Portland storekeeper, about the weather. He already knows I'm gay and thinks my buying such a magazine is as noteworthy as the fact that hundreds of other men buy *Sports Illustrated*. (And I'm one of the men who'll buy

SI, especially when it has a photo feature on Australian life-guards in their rolled-up bathing briefs.) Things have changed.

Traveling from my youth with its clandestine homosexuality to my middle age with its public announcement of my gay life has been a trip that was aided and abetted by pornography. There are certainly other things that have happened in the intervening years, and there are certainly many elements of who I am politically and socially that say I might have found this way without pornography, but it certainly wouldn't have been as easy, nor as pleasurable.

Michael Bronski has written about the place of porn in the lives of gay men like myself ("Art and Evidence," *Gay Community News*, October 21–26, 1990). He points out that, even before there were such magazines as *Physique Pictorial*, gay men had pornographic icons. He recalls the presence of the reproductions of Michelangelo's *David* that were displayed in many gay men's homes in the fifties and, in fact, earlier. The *David*s were not just erotically pleasing pieces of inexpensive art; they were also signals to visitors in the know that the home-owners were homosexual, functioning as a kind of aesthetic morse code of sexual identity.

Whether it's that mass-produced Michelangelo or an early "physique" magazine or today's commercially driven *Mandate*, pornography has real functions in gay men's lives. Bronski refers to two of them:

> By making the desire flesh, the representation immediately brings the desire into the world of the physically possible: out of the mind and into the realm of potential interaction. Desire becomes a physical object. [Then] once this sexual object has been acknowledged, the sexual identity of the viewer is reinforced.

Those are precisely the purposes that pornography served for me in my adolescence. No matter how coy or how vulgar the representations of men as sex symbols were, holding those magazines gave me a real statement about what turned me on. It was both safer and more pleasurable to look at images of men who were straightforwardly posing for me. There was a strange anxiety about my fantasies of the captain of the high school basketball team, an inherent understanding that exposure of that lust could produce violence. There wasn't that same danger when I looked at a model from Kensington Square Studios of London. It also felt more realistic, whether or not it was true, to think of myself in a relationship with one of the models. Whatever else that model was doing, I could believe he was posing for me. I didn't find him in undress by mistake, the way I felt I did with my Sears models.

I wasn't simply consuming those images. I was beginning to conceive of myself as one of them. One of the excitements— and confusions—of being gay was understanding that I could be, in so many different ways, both the active and the passive partner. Sexologists might use those terms only in relation to who performs what physiological acts, but I was quickly aware that there was a whole range of possibilities, emotional as well as sexual. Bronski again:

> While it is true that the viewer [of pornography] with his lust incited may want to hold, own, or have sex with the object, it is equally true that he may also want to "be" the object. As opposed to heterosexual porn, there is usually an element of identification with, as well as desire for, the sexual object.

Whatever the power of these visual images, it was reading that led me to seriously explore sexuality. I consumed great numbers of books. My parents were proud of my literary leanings, and they were careful not to censor my reading material. In fact, they often sent me to visit an older cousin who was studying literature at Boston College and who, with their encouragement, gave me access to the latest writing. I remember that avant-garde literary journals like the *Evergreen Review* were some of the first places I found contemporary accounts of homosexuality, and I know that cousin introduced me to those publications. (She probably also introduced me to Harvard Square; she still lives near there today.) Reading anything that was homosexually oriented was exciting in the sixties. A simple passage of a Nelson Algren novel that acknowledged a gay character's sexuality, no matter how sordid the context, was important to me.

(There were moments of homosexual lust and life in the classics, as well. Petronius was only one of the many Greek and Roman authors whom I read for sex. No matter how much my high school English teacher insisted that Walt Whitman was only talking about friendship—and she did insist on that—I knew better as soon as I read *Leaves of Grass*.)

For years I could only find myself and the life I wanted reflected in these occasional moments of publishing. Whenever something came out that was focused on homosexuality, I was first in line at the bookstore, having scanned all the reviewing vehicles for even the briefest mention of the word. But such arrivals were few and far between and often had miserable endings, not the sort of climax that was going to feed my fantasies of how such a life could be led. Moreover, they usually dealt with sex in a circumspect manner; they couldn't help me deal with my burgeoning sexuality.

I also began to notice that there were printed books available in the kinds of shops that had come to carry *Physique Pictorial*. Such books may not have been stocked in the literary bookstores near my college in Chicago or near my parents' home in suburban Boston, but they certainly met much of my desire for sexually explicit and educational reading. These books made the fantasies of happiness I'd imagined when looking at the photo magazines even more complete. In a real sense, their stories laid the groundwork for my eventual coming out as an activist. They were helping me and others perceive of a happiness that we had been told homosexual men couldn't achieve.

In another article, "Classics from the Closet" (*Guide*, February 1991), Michael Bronski examines some of the pre-Stonewall dirty novels. He points to *Gay Whore*, a novel written by "Jack Love" that was published in 1967, two years before the Stonewall Riots, which supposedly marked the beginning of gay liberation. While writers and publishers in 1967 were limited to a much more soft-core approach than would be used in por-

nography later on, a description of a sex scene between the
main character, Jack, and Bill ended with a paragraph that
Bronski finds "extraordinary":

> They lay back, breathing heavily, limp. They cuddled to-
> gether, holding on to one another without embarrassment
> and it seemed obvious to Jack that he had never been so
> satisfied in all his life.

What's so noteworthy about the passage is the idea that sex
with another man would lead a character to such happiness.
Even most porn before that date seemed to feel a need to leave
its heroes in at best an ambiguous position. As Bronski goes
on to say, "Gone are the angst-filled gay boys who are endlessly
confused. Here is gay sex for its own sake—without compro-
mise and without apology."

From these small beginnings there formed a gay literature
in the seventies—not just an occasional volume that featured a
gay person nor a few volumes done by avant-garde or underground publishers—but a literature that came out of the activist movement that exploded after Stonewall. Some of it was
self-consciously literary, but there were also the new magazines—the *Mandate*s—with their full-color centerfolds whose
models were actually given names and personalities. Even if
those biographies were fictional—and I correctly suspected they
were—the idea that they were real men with real lives made
them even more exciting to me because they became even more
accessible. Those magazines contained stories and articles about
the gay life that was coming into the open; they were writing
about it, making it more real to those who hadn't yet experienced it.

I didn't really think of myself as becoming a writer of
these stories any more than I thought of myself as a creator of
male nude photographs, which I later did become, a comple-
tion of Bronski's perception that the consumer of gay male
pornography is capable of assuming all its roles. It wasn't that
gay writing wasn't an option; I simply hadn't thought of myself
as a writer at all.

It was, in fact, much easier for me to begin with activism, which I took up after college, and then create the world being written about. I moved from activism into editing, eventually becoming the editor of the *Advocate,* the largest gay news magazine, when I was twenty-nine. Even as I shaped a periodical for gay men, I didn't see myself as an originator of the material. That was editorial product I bought from others.

Things in my life changed about two years after I left the *Advocate.* I had moved to New York and found myself in a nothing job. It felt horrible at first, it was a great fall from the California heights of gay editing. Then I realized I was being given a great opportunity. After all those years of all-consuming activism and eighteen-hour days as an editor, I suddenly had a boring nine-to-five job that left my imagination and my evenings free. I could do anything with this time and energy. I could even become a writer.

My favorite of the new gay male periodicals was a magazine called *Drummer.* It was rougher than the others, most of which were attempting to be a gay version of *After Dark* or *Gentlemen's Quarterly* or some other entertainment or fashion publication. *Drummer* went right for the groin. It was full of smells and sensations and fantasies. I could, I thought, perhaps write something for a magazine like this. I wouldn't be noticed, I thought; if I failed, it wouldn't be like having something terrible in a periodical my friends would see.

I wrote a short story that rambled on for twenty or so pages, composing it on a portable typewriter in my half-basement apartment in the East Village. I mailed it off to *Drummer* and thought I might hear from them in a couple months, if ever. Instead, I got a call at work only two days later from the publisher, John Embry. "Do you think you could turn this into a novel? Say, in chapters that we could serialize, then publish as a book?"

The result was *Mr. Benson.* Far from being unnoticed, it made me something of a celebrity. I got to sell T-shirts by mail order that read: LOOKING FOR MR. BENSON. There were versions with or without a question mark. (My boss's husband understood I really was a writer the first time he saw someone wearing that T-shirt and reading the *Times* on the New York subway.) I got fan mail and there were even fan clubs that met to read each installment and then act it out among themselves. There were people in all parts of the country that were actually doing the things I wrote about.

I enjoyed writing *Mr. Benson,* but I didn't write it with a serious design, no matter how seriously people eventually took it. Still, I had proof of my audience, something I'd learn was essential for me to create a writing life. I began to write more, and to take more care in writing. I did essays for *Drummer* and its sister publications, covered the art scene in New York for them (they were headquartered in San Francisco), reviewed books, and continued to write more pornography.

I was fascinated by the response I was getting to my writing and to the place it had in my readers' lives. I began to meet more people who were doing this writing and to learn about still others. I discovered the real name of Phil Andros and went to San Francisco to meet Samuel Steward and to learn about his life as a writer. All the writers I would meet had lessons to teach me, but Steward's were the most pervasive. He had a literary career in his twenties, when he was teaching literature, and became a protégé of Gertrude Stein and Alice B. Toklas, whom he visited regularly in Paris. After he left academia, he became a tattoo artist on Chicago's South Side. His adventures in the demiworld led him to write up the stories he heard. He created the Phil Andros novels. One of the best instructions I received was his advice never to separate my erotic writing from anything else I might do. True, there were some lousy pornographers in the world, Sam told me, but that didn't mean someone else couldn't be a *good* pornographer. As he later wrote in *Chapters from an Autobiography* (San Francisco: Grey Fox Press, 1981):

> How then to write porn in the most effective way? Phil Andros can give no lessons, but merely say that he has always approached a scene slowly, never plunging into the action too fast; that he has attempted to use vivid and sensory images from all the senses, thereby drawing the

reader along with him into the sexual encounter; that he has always trusted the accumulation of details, knowing that each one plucks at a harpstring somewhere inside a person, and that those stimuli compel the imagination to emerge slowly—throbbingly alive—causing the corpus cavernosum to be gradually inflated and pumped full of blood. Then—if Phil has taken his own advice and been diligent—perhaps the ultimate reward will follow: the sudden involuntary clutch of the vesicle muscles around their contents, the convulsive shudder, the thrusting spurt through the urethra, and the deposit of literally billions of tiny invisible tadpole-things upon the silken ribbing of the pouch of one's athletic supporter.

And the porn-writer's version of such a sentence? "He came in his pants" or "he creamed in his jeans."

For myself and for many other gay men, pornographic writings were how we learned the parameters of our sexual life. We could have more than a simple ejaculation with a nameless partner, if we wanted. Pornography was how we developed our fantasies, both sexual and emotional. The eponymous Phil Andros was a hustler and a porn star who was not only showing us how to come with some literary flair, he was pointing out how life worked, where the decent folk were, and who should be avoided. In a precursor to AIDS consciousness, Steward also gave health information in the midst of his fiction, warning against the dangers of hepatitis and other sexually transmitted diseases. But those warnings seemed vague and not all that important when we read them.

By the late seventies, there was much more sexual writing of all kinds. Court rulings and a new air of sexual freedom led more writers and publishers to explore the erotic imagination. Not all critics were pleased with the changes, and they were especially upset by "hard-core" representations of sexual activity that seemed to be gaining acceptance. British critic Kenneth Tynan both defined the issue and answered those critics in a wonderful essay called "In Defense of Hard Core" (in *Dirty*

Movies: An Illustrated History of the Stag Film, edited by Al Di-Lauro and Gerald Rabkin, New York: Chelsea House, 1976):

> Because hard core performs an obvious physical function, literary critics have traditionally refused to consider it a form of art. By their standards, art is something that appeals to such intangibles as the soul and the imagination; anything that appeals to the genitals belongs in the category of massage. What they forget is that language can be used in many delicate and complex ways to enliven the penis. It isn't just a matter of bombarding the reader with four-letter words. As Lionel Trilling said in a memorably sane essay on the subject:
>
> > *I see no reason in morality (or in aesthetic theory) why literature should not have as one of its intentions the arousing of thoughts of lust. It is one of the effects, perhaps one of the functions, of literature to arouse desire, and I can discover no ground for saying that sexual pleasure should not be among the objects of desire which literature presents to us, along with heroism, virtue, peace, death, food, wisdom, God, etc.*

I had moved on with my own writing and had published books that were far from my origins as a pornographer—not that I left those origins. People like Steward and Tynan had shown me there was no need to do so. While I was writing *Franny, the Queen of Provincetown* and getting my first mainstream notices, I was also collecting the stories that became *I Once Had a Master and Other Tales of Erotic Love.*

I continued to write pornography for many reasons, including money. Supporting myself as a writer wasn't easy and the occasional checks from sex magazines often made the difference between paying the rent or not. I also kept on writing porn because it was important to me, because I had come to realize that the creating of it was, for me, accomplishing the same purpose as the reading of it was for my audience. It was how I explored my sexual feelings, how I experimented with my sexual fantasies, how I came to envision my sexual partners. I read other writers in gay sex magazines and books for help in answering the same questions and searching through the same terrain.

AIDS presented an awesome challenge to our sexual vision in the eighties. I certainly found my own imagination tightly constricted by the idea of a deadly virus that was spread by sexual intercourse. The knowledge that seminal fluid, the majestic come that starred in so much of my writing, was the actual vehicle, was paralyzing. It was writing about sex in the midst of the epidemic that helped me face the plague and the fear that it meant an end to our sexual exploration.

I organized a group of pornographers to create a book to use these very elements to help spread the word on how to avoid risk of the disease. *Hot Living: Erotic Stories about Safe Sex* (Boston: Alyson Publications, 1985) was followed by another book I wrote with Glenn Swann, *Safe Sex: The Ultimate Erotic Guide* (New York: NAL/Plume, 1986). They were just two parts of a movement among AIDS activists both to salvage gay men's erotic imaginations from the disease and to use pornography, now correctly seen as gay men's vernacular literature, to stop the spread of the disease.

It's from these many years of learning to respect pornography that I came to put together this book. I both want to record some of the material that's been important to me and to other gay men and to lift up some of the examples of the best writing aimed at gay men's sexuality that I could find.

I make no claim that the writing here is anything but pornography. For as long as I've been involved with pornography, there's been a great deal of pressure to disown it. As I gained some stature as a writer, critics and friends invited me to classify my sexual stories and novels as "erotica." There is an attempt to somehow separate out some sexual works as being aesthetically or politically more acceptable than other works. People would try to say that my sexual writing—or Samuel Steward's or someone else's—was "too good" to be discarded as pornography. I disown that distinction completely. Pornography and erotica are the same thing. The only difference is that erotica is the stuff bought by rich people; pornography is what the rest of us buy.

In all seriousness, there isn't any workable definition of what is pornography *vs.* what is erotica. What goes as erotica is usually that material that's packaged between hard covers or some other more expensive means of production and sold through more acceptable channels. The same book that would be called erotica if it were presented in a bookstore with the trademark of a major publishing house would be dismissed as pornography if it were found with inexpensive paper covers in an adult book store. I suppose that some people will say that what I'm doing is taking a lot of work that would be labeled pornographic and making it into erotica by presenting it in this volume, brought to you by a division of one of the largest publishers in the world. It's an amusing thought.

With this volume, I want to show some of the range of gay male sexual imagery and thought. I have not been shy about including highly graphic work. Some of that is among the best writings we gay men have, and the idea that it might offend some sensibilities—that it might be too pornographic to be erotica—hasn't censored my decisions.

Because the purpose of this book is to explore as wide a range as possible of gay erotic imagination, there are, in fact, some elements that will surprise some readers, and some that will upset them. In many of these stories, for instance, you will find a belief that all men are homosexual and that they only need to find the right partner or be given the right experience, even if that experience is rape. There is also a large element of S&M in this writing. There are many reasons why so much gay male pornography moves into S&M. Much porn of any kind moves into this arena because the context provides the writer with a form that is automatically dramatic. There is movement in S&M that isn't always there in other kinds of pornography—the theme of initiation and an exploration of the hidden and forbidden that makes S&M writing more vital. The contemporary fascination with men's consciousness epitomized by the popularity of Robert Bly's *Iron John* gives another clue to the fascination with S&M for both gay writers and readers: it involves a theme of submission and mentoring that's not present in simple romantic erotic fiction. It includes a form of the rite of initiation for the male that isn't present in other contexts. S&M writing also keeps the writer on the cutting edge, keeping the author from being seduced too easily into attempting to present material as something that should be validated by others. The author says: This is what happens, not what you want to think happens.

The book starts with some of the earliest stirrings of a truly gay life, a time when people were beginning to form their lives around their sexuality. It includes both fiction and non-fiction work that enunciates gay sexuality. It ends up with the present, with sexual writing that takes into account the reality of an epidemic and still strives to maintain the vibrancy of gay sexual being.

JOHN PRESTON
Portland, Maine

PART ONE

THE

FOREBEARS

Of course there was homosexual desire before it was written about. Sexual stories and sexual experimentation were shared before there were printing presses to validate anyone's endeavors.

While Samuel Steward was working as a tattoo artist in Chicago under the name of Phil Sparrow, he met the fashion photographer George Platt Lynes, who lived in New York City and who was famous for his work in *Vogue.* The two began to share their exploits, each in his own way. With Lynes's encouragement, Steward would write vignettes about his sexual encounters, short stories that presaged his later publications. I'd discovered these two stories and Steward's accompanying letters to Lynes years ago and had cajoled Steward into giving me copies. When I went to compile this volume, Steward thought this erotic correspondence with Lynes had been lost, but I still had these in my files. They've not been published before.

While Steward was writing his vignettes, Lynes was engaged in his own form of narrative. He was photographing young men, many of them sailors, in the nude. As Steward sent him stories, Lynes sent back cut-up photographs of his own trophies. Eventually, when Steward visited him in New York, Lynes allowed him to take a set of fifty 8 x 10 photographs from his collection.

When Lynes died, there was a great deal of confusion and upset when his male nudes were discovered. There was some attempt to destroy all the evidence that the famed artist had even done such work. When publisher Jack Woody found out about the pictures years later, he also discovered that Steward still had his collection. That series became the core of the first of many books published of Lynes's males nudes, *George Platt Lynes Photographs, 1931–1955* (Los Angeles: Twelvetrees Press, 1980).

Steward himself was one of the first American gay writers to publish explicitly homosexual work. He began by sending his stories to European magazines that were produced in Zurich and Copenhagen. "The Sergeant with the Rose Tattoo" was one of the first of those efforts. It seems sweet and far from pornographic, but when it was published the magazine in which it appeared, *Der Kreis,* was regularly seized and destroyed by U.S. Customs agents. The very mention of homosexuality was too much for the censors in those pre-Stonewall days.

Another of the writers who began to work in the sixties was "Lance Lester," a Walt Disney illustrator who used this pseudonym. His boss at Disney actually got him started, giving him a copy of an underground pornographic book and saying, "You can do funnier than this." The result was Horny Corners, a gay town in the middle of the American heartland.

It's really valuable, while reading about Horny Corners, to remember that it was being described in pre-activist days. The writer, a comic pornographer, was making pointed and detailed comments on the closet, not just the closet into which gay men put themselves, but also the way that the rest of the world refused to acknowledge the fact of homosexuality, even as it was going on all around them.

Pioneers like Steward and Lester certainly didn't have an easy time with their pornography. Steward's first U.S. book publisher operated out of the psychiatric ward at St. Elizabeth's Hospital in Washington, D.C. Steward claims he never did figure out if that was one of the great scams of all time—hiding in the hospital to avoid criminal prosecution—or if the publisher was actually crazy.

Lester began publishing with Greenleaf, one of the original hard-core houses. The head of the company was Earl Kemp. Kemp was able to maneuver through the seas of government interference for years until he made the mistake of publishing an illustrated version of the federal *Report of the Commission on Obscenity and Pornography*. The illustrations were far from official, and Kemp ended up being convicted to three years in prison for a sex offense. The sentence was reduced to six months on the condition that he promise not to publish erotic material again. He hasn't been heard from since.

SAMUEL M. STEWARD

CORRESPON-

DENCE WITH

GEORGE

PLATT LYNES

5441 N Kenmore, Chgo 40
December 7, 52

Dear George,

Well, you have made me real ashamed of myself, for all week I have been wanting to write to you, and there has been a succession of committee meetings and furtzing around until today, and when I began to think of writing at last, I went down to the mailbox and found those wonderful cuttings of the little corporal there, perhaps he really may look better in the uniform if you say so, but in or out of it, that boy can eat at my table and drink from my glass anytime he comes to Chicago, of that you can be damned sure. I loved them, you wonderful creature, and have already looked a soft hole through them. And I wish there were really something I could do for you besides writing little paragraphs of my adventures, which seem all too silly and slight when you are so nice to me. Like your not having someone to sit for you every week, I don't have things happening to me all the time, and to keep pace I would have to dip into me lurid past and dredge up little things as I did once in a "correspondence" which Glenway [Wescott] read in Bloomington and seemed to like a lot. So if you would be content with small narratives from the past—well, there are millions of those. Meanwhile, however, something lovely happened last night. I know a guy from Chicago's west side who's a young executive downtown, and like me, he leads an extraordinary double or triple life—he's one of the "wild ones," about 34, and he likes me because he thinks I'm one too. At any rate, he lives in Logan Square, because he was born there, and it has sunk to one of the real tough neighborhoods of the city, full of the swaggering hard-muscled cropped-head little toughs that Chicago seems to be producing nowadays in greater numbers than any other kind. He called me up last night to say he'd met one of those, and did I mind if he brought him over? Of course not, I said, except I've just painted my sailor-screwing-woman mural off the wall behind my bed and the place is a mess. Small matter, he said, and after a little while they came. The kid was eighteen, and cute as hell—and his clothes just right. He had dressed up—which means that he had put on a clean but rubbed-white pair of jeans that fit him like a glove both fore and aft, and he was wearing his new shiny quilted black jacket, and a turtleneck sweater—dark blue with gray arms and V at the neck. He had slick black hair and was very polite, and yet damned near took my hand off with his grip. . . . He was very naive still about the H life, Wally having introduced him to it not very long before. Well, it wasn't many minutes until we were all undressing—I was sitting on the edge of the bed naked, and Wally cross-legged in the middle, and the kid was wrestling himself out of his jeans and jockstrap, and then he suddenly paused and looked over at us and said in a little boy voice: "Cheez! I feel just like da T'anksgiving turkey!" It damned near broke up the whole party . . . but didn't. We got him down on the bed and I went down on him while Wally straddled his face and came in his mouth, and

then Wally and I changed places while a coupla stars went off
in my head. . . . After that, we turned him sidewise while Wally
continued, and I rimmed the kid. When he came, he said a little
after: "Youse guys sure treat a fella okay. I hope I kin come
back." And after the two of them left I sat there a little cold for
a moment, thinking about two old queens using a kid that way—
but if it's evil, I'm glad, and I'm for more of it. . . . So do tell
me if you mind if I go back into the past a little farther, for I
love to write down these little excitements, and if you can stand
them, that's a wonderful incentive to me, because—strange as it
seems—I'm actually a very shy and timid lil' sensitive plant. . . .

88,

Sam

IN THE HAYLOFT

When we were in high school, Lou Cline always used to fasci-
nate me—partly because he was so big (about six feet tall,
I guess) and partly because he was always telling us about how
he screwed the girls. He used to sit beside me in class and get
a hard-on, and then say, "Hey, lookit dis—ain't dat sumpin?"
and he'd make it jump up and down in his trousers, right
under the teacher's eyes, until I was terrified she would see,
and yet I couldn't take my eyes off it. He was very wise, and
although I already knew what it was all about, he'd had a lot
more experience than I'd had. He was always putting his arm
around me in the corridors, and running one of those big strong
hands of his over my ass and around and feeling my cock, and
saying things like "Boy, how I'd like to get in that tight little
hole of yourn" or "How'd you like to wrap your lips around
that?" and grabbing my hand and putting it down on his hard
cock, and then making it jump in my hand.

One day we went swimming together. He was beautiful.
Just the two of us, in a little pool down near Sunfish Crick. He
had a kind of bulldog face with a butch turned-up nose, and

long legs—tanned and strong. He had shaved off his pubic hair, because—as he said—the bristles as it grew back in kept him with a half hard-on all the time. After the swim we stretched out on the rocks naked in the sun, and I started feeling around his cock, which grew hard in a minute, and then he said: "We'll go up to old man Thompson's barn. We might be seen here." So up we went. It was a nice barn, high with hay in the mows. "Go on up the ladder," he said. "Chee, I can't wait." I went first and he followed me close, reaching up his hands one after the other as he reached for the next rung, to cup it around my cock and balls. I was excited when we got to the top and stepped off in the hay. "Come over here in the corner," he said, where it was fairly dark. He put our towels down on top of the hay, and then slipped out of his old patched dungarees quickly, and I undressed too. He lay down on the towels and put his arms in back of his head. "C'mon, kid," he said, "you're gonna give me a tongue bath." I said I didn't know how. "You just lick me all over," he said. "Begin up here at my elbow and all down the sides and over the front. I'll tell you." So I began. I licked him down his arms to the darker yellow hair in his armpit, and when I sort of went around that, he reached over with his other hand and forced my head down in it, and said, "Go on, tickle it with your tongue." Then I went on to his nipples, which were standing out hard, and across the ridges of his belly. I could feel his cock beating at my ribs, but I went on past it; I buried my face in his crotch and licked around his balls and then went on down one leg. My mouth was real dry, but I went on licking. "The feet, too," he said, and stuck his big toe in my mouth. "And between each toe, too," he said, "or I'll whop you good." I looked up at the odd perspective of his belly, and his bursting cock, the head of which was enormous and red. With one hand he was slowly moving the skin on it up and down. "Now the other foot," he said, and I went at it, over the bottom and smelling the faint odor of leather and socks from his loafer moccasins, and then went back up the other leg to his crotch. "Now start at my heels again," he said, turning over, "and go up each leg to my asshole. And then you're gonna do *it*." I was

5441 Kenmore, Chgo 40
October 18, 53

Dear George, Beauty-catcher,
    Surely you will never forgive this time. Over a month ago
your letter arrives; I say it must be answered at once, I have
so much to tell that one about San Francisco and the Embarcadero Y.M.C.A.—and then dillydally, and postponement, until just now. There might be some excuses. I had to start teaching in August when I got back, a five-week summer course,
and then in the middle of it I came down with the vapors—
some odd malaise that gave me the loosies and the nausies—
and I thought that certainly it must be the Great Pox, having
just had the sexiest six weeks of my life—and so I had endless
tests and such like, only to discover after a week that I had
jaundice, induced—so the medico said—by too much sunbath-
ing. Luckily I was still heavily tanned and so my skin didn't
show yellow, but my eyeballs turned yaller and glaring as a
wildcat's, and the skin of my bathing-suit mark turned old
Ming Toy. I resisted the hospital and went on working; it was
quite a drag, and I'm glad it's all over now. But San Francisco,
my lad, was a marvel—my town in this old U S of A—real
Mediterranean in quality, with mature people and attitudes
and benevolent policemen. Sometime you should walk down
Market Street about two ayem, to see the leather-jacketed, dun-
gareed, and booted handsome young toughs of San Francisco
fingering themselves and announcing by word or glance their
easy availability. What is there about it? I dunno. Something
frontier? Sex in Chicago's an old tired thing with little excitement of the chase—but there's a kind of frenzied wonderful
excitement surrounding it out there. . . . I stayed at the 'most
notorious Y in the States (says Kinsey) and took elaborate notes
for him and myself on the activity. It's called the Armed Services Y—and cockfull (make that chockfull—Freud pushed my
finger) of sailors, soldiers, marines, and flyboys, but mostly
sailors—the wonderful handsome dears! It may give you some
idea of things if I tell you that I—shy, timid, and retiring as I
am—had in six weeks there more than the number of "con-

tacts" I had the summer before in thirteen weeks in Paris and Rome! It was a kind of Christian bordello, and I am full of tales about it to tell you on the long winter evenings—one of which is enclosed herewith (although I seem to have lost my touch for pornies, I fear). All in all, I don't know when I've had a more sucksexful summer. . . .

And your own sounds pleasant, and I wish I could see your new apartment and the vast additions that you must have made since last we met. You tentatively promised to send me a little evidence—and I hope you can pull yourself away long enough from those fresh young arms to do so . . . even snippets—I love 'em all, you genius, you.

My novel is in the hands of an agent, Greenberg being afraid to publish it although thinking it publishable. I take it they were afeard because of the three lawsuits in which they are involved in southern states over the publication of the *Divided Path* and *Quatrefoil*. I am not sanguine about anyone's taking it, however, this side the Atlantic. For the next winter I'd like to do a kind of *Grand Hotel* about the Embarcadero Y, but am not sure the subject could ever be cleaned up enough to be written in a saleable nonporno book.

I wonder if Will Schultz gave you a ring sometime in September? He's a kind of nice stupid boy, good body, big dong—and he was on his way to Germany on a Fulbright I helped him get. I gave him your number but had no chance to write you, being then a-failing.

I haven't seen the [Margot] Fonteyn pix because I haven't seen *Time* regularly, but next time I'm in the liberry I'll check 'em, eager as always to drool over everything you do. So now gbye and I'll hold a sweet sex thought for you and your desires. . . . Sam

AT THE EMBARCADERO Y.M.C.A.

The first guy I had out at the Embarcadero was a negro named Johnny, a corporal in the Air Force. There weren't many people around the Y that Saturday night—it was about ten-thirty and I was thinking of dressing to go downtown at midnight to meet a friend. So the corridors were empty and the rooms were quiet. I wrapped a towel around me and took some soap and headed for the showers, and as I got closer I heard the water running. When I walked into the washrooms I saw the light was off in the shower room although the water was running, and so I stepped inside and took off my towel businesslike and hung it up. When I turned around I saw it was a young negro, as black a one as I ever saw, made even blacker by the white lather that was on his skin. I said "Hi," and then, "You just getting ready to go out, or getting in?" He said, "Neither; I'm getting ready to go to bed." We went on talking for a minute, and the steam grew heavier and his body looked blacker than ever in the dim room—only a little light from the doorway—and then finally he sat down on the floor with the hot water running down his back, and looked over his shoulder at me, and said this was the only way to enjoy it. Meanwhile I was getting a half hard-on from watching him, and when he got up he saw it and sort of laughed huskily and said, "Hot water gettin' you?" and I swallowed hard and said, "No—*you* are." Then I reached over and took hold of his cock and he laughed a little but didn't stop me. I fingered it for a moment and it got stiff at once and stood up close against his belly. He moved his hips back and forth a few times and said, "Mm-m-m, that feels good," and then suddenly I was on one knee, even though it was dangerous as hell—anybody could've walked in—and managed to pry it far enough away from his black belly to get my mouth over it, and then I began to swing on him, with the water from the shower running down my face and blinding me, and he put his hands on top of my head and pushed down so that his cock went clear to the back of my throat and stayed there, with me almost choking but loving the several electric throbs that it was making against the back of my throat. Finally, half drowned, I managed to get loose from that rod down my throat, and got up gasping and said, "C'mon down to my room where it's safer," and he said okay, he would. I was trembling as I partly dried myself and told him the room number, and then I went back, still shivering, and left the door unlatched and turned off all the lights and lay down naked on the bed. Soon he pushed the door open and came into the dimness like a dark shadow. He took off the white towel, and I could see he still had a hard-on. He stood there with his cock in his hand, moving the skin on it back and forth slowly, and I could see his white teeth shine in the black oval of his head. I made him lie down on the bed and started a trip around the world for him—into the black tightcurled hair of his armpits, across his wonderful chest, tugging at the nipples with my teeth and tongue, down the ribs and across his flat belly, and into his navel and then skirting the little bramble patch of pubic hair, and down the inside of his legs. He was half moaning, little animal sounds of pleasure—and down to his toes, sucking them one by one, then back up to his cock, and then turned him over and buried my face for a long time between the cheeks of his lovely tight little black ass, while he squirmed with delight. Then I turned him back over and gave him a good long slow blow-job, my own cock hard as a brick—if he'd have touched me I've have blown in a minute—and I kept on with his cock, nibbling it up and down the sides, and putting heavy suction on it, and using my tongue on it, running it all around the black and fairly large head. He wrapped his firm young legs around my neck and locked my head there, and then started to fuck my mouth. I was struggling after a while to get loose because he was choking me to death. So he stopped and said, "You got any Vaseline?" I reached for the tube and turned over, and he guided it into me—I felt it push past the guardian sphincter and gradually in, in, clear up until I felt the electric roughness of his pubic hair against my ass, and then he began to fuck me, slow, from side to side, until after a few minutes he began to go faster. I was pumping my ass and gripping him for all I was worth, and he was panting on my neck and biting my ear, hot and sweaty, and his hips moving rhythmically, and pretty soon he let out a muffled yell and I felt his hot juice shoot into me, and gradually it slowed down, and he lay on top of me, joined to me, panting, for ten minutes before he rolled over. It was a lovely way to open my six weeks' stay.

SAMUEL M. STEWARD
WRITING AS PHIL ANDROS

THE SERGEANT

WITH THE

ROSE TATTOO

HE WAS ALMOST THE FIRST PERSON IN MY LITTLE shop, for I had been officially open only three hours. He came tentatively to the door and stopped there, outlined against the lovely pale pearl of the Paris dusk, his face turned a little sidewise so that the red and green and yellow of my new neon sign made a kind of jewel around his head. His uniform was neatly pressed, the ugly familiar khaki of the American army, the three stripes of a sergeant's rank on his left sleeve.

I was more than astonished, for when one opens a tattoo shop in Paris, somehow one thinks the first visitor will be a Parisian. How he ever found his way up the high hill of Montmartre to the dark little alley near the white dome of Sacré-Cœur was almost a major mystery. I turned from putting up the last of my design cards and said, "Oui?"

In a dreadful halting pidgin French and English, he said, "Vous—you . . . er . . . ah remuer les tattoos?"

In the smoothest French I could muster I said, "No, I

regret it—you must go to a plastic surgeon for that; the whole
cell structure must come out."

He looked so comically blank and woebegone that I had
not the heart to deceive him any longer. "C'mon in, Mac," I
said in English, "and take the load off your feet. You got a
problem with a tattoo?"

His mouth opened slowly and then closed. "You—you're
American," he said. It was almost a gasp. It had wonder—and
lonely heartache—in it.

"I sure am," I said, "and you're the first customer." I
turned to look at him more closely. I had been wrong in thinking the last rays of the sun had somehow illumined my shop
when he came in; instead, he brought the light with him, in
his golden close-cropped hair and the brilliance of his friendly
smile. He was a distillate of all fraternity men and young football players and husky farm boys from the Midwest that I had
left so far behind, and I found myself in a kind of homesickness
opening to him, as I knew he opened to me—a compatriot in
a foreign land.

"Holy cow," he said, "how'd you ever come to be working
here in—in this place?"

"It's a long story," I said, and it was. I hardly knew how
to tell it, nor that I even understood it myself. I remembered
reading long ago somewhere in Gide that a man should make
at least one decisive break in his life—with his family, his
thoughts, or even the room in which he lived. And I had made
two—one, when I gave up being a music and drama critic for
a San Francisco paper and shocked my friends (most of whom
could not survive the blow) by becoming a tattoo artist. But
the second—and greater—separation came when I renounced
my country, tired to the death of its phony optimism, its stifling
puritanism, its bigotry, but most of all its hypocrisy—a kind
of idiot dance-of-death publicly denying that it tolerated what
nearly all of its citizens practiced in private on the sly. So I
renounced its sham, rejected its money-grubbing ideals, called
it the only country that had ever passed from youth into decay
without going through maturity—and left. My first papers of

application for French citizenship were already among the bureaus.

"Pull up a chair and sit down," I said, and he did. He moved with an easy grace, throwing one leg over the back so that he straddled the seat, and clasped his hands on the chair edge in front of him. I saw the handmade letters on the lower phalanges of his fingers, but said nothing about them.

"You asked why I was here," I said. "Well, it was just a case of my geographical birthplace not coinciding with my so-called spiritual home. I never liked America or its attitudes."

He thought about that for a moment. "I guess I don't know where my home is," he said. "I kinda think it's not in Germany, where I'm stationed."

"What are you doing there?" I asked.

"Military police," he said. He made a fist and rubbed it into his palm. "But I've been doing a lot of boxing for the company. Even some exhibitions. If I can get permission, I been thinking about doing some pro work around the German towns."

"I thought you might be an athlete of some kind." His shoulders were broad enough so that you had to turn your head slightly to see both of them and his waist so narrow he could have swapped belts with a chorus girl. "What are you doing in Paris?"

"I got a week's leave," he said. "Another guy and I came over. He knew a babe here, and he's shackin' up with her."

"That kind of leaves you at loose ends, doesn't it?" I said.

"Yeah." He looked at the floor a moment, and then caught the side of his hands down between his legs, clasping the chair. "See?" he said, holding them out for my inspection. "I did that with a needle and some India ink. I wish to God I never had."

I had seen similar lettering before. On the fingers of one hand were the letters: L T F C; on the other—well, never mind. When you put both hands together, palms down with the fingers interlaced, it spelled out an obscene invitation. "That was a foolish thing to do," I said, but without reproach.

"Guess I thought it was funny at the time," he said rue-fully. "Can you take 'em out?"

"I'm working on a simple method," I said, "but it's not ready yet. The only way now is sanding or skin graft."

We talked for a half hour, a kind of nuzzling little conversation like two dogs sniffing each other to find the extent of our friendliness. His name was Buck, he came from Seattle, where a girl waited for him. Before he left, she had tried to use on him the oldest of the devices to snare a man. "But I didn't quite believe she was gonna have one," he said. And now the letters were spacing themselves farther apart; either she had cooled, or he had—he didn't know which. His father and mother had separated. His mother, he indicated with more delicacy than I would have thought possible in him, was a tramp; he adored his father, but had lost him somewhere—a simple case of desertion when his old man had caught his mother in bed with a sailor.

A tattoo shop is usually a friendly place. The intimate nature of the operation stimulates confidences. In my long and battered career, I had seen thousands of young men and, with greater patience than a bartender's, heard their tales of joy and woe and defeat and triumph. But as I listened to Buck, and urged him gently on like a father confessor, I was amazed at what was revealed. There were no tough and artificial overlays of brutality and sophistication to be cut through; his very real purity lay close to the surface. Oh, he had been in bed with a few women—but somehow he seemed to have retained a virginal quality that was most attractive. And like the romantic that I am, and have always been, I began to project my own desires and idealizations upon the screen of his youth and charm.

He had a wonderful body; its beauty shone through the drab mustard-colored cloth. A few courses in life-drawing years ago had taught me how to see through clothes. I noted that the definition of his muscles was superb; in the position in which he sat, the cloth was drawn taut across his magnificent thighs, and his calves were strong as the fabric tightened down to his well-polished army boots. His hands, big and well shaped, a farmer's hands, lay quietly powerful as he talked, or moved a little to emphasize a point.

It has been said that no one ever asks another person to
stay the night without having an ulterior motive in mind. But
I can honestly say that such a thing was not in mind. I suppose,
in a sense, I was as lonely as he was, for the wrench of leaving
my homeland had been a strong one. So it was with a heart
nearly as clean as his that I asked him . . .

"Where are you staying?"

He gestured down the hill. "At a dump on the Rue Notre-
Dame de Lorette," he said. "I think maybe it's a—how you
say it?—maison de passe. Girls keep screamin' and runnin' up
and down the hall, and drinkin', and people rent rooms but
they're in 'em for only about thirty minutes."

I laughed. "And you trapped there, the innocent in the
whorehouse. I have an idea. How would you like to come stay
in my apartment? There's an extra twin bed so . . . so you
won't be bothered, and I . . ." But I need not have felt guilty.
His face lit up, and his warm friendly grin was that of the long-
lost returning home.

"Chee!" he exploded. "Wouldja mind? I'd like that a helluva lot. And say . . . ," he leaned forward and laid one of his
great hands on my knee. Mentally I shivered and almost moved,
but I controlled my reaction. ". . . wouldja have any time to
show me a little of Paris?"

If I haven't, I'll make it, I thought, and nodded. "As much
as I can," I said, "and I'll steer you where to go for the rest."

"That's swell!" he said. His joy was touching, and his
excitement grew. "Tell you what—I'll go down to that flop-
house and get my gear, and bring it here, huh?"

"That's the best idea," I said.

He laughed in high glee, and sprang to his feet, knocking
the chair over. He picked it up, smacked his fist into his palm,
laughed again, and tilted his cap forward until the visor came
down on his nose so far I did not know how he could see
underneath it. He almost pranced. "Gee!" he said again, grinning. "I'll get goin' right away. Now . . . now you wait for me.
You won't go away, huh? You'll be here? For sure?"

"For sure," I laughed. His excitement was catching. "I'll
be here."

And I watched him move out into the deepening night, jaunty, alert, handsome, trim. The streetlight picked out the spots of shine on his boots and belt. A few feet away he turned, gave me a half-salute and another grin, and then walked rapidly down the hill.

And thus began an odd and troubled week for me. I was disturbed in the first place because I had broken a cardinal rule: never mix business with pleasure. It might be hard to believe, but of the unnumbered thousands of young men who had passed under my needle, I had never in any way overstepped the bounds with a single one. It was too dangerous, in a business sense. Amongst the young of a city, such a bit of gossip would flash like a fire through a forest, and had any of them known my secret—well, I would have been popular, no doubt, but I would never again have made a cent in my business. Thus gold conspired to keep me pure, as far as my clients were concerned; certainly the strangest thing gold ever did. The motivation, I'll grant, was hardly of the kind to gain me admission to the *civitas Dei,* but it did for all practical purposes make me keep my hands off my customers.

For the rest—well, I was no different from most of the brotherhood. Any handsome young man, provided he was not a customer, was a direct challenge. By cajolery, flattery, outrageous bribes, talk, the bait of records or books or pictures or liquor, or money itself—I'd get him sooner or later. But what was Buck—customer or handsome young man? Distressed, I pushed the problem away and refused to face it for a while.

That first night was both a pain and an ecstasy. We hailed a taxi when I closed the shop and piled his gear inside, then crawled in ourselves. I directed the driver to pass by the Place de la Concorde, to show Buck the lights, and the great jewel box that was Paris by night. He laughed and hollered and asked continually, "What's that building?" or said, "Chee! lookit dat babe!" and pummeled me on the shoulder and back like an excited child. And when we reached the Rue des Saints-Pères, where I had an apartment formerly occupied by two fairly wealthy Americans, his enthusiasm overflowed.

"Chee, what a pad!" he exclaimed. "Have you read all dose books?" He walked to the one wall where I had shelves to the ceiling. And then he peered through the door into the bedroom and saw a bath beyond. "And a real honest-to-god shower!" he said. "That's the first one I ever seen in Europe, outside the barracks! Does it work?"

"It sure does," I said.

He started to unknot his tie. "I'm gonna take one," he said. "You mind?"

"Of course not," I said, "the place is yours."

He stripped off his shirt and then his T-shirt and quickly stepped out of his trousers. And the room was filled with radiance. I had not been wrong in picturing his body—like a warm and living marble, sculptured with the hand of Praxiteles, descended from the Parthenon frieze to grace my living room. As he turned his head, a great muscle on his neck flowed smoothly down into his excellent shoulders; the torso was flat and ridged, and the great ligament that held his belly swooped down like a birdflight into one side of his tight white shorts and up the other to vanish in the warm curve around his back. The torso of a faun . . . *Behold my beloved, he cometh leaping upon the mountains.* . . . In a moment of near faintness, I shut my eyes for a second, and then turned to busy myself. My mouth was dry.

"I'll get you a towel," I managed to say, "and then I'll wash my face while you're in the shower."

He strode like a conqueror into the tiled cubicle, and a moment later I heard the rush of water. I shook my head, took a deep breath, and took off my own shirt. Then I got him a towel and went into the bathroom with it. I drew the water and washed my face and then sat down in the bedroom until he finished. The April air was cool, but not unpleasant. From a corner of my window, I could look out at the lights along the Quai Voltaire and see the black shimmer of the Seine. The trees were misted over in the circles of light with the first faint green of their spring leaves.

The water stopped running in the bathroom. I heard the shower curtain being pushed aside and the small soft sounds as he dried himself. And then he burst into the room like a blond panther, the towel wrapped around his middle.

"My gosh," he said, electrified. "What a beautiful tattoo!"

I looked down at the garland of roses and flowers that hung across my chest from each shoulder. "You like it?" I said, feeling as foolish as a high school girl in her first formal.

"I never saw anything like it!" he said with real enthusiasm. "Does it go clear around the back?"

"Yes," I said. He put his hand on my shoulder and pulled it around to see. "Beautiful," he said. Then, "Gee, you're all goosebumps."

"Your hands are cold," I said, but it was not that. I stood up and put on a light dressing gown and threw him a dark red one. "Be careful you don't split the back out of that with those shoulders," I said.

"I'll be careful," he smiled. "Don't worry."

Then we talked some more, and I poured him a glass of cognac, and at last we went to bed—he to his, and I to the twin beside him.

To judge from his breathing, he was asleep almost at once. But I—I lay for a long time listening to the night sounds of the city. The strong silhouette of his shoulder and back under the covers lay between me and the faint light of the window.

And I concluded, finally, that I'd rather have him as a friend. . . . and then, partly at peace with myself, I fell asleep.

It was a wonderful week, but I must confess that I neglected my business—a bad thing to do when one is just beginning in a new place. Together we did all the silly and wonderful things that tourists do, and the thrill was great for me. I was continually refreshed and stimulated as I saw Paris through his young eyes; it was almost like a first visit again, and once more I fell captive to the sweet gray spirit of the old city. We walked up the Champs-Élysées, had aperitifs at little sidewalk cafés, and strolled through the Bois de Boulogne, marveling at the recurrent miracle of spring in Paris. I introduced him to cafés of the St. Germain district, and we went once to the Folies Bergère. In the mornings the air was cool and sweet and thin as a golden sauternes, with little sparklings in it; the evenings were sometimes chill and lemon-colored still—but it was all beautiful, seen with the eyes of love.

And I must confess, again, that the wall of my resolution lasted about three days; then it began to crumble from the repeated onslaughts of his beauty. His shyness disappeared, and whenever we got into the apartment the first thing he did was take off his clothes. Not that I objected, of course, but the effect weakened me, to see him walking in his young glory nearly naked around the room, or playfully taking the boxer's crouch, or showing me a few judo holds over my protestations. Contact with his body chilled and frightened me, for I saw the end of it that was hidden from him. And then gradually I began to say things, leading statements that he could hardly misinterpret—and he was not stupid.

I think it was the fifth evening. We had gone to bed, both mildly soused from a good deal of wine at dinner and cognacs afterward at La Reine Blanche. The light was out. I was greatly depressed and lay on my back in bed, biting my wrist and aching with desire.

Suddenly he switched on the lamp between us and propped himself on his elbow. His handsome face was serious. He bit his lip a moment, and then said, "I'm sorry."

I stopped acting like a cheap theatrical ham and turned to face him. "Sorry for what?"

He flushed with embarrassment and looked down at his pillow, and punched it. "I—it's kinda hard to say. But—but I guess I know what's in your mind, these last few days. . . . "

I said nothing.

"Well, the thing is, I just *can't*. The idea of it . . ."

"That's okay, Buck ole boy," I said. "I'll get over it." And then out of my frustration or spite or something like it, I added with some bitterness, "Besides, there'll be others coming along."

He looked at me for a long moment without speaking, and I saw the cornflower blue of his eyes turn frosty and darken. Then, abruptly, without saying more, he switched out the light and turned on his side.

But by the next morning it was as if nothing unpleasant

had happened at all. He had to leave the day after, so we made a real celebration of the last twenty-four hours. We even went up the Eiffel Tower over my loud complaints, for in all the years I had been going to Paris I had carefully avoided that excursion. Then in the afternoon, a lot of Pernod, and in the evening an excellent bouillabaisse. At the end of the meal, he leaned across the battlefield of our dead dinner and said, "I've got just one more favor to ask of you."

"Name it," I said through a happy haze.

"I want you to put a rose in the middle of my chest. Like in your garland. And someday I want the rest of it, too."

His request shocked me a little, and pleased me a lot. "You quite sure you want it?"

"I've thought a lot about it," he said. "Yeah, I want it. And in addition . . . that's one way I can be sure I won't ever forget this week." He toyed with a fish bone fallen to the tablecloth. "Or you," he added in a low voice.

So we got into a taxi and climbed back up the hill of Montmartre to the Rue Gabrielle, and opened up the shop. Then I went to the back room and got out the slanted bench. I put the screen up and did not turn on the shop lights—just those in my working area.

"Well, uncover the muscles," I said, and he took off his shirt. "And lie down." I put a pillow under his head and got my needles ready. Just before I started, I looked down at him stretched out on the bench, and said, "It's not too late to change your mind, you know."

He shook his head. "Nope. I want it. The big one just like yours." And then suddenly he put his arms up and clasped his big hands around the back of my head. He drew me down toward him, as startled as I had ever been in my life, and kissed me full on the mouth. Then he let go, and grinned up at me. "Now, go ahead," he said. "I just wanted you to know how I felt."

Trembling, shaken, I dipped the needle in the ink, and drew the first lines of the great scarlet rose upon the smooth and swelling plateau of his chest.

■   ■   ■

It was a little over a year later, almost at the beginning of May. My shop had begun to prosper somewhat, and although I was not yet the rage of Paris, I had a good flow of customers. The number of women wanting tattoos surprised me, and to protect myself from the predatory females of Montmartre (and their vengeful *macquereaux*), I had bought a plain gold wedding ring, which helped to scare them off.

I still remembered Buck, of course, but in the deluge of young French *durs* and hoods, of sailors and soldiers, and in the making of new designs to satisfy their tastes, he had begun to recede into that pleasant opalescent realm of the past where we keep our best memories. My frustration had lost itself in a vague glow of pleasure that I always felt when I thought of him. He had written three letters to me, each enclosing some clippings. He had won bouts in his company and regiment, and the write-ups in the Army paper were flattering—"The Rose Boy-Cop," they called him. And then there were some clippings from German papers, and one victory picture of a referee holding Buck's hand high in the air, and he grinning like a Cheshire cat, with the rose plainly visible on his chest. When he went "pro," the crowds went wild over him; he turned out to be one of the most popular young boxers in Germany. And what was his name in Frankfort and the other towns? Why, it was natural: *Der Rosenkavalier!*

It was ten at night and I was getting ready to close. I heard my doorbell tinkle, and looked up. It was Buck. He had on slacks and a windbreaker, and was bareheaded; his golden hair shone in the light.

"Well, here I am," he said.

I played it very low-key. "So I see," I said quietly.

He came into the working area through the swinging gate, and sat down. "I'm outa the army."

"Really?" I said. "You're a pretty famous boy now."

He grinned in the old way. "Mostly your doing," he said. "That rose sure caught on. I guess you made me all right."

The opening was there, and I said with a faint bitterness, "Hardly the way I intended however."

He smiled briefly, and then sobered, and moved his toe

in a small circle on the floor. He said, without looking up, "I guess I've learned a lot in the last year. They always said travel was broadening. So what I'm really here for, in a way, is to apologize."

I felt a churning inside that formed into a tight knot, and then suddenly released. "No apologies needed, Buck ole boy," I said. "It's all in the past."

He looked up with his eyes, keeping his head down, and smiled. He said nothing.

"What's all this leading to?" I asked.

He stood up, raised his arm high in the air, and stretched like the handsome young animal he was, and looked down at me.

"To a final question," he said. "How's about putting me up for the night?" He lowered his arms, and put one hand on each of my shoulders. "We've got a lot to make up for," he said, and playfully cuffed me alongside the ear.

I looked at my ink-stained hands, lying in my lap. I had made myself a good life with them, and regained a measure of self-esteem. Why should one be at the mercy of the Bucks and Tonys and Chucks and Johnnys of this world? For me, there had been too much experience, it had multiplied itself until I was no longer under coercion from any person or thing. It was not my fault that it had taken this young man so long to learn, under how many faceless tutors I would never know. And it was not flattering to hear him say something that I had known for many years, and had once told him was true. It would be so easy to show him the wedding ring, and tell him I was married, and that my wife would not understand.

And yet, from the slowly unrolling frieze of the young men that had passed before me in life, there were few that had stepped down to join me, and call me friend; and fewer still who had offered me love. And was not love the answer, the bridge between soul and soul, the joyous agony at the very heart and end of being?

It took me less than three seconds to have these thoughts. Then I looked up and said, "Okay, Buck. I'm glad to see you back."

"CLAY CALDWELL"
WRITING AS LANCE LESTER

FROM

CRUISING

HORNY

CORNERS

OUTSIDE THE GRAND VISTA COFFEE SHOPPE, THE main street was as peaceful as it had been ever since the highway was rerouted, and Mike and Johnny sauntered along the sidewalk, talking casually. From time to time, Johnny pointed out one of the points of scenic or historic importance—the police station, the oldest fire hydrant in continuous service south of Sacramento, Miss Angelina Patterson's bookstore, which catered to adult males only and was run by a lady who occasionally showed a definite five o'clock shadow. The Dignified Order of the Matterhorn Clubhouse—but in his innocence, he ignored some of the places that might have been of greater interest to Mike.

There was Carter's Clothing Store with the CLOSED FOR ALTERATIONS sign in the window. At the moment, Mr. Carter was in the back room tailoring the Y gym shorts of young Harry Ford. Harry had long since completed the youth-development program at the Y, but he often had Mr. Carter tailor his shorts again for old time's sake. Mr. Carter looked forward to these visits, recognizing Harry's appreciation of his talents, and when the young man appeared the sign was put on the door while they adjourned to the world's only dressing room complete with air-conditioning, towels, and a Coke machine. There, Mr. Carter was presently devoting himself to young Harry's alterations.

Farther down the street was the Y, which Johnny pointed out, and the adjoining parking lot, which was quite obvious and completely filled. Several members of the youth-development program were on duty as car attendants, and they wore the uniforms Uncle Phil had designed: formfitting crimson shirts split to the navel and white trousers that were not split but appeared to be in momentary danger of being so. Two of the attendants were getting up from the backseat of an automobile, smiling and zipping up their flies, when Johnny passed with the husky, rugged-looking marine, and after watching them for a moment the attendants unzipped in silent agreement and returned to the backseat.

Opposite the police station was Harvey G. McDaw park, a tribute to a pioneer who had maintained a lifetime program of youth development long before Uncle Phil got into the act, and Johnny paused for a drink at the public fountain while Mike read the bronze plaque unveiled the preceding year as a memorial to the late Mr. McDaw. The plaque described Harvey as a community leader who had left his impression on several generations of Grand Vistians; it did not mention that he had departed this life, at the age of ninety-seven, in the steam room of the Y. He had died with a smile on his lips, and the solid marble column above the plaque graphically described the balance of his remarkable physical condition at the time.

Turning from the plaque to Johnny, Mike discovered a feature of the young athlete he had not fully observed before. Two features, to be more exact. Johnny was bent over the drinking fountain satisfying his thirst, and the two features were clearly marked beneath his tight trousers, sleek and firm

and smooth-curved. Mike found himself suffering from a somewhat different thirst than Johnny's, one that had been stirred
by the events in the storage room of the Grand Vista Coffee
Shoppe and was now becoming most distressing.

"For such a big stud, you sure got a neat pair," Mike
murmured, concentrating on the upturned arcs with an ap-
proving gaze. "I'd sure like t'—"

"Want a drink?" Johnny asked, straightening and turning
to Mike with innocent brown eyes filled with pride. "Grand
Vista water is the purest in the county. Everyone says it makes
a difference."

"Something around here sure does." Mike suddenly felt
the responsibility for escorting the only thing in Grand Vista
purer than the water. "Johnny, are you sure you want t' go t'
LA? I mean, maybe you won't like th' way your problem gets
solved."

"I've got to solve it," Johnny said earnestly. "You said
you'd help me, remember?"

Mike blinked away from the clear-eyed directness of the
youth and noticed the men's rest room nearby. He could take
Johnny inside and solve the problem—and his own—right then
and there. Then he noticed the police station directly across
the street and thought better of the idea.

"Okay, buddy. Only don't say I didn't warn you." Mike
took Johnny's place at the drinking fountain and purposely
offered a view Harvey G. McDaw would have appreciated,
wherever he was. When he finished drinking, he turned to find
Johnny studying the architecture of the police station. "Maybe
my pants have stretched," he muttered to himself and then
walked over to clap Johnny on the shoulder. "C'mon, let's move
out for LA. From what I've heard, you ain't never gonna solve
your problem in Grand Vista. Especially right across th' street
from th' police station."

What Mike didn't know was that a number of problems
were being solved at that very moment in the nearby rest room.
Several gentlemen had arrived at the Y without room reservations, and the management had thoughtfully arranged to have
them quartered in this public establishment on a space-available

basis. Uncle Jerry had designed the building after considerable thought, and beyond the traditional cubicles and washstands in the front, a short corridor led to a series of less traditional rooms capable of holding fifty persons in a standing position—and somewhat fewer in other positions, which is what most of them were in at the moment. Music was piped in direct from the Y steam room through the courtesy of the local phone company, and the president of the company was even now checking the equipment in one of the rooms.

Mike and Johnny walked several blocks—past the bookstore where Miss Patterson was preparing a window display of sunbather magazines from Sweden and past the D.O.M. hall where the cleanup man had just discovered a pair of G.I. shorts among the rubbish from the previous night's business meeting. Then they met a middle-aged man climbing into a government-owned automobile.

"Hi, Johnny," said the middle-aged gentleman. "Can I give you a lift?"

I'll give Johnny all the lift he needs, Mike thought, and from the look on the man's face, he was sure he was thinking the same thing.

"Mike and I are going to the freeway, Mr. Mortimer," Johnny said, innocent of the uplifting thoughts concentrated on him. "We'd sure appreciate a ride."

"Hop in."

Mr. Mortimer was the postmaster of Grand Vista, which explained the government car. He had been appointed postmaster some ten years earlier because he had obtained some photographs of the local congressman enjoying the fruits of harvest with a handsome young grape picker and because no one else wanted the job. When the congressman retired to do some grape-picking of his own, Mr. Mortimer doctored the photographs to include the new congressman, and he had no trouble being reappointed as postmaster. He spent more time interviewing potential carriers than he did learning the postal rules and regulations, but the mail continued to be delivered on time so nobody thought to question his abilities—as postmaster, that is.

During the ride to the freeway, Mike realized that Johnny knew Mr. Mortimer fairly well; they discussed the high school senior play, the band concert, and the forthcoming graduation. Mike was relieved when Mr. Mortimer let them off at the freeway.

"That old guy's gay as hell," he said as he watched Mr. Mortimer's car head north.

"I guess he's always in pretty good humor," Johnny agreed in the only way he could—innocently. "He's the postmaster in Grand Vista."

"He ever invite you over t' lick stamps with him?"

"No. He lives north of town with one of the postmen."

"His nephew?"

"How did you know?" Johnny put out his thumb to a passing car without success. "It's a funny thing about that. His nephew worked at the post office for almost a year before anyone knew they were related. That was when they moved out north of town."

"An' brought a station wagon an' a French poodle, I bet."

"How did you know?"

"Wow," Mike murmured and offered his thumb to the next passing car.

Johnny and Mike stood on the edge of the roadway for some time without getting a ride. At last Mike viewed Johnny critically and then clapped him on the shoulder.

"Do me a favor, buddy. Unbutton your shirt."

"What for?"

"It's sorta good luck for hitchhikers."

"Okay." Johnny unfastened the top button of his shirt. "Think it'll help?"

"Th' next one down, too."

"All right, if you say so."

Mike blinked at the expanse of high-curved, bronzed chest sprinkled with sun-bleached hair. "Now, hike up your pants high as you can."

"Like this?"

"You wearin' Jockies?"

"No, skivvies."

"Yeah, I can tell now." Mike licked his lips. "One other thing—when I tell you, suck in a deep breath. An' smile." He viewed his workmanship. "Yep, that sure as hell ought to do it."

Several cars passed: a family headed for Disneyland, a prominent lawyer picking his prominent nose, two Volkswagens in tandem. Then a large, highly polished convertible sped into view, a lone male at the wheel.

"Now," Mike said, and Johnny sucked in a deep breath and smiled.

The convertible left a considerable trail of smoking rubber as it swerved to a stop.

"Where to?" the young man behind the wheel asked, beaming from Johnny's chest to Mike's crotch.

"LA," Mike answered, pushing into the car ahead of Johnny.

"Anything you say, lover."

"I'm Mike."

"And I'm Johnny."

"And I'm in luck," the driver announced, flinging the car back onto the highway.

Luck's name was Lance. He was twenty-six, medium-tall, and dark-haired. He gave Mike a smile and Johnny a look of indecision, and the car sped down the concrete roadway toward the distant mountains separating them from Los Angeles.

The roar of the wind in the open convertible made it impossible for Johnny to hear the conversation between Lance and Mike, so he sat back and closed his eyes. Being in the middle, it was logical for Mike to spread his arms across the back of the seat, and the pressure against Johnny's shoulders was pleasant and friendly. Johnny reviewed the topics of Monday's exam in chemistry.

"Nice car you got here," Mike said to Lance.

"A friend gave it to me."

"I wish I had a friend like that."

Lance grinned and nodded toward the youth apparently dozing on the other side of Mike. "And I wish I had a friend like that."

"I just met him. He don't know from nothin'."

"If you were a real buddy, maybe you'd teach him."

"I dunno. It seems a real dirty trick t' spoil somethin' that innocent. An' it seems a real dirty trick not t' 'cause he wants it spoiled so bad."

"Maybe he hasn't got anything worth spoiling."

"Better look again, buddy."

"You're right." Lance settled back, his foot firmly on the accelerator, his hand on Mike's knee. "I'm not sure I can do him any good, but I certainly wouldn't mind trying with you."

"You go right ahead an' try, buddy. I can be had."

Having completed the review of his homework, Johnny opened his eyes. To his right, the hypnotic rows of cotton fields spun past, and to his left, Mike was half-turned to Lance, their words lost in the rush of air. He glanced down and saw Mike's legs spread wide, one thigh pressing against his own. He studied the fullness beneath the khaki trouser and the muscle ridge showing through, and he shifted his gaze to his own thigh and noted it was wider with the same muscle even more clearly outlined. Anatomically most interesting. He went back to Mike's exposure and followed the arc of his crotch to the heavy bulge extending down the inner thigh on the left side. He viewed it critically, then shifted his gaze again to compare it to the mound straining his own trousers. It appeared to be larger than Mike's, and he was relieved that the doctor had assured him only yesterday that he didn't have a hernia.

Johnny felt the pressure of the marine's arm against his shoulders and the thigh against his leg, and he watched the mound begin to strengthen. Anatomically, this was most interesting—but physically, it was uncontrollable. He glanced out of the car to his right and saw that the cotton fields had given way to new orange groves irrigated by the massive state project bringing water from the northern end of California to this formerly arid region. It was economically interesting, but he wondered if the state had included cold-shower facilities for growing boys from Grand Vista.

■ ■ ■

It was early afternoon when Lance let his car swoop down the final grade from the mountains separating the Central Valley from the Los Angeles basin.

"I live out here in the San Fernando Valley," he said to Mike. "Suppose you stop by for a swim in the pool."

"You—an' the friend that bought you this car—live in the valley," Mike opined wisely.

"Th' friend is out of town for the weekend."

Mike grinned broadly. "An' I could use a swim." He nudged Johnny, not with an elbow as might be expected, but with a knee that was more convenient. "Hey, Sleeping Beauty, how about swimmin'?"

"I wasn't asleep," Johnny assured him, opening his eyes. "I was thinking about what my father will say when he finds out I'm not staying with the Wilkins boy."

"How old's th' Wilkins boy?"

"Four. And he wets the bed.'

"He ought t' wise up."

"The Wilkins boy?"

"Your father."

Lance slowed the car onto an exit ramp from the freeway and turned down the wide, divided street.

"The tract where I live is just ahead."

"Monumental Acres?" Johnny asked, reading a huge billboard in turquoise-and-puce lettering beside the street.

"We call it 'Horny Corners.' "

"Why?"

"You'll find out—I hope."

Shortly after the end of World War II, Colonel Harper L. Faries settled in the then-emptiness of the sprawling San Fernando Valley and decided to pursue a career in politics. His title was the result of devoted membership in an organization known as the Army of the Righteous, which served the war effort with a kind of recreational program the U.S.O. never dreamed of. His duties were to meet incoming troop trains and pass out goodies to the servicemen; the type of goodies depended on the proclivities of the servicemen, and it was said that his efforts short-

ened the war in the Pacific by six months due to the eagerness
of the troops to return for fresh goodies.

"They also serve who only stand and wait—or bend down,
or over," Harper explained to his draft board when they called
his number. He also demonstrated just how he served, and the
board promptly awarded him a 4-F classification with an E for
Excellence. "Bless you, honey," he murmured in response and
returned to the Army of the Righteous.

By the end of the conflict, he had discovered that there
was a singular difference between the officers and the enlisted
men in that other army (the one the government had); the
difference was that the officers had money and the enlisted men
did not. The more baubles and bangles on an officer's shoulders, the more jingle in his pockets, and soon that jingle found
its way to Harper's bank account. Thus was laid the financial
basis for his venture into politics.

The venture was an instant disaster. Even in those halcyon
postwar days, the natives were unconvinced of a program of
"free trade, free enterprise, and free love," and Harper was
defeated 38,469 to 2; the other vote came from a returning
enlisted man who had been entertained by the Army of the
Righteous in those early days before the prices went up. Harper
studied the election results carefully and determined that the
only way to get elected was to change the complexion of the
voting population. Thereupon, he went into the real-estate
business, investing his righteously gained savings in a housing
development he called "Harper's Happy Homes."

The last of "Harper's Happy Homes" was sold the day
before he was judged guilty of 487 zoning violations, and during the tax-free vacation that followed, Harper put his training
in the Army of the Righteous to good use and was released
even richer than when he entered. He was also more experienced, both in prison life and in business methods, and before
building his next tract he thoughtfully bribed the zoning in-
spectors.

Soon the San Fernando Valley was well covered by two-
bedroom, one-bath, no-good houses known as "Faries's Family
Facilities," and Harper gave up all thoughts of politics, real-

izing that he was making a better profit from houses than a politician could ever make from graft. The secret of his success was that he saved all the engineering expenses by using a single plan he had traced freehand from a book, *The Care and Spawning of Tenements,* that he had stolen from the local public library.

The triumph of Colonel Harper L. Faries's building genius was called "Monumental Acres," a massive tract that was completed and sold out just before winter arrived; the tract was built in a dried-up river bed, and when the first rains came the first fourteen houses went. Colonel Faries was already in Argentina by this time, however, and the last record of him is as a leader of a paramilitary group dedicated to starting another war so the Army of the Righteous might be reactivated.

By careful application of additional stucco, supports, and a million-dollar flood-control project, Monumental Acres was saved for the day when Lance brought Johnny and Mike for a swim in the pool behind his house. As they drove up the main street of the tract, Johnny had some difficulty telling one house from another; as it turned out, so did the occupants. The designs were all alike, the colors were all the same, and in many cases, the tenants were interchangeable.

Lance's home had been described in the ads as "a charming, California ranch house." Beyond the combination living-dining-family-room-kitchen and walk-in freezer, there were two closets called bedrooms separated by a short, dark hallway; Johnny was assigned to change clothes in the one smelling of mothballs, while Mike shared dressing-room facilities with Lance.

Alone, Johnny stripped down and pulled on the swimming trunks Lance had lent him; they were considerably too small, and he wished he could swim bare-assed the way the coach at high school let him when no one was around.

"Gawd!" Mike murmured as he came from the house to find Johnny poised on the edge of the swimming pool, carefully tucked into his trunks.

"No lie," Lance agreed, following with the beer.

Johnny tensed, about to dive. The afternoon sun caught the blond of his hair and etched the deep-tanned outline of his body with a copper glow. The thick, powerful muscles of his shoulders and arms tightened as he drew in a long, deep breath, his full chest rising beneath the spattering of golden hair, his amber nipples showing clearly.

"Strawberries," Lance muttered.

"Raspberries," Mike countered.

"And awaiting to be harvested."

Johnny's flat stomach sharpened, the thick volumes of muscle sloping to the smoothness of his slightly curved belly. Wisps of wiry hair escaped about the elastic-tight shorts clinging valiantly to his solid hips.

"Basket," Lance muttered.

"Bucket," Mike countered.

The breadth of untanned flesh showed above and below Johnny's shorts, and then the bronze began again, hair glistening over massive thighs and swelling calves. He jerked up sharply and dove into the pool.

"God, Queen, and Country!" Lance bellowed, leaping into the water.

"Semper fi!" Mike shouted, following Lance.

"My goodness," Johnny murmured, climbing out some moments later with his shorts down to his knees.

Johnny blinked his eyes open and watched the fading sunset for a long moment.

"Mike, maybe we ought to get going and—"

He sat up and looked around. The pool was empty and growing shadows ran along the high fence surrounding the equally empty lawn.

"Too much beer," he muttered thickly and dragged himself to his feet. "Two beers are too much for me."

He yawned and stumbled heavily toward the house. The side door stood open as if left that way by those more concerned with other things—as indeed it had been—and he wandered into the living room rubbing his eyes, still half-asleep. The house seemed deserted, and then he heard faint music. A radio playing softly. From Lance's bedroom.

He started down the hallway and saw that the door was

closed, but that was definitely where the music came from. Then something else came from the other side of the closed door. A sort of laugh, only not like any laugh Johnny had heard before; a mixture of pleasure, excitement, and strain. It was followed by an even more peculiar, gurgling sound, something between the last draining of water from the bathtub and the lapping of the Wilkins's dog as he washed himself. And then a gasp that might have been pain-filled if it hadn't been followed by a sigh that was not.

Johnny knew instantly that he must do something. Beyond that door, Lance or Mike—or maybe both of them—might be . . . well, he wasn't sure what they might be, but he did feel that he should help. If they needed help. On the other hand, they might not need help, and then it would be most impolite of him to burst in on them. Faced with the choice of breaking in and possibly angering them or walking away and possibly leaving them to a terrible fate, he did the logical thing; he stooped down and peeked through the keyhole.

Neatly framed in the horseshoe of the keyhole was part of a large bed and part of Mike—the upper part of each. To be exact, Mike was lying on his back on the bed, and he was stripped at least as far as his hips, the edge of the keyhole making it impossible to determine his condition below that point. His eyes were closed and he seemed to be smiling, but even as Johnny watched, another of those gasping sighs came from the young marine's half-open mouth.

Johnny felt that the reaction was the result of something happening in that area of the marine's anatomy hidden from his view. The young man might have been exploring those mysterious regions with hot little fingers except that his arms were comfortably folded under his head; Johnny noted with academic interest that his exposed armpit was quite wide and well filled with silky black hair, much akin to the hair rising across his chest.

"Man," Mike murmured, "it tears me up, gettin' turned on like that."

This announcement puzzled Johnny, for in spite of his protests of being turned and possibly dismembered, Mike did not appear interested in escaping. In fact, he began squirming slightly as if pressing himself down closer to whatever it was that threatened to destroy him.

"Dammit, you got me goin', buddy."

But Mike did not appear to be going anywhere, either. If anything, he seemed quite prepared to stay where he was.

"Baby! Oh, baby!"

Even Johnny knew it was highly unlikely that Mike was having a baby.

"Yeah! More!"

Mike jerked his arms from under his head and reached down to whatever was out of keyhole sight, writhing rhythmically on his back.

"Go, you hungry bastard! Go!"

Evidently the hungry bastard did not go, and a moment later, Mike sat up abruptly and doubled forward out of sight.

"Take it, buddy! Ohhhh, that's good! Damn good!"

With that, Johnny decided that Mike did not need his assistance, and he relinquished his observation post at the keyhole.

As he walked down the hall to his room, he considered what he had seen—or not seen, as the case might be. He felt it had meaning (one of his teachers had told him all things in life have meaning), but he failed to understand the meaning. He understood something else that had happened, however, and went to take a cold shower.

Temporarily calmed—and half-frozen—Johnny put a towel about his hips, drew the drapes across the bedroom window and lay down. He watched the fading light play across the ceiling overhead and tried to analyze the events seen through the keyhole. This threatened to force him back to the cold shower, and he concentrated on his chemistry again. This put him to sleep.

PART TWO

THE SEXUAL

GRUBB

STREET

Paychecks have been one of the great contributions sex writing has made to gay literature. Many writers have been able to support themselves—in the beginning of their careers, at vital moments, or for many years—by putting their erotic fantasies on the page. For some, like Roy F. Wood and Lars Eighner, the stories that were written were the author's best work, and they would later be collected into books that would receive some real critical acceptance.

Eighner went beyond publishing his own stories and wrote a guide for hopeful writers (for which I wrote the introduction). *Lavender Blue: How to Write and Sell Gay Men's Erotica* (Austin: Caliente Press, 1987) didn't exactly transform the writing world in the way that Eighner might have liked—he was greatly upset at other writers' low standards for their work--but it gave many aspirants a look into how the pornographic world worked.

One of my most beloved peers in pornography is T. R. Witomski. T. R. and I were in this world for a living for a

long time. We wanted to find out how to make the most money,
not just get the most words published. We discovered one of
the formulas from heterosexual porn magazines. It was simple:
you tell the story of how some sexual kink saved your marriage.
One of the best examples of the genre, always treasured by the
gay porn magazines that were anxious to show their socially
redeeming qualities by publishing marital aids, is "Peekers,"
where a narrator learns to accept voyeurism and use it to turn
on his lover.

Many other magazine writers are like Michael Lassell, a
poet (*Decade Dance,* etc.). Lassell was unemployed in 1983 and
wanted to try to be independent. "I didn't know if I could
write," he explained to me in a letter, "but I knew what turned
me on. . . . 'Negative Image' is based on a real incident from
my college life at Colgate University, . . . but it is also inspired
by my longtime friendship/infatuation with Gavin Dillard. I
had loved Gavin once upon a time, from close proximity chilled
by a sexual gulf we never crossed. One day in San Francisco I
was walking down the street and there was Gavin's picture
from *Track Meet.*" Dillard, also a published poet (*The Naked
Poet,* etc.), and Lassell used to visit each other's dormitory rooms
when they were both students at California Institute of the Arts.
One of Lassell's favorite memories is the image of the teenaged
Dillard in miniscule flimsy shorts, sitting across the room on a
bed, reading his poetry aloud. Unbeknownst to Lassell, Dillard
had gone on to a short, but highly visible and successful, career
as an actor in pornographic movies. The poster Lassell refers
to was publicizing one of Dillard's first successes.

Robin Metcalfe, far better known for his essays in Canadian political journals than for his erotic writing, is a more
common example of someone who writes pornographic material regularly, but not as the center of his career. Entering into
the erotic world is something Metcalfe values, as shown in "The
Shirt," but this is an ongoing part of his work, neither a short
chapter nor the central theme.

Leigh Rutledge is another writer who continued to write
porn as he pursues a career as a book writer (*Gay Decades,*
etc.). Rutledge is part of a school of gay writers I greatly ad-

mire, one that's made up of people who won't deny their sexual compulsions. In fact, he's open about the energy that writing erotic stories gives him. He is even one of those who'll deal directly with a question very often asked of pornographers but not always answered: Do you masturbate to your own stuff while you write it? Rutledge wrote to me recently:

> One of the big problems is when a story I'm working on turns me on too much: it has to be finished in five or six sessions, because I barely get a couple pages done and— wham! I sit there increasingly torn between the torment of feverish images in my head (and trying to get them down on paper before they evaporate) and the raw de- mands of my dick. At the risk of sounding totally bizarre, it isn't just porn writing either. I once read an interview with Harvey Fierstein in which he said he's often nagged by an increasingly irresistible compulsion to jack off while he's writing during the day, no matter what the subject matter. The urge isn't as frenetic as it is with porn (and sometimes it works in exactly the opposite way: I'm too exhausted as the hours wear on to think about sex), but I know what he's talking about.

"D. V. Sadero" is another example of a writer with a career outside the world of pornography. Sadero is a private eye who uses his special talents to extract from the regulars in San Francisco gay bars the answer to a question that often produces the stuff of his stories: What is the weirdest sex you've ever had? The answers often end up on the printed page, un- censored, to say the obvious.

Steven Saylor has been one of the bulwarks of gay por- nography for the past decade. Both as an editor for magazines including *Drummer* and *Inches* and as a writer, usually under the name Aaron Travis, he's contributed immeasurably to the gay imagination. He is, in many ways, the Samuel Steward and the Lance Lester of the eighties, the man who has been chron- icling the sexual exploits of an entire generation.

When I began to put together this volume, the one story

that everyone I talked to insisted had to be included was Saylor's "Blue Light." A strange, eerie tale of sexual danger, it exults in the same bodily fluids that would later become forbidden because of AIDS and the danger they represent in its transmission. "Blue Light" is one of the stories that will most assuredly stay with any reader's mind.

"Getting Timchenko" is a much more recent story by the same author. It shows a much more tender exposition and is a more subtle example of Saylor's craft.

ROY F. WOOD

WORKOUT

I WAS LIFTING A BARBELL LOADED WITH 350 POUNDS of weights when the phone rang. Should just let it ring, I figured. Sure as hell wasn't gonna be a business call. Ric's Gym in Tilton, Georgia, wasn't exactly the bodybuilding mecca of the world—or of the state either, come to that.

Only reason Ric opened it was 'cause he had money to throw away—or at least his wife did. Betty Lou was quite a woman and it was known in the community that she liked her men with muscles. Ric used to be in pretty fair shape but after he married Betty Lou and her bank account, he sorta let himself go to belly. I think the reasoning behind Ric's Gym was for Ric to work his ass off and get in the kind of shape his hot little wife wanted.

But like most things Betty Lou got involved with, it didn't work out that way. For one thing, I came along.

Me, I'm gonna be Mr. Olympia one of these years. All I ever needed was a place to train and a job while I worked at getting ripped. Ric provided me with both.

Which is about the only reason I reluctantly halted my workout to answer the phone. Figured I owed Ric some enthusiasm.

"Calling to see if you guys are open," the voice on the line stated. Sorta gruff like.

"Yeah," I said, "we're open, but we ain't fancy. Not nobody here but me and I'm doing my own routines now. We're supposed to close at seven. But I reckon if you can lift without supervision, you're welcome. I'll be another couple of hours.

"All I need is the equipment," the guy told me. "I wouldn't expect to find Gold's Gym in Tilton."

I shrugged my shoulders, which didn't do no good since I was on the phone, not television, but I told the voice how to reach the place. We hung up and I went back to my workout.

I love bench presses. Lifting heavy is a real turn on. Watching the weights go up, come down, feeling my muscles strain, tense, push, sometimes just watching my body respond to the demands I make on it can be a trip.

I'm only nineteen but I already got a couple of amateur titles to my credit. It won't be long, another year or two, and I'll be ready to leave Tilton, move into the big time. Maybe go to California and work out with the Golden Boys.

For that to happen, I've gotta lift my ass off. Not screw around, wasting time. Most importantly, I gotta be careful not to pay too much attention to the other guys.

Yeah, fact is, I dig guys. Hell, you'll never convince me that these studs who manage to get a forty-five- to fifty-inch chest and massive arms and legs ain't in love with themselves or other guys. Maybe both.

Happily for my concentration, Ric's Gym don't attract anyone who can compete with me. I'm not tempted by the dudes who work out here, not that I ain't had the come-on from a few of 'em. Considering how small and conservative our town is, that's pretty good. I gotta admit, I love it, having 'em watch me, seein' their eyes follow me as I move about the gym. Feeling them stare as I go through my routines. Knowing when I'm all sweaty and pumped up, they'd like to come over and pour their faces down into my crotch, lick the beads of sweat from my balls, then take my dick in their mouths. They'd love it! I bet they dream about caressing my body, feelin' the ripples on my stomach, the curves I've carved out of my flesh. I ain't above temptin' them. Once in a while I'll accidentally let my balls drop out of my jock. I've even let my big hunk of cock flop out if I feel like bein' real nasty. Don't hurt none—they can't say nothin'; they know they're supposed to ignore it—and they do. When it happens, I keep pumpin,' glancin' at 'em, watchin' 'em get hotter and hotter. After a while most of 'em go to the john and whack off!

Yeah, they want to get their hands on me bad. So fuckin' bad!

But I never give any indication I'd be interested. 'Cause I wouldn't—not with the likes of them.

I was working hard when the door opened and my caller of a few minutes earlier walked in.

Goddamn! I almost dropped the barbell 'cross my chest. He came over to where I was straining with the weights, reached down with one hand and took off just enough pressure for me to get it up and onto the rack.

"Don't you have sense enough not to lift alone? At least not with poundage that high? Goddamn it, Kid, where's your brain?"

I felt my face flush. I sat up on the bench and eyed the dude. I almost shivered and it wasn't cold! Minute I set eyes on him something happened.

I wanted his approval so fuckin' much!

"Your bangin' the door spoiled my concentration," I protested. "I don't usually have trouble with this light a set."

His eyes bore into me. Then he glanced around, scornful-like.

"I suppose you must work here, since I don't see anyone else. What's the problem? Nobody in this town work out? Or don't you have any business?"

I shrugged. "I work here," I admitted. "Our business, what there is of it, comes in the early afternoon—four, five o'clock. We're open till seven, but Ric lets me stay a couple of hours afterward for my routines. I usually keep the place open."

"You still need a partner, Kid."

"Ain't no guys around town able to stay with me," I said.

He grunted. Then did something nobody else in this town would have dared to do. Walking over to me, he placed his hand on my biceps, felt them, almost lovingly, then let his fingers roam up and down my forearm.

It got me bothered, but I reckon he didn't notice. All he said was, "Not bad. Twenty, twenty-one?"

"Twenty-one and three-quarters."

He moved around in front of me and raised both my arms.

"Flex," he ordered.

I obeyed. He was standing squarely in front of me. I could smell his musky odor, that scent of sweat and maleness that you always notice after a heavy workout. Or maybe after a heavy sex session with another guy. Only I ain't never had many of those.

He kept runnin' his hands over my arms like I was a bull on the market. Finally he tapped my wrists, indicating I could lower my arms. I did, and we stood there, staring directly at each other. I knew I oughtta be embarrassed, but I couldn't be. He was too much man. And what the hell, if he knew what I was thinkin' it was his own fault. You don't come in a gym and carry on like this guy was doin'.

I should have been gettin' started with my workout. Instead I found I was wonderin' what I'd do if he suggested we do something else.

Instead, what he said was, "How about it, Kid? Wanta get started?"

"Huh?"

"Come on! We're both here to work out, right? Let's see how damned good you are!"

So we commenced our lifting.

"What body parts you working today?" he asked.

"Chest, arms, stomach," I told him.

He nodded. Did a few sets of quick warmups and we were ready to go.

The bastard put me through the roughest series of routines I ever handled.

But tired as I was, whenever it came his turn, I was eager to watch, not just wait for him to finish so's I could get done with another set myself.

His flesh was fantastic. Maybe not quite as good as mine, but what the hell. I guess it was all relative. When he lay back on the bench to do his presses I stood up to spot for him and got a special look at his body. Watching his arms strain and bulge, seeing his crotch arch briefly as his back left the bench when he tried cheating on the last rep, I knew I wanted him in the worst way.

"Come on," I snapped at him. "Keep your goddamn back on the bench!"

He kinda jerked the last rep, but he got the bar back in place and lay there, breathing hard. Drops of sweat formed on his forehead and ran down his face. His gray T-shirt was growing dark now, wet, molding itself to his chest. Outlining his nipples, which were erect, as hard as the rest of him.

I startled myself by reaching over to feel his arm.

"Getting a nice pump," I congratulated him. What the hell! He'd done some feelin' earlier.

"So I am," he acknowledged. Adding, "We both are."

We should have been gettin' tired, and I suppose, in one sense, we were. Yet the harder we lifted, the more we challenged each other, the more we drew strength from the other man's body. It was as if I could feel my energy going into him when he was straining to raise a barbell or dumbbell packed with iron. When my turn came, *he* supplied the power, channeling it through me, forcing me to better my performance, aiding me in reaching new heights of glory.

'Cause that's what it was—pure, uncontaminated glory! A good session with the weights always makes me feel great— almost religious if you can imagine that. The surges of strength, the strains that can hurt like hell but at the same time tear into your muscles, pulling them apart and putting them back together—stronger, more powerful, more beautiful than before.

I've always felt that—but this time, working out with him, it was all magnified.

In all my days of lifting, I've never felt anything like what he was doing to me.

By now we were approaching our last sets and I knew I wanted to do more'n work out with him. Not being experienced, I couldn't even be sure just how I wanted him. But I knew I didn't ever want that strength he was giving me to leave.

And it seemed to be working both ways. As I watched him struggle to lift the weights, cussed at him—forced him with the power not of my voice but of my body—to achieve his goals, I could see him respondin'.

He finished his last rep and lay across the bench. A tiny smile flickered over his face.

"Pretty good workout, wouldn't you say, Kid?"

"Yeah. Better'n most I've had." I didn't want to spoil a perfect moment, but I had to know. I had to do something to make him understand that this workout had been different— that he was different.

"How'd we manage it?" I asked in a whisper.

He did a modified sit-up and stared at me.

"We managed it by being on the same wavelength, Kid. Our minds and our bodies melted together. Maybe we're Vulcans." He laughed. "Somehow I don't think we've had enough yet, either. I haven't. What about you?"

"I don't understand," I mumbled.

"Sure you do," he protested. "Come here."

I walked around and stood at the head of the bench he was sittin' on. He lay back down on it, reached his arms out and pulled me forward to where I was standing at his head. His hands on my legs were electric. I could have sat down on his face, I was so close to him. He stared up at my crotch, moving his hand up my thigh, exploring the deep, muscular cuts in my legs almost like a doctor. What I was feelin' wasn't like a patient, however. My cock grew harder, stiffer, almost escaping from my jock in its eagerness to his touch.

He guided me around until I was astride his middle, then

he pulled me down on him. Through his gym shorts I could feel his own cock grow thick and hard, pulsating beneath me.

I was losing control, assuming I'd ever *had* control. My cock was so hard it almost hit his face. His hands, meanwhile, were playing with my chest, and my nipples responded to the touch of his hands. He pinched them lightly, then harder, eliciting a gasp from me. Nobody had ever done that to me before.

Then he stirred beneath me, and almost like I was a twenty-pound dumbbell, he moved me aside and suddenly we were on the floor. The floor was cold, but his furious onslaught of motion made me forget everything except his body.

His fingers dug into my arms as he tried wrestling me into a position where I couldn't move.

"Come on, Kid," he gasped. "Let's see how strong you really are!"

So we tussled around on the floor. It wasn't to test strength, however, as much as it was simply to feel the other's flesh moving beneath our hands. There was no doubt now in either of our minds about what we wanted, nor, I suspect, how we were going to go about it. But we both had worked almost forever to become the towering mountains of flesh we were: I, at least, wanted to devour his body. I wanted to feel his warmth, yet know underneath my fingers I was in contact with hard, solid, unyielding manflesh. In my frenzy of exploring his body, I finally, hesitantly, allowed my hands to cup his crotch, felt the largeness of his cock and squeezed it in the excitement of discovery.

He laughed—I hoped at my naïveté—then rolled me around until he pinned my shoulders to the floor. His hand went for my crotch, and with one violent motion he stripped my shorts down to my knees and began rubbing his hand over my cock with obvious satisfaction. My jock strap wasn't doing much to contain me, so he pulled that off too. My cock lay stiff and hard on my stomach, reaching up past my belly button, demanding attention, craving release.

I tried movin' 'round so's I could take down his shorts but he shoved me back to the floor, then he put his face down to my chest and took my nipple in his mouth, biting it hard.

As the pain shot through me, his fingers started manipulating my cock. He explored it length and width and cupped my balls with his large hand. And the warmth of his hand, the playful touches and caresses he used to arouse me were almost more than I could stand. I lay there moaning while he towered over me laughing softly.

He moved his face over my stomach . . . using his tongue to lick the sweat from my body. At last his mouth reached my large, throbbing cock, which he slowly took in his mouth, sliding his face all the way down my shaft until he had my whole cock buried in his throat. He sucked on it almost casually, then withdrew his mouth and tongued my balls, all the while keeping his hands moving over my mountainous pecs, caressing and exploring all the muscular cuts of my flesh. As he carefully worked his way down my body, I was finally able to get his pants off him.

Now I gotta admit I ain't never seen too many hard male dicks before but even takin' my own into account, I didn't think they made 'em this big. My hands could have both fit 'round it and some would have stuck out over the top. His balls were large, heavy, and low-hanging. When I buried my face in them, the smell of his crotch enflamed me.

I grabbed his cock with my lips and moved my mouth up and down his splendid shaft of meat. Bein' inexperienced, I don't reckon I was as good at it as he was, but nothing was said, about that.

We moved our bodies together in a frenzy of motion. . . . My hands tried encircling his massive chest and when I couldn't quite do that, I found myself feeling his firm, rounded ass.

I could have lain there with him forever. The muscles of his back and shoulders filled my hands; his arms, almost as massive as mine, rubbed against my own and started that same sort of connecting power I'd felt earlier with him. And before I knew what was goin' on, he was rotatin' his body against mine, pressin' himself into me. His mouth reached for my earlobe and he bit me hard. I tried matching his actions and moves, but the urgency of my cock was all I could think about.

And suddenly he sat up atop me, straddlin' my rock-hard stomach. With one hand he grabbed saliva and applied it to my cock and the next thing I knew he had my hard dick in his ass—moving his body around my hot shaft as I drove it deeper and deeper into his explosively hot hole. At the same time as I was thrustin' up into him, he was jerking off his own massive meat, and all at once I felt that awesome surge of pleasure/power as my cum started erupting in his flesh.

"Oh damn, I'm gonna shoot!" I gasped and a second later filled him with my load. He grabbed me as I came, and a split second later I could feel hot cum spurting out of him onto my chest and stomach.

We groaned and lay there holding each other in a hard, firm, deathlike grip. It was only when the last shuddering spurts of cum had emptied from us that we relaxed, slightly, our hold on each other. I bent my head beneath his chin, unable to look him in the eye. I knew, when I thought about it, this experience was gonna unnerve me.

What was worse, I didn't want it to end. Not ever.

But of course it did. Rather abruptly, in fact. The door burst open and in rushed Betty Lou. She took one look at us in our naked splendor and exclaimed, "Oh goddamn! I was looking for a man, for that Ric of mine!" She chuckled, adding, "I think I'd do better with one of you. Maybe both of you!" Betty Lou never had been bashful.

We disentangled ourselves and sat up.

My face got red and I tried offerin' some kinda explanation.

"Oh shut up, Tony! I've never been blind! Maybe a bit on the gullible side, but that's coming to an end. When I get hold of that sorry Ric. . . ." She eyed my partner speculatively. "Don't suppose I could interest *you* in a gym, could I? Real cheap?"

He stood up. His cock, while not fully hard, wasn't all that flaccid either. He and Betty Lou stared at each other with more admiration in both their eyes than I'd have expected to see.

T. R. WITOMSKI
WRITING AS RAY WALDHEIM

PEEKERS

I NEVER ONCE THOUGHT ABOUT THE WORD *voyeurism* or its meaning—until about a year ago. In fact, I had never given sex a lot of thought—until the past year. I am just beginning to realize how naive and even ignorant I have been about sex and the many human emotions related to it.

In the past year I have gained some understanding; I have found that awareness and fulfillment of sexual needs can improve every other emotional part of my personality. I have always considered myself a fairly ordinary person, possessing more or less the same feelings as other people. The idea of being different, of having my own unique sexual and emotional needs, had never occurred to me until I was twenty-five years old.

I experienced a normal childhood. My school years were reasonably happy and content. I had numerous adolescent sexual experiences; none were particularly memorable. I remember knowing that I was gay from a very early age; thus "coming out" proved an easy passage for me. I was born and raised in

San Francisco, which in the mid-1970s, when I began my sexual exploration, was probably the most gayly liberated city in the history of the world.

The sexual experiences I do recall are the earliest ones, when I was first being introduced to sex—those first clumsy attempts in the school gym and in the backseats of cars. Still, I never could quite understand why all my friends were so preoccupied with sex; it was just not all that exciting to me.

During college, I started a relationship with an attractive man named Steven. Though we soon started living together, I was not drawn to him because of passion, but because of a need for emotional and financial security.

Of course, I liked Steven very much and enjoyed being with him, but something important was missing from our relationship. Our sex together was relatively frequent and very pleasant during the first few years of our relationship, but nothing to brag about or to discuss in erotic magazines. Steven and I never experimented with sex, never went much beyond basic sucking and fucking. Steven always seemed satisfied with two or three quick lovemaking sessions a week—or so I thought then.

Yet there were times when I would walk past the bathroom when Steven was standing there in his jockey shorts, shaving and not knowing that I was watching him. At those times I would have an uneasy stirring in my stomach, a slow burn that seemed to be fanned by the knowledge that he did not realize I was looking at him. Or I would watch him jogging or working in the backyard wearing only an old pair of threadbare cutoffs. At those times I would fantasize about him stripping off his running shorts or cutoffs and running or working naked. I was constantly trying to spy on him taking a piss behind a shrub in the backyard, as he often did when he was working outside.

Once I secretly watched him through the window as he pissed against the garage. The muscles in his thighs and buttocks flexed as he shook and squeezed the last drops of piss from his thick cock. He almost looked like he was jerking off. I flashed hot all over. After that incident, I desperately wanted to watch my lover masturbate, and I fantasized about his beautiful cock until it exploded into an ocean of flowing hot man-lava many times. But I was too embarrassed to mention my fantasy to him.

I suppose I never would have discovered my sexual well-spring had it not been for an experience that took place by chance on an innocent shopping trip. (Or, if Freud was right and there are no accidents, maybe the expedition wasn't so innocent.) I was killing time at a shopping mall when I had to take a shit. I headed for the public rest room that was located at the far end of one of those long, forbidding cinderblock corridors. The corridor was empty and gray. The sharp sounds of my footsteps reverberated in my ears as I hurried to the john.

Entering the rest room, I glimpsed myself in one of the wall mirrors as I turned to one of the four stalls lining the other wall. I was seated, my shorts and pants down past my knees, and about to relieve myself when I noticed a small hole in the partition to my right. It was about elbow level as I sat and the size of a dime. Curiously, without thinking, I leaned forward and put my eye to the hole, expecting to see the interior of another stall. Instead I saw a strong-looking hand slowly pulling on a huge, erect cock.

My face felt like it was welded to the partition, blood rushing to my head as my body caught fire. My breath stopped short and I was scared silly that I would gasp for air and the man I was watching would hear me. The thought quickly went through my mind that he was too occupied to have heard me enter and did not know I was there. Later, I realized that the stud may have been jerking off for my benefit, perhaps trying to lure me to lend him a helping hand.

Immobilized with fear that the man I was watching would realize I was sitting there just inches away, I stared at him masturbating. I felt physically paralyzed, my nervous system frozen. I could not pull myself away from the spy hole. I was mesmerized by his hand sliding up and down his huge, purple-veined, rock-hard cock. His muscular thighs were taut and his flat stomach shook with pleasure as he brought himself closer and closer to shooting off his load. Occasionally his left hand would stray to his chest and tweak his hardened nipples.

I thought of getting up and running from the stall before he could finish, but I didn't want him to hear me moving. I steadied myself with my hand on the tissue holder and realized that my own cock was stiff, pre-cum dribbling out of the piss-slit. I wondered how it would feel if I jerked off while watching the stud in the next stall working his meat.

The aroused man grunted softly, and a chill caressed my whole body. I was envious of the man I was watching, jealous of his total abandonment. He was pulling his cock with ever increasing speed, now and then spitting on his pulsating prick to lubricate it. I fantasized about his cock entering me, shaking down my throat or pushing deep into my asshole.

My cock was so hot it was almost unbearable. I thought of running to the sink and running cold water over it. My "sex partner" grunted again. I wanted to reach out and touch him. His rhythm quickened and I could see his deeply tanned legs and one side of his muscle-bound thigh as he moved slowly back and forth in a rocking motion on the toilet seat. I gasped for air as his thumb massaged his pre-cum-covered cockhead.

At that moment I wanted more than anything to kiss his beautifully erect cock, but I had to control myself. I tried to regain my presence of mind by looking at other things in his stall: his scuffed work boot, his half-opened flannel shirt, the leather band on his wrist. I knew that I would not leave him now. I wanted to see and feel the orgasm with him.

He came softly, his legs and ass making little spasm-slaps against the toilet seat. I sat upright, looking down at my own steely cock. A long, low sigh came from the next stall, and I heard the rustle of clothes as he put himself back together. Though I hadn't gotten off, I felt numb and exhausted.

The latch on the door made a loud sound as my "friend" let himself out of the stall. There was a rush of water while he washed himself off, seemingly unconcerned or unaware of my presence. I continued to sit perfectly still while he dallied at the sink. He took what seemed an inordinate amount of time. I dared not think he was waiting for me.

A heavy quiet fell over the room as the door closed behind him. The pungent scent of cum and piss wafted over me. My pulse was still racing. I was still so fuckin' hot. I wanted to call him back, shove his mouth down on my cock, fucking his face until I shot a huge wad of hot jism down his throat.

I tried to stand and had to lean against the partition wall to keep from sinking to the floor. I pulled my shorts and pants up. I rushed out of the rest room and down the long empty corridor, feeling as though a thousand eyes were on me. I burst into the mall shopping area with my eyes downcast, certain that the man from the rest room was watching my every move. I ran from the mall and frantically drove home.

For several days after the rest-room encounter, I was terribly agitated. Steven noticed my behavior and asked me what was wrong, but I couldn't bring myself to explain it to him. I couldn't even explain it to myself. I had no idea what had happened to me inside, what emotional layers had been stripped away. I had no previous similar sensations to compare my confused feelings with and no one to talk to.

Gradually, I recovered from the rest-room episode or, at least, I regained control of my outward emotions. Inwardly, I remained very agitated and unsettled, very unsure of myself. Yet I must have relived that scene dozens of times in my mind. I lingered over each sight and smell, savored each moan and flash of flesh. I would roll and writhe in bed and think about my rest-room lover's magnificent cock. I also caught myself thinking frequently about watching my lover jerk off and about a stranger watching me as I pulled my hard dick until jets of hot cream shot out of my pisshole.

Those fantasies continued with increasing intensity until one night a few weeks later, a night when I "found" myself sexually. There is a hospital in our town surrounded by some nondescript brick buildings that are the dormitories for the student nurses and residents. Some of the dormitories face a little-used side street, their first-floor windows not more than twenty feet from the street.

On a night when Steven was out late with a couple of his

friends, I took a drive through town just to get myself out of the house. I happened to turn past the dorms and caught a glimpse through a near window of a resident pulling his green tunic over his head. The scene seared my mind.

Without so much as a thought, I jerked the car to the side of the road, cut the engine, and got out. I looked up and down the dark road and slipped quickly onto the lawn and up to the window where I had seen the flash of cloth and exposed flesh. Trees and shrubs hid me from view from the road, but it would not have mattered had they not been there. I had no control of my actions. My cock ruled me completely.

I peered through the screen of the open window and saw a handsome young black-haired guy washing his hair in a small sink that was part of a private bath adjoining his bedroom. I have since been amazed at my boldness, but at that moment I gave no thought to anything except that wonderful scene.

The man was tall and muscular and totally naked, his body the stuff of centerfolds and wet dreams. His head was bent into the basin, his hair white with soap lather that he was working with his fingers. In his bent-over position, his firm, well-shaped ass stared at me and jiggled in rhythm as he massaged his head. His pecs undulated softly in unison to the movements of his arms. I could see his cock, half-hard and succulent-looking.

I leaned against the cool bricks of the building and ached to touch this man. I rubbed my own cock through my tight jeans. I could almost smell him.

The young doctor ran his hand through his soapy hair and scooped up a glob of lather. He pressed the soap into his pubic hair and began to rub it up and down his rapidly hardening cock.

He turned around, facing the window, and for a panicked moment I was afraid he had seen me. But he was absorbed in what he was doing and merely leaning against the sink for support, his hot ass pressing into the cold porcelain. He took another handful of soap from his hair and stroked his cock alternately with both hands. His leg muscles strained as he became increasingly aroused. He threw back his head and swayed it slowly from side to side. Small groans began to escape from his lips as he gave himself over to pleasure.

The object of my eyes threw his head forward and watched his hands as they stroked his erect cock, a real monster of nine throbbing inches. His nipples stood out hard from his lightly hairy chest. One of his hands left his crotch and massaged his muscular pecs.

I was drinking in his movements as I roughly stroked my fully erect cock. My asshole was twitching. How I wanted to feel the young doctor's great cock fucking my tight hole!

The doctor's moans seemed suddenly louder, but the sound I was hearing was my own groans coming involuntarily from my dry throat. I matched him sigh for sigh, grunt for grunt, and stuck a couple fingers into my mouth, pretending that I was sucking the doctor's big fat cock.

The guy's strokes speeded up. His eyes closed tightly as though he was in pain. His mouth was wide open, his face a mask of lust. I tried to imagine what he was thinking and feeling.

It seemed as though the pleasure had become too much for him because his knees buckled and he dropped to the floor on his knees. He moved one hand to his ass and I knew from the movement of his arm that he was inserting a finger into his fuckhole. I shuddered, imagining that it was my asshole he was penetrating.

My doctor knelt that way for several minutes finger-fucking himself, one hand pulling his huge erection, the other hand diddling his asshole, thrusting first into his fist and then back, impaling himself on his fingers.

I heard a deep growl and watched as his cum spewed from his cock. As he shot his load, he moaned sharply, pumping his pulsing cock with a mad frenzy of passion, as glob after glob of delicious-looking cream splattered the floor in front of him. As his orgasm subsided, he moaned contentedly, looking and sounding as though he had been released from some trying ordeal. He collapsed exhausted on the floor.

Racing back to my car, I pulled down my pants and shorts and roughly jerked myself off. I came violently, my jism squirting on the steering wheel and dashboard. I thought I'd never stop creaming! I must have shot off for a full five minutes.

When I came back to earth from my orgasmic orbit, I drove home. Steven's car was in the driveway when I arrived. The house was dark and I assumed he was asleep, for which I was thankful. I quietly let myself in and tiptoed toward the bedroom. A dim shaft of light shone from the bottom of the bedroom door. I peeked in. What I saw jolted me: Steven was stretched across the bed naked jerking off into one of my jockstraps. I was instantly aroused again, as excited as I had been spying on the doctor not a half hour ago. Here was my most constant fantasy realized in the flesh!

My lover was oblivious to my pleasure. He was rolling and grunting, rubbing my jock in his face, sniffing my crotch sweat, and then placing the jock over and around his big stiff prick. I started to undress, never moving my eyes from his writhing form. Finally, with a loud groan, Steven shot off into my jock, tossing and jerking and driving his throbbing cock into the sexy cloth.

I waited a couple of minutes until he had recovered and then walked into the room, sat beside him, and started to kiss him all over. He must have been shocked at my entrance, but I did not give him time to think. I smothered him with kisses and caresses, rubbing him all over and talking softly.

I began to tell Steven about my frustrations. I told him of spying on him when he pissed, of my desires to watch him jerk off, of the bathroom and dorm scenes. I included all the graphic details and described my feelings as best as I could.

My mind tried to prepare for my lover's reaction. Would he be angry? Jealous? Would he understand? But I was not prepared for what Steven did: he smiled at me, took me in his arms, and we made the most intense love we had ever experienced.

Steven, it turned out, had been as uncertain and frustrated as me and, like me, was too unsure to talk about it. After that beautiful night of sex, we opened up to each other about our sexual desires and discovered we had much in common. Steven was thoroughly aroused by my talking about my fantasies and was able to reveal his own.

One of Steven's biggest turn-ons is my talking about making love to another man. We now often begin our fuck-play with me describing such a scene. I have learned also the pleasures of jerking off with Steven watching, and he enjoys pulling himself off while I spy on him through a keyhole.

We both feel good about our sexuality now. Our sex life is varied and fulfilling. We are able to act out our sexual desires in the privacy of our own home. We're devoted to simultaneously pleasing ourselves and each other.

We are happy.

D . V . S A D E R O
WRITING AS RICK LANE

THEY

CALL ME

"HORSEMEAT"

BACK A FEW YEARS AGO, WHEN I WAS TWENTY-two, the thing I wanted most in all the world was to get my ass out of the boring little nowhere town I was born and raised in. It looked impossible to me, though. My parents both had died in a car crash a few years before, all the family I had, and what I inherited from them was mainly the bills for their funeral.

So I up and quit high school in my last year, which was no big sorrow for me, and surely no loss to education, and I went to work. I'm a helluva good motorcycle mechanic, if I say so myself. Harley to Honda, I don't have any prejudices at all.

Besides ridin' around on my big ol' Harley and my sex life, which was that small-town kind of stuff, all quiet and sneaky and never enough of it, I didn't have much except dreams. Like livin' in a big city and fucking all the time and partying, maybe getting into a gay bike club, bein' all open and free. And in a few years I was going to make the dream come true, when I'd got enough money saved up. It looked like a long, dull stretch of time ahead of me, though.

Then my life brightened up when I got to know Doc Zane. He was the last of the old family that founded the town, a real bright guy, kind of a thin, handsome dude in his forties. He lived all alone in this huge house with an acre or so of yard all around it. Doc lived on the family money and didn't work for a living, which some people in town thought was terrible. I wasn't one of them, though. He didn't care about anything but his chemical experiments he did in his basement, which is why everybody called him Doc, even when he wasn't any kind of doctor.

We happened to meet one night at a rest stop on the highway north of town, and one thing led to another and we were making it on a fairly steady basis. Doc was older and all, but he was wild and had the bucks too, so he could arrange three-ways and all kinds of fun stuff like that. He seemed to be just about the only *living* person in that town, besides me.

One time I asked him, "You got education and money and class, you dress to beat the band, and I'm a mechanic and a biker. How come we get along so well, huh, out of bed? In bed, I understand."

"We're both rowdies," he said, "you physically with your beefy, muscular body and your suicidal racing-about on your motorcycle. And I'm a mental rowdy. And both of us have a don't-give-a-shit attitude, and we both hate this flat little no-where town. And of course we've both lost our parents and are alone in the world full of jocks."

I couldn't disagree with a word of that, and we hung around together a lot. I was over at his place all the time. One night I was sitting on the couch in his living room, which was furnished the same as it was a hundred years ago, I reckon, and Doc was in a huge old chair, and we was watchin' some stupid shit on the tube, and when a commercial comes on he shuts it up with his zapper and he turns to me and says, "Beau, tell me honestly, would you like your cock bigger?"

"What?" I asked, like, you know, very surprised.

"And your balls, too," he says.

"Sure," I say, figuring there's a joke coming up, "of course. Who the hell wouldn't?"

"Exactly," he said, "to be sure." That was the way he talked.

"Too bad it's impossible," I say.

Doc looked up at me out of that thin, handsome face of his, smiling a real odd smile, and I could see his eyes were glittering.

"Isn't it?" I ask. "It can't be possible."

"Why not? Who has ever tried? Modern science has never addressed the problem . . . until now."

"Oh, Doc, come on," I say to him.

"Beau, I've been working on this problem for years."

"Sure," I say, figuring he's trying to blow my head out.

And he says, "Beau, when was the last time you saw my cock?"

"About two weeks ago," I say, "with that farmer's son who was hitchin' a ride into town."

"Exactly," Doc says. Then he stands up out of the big old chair, gets square in front of me, and opens his slacks and skins his shorts down his thighs.

Now I knew Doc's meat pretty well, and nice stuff too, but nothing out of porno flicks. Now, though, what he had looked to me about three times bigger. I mean large. A fat red pipe hanging way down, big head on it like a mushroom, and his 'nads were about the size of a coupla tennis balls.

All I could do was stare. I wanted to believe it so much. I reached out and felt around, up the crotch where his dark hairs could hide something fake.

"You think I'm wearing some sort of plastic or rubber appliance, Beau, don't you?" he asked me.

I didn't say anything, just cupped his balls for a few moments, then took a hold of his cock. Both felt nice and warm and real, and when I sniffed my hand there was a clean mellow smell of fresh ball-sweat.

"Okay," I said, letting him go and looking up at his face. "Where do I sign up? How much do you want? I'm poor, but

I have some savings, I can make time payments, and sell my motorcycle and . . ."

"Beau, Beau, calm yourself," Doc says, tucking all his beautiful meat back into his undershorts and zipping up his pants. "Of course, I'm going to give you the treatment too. We are going to be partners and become richer than anybody has ever been."

Doc's idea was to sell the treatment to a few rich men and let the word spread all quietlike. I was going to be his partner if I'd go for the treatment and pose for before and after photos, "because nobody'll believe us without them, just as you didn't believe me."

Me being big and muscular and, well, maybe a little tough-looking, was part of the deal too. "There will be those who will try anything to get at my discovery," Doc said. "And the treatment is sure to be illegal as well. Both brains and brawn are necessary. Are you game?"

"When do we start?" I asked, out of my head with excitement. Me, Beau, being both rich and hung.

"When you can stay overnight," Doc says, "this coming weekend."

That was a Thursday evening, I remember, because the next day at work was the slowest in the world. At five I split like a shot, got on my Harley and roared out to Doc's house.

In one of the many empty rooms in that big old place Doc had me strip down and pose for like thirty or so photographs, all different angles, me limp, then hard. After that we went down into the basement. He had me sit in a kitchen chair covered with a sheet and some towels, and he fitted a plastic sack-type thing around my cock and balls. A hose of clear plastic tubing led from it to a big glass vat that had some dark, greasy-looking liquid in it.

I asked Doc if I shouldn't be sterilized or anything, and he said that wasn't necessary. "It's beautiful in its simplicity," he said. "Invented right here in this basement. I merely brought together a number of facts scattered in a lot of publications in several widely separated scientific disciplines," or something like that. I think he used words that were even bigger. He was a proud man that day.

So he tells me to sit still and keep my legs wide apart, and he goes over to the vat and pours another liquid into it, clear stuff, and all at once there's a big fizzing sound and smoke or fumes pour out of the vat through the tubing, and then the plastic sack begins to puff up like a balloon, sort of, and my meat can't be seen for all the smoke around it, but it feels real warm. I'm expecting it to hurt or get real hot, but it doesn't.

An hour later it's all over. Doc is real careful about not letting any of the smoke escape, so I ask him if it's poisonous. He says, "No, just incredibly explosive. That's the only drawback, the only real difficulty in the whole treatment . . . except for the pain."

"The pain?" I ask. "You didn't tell me about any kind of pain."

"Beau," he says, "have no fear. It'll last only a day or so, and if it gets very bad I have a nice pill for you."

He said I shouldn't wear pants or underwear and gave me this big new bathrobe, a real pretty blue color. I put it on and we went upstairs where everything turned back to normal. We had dinner and watched TV.

Then I began to hurt really bad down there. Doc gave me a big white pill. I swallowed it and lay down on the couch. Next thing I knew it was morning. I pushed off the blanket Doc must have spread over me and looked down at my meat. My cock was layin' there just like always, kind of dark, but now it was about three times as long as before, and a lot thicker too. I lifted it up in one hand, and man, it really *weighed*. And it didn't hurt at all anymore. My nuts were two big beauties in all that reddish, wrinkly sac. I had just what I told Doc I wanted when he asked me before the treatment. I'd said I wanted a salami and tennis balls, like he had.

And there they were.

I was so happy, I was almost scared to feel that overjoyed. I got up and threw off the robe and stood there naked in front of this huge old mirror that hung over the fireplace. And I admired the hell out of myself, looked at myself from every side, held my cock up out of the way, and swung my balls back and forth; then I let go of my dick and watched it flop down, and I could feel the pull.

All of a sudden my scrotum tightened up, made a big hairy fist under my cock, which was beginning to curve and thicken, starting to get hard. And I just stood there with my legs apart and started stroking my big cock, watching every move I made and feeling it too.

"Stop that!"

"Aw, Doc, I . . ."

"Do you want to spoil everything?"

"No, of course not."

"Then put your robe on and relax."

I did what he told me, and he said that the change wasn't complete yet, that it would take a couple more days.

Doc said that on the next Tuesday night he'd have a young, good-looking guy at the house for me, that I could have sex then, under his supervision. Then he leaves me to fix my own breakfast and goes down into the basement to do some more of his experimenting.

I'm eating my fried eggs in the kitchen, at the big wooden table in the middle of the room, when I hear a noise. It sounds like snorting, and it seems to be coming from the spare room down the little hallway that goes back from the kitchen. I think this is kind of odd, since Doc hasn't said there's anybody else in the house, so I go down the hall and push the door open just a crack. A rich and mellow, man-type smell comes out, making my cock come to life. And lying on the bed, naked and uncovered, is this young guy, maybe eighteen or twenty, a little scrawny but nice-looking, sort of cute and kind of short, probably about 5'5". or so, though it was hard to tell with him lying down.

What had me staring was that between his legs were his balls, of course, but I swear they were the size of basketballs. Two hairy basketballs. And his cock lay up on his flat little belly. It was big and almost as long as a full-grown man's arm. I just stood there, looking and looking.

When Doc came back upstairs, hours later and looking tired, I asked him about the guy in the spare room.

"So you discovered Leo," he said. "He was my first try at giving the treatment to someone besides myself. What I did was dose him the same as I had. I didn't realize that the younger a man is, the better the formula works. Now I must find a way to reverse the process. And if I can't, well, I suppose I'll have to care for the poor thing for the rest of my life."

"Who is he?" I asked. "Does his family . . ."

"His name is Leo, no family to speak of, a youthful adventurer, hitchhiking across the country when we met."

"He can't even walk with all that meat on him."

Doc says, "I've made a sort of jock for him to wear, out of heavy netting, with a supporting rope that goes around his neck."

"That won't happen to me, will it?" I ask.

For the next few days I don't do anything sexy at all, and on Tuesday night I'm in Doc's living room, waiting for the guy he's hired from a "models' club" in the nearest city to this town, which wasn't very near, and the guy would get here on a bus and take a taxi out to the house. I knew all that had to cost a bundle, so I expected a pretty hot young hustler.

The doorbell rang about eight o'clock, and Doc lets in this movie-star-lookin' guy, all smooth tan skin, super-handsome face, lots of dark, wavy, gleamy hair, and a body the opposite of mine, muscular but kind of delicate, with narrow hips and a little high-riding butt on him. We all went into Doc's bedroom, and for once he had made the bed. Then Doc left, saying he'd be back in a little while. I told the hustler—he said his name was Ron—to strip, and he got naked and he was a real beauty, and real nice hung, too, though not like me, of course. I kind of tore off my clothes, dived at him and brought him down to the bed. Then I got up on all fours over him, put my stiff prick right at his face, and said, "Suck it."

He went at it in a real enthusiastic way, after he got over his surprise at its size. All he could get in his mouth was the head, but he did a hell of a job on that, so I was feeling good.

Doc came in and sat on the edge of the bed. He was bare-ass naked and getting off watching. I kind of slid down the hustler's great body and turned him face down. I smoothed that pretty little behind with my hands—it was the most beautiful ass I'd ever had up to that time. And there was Doc, lube on his fingers, so I let him grease up Ron's hole and my cock, and then, straddling the guy, I just sort of moved forward and sank my stiff meat into him—slow and steady. It took a while, but I got it in all the way.

This made the hustler groan and spread wider, but I knew he was finding it maybe a little hard to take, but I'd never felt better in my life, with the hot grip of his hole tight around my cock all the way from its head to the root.

I really made it last as long as I could, and all the while Doc was right beside us, watching everything, his big slab of cock sticking out hard and shiny from between his legs.

Finally I can't stop myself from shooting, and it's like I'm overcome by an attack, a fit of some kind, only I feel the most pleasure I've ever felt in my life.

I try to make it last, but pretty soon all that's left is the grunting, so I pull out and lie back on the bed, totally wasted. In a few minutes I get up and stagger out to the bathroom, and when I come back Doc is on top of the hustler, just wailing away. Doc takes his time, too. He's older, which helps, but he really knows how to hold back. Ron is looking all sweaty and he's breathing hard. But there's a smile on his face.

At last Doc finishes up and flops off, then lies there heaving in deep, noisy breaths of air.

Then Ron, the hustler, lets out a yell of pure fright. I look back over my shoulder, toward the bathroom door, where he's looking. Leo's standing there, his great mounds of balls filling this bag of, like, hammock netting that has a rope going around his neck to hold them up. And Leo's holding his stiff cock in his arms. Huge as it looked to me before, now it's like a piece of flagpole.

Before he realized what was happening, the hustler had grabbed his clothes. Now, naked, he runs past Leo and out the door.

Leo's just standing there, looking disappointed. "I only wanted to watch and jack off," he said.

We all heard the big front door slam shut.

I look at the kid and I'm feeling horny again, so I say, "Hey, Leo, let me fuck your ass, huh?"

Leo smiles and goes and lies face down on the bed. Doc helps him get rid of the net thing and arrange his balls in a huge "pile" just against his right hip. I put my legs over Leo's body, being careful and all, and after I get my cock into him and am feeling really fine having my second grade-A young butt for the day, I realize Leo is getting off in his own way, by kind of sliding up and down on his own hard cock that was lying between his hard, flat torso and the mattress. It must have been like lying flat down on a hot fence post.

All the while Leo and I were going at it, Doc was going ape. He clearly couldn't decide whether he wanted to watch us or lick all over Leo's huge mound of balls, and he was desperately trying to do both.

Leo began to shoot, and his hole played my cock like a flute, and I got where I couldn't hold off any longer. Doc was jerking off as he ate balls and sped up his hand to join us in going over the falls.

Incredible. I didn't know I had that much juice in me, especially for a second shot. The bedroom reeked of cum; it was wonderful.

That night, for hours, Doc and I made plans for the future. Like moving to a big city, for a start, to set up our business. But Doc didn't want to leave just right then. He said he was very, very close to figuring out a way to reverse the process, and in a few weeks or a month, when that was accomplished, then we'd leave Zanesville forever.

I was disappointed but, all considered, I could stand to wait a little while longer, now that leaving was sure.

A couple of days later, after work, I biked on out to Doc's to visit, and I found the street was blocked off, the air stank, and that big old house was nothing but a huge black hole in the ground with little whirls of smoke coming out of it here and there.

The town cop asked me a few questions, but I didn't say much, and the next day he let me look through the ruins. Chances of a book or a paper with the formula on it were real slight, I knew, but I had to look—and I might as well have been wading around in a coal bin. One of the firemen, friend of mine, told me they thought the house burned for a while, with the guys overcome by some kind of fumes, probably, and then exploded.

The next morning I revved up the Harley and left that town forever. But now I didn't have anywhere to go or any hot plans for the future. All I owned in the world was on my back, in my saddle pack, and between my legs.

I had a lot of adventures after that, but anyway now I'm living in LA, in Beverly Hills, to be exact. And a very big movie star keeps me. I'm real expensive, known around town by my nickname, Horsemeat, but he can afford me. And sometimes I laugh to myself, thinking how all his fans would react if they could see him with me, his legs in the air and begging for more. . . . See, my superstud movie star friend has a thing about bikers and cocks. . . .

It's a great life, swimming pool, private gym, big estate, parties and all, but sometimes I kind of miss Doc. He'd love to know I'm called Horsemeat, he'd just love that as a tribute to his scientific genius. I owe Doc a lot, my whole way of life, in fact, and escaping Zanesville, bless his ol' dead ass.

LARS EIGHNER

A COWBOY

CHRISTMAS

WE DON'T GET MANY CALLERS HERE. YOU WERE IN luck. Cookie outdid himself on account of Christmas Eve.

Now if you'll join me in the parlor for a little brandy and a smoke, I'll show you to the bunkhouse thereafter. The boy's gone to bathe in the kitchen. We celebrate Christmas special, as you will know presently.

I don't mean to inquire of your business, but if you are at liberty, we could use another hand. You'd be expected to make up your keep come springtime.

Well, I didn't want to say so, but I noticed you were particularly attentive to Cookie's offerings. You sleep on it. But if you are considering the job, there is a story you ought to hear.

You understand, I speak for the boy as well. What I say goes.

Let me draw aside the drapes. This is the biggest window on the Western trail. It was carted out, all in a piece, from St. Louis. See that pass, you can just make it out in the moonlight.

Through that pass, the notch south of the big peak, lies the high range.

This brandy is supposed to be good, but I wasn't born to brandy. You can see that. No, the old man left a quantity of this when he passed on. He favored it a great deal in his last years.

Seven years ago last October, we were a crew of five or six on the high range, the boy and me and the straw boss Will and a couple of the others. You're a sheep man, aren't you? Well, we run some sheep up there after the cattle come down. Not like the old days in Texas.

We had a flake or two of snow, but nothing to amount to anything. Still and all, time was getting by. Damned if the boy didn't break a leg.

The rest of us, all pulling together as hard as we could, managed to splint it straight. He tried his best not to show it, but I reckon we hurt him pretty bad.

We sent the others down with the stock. Will fashioned a pretty fair sled from the remains of an old wagon that must have broken down when they built the cabin up there. We waited for the boy to feel more himself until we could wait no more. One evening, at dusk, the snow began to fall in earnest. We knew it meant to close the pass. But the boy didn't want to move.

He had a pistol that we had left him some time when all of us had left him alone in the cabin, so there wasn't any arguing with him. Will and I drew straws and determined that I'd stay.

Of course, I was just as happy not to be the one to have to tell the old man that his boy was going to winter it on the high range.

We had beans and flour enough, so Will left me the rifle. But the boy suspected a trick. He lay awake all night with that pistol, and most of the next day. But by that time any fool could see that the two of us were snowbound.

Have some more of the brandy.

The boy was up and about by Thanksgiving. He felt fool-ish about keeping us up there, but done is done. His traps kept more than a little meat on the table, which is well because I don't do much harm with a rifle at any range to speak of. In fact, we resolved to lay some by for Christmas and I made a little lean-to which served for a smokehouse.

Once he was on his feet, the boy was frisky and full of beans. He thought he'd fix up the cabin to stay the year around. The old man had been in his cups since the boy's mother died. He beat the boy pretty regular, and weren't too nice to the rest of us either. I can't blame the boy for wanting a place of his own.

One more brandy and I'll take you to the bunkhouse. Be generous with yourself. You'll find it nippy when we step out.

You see the boy's filled out to be quite a man. You should have seen him that winter. He has put some meat on his bones since then, but he was a fine young buck then.

Yes, you know what I mean.

As December went by the game got scarce. I could not pretend to be hunting. We didn't go far from the cabin. The storms come up quickly. I began to get somewhat restless.

The boy, well he's religious about his bath. When his snow was melted in the evenings, he'd have his bath and stretch out naked in front of the fire to dry. You know, the wind would be whipping the loose snow around outside. I'd be sitting there. And his little rump would be all red in the glow of the firelight, with those golden furry hairs just aglitter.

You know how long the nights get up here.

By and by, it was getting to be Christmas. He kept saying that he thought Kriss Kringle had lost track of him. He only meant it didn't seem much like Christmas. All the time, the thought of that tight little butt was preying on my mind.

I'd go out behind the lean-to for some relief. But it couldn't freeze enough to cool me off.

I was losing sleep. My temper got short.

Still, we wanted to make the best of Christmas. He melted down snow and made a regular laundry so we would each have a change for Christmas Eve. While he went to check the traps, which was pretty useless by then, I decided to have a bath—I don't suppose it is all that healthy to bathe like that in winter, but he had shamed me into it. I spread out the table with meat and tortillas, and the bit of whiskey left from splinting his leg. When he got back and saw me in the clean duds and the whiskey on the table, he brightened a bit and admitted he had some applejack stowed away.

Dinner went well enough. We warmed to the liquor. But I have spent merrier Christmases. He cleared away the table. Then he began to make his bath, just like any other night. I pretended to clean the rifle, like I did every night, to keep my hands busy.

Pour yourself another and put on your boots. I'll show you to the bunkhouse.

He's always had those big round shoulders and a flat belly. He didn't wear that beard then. He didn't seem to notice or mind my watching him. He'd squeeze out the sponge and the water would run down his back, right into the crack of his ass. When he would bend over to wash his legs, it hurt in my pants.

With the liquor in me, I just leaned back and almost shut my eyes, watching the flicker of the fire as he scooted his belly onto the sheepskin and turned his head to the fire.

"Joe," he says when I thought sure he was asleep, "why don't you show me how." He wiggled his ass, which looked all the whiter on the black sheepskin. "I seen you one Saturday night with Will. I watched you through the loop of the bunkhouse door."

I knew he was telling the truth. I remembered the night he meant. The others had gone off. Will and I had got going before we thought to blow out the lamp.

"Do with me what you done with Will," he says.

A man is only flesh and blood. I figured the old man would kill me if he got wind of it. But I thought I'd have a feel of it. Ain't no harm in that. If they start shooting cowboys for patting each other's rumps, they'll run out of rounds in a hurry.

I squatted next to the boy. I swear, I really thought I'd just have a feel of it. I laid a hand on his flank. Those cheeks flared up, and pressed firm against my palm.

I began to suspect that I would have to have some.

"I'll be good," he says, all the time churning his belly

against the sheepskin. "I've practiced all I can by myself. I'll be as good as Will."

"I know," I says.

I stood up. In the back of my mind I was thinking that I ought to reconsider. But while I was reconsidering, I was letting down my jeans.

As soon as he saw mine, he got his hands on it. He sat up and stroked it a bit, as you might stroke a cat.

I reckon he wanted it real bad. All he knew about was from watching me and Will that once and however he had contrived to practice by himself. The instant he touched mine, his cock stood right up.

I hadn't seen it hard, except for glimpses when he rolled about on the sheepskin in his sleep. He had a man's cock then, as he does today. I took it in my hand. It was hard as a saddle horn, bouncing against his belly. I gave it a couple of healthy strokes. He got the idea and gave mine a good squeeze back. He was already gasping like a trout out of water. I thought that might be the end of it right there.

But he stopped and looked me dead in the eye like he was going to say something. Instead he flopped on his bunk, beckoning me with his fanny.

"Please give it to me, Joe."

I lowered myself down over him, thinking I'd just rub up the crack of his butt a bit.

I was still thinking he would never take it in. Then I looked down at the red head of my prick, plowing up the valley. It just made me wild.

I spit on my cock, saying to myself the whole time, *Cowboy, this piece will be the death of you.* I figured I'd go in hard and fast, and then I'd lay there until he settled down from the pain. But when I pressed firm against his tight little knot, it swallowed me up.

He just took it in.

Then he clamped down.

I've held onto reins for my life, but I've never grabbed nothing like his butt grabbed me. I stopped dead. I could have lost my load that second.

After a moment I gave him one of those long, slow strokes, everything I had, just to see how much he wanted. He squirmed, but just whispered, "Please, Joe." And that weren't a complaint.

When I pulled back, his whole body came halfway up with me, like he thought I wasn't about to put it right back.

The fire was low. The room was chilly. I hadn't given him three strokes. I looked to see my cock half in him. I was dripping sweat. A pretty picture, those cheeks tense and all aquiver, rearing back and trying to pull the rest of my cock back in.

Presently he was up on his elbows and knees, pressing his spine against my belly, milking my cock. I reached under him. It was harder than before. The head of it was already as slick as a sheepshearer's hands. When I got my fingers around it, he dropped his first load. "Don't stop on account of me," he says.

And I didn't.

I twisted him over on my prick like beef on a spit, kissed him soundly, and kept on pumping.

I thought of those nights he'd lain out bare-assed. I thought of the times I'd watched him fall asleep, waiting to hear him snore so I could get some relief in the corner. I thought of my cock rubbing itself red inside my jeans, aching for that tail, never thinking it would get there.

The more I thought, the harder I fucked him, looking him square in the eye, thinking of how I had hurt to get where I was. And he was looking back at that look, daring me to fuck him as hard as I could, teasing me because he knew I couldn't make him hurt. "Say it's good, Joe."

"Damn right," through my teeth, I says, "damn right it's good."

He pushed my chest back with his legs, so he could get his hand on his cock. I reckon it never did get soft. I got another eyeful of his butt taking my cock, so I slipped it all the way in and out. He whimpered when I pulled it out. "Give it back, Joe, now."

His cock jumped again, with those big nuts hanging in tight. His gut twisted over my cock. I could see the ripple in his gut. His first wad whipped over his head, thick and white. He ripped my load out of me. I spent inside of him until it was flowing back all over us.

I'd never spent like that before. But I wanted to keep on fucking him. He begged me to keep it in. I did.

I don't know if I fucked him all night. I just remember that when the gray light came, he was sitting up on top, riding it.

I never thought I could get it on my back, but he proved me wrong. He didn't seem to be done, so I put him in me. That didn't last as long as it takes to tell of it. He's learned a lot since then.

"Looks like Kriss Kringle brought me something after all," he said. That day to this, that's how it's been—partners.

When the thaw came, we got down. The old man had a fit of apoplexy while we were gone. I don't say it was just as well. I just say, sometimes things work out for the best. We made short work of mourning him.

Will, I think, had it in his head to run the place once the old man was gone. Will's a gentleman, though. When he saw how the boy looked at me, he asked for his references right then. He's doing well now, I hear.

I can see you don't mind my tale. I've got to get back to the boy now. There's the bunkhouse.

All the hands here know the story. We don't keep none that think ill of it. I reckon if you keep your eyes open around the bunkhouse, old Kriss Kringle will find something for you too.

Now, good night, sir. And a very merry Christmas.

ROBIN METCALFE

THE

SHIRT

THE STREET WHERE RANDALL ZINCK HAS HIS STORE is bracketed between busy thoroughfares. A torrent of traffic rushes past on either side of the little neighborhood. Occasionally a stray car wanders down the street as if lost. In the park across from Randall's store, sunlight settles through the trees like silt in a deep, slow pool. You can just hear the sound of traffic above the rustling of the leaves.

The faded letters on the tall, old-fashioned windows of Randall's store say ZINCK'S ARMY SURPLUS, but one can find all sorts of old clothes, not to mention camping supplies, among the dusty racks. Randall is both the proprietor and the only sales clerk. A tall, thin man on the elderly side of middle age, Randall has the air of a dealer in rare and erotic antiquities, a connoisseur of the most exquisite taste. His smile, while perfectly proper, is also somehow suggestive, as if it harbors an indecent secret. I know what you are looking for, it says, and I am quite certain you will find it here.

It is Randall's preference to deal in used clothing. For all their flashy stylishness, new clothes are cheap and shallow things. They have no history. Used clothing, even the most drab and tattered, is steeped in the past, in that most mysterious kind of history, the personal, the unknown. For what is unknown must be imagined, and how much vaster and more complex is the geography of the imagination compared to the plain streets of daily reality.

The first time I visited Randall's store, I found the jacket of my dreams. An old high school jacket, probably of the fifties or late forties, judging by the quality of the sturdy, navy wool cloth. The white satin lining under the collar was yellowed but still intact, the pockets bordered with white leather piping. And on the shoulder—what joy!—the name Steve, embroidered in silver thread. Who is Steve, what is he? By now, he is probably married, middle-aged, dead. I don't want to know. I can see him bundled in blue wool, during some ancient, innocent winter, going to basketball practice, walking his best friend home along the railway tracks, jerking off in his bedroom surrounded by pennants and Hardy Boy novels. I am in love with him. Every time I put on his jacket I become him, I put on his youth and his unknowing beauty. Strangers, misled by my small deception, address me by his name. Sometimes I correct them, sometimes I do not.

Randall always calls me Steve. He knows my real name, having seen it on my credit card when I made my first purchase. Nevertheless, he calls me Steve, out of respect for my fantasy. It has become our private joke. Since that first visit, he has treated me with a polite familiarity, as if he recognizes in me a kindred spirit. He smiles as the bell tinkles above the wooden door to announce my arrival and leads me to the bin of army-surplus footwear, where a pair of white canvas sneakers is waiting for me. A label sewn neatly to the underside of the tongue says that GAUTHIER, P. L., pulled these onto his sweaty feet more times than he would care to remember. I am enchanted, of course, and wear them home.

Three blocks from Randall's store, across from the army base on Gottingen Street, I crouch on the sidewalk to retie my shoelaces. A young man walks slowly past me, pauses, stops. I look up into the blue eyes of a pretty soldier with curly blond hair. He asks if I am from Windsor Park. Not understanding his question, I grunt noncommittally. He takes this to mean yes, and suddenly smiles at me as if I were a long-lost brother. I am from his regiment, it seems—he recognizes the sneakers. Can he walk with me? (Can he!) Used clothing can be one of the most powerful aphrodisiacs.

It is a fine bright day in early summer. Too fine—I know I won't get any work done today. A good day to visit Randall's store.

The air is warm enough to get away with wearing only a T-shirt. Light green, armed-forces issue, with darker green trim at the neck and sleeves. A gift from the pretty blond soldier, who left in the halflight of morning wearing one of mine. I can smell the odor of his golden skin trapped in the soft fabric. My armpits sprout dark hairs from under the sleeves, where his blond hair would have glistened before. And after he left my bed—embarrassment of riches!—I found his jockey shorts, lost between the tangled sheets. The horny god of love smiles on me. I have them on now, beneath my blue jeans. The white cotton that cradled his hard little nuts is wrapped snugly around my balls. They roll inside their hairy sac as the juices stir within. My cock nuzzles against warm cloth.

Randall's street is nearly deserted in the lazy afternoon sun. Two old men doze on a park bench in the little square. The shop is hazy with dust as I open the front door. A tinny aria from *Tosca* drifts up from a portable cassette player propped against the cash register. Randall is bent over a newspaper that is spread out in front of him on the countertop. He looks up to greet me with a genteel nod and returns to his reading. The smoke from his cigarette plays hide-and-seek with the shafts of light that filter through the dirty windows. The air in the store is warm and stale.

Randall always lets me take my time poking through the tumbled bins of clothing. I linger over piles of combat boots, sneakers, T-shirts, dark-green army sweaters peppered with moth holes, military caps with the insignia removed. I try one of these on, but as usual it is far too small. Do soldiers all have tiny heads? Nothing here catches my interest. I move over to the other side of the store, passing over the boxes of manufacturer's rejects and secondhand jackets. The table of used shirts is a circus of colors. I sort absently among garish paisleys and stripes, sniffing for the special find that makes the search worthwhile.

My fingers catch at a patch of dark cloth. I pull out a knit shirt with short sleeves. It is burgundy with fine yellow horizontal stripes. Nothing beautiful, but something about it holds my interest. Stretched and rumpled, it long ago lost its shape—or, rather, it gained a shape, that of the body it once clothed. The ghosts of biceps bulge at the sleeves, swelling pectorals stretch the chest, an invisible neck surges from the open collar. A faint male odor lingers about the fabric. Some unknown man has left his imprint here for me to snuggle into, as in the morning one might curl into the warm hollow left by a body that has gone on its way.

Ah, I see that one has found you. Randall regards me from behind his counter with that secret smile of his. That shirt is very special. You must try it on. He pauses to extinguish his cigarette with a delicate tap, then walks around the back of the counter and out into the store. Come. I'll open up the dressing room.

I follow Randall down the twisting aisles to the back of the store. The path to the dressing room leads through a rack of World War II greatcoats, looming shaggy and black like old bison. We push through the herd of coats and out into a small back storage room, crowded with dusty boxes. To the left is a familiar cubicle with a curtain stretched across the opening. I move toward it. No, says Randall, not that one. Over here.

Randall turns a key in a lock and pushes open the door to a small room that I have not seen before. He flips on the light and it glares off of white walls and ceiling. Here we are, says Randall. Take as long as you like. I step into the room and pull the door shut behind me.

The bareness of the room is a relief after the musty clutter of the store. It is larger than an ordinary dressing room. A chair upholstered in blue vinyl is positioned against the wall to my left. Across from it stretches a large mirror. And beneath the mirror, a clean white shelf, with a glass bottle, a neatly folded towel, and a book.

I strip off my T-shirt and pause to admire myself in the mirror. I run my fingers lightly over the ripples on my stomach, bought with the agony of many thousands of sit-ups. The burgundy shirt is soft to the touch and tickles my nose as I pull it over my head. It flows like a cool hand across my skin. What man has worn this shirt before? I feel as if I am in contact with him now, through my contact with the shirt. I regard myself in the mirror. I have deliberately let the shirt fall carelessly. The collar is crumpled and crooked, the tail hangs out rumpled over my jeans. My hair is mussed up. I look like a tough. For a moment I experience that delicious sensation of seeing myself as a stranger, someone glimpsed briefly on the street, perhaps a laborer. It's an ugly shirt, and shows its age, the sort of shirt a man would wear to perform heavy physical work. To hoist garbage into a truck, perhaps. I smile at myself, a come-on to the stranger in the mirror. I strike a couple of poses.

My movements bring my eye back to the articles arranged on the shelf. They have been placed there as neatly and carefully as if on an altar. They are Randall's, I tell myself, and private, but my curiosity gets the better of me. I unscrew the cap of the bottle and take a cautious sniff. Ordinary vegetable oil. In a dressing room? I move on. The towel is antiseptically clean, with a chemical odor, its virginity restored by detergent and bleach. If it has any secrets, it will not give them up. At last my hand hovers over the book. It is large with a black cover, a looseleaf binder I now realize, not an ordinary book. Carefully, as if trespassing, I turn back the cover.

The image startles me. For a moment I think I am looking again in the mirror. A dark-haired, muscular man gazes at me, his build as stocky as my own. He is wearing the same burgundy-and-yellow knit shirt that I am wearing now. But he is not me, of course. The man in the polaroid photograph has a ragged moustache; I am clean shaven. His hair is a cluster of playful curls, like that of a Greek faun. Mine is straight. Nevertheless, the resemblance is striking.

The next page holds another surprise. The same man, only now his hand has moved up from his side and reaches in toward the center, to grasp his cock, which is hard and exposed. The cloth of his jeans is peeled back in a wide V, his balls dangle free like pale fruit, the pink shaft points up toward his navel. More images follow, showing him pushing the shirt up over his chest, squeezing his balls, closing his eyes—and finally, in the last photograph, trailing his fingers through a shiny puddle of white smeared across his belly. I gaze at this last image with rapt attention, my hand pressed against the growing bulge in my jeans, gently kneading the eager flesh.

Did I say the last photograph? I meant the last of him. For the next page begins a new series, this time of a slender young blond man with long lank hair. The burgundy shirt hangs loosely over his flat belly. This one has his pants off entirely, posing with his cock in his hand, smirking at the camera. His eyes remain wide open right through to the final photograph, watching the white liquid come threading out into the air. My own cock is pounding at the tight fabric of my jeans.

The photographs continue. I plunge into them as if deeper into a dream. There must be at least a dozen men. I start to count, but keep losing my concentration. A thin man with close-cut brown hair, as stern and serious as a schoolteacher, his cock a ruler pointing upward. A middle-aged man, grizzled and masculine, thick hair sprouting from his powerful arms and from the open neck of the burgundy shirt. A soldier with a tiny black moustache and a tattoo on the bulge of his upper arm, gazing from the photograph with deep, liquid eyes. His cock aims straight out of the picture like a gun. A dozen men, standing before a white wall, their cocks hard for the camera, jerking off one by one. Eyes open or closed, cocks straight or curved, cut or uncut, all joined in the animal ritual of coming.

The mirror presents me, spotlit in a white room like an actor in the opening scene of a play. The script lies open before me. I examine the mirror more closely. The glass is dark, like the mirrors in police questioning rooms. Not all the light is being reflected. I press my face against the glass and peer into a silver void. I see my own eyes glistening in the shadow of my hand. My reflection steps back and smiles at me. We know what to do next.

I take my time starting, rubbing the hard ridge that has risen in my jeans. Deliberately, with a tantalizing slowness, I open the fly, gingerly lift out the tender balls, the long pink root of my cock. The edge of the shirt brushes against the tip of my cock, a maddening sensation that makes it stiffen and point upward. My hand strokes soothingly up and down. Horniness seems to flow into my groin from the shirt. The mirror turns me into my own porn star, one of a series. Tinker Tailor Soldier Sailor. Me, I'm the Garbage Man. Stick out yer can. I have ceased to be me and have become an ideal type: Man with Hard-on.

My balls are framed by the folded-back flaps of my jeans. The pressure of the underside of my cock is pleasant, but the pants are becoming an encumbrance. I peel them off and feel the sweet freedom of air tingling against my bare ass. My cock waves in the air like a flag. I prance about the room, horny as a goat, grabbing my stiff dick and eyeing myself in the mirror. My cock feels as if a dozen hard cocks were stuffed inside it, the dozen hard-ons of the men who have worn the shirt before me.

The mirror makes the room a closed circuit. There is nowhere to look except at my own reflection. My flickering glance cruises the stranger in the mirror. I am alone with my eyes, my cock, and the burgundy shirt. I leer at myself lustfully, strutting and grinning like a bare-assed satyr. The joy of prancing begins to fade. I settle into the chair for some serious pleasure. As my sweaty behind makes its clammy contact with the cold vinyl, I remember again that I am bare-assed. The sticky surface squeaks the word as I wriggle about, whispers it to my cock, which is trembling with frustration, but I won't let it come, not yet.

Ever so slowly, I peel back the soft velvet blanket of my foreskin. The flesh beneath is swollen to a slick, glistening red. My dry fingers are raw against the tender skin. As I reach toward the shelf, I thank my thoughtful benefactor for the provision of the slippery golden oil the bottle contains.

I cannot put it off any longer. As the pressure mounts, I give in to the pounding rhythm of my fist, give myself over to the spirit of Horny Man that inhabits the shirt, that is possessing me as the hot tide rises within me. Even the image in the mirror is squeezed out of consciousness as my eyes close and I am lost to spurting, surging pleasure. In the moment of serene silence that follows I hear only my own heartbeat and a faint mechanical click and whirr from somewhere behind the glass.

Randall is sitting behind the counter when I come out again into the store. He smiles and raises his head from the paper before him. An interesting garment, is it not? I nod and smile in return. Too bad it is not for sale, he sighs—it is part of my personal collection; it would never do to break up the set.

The bell above the door tinkles over my head. The sound of *Tosca* trails after me, out into the sunlit street.

MICHAEL LASSELL
WRITING AS MICHAEL LEWIS

NEGATIVE

IMAGE

THE CITY HAD BEEN BEASTLY—HOT AND HUMID, THE way it always is in New York in August. You could feel the fever of the pavement come up at your feet through the soles of your shoes. Racial tension was running high as usual, but everyone was equally miserable, complaining ad nauseam about the relentless tropical weather and saying how it wasn't the heat but the humidity that made summers so unbearable. I thought if I heard one more person drop that irritating cliché into a conversation with a stranger I'd have to kill them both. I understood why the murder rate soared with the temperature.

I'd gone up to Times Square to see if I could snag a seat in an air-conditioned theater at the half-price TKTS booth, but I was too early to get on line and had to waste some time. I was watching a group of German tourists, all blond and rosy, the boys with their muscular hiking legs bulging through thin blue shorts, and I bumped into a cute little black dude.

He had his T-shirt tucked like a towel into the back of cutoff Levi's. His skin was gleaming from sunlight on sweat.

We exchanged apologies and more than casual eye contact, but he moved on down Broadway without breaking stride. He wasn't even a block away when I noticed that this slight, accidental human contact had triggered a hard-on in my jeans. It'd been days since I'd had sex. Something about the heat was making me angry, and something about the anger was making me horny. I was primed.

I looked around to see what was up and found myself standing in front of a small "all-male cinema." I could hardly believe my eyes. There on the poster, under sooty rain-streaked glass, was good old Ray Asher. I'd have recognized that face anywhere, it was so burned into my brain. After all, Ray was the first guy I'd ever gotten it on with. The first guy I'd ever smoked dope with, too, which made him pretty memorable. And he *was* pretty. At least to my way of thinking.

I'd known Ray a little around our college campus, but we'd never talked much. Then one night we found ourselves sitting next to each other at my favorite Brando flick, *On the Waterfront,* which the film society was showing in the science lecture hall on the main quad. It's one of those brutal black-and-white films that makes you feel depressed and really good at the same time, kind of morose but ready to kick ass. When the movie was over and Ray asked me if I wanted to come up to his dorm room to sample some pot he swore was Hawaiian, I said sure. But it wasn't the weed I was hot for.

I don't know what his ancestry was, but Ray looked like what I thought an Italian should look like, or a Sicilian anyway. He was shorter than me, about five-seven or -eight, and had dark skin and black curly hair. Which made him pretty much my opposite. If he'd been a magnet, I'd have been a billion iron filings clinging to his poles.

His nose was typically aquiline, and he had a thick beard stubble that always looked like it needed shaving. He had full fleshy lips that were most comfortable when slightly open in a kind of pout and the bluest eyes I'd ever seen in so dark a face. He was like a boy with a man mask on, an acolyte pretending to be priest for the Festival of Fools. I'd never managed to catch him in the shower, but I'd seen him in shorts. His arms and legs were covered with hair. He had a compact little butt and a basket that looked like it held more than you'd expect from a man his size.

When we got to his room, he peeled off his jacket, shoes, and socks and opened the top button of his jeans. He was wearing a loose sweater than hung nicely across his hard chest. Since we were making ourselves at home, I took off my boots and sat on one of the two beds. Ray sat on the other. His roommate had dropped out midsemester, so he had the room to himself for the rest of the year. I leaned forward, my elbows on my knees, my eyes glued to every move he made.

He rolled a couple of reefers and lit one, taking a deep toke, squinting his Mediterranean-blue eyes. When he handed me the joint, I had to tell him I'd never smoked marijuana before, but he told me what to do, then showed me. He stared at me intently as I tried to follow his lead. At one point, our eyes locked into the kind of open invitation that would have spooked both of us—if we hadn't been so stoned. He broke the tension with a wink.

I don't know what was in that shit we smoked, but I blasted off, higher than I was prepared for, certainly as high as I've ever been on grass since. It was *great* stuff.

Well, Ray stretched out on one bed and I stretched out on the other, and we started groovin' on the ganja, each of us in our own private world. It wasn't long before I was getting that nice warm feeling in my lap that meant an erection was coming up . . . like daffodils in spring. I had no idea how horny grass would make me. I looked over at Ray on the other bed. He had kicked off his jeans and was lying there in his jockey shorts and sweater, which was pulled up to his chin. He was stroking his nipples with one hand and rubbing his hairy stomach with the other. He had achieved an enormous piss-hard boner that was peeking over the waistband of his briefs.

I came to immediate full attention. My balls were pinched against the crotch of my jeans, so I stripped them off. I took my shirt off, too, so I wasn't wearing anything but my underpants and socks. When Ray happened to look my way, he saw me propped up against the wall staring at him, my own blood-swollen cock straining against the fly of my BVDs, oozing a drop or two of slippery juice into the absorbing cotton. Ray slid his hand down to his groin, stuck his hand under the elastic, and started massaging his cock and balls. He kept his intense blue eyes riveted on me. I thought I would cum just looking at him.

He was tugging on his prick now, and the jockeys were slipping farther and farther off it with every motion of his hand. I was getting a better and better look at the thing. I'd never seen one so big and dark. The veins of it were enormous. I liked what I was seeing. A silent voice inside my head was screaming at me to do something when Ray said, "You ever done it with a guy before?"

I was embarrassed by the question, but I was more shamed by the truth, which was that I'd wanted to—God, I'd wanted to!—but I never had. So I dropped my hand into my lap, took hold of my throbbing tool, and said, "Yeah."

Ray shifted his weight onto his shoulders, lifted his knees into the air, and with one motion slid the jockey shorts down his hips and kicked them off with his feet. He spread his legs— one knee up, one leg extended—exposing two huge balls totally covered with curly black fur. They looked like two goose eggs in a hair nest. His thick, uncut dick tapered to a hot purple head that pointed up past his navel. He lifted the sweater over his head and posed there on the bed, totally naked and ready to be had.

"Well," he finally said, "then what are you doing way over there?"

Now, I said I'd never done it before, and I hadn't, but I'd read some choice books and had a vivid imagination when I wanted one. I had a pretty good idea about the basics going in, and I managed to finesse the more sophisticated moves without too much fumbling. I stood up and dropped my drawers. My cock was sticking straight out across the room—right at Ray's eye level. I was smaller than him, but I came to a full round head, so I figured we were about even. He sat up on the bed as I walked toward him and opened his mouth. I popped in without so much as an implied hesitation. I thought I'd shoot the minute that warm, wet mouth of his took me inside it, but Ray had other ideas.

After sucking me to the brink of bursting, he pulled his head off me and started to tongue my balls, by this time as tight up inside me with pleasure as they get before I shoot. I could feel him pulling at the hairs behind my nuts with his teeth. Then he turned me around, bent me over, and started lapping my ass like a thirsty dog.

I'd never felt anything like it, and I didn't know how much I could take before my skin split its seams. He zeroed in on my virgin hole, prying it open with his thumbs, and stuck his tongue as far into it as he could, his hands spread across my butt cheeks. "I'm going to cum," I moaned. Ray wheeled me around and took my cock in his mouth so he could drink the hot milk that was gushing out of me. I thought I'd squirt a gallon, but he kept taking it, gulping it, crooning as he swallowed, each contraction of his throat coaxing more liquid out of me.

When I was finally done jerking, he took my pecker in his hand and licked the end of it, like a kid with a Popsicle, then he scratched that hard black beard stubble of his across the tops of my legs and I thought I'd collapse with satisfaction.

Ray looked up at me with those fabulous eyes of his and leaned back on the pillow, offering his big, hard hunk of meat. It was already dripping into the raven hair of his taut abdomen. He had his knees pulled up and wide, and I could see between his thighs the white hemispheres of his lower ass. It shone like an oasis in the desert. He put his hands behind his head, showing off two tufts of moist glistening hair, then smiled and said, "Go to it, man. You're the best."

I'd never gone down on a guy before, especially one hung as big as Ray, but I took to cocksucking like my mouth had been made for it. I started with the small pointed head of the cock and took as much of the shaft as I could. I had a little trouble at first, but as I relaxed into it—excited by Ray's obvious increasing pleasure and the man smell of him—I was able to take most of the hot rod into my mouth. I started to lick his cum-heavy balls and his musky asshole, but before I could get into it, Ray let out a loud, guttural cry, and his stomach muscles clenched violently. His scrotum tightened and a huge wad of hot cum landed on my left shoulder. I straightened up and let the rest of the semen spurt into my face. I was trying to lick it off as fast as possible, but he was shooting the stuff all over. I was dripping with it.

When his spasms finally subsided, he licked the rest of his cum off my face, and stuck his tongue, which was loaded with it, into my mouth. I loved the salty taste of his rigid tongue. It made me hard all over again. I asked Ray if I could fuck him. He said he wasn't into that, so he had me straddle his hips, the great bulk of his semihard cock now nested in the crack of my ass.

As he gently rocked his hips and stroked my thighs with his hands, I jerked myself off, shooting onto his hairy chest almost immediately. I stayed like that, running my hands around in the sticky hair, until it started to dry. Then we stepped into a steaming shower. It took us nearly an hour, we spent so much time soaping each other's privates and sucking each other's tongues, and Ray wanted to get off again. It was a night to remember, and I've done my best to retain every particular.

Naturally I wanted to get it on with Ray again as soon as possible, but he said that he didn't like to mess around with the same guy twice, and that he preferred women in any case. I was pissed off, but by then I'd found another dark little man to play with, this one a Panamanian. His ass wasn't quite as perfect as Ray's, but he liked it stuffed regularly, so I wasn't complaining. Then I heard that Ray knocked up one of his girlfriends and they both got tossed out of school. I never saw him again—until that day in Times Square when I happened to spot his picture on a porn movie lobby card.

I paid my money and sat down in the small, dark theater. There were twenty or so other guys in there, spread out. The air-conditioner was turned up full blast, but nobody was shivering, at least not from the cold. One guy in front had his pants around his ankles, and another was diving into the lap of a fat man in the back. I sat down near the middle of the auditorium.

It was a pretty standard flick as these things go: sucking, fucking, and a lot of moaning on the soundtrack. There wasn't any plot to speak of, but it was Ray, all right. He was playing this supposedly straight guy who keeps getting involved with impossibly perfect blond studs. Each scene became a contest to see who could be hotter and hunkier than the other.

Ray had obviously done some serious bodybuilding since that night I first sucked dick. And whatever experiences he had had or not had before I met him, he was giving his paying customers the full range of the male repertoire—from jerking off to getting fucked fore and aft by a pair of look-alike muscleheads. The scene reminded me of Chinese handcuffs, those woven bamboo tubes you can't get off until you stop pulling and start to push.

I sat in the mildewed darkness with my hand through the open fly of my 501s and watched the engagement of lubricated organs, tongues in mouths and assholes, sweat sliding between nipples rubbed raw by admiring partners, and I thought about that flash of white ass I caught a glimpse of that first night with Ray all those years ago. By the time the scene came where a huge black man was slamming himself up Ray's chute, I was frigging my own cock so hard I was about to cum in my pants.

I turned my head and caught the eyes of a Latin-looking kid who had moved closer to me twice. He didn't look old enough to be in here, but I figured he probably knew what he was doing—even if he didn't speak the language. I closed one button of my jeans and walked past him, nearly rubbing my crotch in his face as I went by. I could feel his desire, his heat. I could feel a drop of moisture leaking out of my dick into my knotted pubic hair.

I walked through the draped-off "lobby" and downstairs into the toilet. There were two older guys in there with their hands in each other's pockets. They stopped when I walked in, but got back to business within seconds. There weren't many places to go in this theater, so I knew the kid—and I wanted him to be a kid—would show up here if he was going to follow at all. He did.

Our eyes did a quick inventory. He was older than I thought in the dark, but more attractive, like a saint being tortured by the Inquisition in some Spanish Renaissance painting. In fact, he looked a lot like Ray, as Ray looked upstairs on screen: on the short and solid side, dark, hairy, overdeveloped. He was wearing tight black jeans with a tantalizing basket and a red tank top that showed volcanic nipples. You could almost see them pulsing they were so big, so full of themselves. He walked past me into the stall at the far end of the bathroom. The two old guys stopped again to see if there was a chance on them getting in on some new action. There wasn't, and they knew it.

The kid was hidden inside the stall, but he hadn't shut the door. I could see his feet under the partition. Then I heard a zipper and he dropped his pants to his ankles. The hook was baited, and I was ready to be reeled in. It would have been plain rude to ignore so direct an offer, especially since I had started this little fishing expedition myself.

He was sitting on the porcelain stool with his shirt off, nude down to his high tops. His tits were the size of quarters and protruded what must have been half an inch. They were wreathed in jet-black hair. His dick wasn't the biggest I've ever seen, but it had a terrific shape to it and was nearly classic in proportion and detail. The head was dark red and was stretching the skin on the underside of the shaft to its limit, he was so hot.

I turned and looked at the two old men, wondering how soon it would be before I stopped being a contender and stepped out of the ring for good. My heart started pounding in my chest, the way it did when I walked across the room with my hard-on pointed at Ray's mouth that first time. I shut the door and slid the little chrome bolt into its slot and moved between the kid's thighs.

He looked up through long eyelashes and, without a word, pulled my belt open. He unbuttoned the one I had closed and pulled my jeans down to my knees, brushing his long curly hair against my stiffening cock. When he sat back up to get a good look at what he'd gone after, he let out an audible "Oh . . ." I was glad he was pleased. I licked my fingers and took one of his tits between the thumb and middle finger of each hand and started squeezing, pulling, twisting, until his mouth was open with promise of things to come and he wrapped his lips around my dick, massaging my butt as I pinched and tweaked. I thought he'd go crazy, he was making so much noise, and I was having a fine time, too.

I dropped my head back and started rocking my hips, pushing farther and farther into his throat. I could see in my mind's eye that patch of white ass from all those years ago, the same patch of ass that was splayed across a movie screen somewhere above my head. I pulled out of the kid's mouth and, before he could offer an objection, I flipped him around. He bent over the bowl with his hands on the back wall for balance and offered me his ass with a demure upward tilt of his hips.

I reached around and stuck the middle finger of my right hand into his mouth. When it was slick with spit I pulled it out and tried his asshole, a loose pucker surrounded by dark moss. My finger slid in without resistance, so I rubbed some saliva onto my cock and pushed into his asshole, which opened to take me. The kid smelled like a working man wearing perfume. He was letting out little "ay . . . ay . . . ays" every time I lunged, and he took his hands off the wall to spread his cheeks farther apart. I was thrusting into him, in and out, in and out, like a popular tune you can't get out of your mind. I was sweating like a horse in the home stretch.

I grabbed hold of the horns of the kid's pelvis, ramming a little deeper and rougher than I might have—because by now, of course, I wasn't fucking a tough little stranger in a porn flick john, I was fucking Ray the way I had wanted to once upon a time. The kid was jerking himself off hard and fast, like he had an appointment to get to, and I felt his knees go limp for a second, then he let out a loud groan. He arched his back and his cum flew all over the stall, hitting the back and side walls and dripping down over the graffiti, melting it. I plunged, fierce and violent, until just before I was about to cum, then I pulled out and gushed like Niagara Falls all over his ass and back, up into his hair. I hadn't had a climax like that in years.

When I got back into the auditorium, I needed a minute for my eyes to adjust to the dark. I stumbled down the aisle until I got to a row I thought was empty. When I finally looked up at the screen, I saw Ray. He was lying on a bed in what looked like a dormitory room. He was wearing nothing but his jockey shorts and was fondling his equipment under the white cotton. "You ever do it with a guy before?" he said, and an off-screen voice said, "Yeah." Ray peeled off his shorts and opened his legs, exposing his stiff cock and heavy balls and that magical patch of white ass. "Well," he said up there on the torn, stained screen, "then what are you doing way over there?" Then a cute blond guy with a huge cut dick and tight, hairless scrotum walked into the frame. Ray sat up on his bed and opened his mouth like a penitent ready for the Host. As the blond guy approached, he put his dick right up to the hilt into Ray's mouth. Then he turned his hard white ass toward the camera, revealing a neat little tattoo that read: THE END—CUM AGAIN.

LEIGH RUTLEDGE

BRIAN'S

BEDROOM

A PAIR OF DIRTY JEANS LYING ON THE FLOOR IN THE doorway to Brian's bedroom. The jeans are like an animal curled up, only pretending to be asleep. They were obviously tossed there in haste, a last-minute thought before his departure. The ass of the jeans is deeply faded and frayed: there are slashlike rips around the rear pockets, at those points where a guy's ass rubs hardest against the inside of the denim. Something about them just lying there makes me ache for a moment, the way the sight of some beautiful boy walking down the sidewalk, a shirtless boy one will never know, can make one ache— the kind of pang you forget a second after it comes and the boy is out of sight. The door to the bedroom itself is half-closed. Walking by it, I get a glimpse inside but see only shadows, indistinct shapes—a volleyball, dirty socks, and a leather belt. . . .

"He's such a slob," Dave tells me good-naturedly.

■ ■ ■

In the morning, on the way to the bathroom to take a piss, I stop for a minute and push Brian's bedroom door open slightly to look inside.

The curtains are drawn. At the foot of the bed is another pair of jeans. There are a couple of posters on the wall. A weight-lifting bench, some ski equipment, a black leather jacket, sleek and luminous, with rows of soft creases down the arms, a sign of the leather adapting to the flesh that wears it—all muted and slightly unreal in the dirty gray light, like objects floating in a dream. . . .

"What are you doing?"

I turn around. Dave is looking at me with a hesitant smile on his face.

"How long is he gone?" I ask nonchalantly.

"He won't be back until Friday. He's in Oklahoma City visiting his parents for a week. Why don't you get dressed so we can go get some breakfast? I'm famished."

Brian is Dave's new roommate. I've never met him, I've never even seen him. In fact, I've only talked to him once on the phone, briefly—a masculine, reasonably sexy voice, easy and flirtatious—the voice of a vain boy always on the lookout for admirers, or at least a good lay. He's twenty-two. Dave describes him as being incredibly hot, a real beauty: smooth, muscular, with darkish blond hair and deep-blue eyes, and "the sweetest ass you've ever seen—white, creamy, flawless." Almost sweeter than his ass, though, Dave tells me, are his lips: full, masculine, and beautifully shaped. "Hungry-looking," Dave adds with that pride, a kind of flaunting possessiveness some people exhibit just having a beautiful roommate they know everyone else desires and envies them for.

He and Brian have never had sex or anything; they're not lovers, just roommates. Dave tells me he thinks Brian is bisexual—or *was* bisexual—or is maybe just a little confused still. "He jacks off enough though," Dave tells me dispassionately. "I mean, I can hear him going at it in there every night." Dave shrugs and laughs. "It doesn't seem to bother him. At least he isn't a screamer like Lawrence was. Remember when you were here last April?"

Dave has to go in to work for an hour or so, and after he leaves, I walk in and look around Brian's bedroom, not with any specific intent, just with a kind of bored and nagging sexual curiosity. Who is this boy? What is he like? Pushing open the door all the way, I feel a strong adrenaline rush, the way I used to feel as a kid surreptitiously exploring my parents' dresser drawers or sneaking a peek at the dirty books my father always kept hidden under some old clothes at the back of his bedroom closet.

The feeling of stepping into the middle of someone else's life is strong.

The curtains are drawn against the bedroom's only window. There's a cooped-up smell of sweat and musty clothes, the evocative smell of a young male body; it's like the smell of a boy's locker room but not quite as pungent.

I walk around a volleyball in the middle of the floor and a wrinkled pair of lime-green gym shorts just beyond it. Brian seems to have left only a minute earlier. Against the right-hand wall is a weight-lifting bench, celebrating the body with incline bench presses, two-arm dumbbell curls, and leg pull-ins—the body as sex tool, as cultural weapon, as political statement. A stack of round weights sits in the corner, along with a wadded-up jockstrap and a scuffed pair of cross-trainers coming apart at the seams. I run my hand along the red vinyl bench and imagine some beautiful boy stripped to his jock and working out hard, with sweat on his neck, pecs, and face; his bare ass slides back and forth along the vinyl as he pumps his muscles. Maybe he jacks off sometimes after a workout, and the cum and the sweat mix in a small pool on his upper belly. He uses the jockstrap as a cum-rag, the fabric stiff and potent from semen and sweat. . . .

There are several items taped to the wall above the bench. A postcard: "Brian, Having a helluva good time (2 cut, 1 uncut). San Diego is HOT. Surfers and sailors everywhere. Flying on to SF tomorrow. Stroke it once for me, buddy—Jeff." Next to that, torn from some newspaper, a photograph of two high school wrestlers, one holding the other down on his stomach, both boys obviously struggling, obviously straining their muscles to the limit; the boy on the bottom has a harrowing and somehow intensely erotic grimace on his face, the kind of wrenched-up face you see on a young male who is being fucked, hard, up the ass, and for whom the feeling is both brutally shocking and a sudden revelation of fulfillment. Next to that, a magazine photo of a shirtless construction worker, his powerful torso sunburned, his low-riding 501s dirty and bulging; it's an ad for a national brand of home insurance.

My eyes scan the top of Brian's nightstand. A comb, a cigarette lighter, a rawhide strap. There's also an ashtray, pilfered from some casino in Las Vegas (in it are the remains of a joint), a gray bandanna-type handkerchief rolled into a ball, and a beaten-up paperback copy of Tom Clancy's *The Hunt for Red October*. Sticking up out of the nightstand drawer is part of an envelope; the return address is from Oklahoma.

Beneath the nightstand is a tall stack of porno magazines. There are the usual gay slicks—"Rock-Hard Nudes!" "Sizzling Summer Fiction!" "Fraternity Flesh Issue!" "True Experiences: Our Readers Tell All!"—plus a few bondage and S&M magazines at the very bottom, as if Brian has occasional, hesitant fantasies about kinky sex he isn't willing yet to fess up to. There are also a couple issues of *Penthouse* and *Playboy*.

As I thumb through one of the *Playboy*s, a Polaroid snapshot falls out from between the pages and lands on my shoe. It's of a tall, broad-shouldered blond boy standing naked; he's smiling devilishly at the camera and holding a huge hard-on toward the lens. Whoever it is—Brian or someone else—has an enormous cock and huge balls. His hair is all disheveled and standing up in the back, as if he had just come from an active round of sex and the lingering traces of grease and sweat in his scalp made the hair stiff and unruly. On the back of the picture someone has written, "Great fun, huh? Love, R."

Browsing through some of the jack-off magazines, I wonder which ones give Brian the biggest hard-ons, which images turn him on the most, which of these pictures—the young blond ranch hand tied to a fence post to get fucked, the sergeant licking the buck private's ass, the football player in his jock-strap and pads—does he go back to, time and time again, for the most intense and satisfying orgasms? Which of these situations and fantasies, if any, most accurately reflect his deepest longings, the sexual yearnings of a indecisively bisexual, twenty-two-year-old male? Or does he swing back and forth between *Penthouse* and the gay slicks, between fuckable women and beautiful boys, building himself up—from one kind of fuckable hole to the other—to a deep messy masculine orgasm that embraces all indiscretions, all combinations, all possibilities. . . .

It suddenly seems as if someone is in the room with me, and for a moment I look up, startled. But—no one is there. The blood vessels in my head pound for a second with a sudden, brief charge of anxiety.

There's a pair of crumpled white briefs half buried between the bedsheets. I pull them out. Jockeys. Waist 28. I raise them to my nose: the white cotton pouch smells of fabric softener and piss. Turning them over in my hands I think of what Dave said about Brian's ass: "white, creamy, flawless." My bewilderment is like touching an autograph in a book, knowing that someone has once been there, where your hand is now, but at a different time. God, how I'd love to have that ass here right now. . . .

Suddenly there are unmistakable noises downstairs—Dave must be home for lunch. I shove the briefs back down between the sheets and get up from the bed.

Leaving the room is like being forced to pull my hard cock away from a warm, pleasing mouth, just when I'm about to come. . . .

Driving round town with Dave (a cursory stab at sight-seeing, even though I only stopped over here for a couple of days on my way to someplace else), I ask whether Brian ever brings any girls home to fuck.

"Up until about a year ago I gather he was still fucking girls," Dave tells me. "But now I think it's strictly boys. He's coming out of the closet with a vengeance."

"What kind of boys?"

"Young athletic types, a couple of years younger than he is. I think he's also into kink. I know he bought himself a black leather jacket recently. And a couple of weeks ago, I found some rope and clothespins in the basement. I *don't* think he was doing laundry."

Shortly after Dave leaves for work the next morning, I explore the bedroom again. In fact I find myself annoyed when, after having left once already, Dave comes back ten minutes later for some work files he forgot. It's the same kind of exasperation one feels trying to get settled down to good sex (or just jacking off) and the phone keeps ringing or a roommate keeps tapping at the door with a gingerly, "I hate to interrupt you, but can I borrow a few dollars?" "I hate to interrupt you *again,* but can I . . ."

Standing in Brian's room, I feel a sensation like vertigo for a moment, as if I'm standing on a high bridge looking down at a river at night: one sees only the glints of reflection off the water, but not the river itself. Like most gay men, I'm fascinated by guys I know about, have heard about, but have never actually met. I don't know why exactly. I remember as a boy I sometimes used to go through my older brother's bedroom when he wasn't home. His room seemed mysterious and exciting to me. I was fascinated by his secrets, the icons of his masculinity, the private souvenirs of his male life; even the smells could fill me with longing, make me ache, as if they belonged to a foreign country I had never visited but was still nostalgic for. I was fascinated by his friends' secrets, too, as if the contents of their jeans pockets or the things they carried around inside their cars had some special significance.

To the left of Brian's closet is an orange crate full of skiing magazines, plus half-a-dozen or so books: *Man's Body: An Owner's Manual, Sex and the Single Guy,* a cheap well-worn paperback entitled *Abnormal Sexual Behavior: 16 Explicit Case Histories of Bizarre Acts,* and others. Whole sections of the *Abnormal Sexual Behavior* book have come unglued from the spine; the book is barely holding together.

Various clothes are scattered around the room: an old green khaki army jacket that smells faintly of old closets, a pair of Adidas socks with filthy soles, hiking boots with dried mud on them, a couple of muscle shirts (one with a button pinned on it, "I Brake for Hot Buns"), a dirty T-shirt with the stains of an afternoon's sweat still on it. . . .

The top of his dresser is neat and orderly. He has one of those tall, narrow oak dressers from the thirties; the edges of the surface are marred by decades of cigarette burns. Some pocket change in a glass ashtray, a couple of toothpicks, a Coca-Cola can from Saudi Arabia. There's also a used disposable razor, with some chips of dark blond hair still on the blade. The top of the dresser smells soapy, of after-shave, as if someone had once had an accident with a bottle of cologne and the wood was now soaked through forever with that overpowering scent.

On the floor at the foot of the bed, partly hidden by the ends of the blankets, is another pair of dirty underwear, as if Brian had slipped them off his hips in the middle of the night and kicked them way down under the covers—or maybe he woke up early in the morning and wanted to jack off.

I pick them up. They're incredibly soft, like the flesh of a boy's ass. Strange to think of all the erections that must have occurred in them. What was he thinking about the last time he had a hard-on in this exact pair of briefs? What was he imagining himself doing? What—who—was he hungering for? I imagine his rear—that "creamy, white, flawless" ass again—tucked into them; and from the front, a trail of golden dark hair starting around his navel and then trailing down to disappear beneath the tight waistband. . . .

Other details. There are two posters on the wall: a poster from some jazz festival in southern California and a ski poster from Switzerland. I hesitate briefly before looking in his dresser drawers. Jockstraps, socks, several brochures from Soloflex. A brochure for one of those "How to Make Your Life's Goals Come True" home-study programs. A generous supply of condoms (Trojan, Regulars). Half a ticket from a Bruce Springsteen concert several years ago. An old beige T-shirt with a fading black message stenciled on the front: "FOR SALE: Almost new chassis with high-speed rear. Must be tested to fully appreciate." Other clothes, the kind with holes and rips in them: the kind of clothes you find in everyone's dresser, favorite clothes that no one can ever bring themselves to throw away.

In one drawer there's a small pile of Polaroids stuck together with a rubber band. The pictures are mostly of young people at indiscernible locations. Teenage friends smiling and making silly faces at the camera. Friends drinking beer, playing cards at a picnic table. A couple of nude shots of some guys at a mountain lake. Good-looking guys, college students. There is, though, one really graphic and sleazy picture (there's no indication of who it is or when it was taken): the snapshot shows a tight, good-looking young ass lowering itself onto an almost impossibly large dildo. In fact, the mammoth dildo is already a good three or four inches into the rectum. On the right cheek of the ass are the words, written with a black-felt pen in big, awkward letters, "Property of J.J.B."

Later that night—it's probably two or three in the morning—I wake up hearing voices from the hallway, and the sound of doors opening and slamming shut. There's a sliver of light coming from underneath my door and shadows moving back and forth across it.

"What are you doing back already?" I hear Dave ask, in a loud whisper.

"A fuckin' drag" . . . "my asshole mother"—a few other muffled remarks. I can't hear any of it very well. There's more conversation, the sound of a guy taking a piss and then washing his hands, and finally a door—Brian's bedroom door—closing shut. I can hear the thud of him tossing a pair of shoes in the corner, then opening some drawers, hanging something in the closet. Silence for a few moments. Then the click of a light. He must have gone to bed. I wait. Nothing.

Sometime after that, after I've dozed off for a while, I suddenly hear the unmistakable sounds of a guy jacking off. There's the muted creaking of bedsprings, a pause, more creaking, some low moaning, another pause, more creaking, and deep breathing. I can tell the exact instant of his ejaculation: it sounds for a moment like someone bursting up through the surface of a pool and gasping for air.

Then, silence.

Early the next morning at breakfast, I ask Dave whether Brian came in last night.

"Yeah. He didn't have a very good time at home. He and his mother are always getting into it. She's constantly hassling him." He mimics the voice of a nagging old woman: " 'What are you doing with your life? When are you going to grow up? Why don't you at least *try* to get married?' He decided to come back early."

"Do they know he's gay?"

"He told them last winter. The father took it okay, but the mother freaked out totally. She started telling everyone, 'I have no son. . . .' "

"So do I get to meet him or what?"

Dave shrugs. "He'll probably sleep till noon. He got in around three-thirty. And we have to leave pretty soon if you want to catch your bus. . . ."

Going back up to the guest room, I pause by Brian's bedroom door, now closed. Strange to think of him in there now, sleeping, oblivious. I hang around outside his room for a few minutes, hoping that maybe, just maybe, he'll suddenly come staggering out—this beautiful boy with the flawless ass— to take a piss or say hello or get something to eat. . . .

Suddenly I hear the shower go on in the bathroom behind me. The sound makes me jump. The bathroom door is half-open. I hesitate for a second, then finally decide to walk in on the pretext of washing my hands.

Furls of warm steam hit my face. There's a small window in the wall behind the shower, and I can see a silhouette against the opaque shower curtain, just the outline of his head, his shoulders, his arms, and—when he turns slightly—the seductive line of his ass and an intimation of his cock and balls. He's lathering up his belly and crotch.

I turn on the water at the sink.

The silhouette suddenly freezes. "Dave?" he calls out, loud

enough to be heard over the shower. "Is that you?" The same masculine, reasonably sexy voice I remember from our brief phone conversation.

"Naw," I tell him. "Just me."

Pause.

"How's it goin'?" he asks, starting to soap himself up again nonchalantly.

"Pretty good," I tell him. "And you?"

"Could be better. . . ."

A single hand suddenly shoots out from behind the shower curtain. "Could you hand me that bottle of shampoo on the counter?" I stare at the hand. The underwear, the volleyball, the leather jacket, the porn magazines, the joint, the rubbers— all of them belong to this hand. Staring at it, I find myself wondering, is this the hand he uses to play with his dick? Or is it the other one? I feel that same sharp pang again, just like the one I felt that first day when I saw his dirty jeans lying on the floor in the doorway.

"Sure . . . ," I tell him.

I hand him the bottle—our fingers never touch—and the hand disappears again inside the shower curtain, back to lathering up armpits and his ass and washing his hair.

Then, hearing Dave yell from downstairs that we're going to miss the bus, I reluctantly walk out.

STEVEN SAYLOR
WRITING AS AARON TRAVIS

BLUE

LIGHT

I WAS NEW IN TOWN, DIDN'T KNOW ANYONE, needed a place. My old apartment in New York had made me sick of cramped quarters; I needed space.

I had no intention of moving into some tacky Houston apartment complex with a bathtub-size swimming pool and nosy neighbors. I wanted something different, something with character. A room in a house with laid-back people. Cooperative living. I'd done that back in my student days. It might be just what I needed to made me feel at home in this fucked-up town.

They say New York's impersonal. Give me those hordes on the subways any day over the automatons in steel modules that cruise the superfreeways in Houston. Forget the sweltering heat; this town is all cold concrete and glass. Maybe that explains the incredible murder rate. There's a lot of mental illness down here.

On Saturday morning I took the Harley over to Montrose and found a health-food restaurant. I leafed through a few of the free underground rags that were stacked in front of the cash register. One of the classifieds seemed to be just what I wanted:

Liberated person needed to share 3-storied house w/2w, 1m. You help in house, garden, get privacy, fresh vegs. $90/mo.

The address was on Beauchamp Street. I asked the cashier if she knew where it was. North of downtown, she said. Pronounced *bee-chum*. Sort of run-down, but gentrified around the edges. Lots of big oak trees and old houses. A mixed neighborhood—Chicanos, blacks, old couples, student types.

I loaded my salad with alfalfa sprouts to get in the mood and then biked up to Beauchamp. I thought about removing the studded leather armband from my left bicep, but decided against it. If I moved in, they'd figure out where I was coming from soon enough. Better to start out being open.

The house was set on a corner and dominated everything around it, a fine example of Texas Victoriana with lots of decorative carved wood, yellow clapboard walls, and a green shingle roof. The successive stories were set back in tiers; a jumble of gables directed my eyes up to the octagonal room at the top, where the domed roof came to a point. It seemed perched on the house like an eagle's nest, high above the tops of the oaks and pecan trees.

The yard was like a jungle, dense and green. Shady trees, century plants, stands of wild bamboo, even a few spindly yuccas. The more I saw, the more I liked it.

Two women were sitting on the front porch. As I walked up, they stopped talking and looked me over. They were both dressed in loose, lacy cotton dresses and sandals, and wore their hair long and frizzy.

Their names were Karen and Sharon. Karen wore thick glasses. Sharon wore contacts. Karen smoked lots of dope and was addicted to science-fiction magazines. Sharon smoked lots of dope and rode a Harley, which gave us something to talk about. Sharon left after a while to do some shopping; Karen gave me a walk-through.

The first-floor ceilings were twelve feet high. All the wallpaper had been stripped off, baring the dark lumber beneath.

The women had separate rooms on the first floor. There was also a big bathroom, a living room, library (shelf after shelf of *Analog* and *Fantasy and Science Fiction*), and a cavernous kitchen with yellow plaster walls. There was a poster of Janis Joplin over the refrigerator.

A back door off the kitchen opened onto a small wooden porch. They had turned the backyard into a big garden, with rows and rows of tomatoes and sunflowers.

"Now I'll show you your room," Karen said.

The stairway was narrow and steep. The second floor was much smaller, with a short, dark hallway that led to a bathroom at one end and a bedroom at the other. The room had a low ceiling and bare walls. It was narrow and U-shaped, with windows facing all around. The drapes were gray with age and dirt. The furniture consisted of an old dresser, a few chairs, and a mattress on the floor. I told Karen I liked it.

As we stepped back into the hallway, I looked up the last flight of steps. They ended in a trapdoor.

"You might as well see the rest of the house," Karen offered. "I think Michael's out. I'm sure he wouldn't mind if we take a peek." I followed her up the short flight. She pushed the door open a few inches and peered inside, her eyes at floor level.

"Just want to make sure there aren't any burnt offerings or spilled entrails on the floor," she said.

"Huh?"

Karen laughed. "Just kidding. Sort of. Michael's into some pretty weird stuff." She pushed the trapdoor open. "Come on up."

At first I couldn't see much for the darkness. As my eyes adjusted, I blinked in amazement.

We were in the octagonal room at the top of the house. There were four walls painted deep purple separated by four windows. The windows were covered by heavy black drapes that admitted no light. I wondered where the faint illumination came from, then realized it was concentrated in a bar in the center of the room. I looked up. A tiny stained-glass skylight shaped like an eight-pointed star was set in the center of the high ceiling.

"Michael owns the place. You may not meet him for a while. He keeps odd hours, eats up here in his room. . . ."

The room was crowded with ornaments and furnishings. There was a large four-poster bed against one wall, ancient-looking wooden caskets with bronze hinges, a huge wooden chair that looked like a medieval throne. Squat candles were set all about the room. Pentacles and other symbols, indistinct in the dim light, were painted in white on the dark purple walls and high domed ceiling.

I glanced at a bookcase close by. Only a few of the authors were familiar: Dennis Wheatley, Aleister Crowley, Anton Levay.

"He's a Satanist?" I asked, mildly curious. I had met stranger types.

"Michael? Oh, no." She laughed. "I mean, he doesn't hold black masses or anything like that. At least I don't think so. Actually I don't know what he does up here. Sharon and I stay pretty much on the ground floor."

I moved in that afternoon.

That evening I ate in the kitchen with Sharon and Karen. I kept expecting to see my third housemate, but he never showed.

After a hard day of moving, I decided to reward myself with an evening out. I checked out a couple of bars and ended up at one of the baths. I stumbled in around four in the morning, trying not to make too much noise on the creaky stairs. I noticed there was a thin edge of light around the trapdoor to the octagonal room.

I woke up hung over and headachy sometime in the late morning. Sunlight was streaming in the room. I got up to close the drapes. One of the windows looked down on the garden. I saw a man there, shoveling.

From the steep angle I couldn't see much except his head and shoulders. He was wearing dirty white overalls. His hair was long and black, almost to his waist, and pulled back in a ponytail. His untanned shoulders were broad and scalloped with muscles that undulated as he dug the shovel into the earth and scooped it out.

He suddenly stood up straight, turned toward the house, and looked up at me.

He was tall, easily over six feet. The overalls fit tight around the waist, emphasizing the striking width of his chest and shoulders. Sweat made the sunlight glimmer in the smooth, deep cleft between his pectorals. His smooth cheeks and forehead were spotted with dirt. I was struck by how white his skin was, like ivory. He rested one hand on the shovel at his side and raised the other to wipe the sweat from his forehead.

I stood naked at the full-length window as we looked at each other—naked except for the leather band around my left arm, which never comes off. I tried to smile, despite the pain cracking my head. Now, why couldn't I have run into *that* at the baths last night, I thought. Then I closed the drapes and stumbled back to bed.

When I finally made my way downstairs, I noticed he was no longer in the garden. Karen told me he was up in his room. Working, she said.

"What does he do?"

"I don't really know," she shrugged. "I say 'working' because he doesn't like anybody to disturb him when he's upstairs."

I took the hint.

There was no sign of him for several days. I wanted another look at those broad shoulders and muscular arms. It became a mild obsession.

I placed my bed opposite the door to my room and left the door open in the evenings. I lounged shirtless on the bed, reading or smoking, keeping an eye on the hallway. Sooner or later I'd see him pass by.

That was how I spent my evenings that first week in the house, waiting for a chance to meet Michael. Somehow he eluded me. I must have read Karen's entire collection of *Amazing Stories* that week.

It became a game. It's my nature to win games. Or so I thought.

Finally, on Friday night, I heard footsteps on the lower stairway. Not the slap of Karen's or Sharon's sandals, but a heavier tread.

I lowered the magazine just enough to peer over it, and watched as a man appeared headfirst in the hallway. It wasn't Michael. But he easily drove Michael from my mind.

He was blond, with short hair, a square jaw, and a mustache, dressed in a tight sleeveless shirt that showed off muscular, golden-fleeced arms and a rippled chest. He looked more than a little like me, in fact.

I glanced at his crotch, but his chinos were too baggy to show a bulge. Instead I found myself studying the way his nipples pressed against his shirt.

He was obviously gay, or so I thought. When his eyes met mine, I tried to lock him in with a steady gaze. I said hello. But he seemed to look straight through me, completely indifferent, and only mumbled in reply. He took the final flight up to the trapdoor. I craned my neck and saw him disappear into an arc of soft yellow light. The pants kept his crotch a mystery, but they couldn't have flattered his ass more.

I got up from bed and tiptoed into the hall. I looked up at the closed trapdoor. It was quiet for a while, then I heard voices, louder than normal, an argument of some sort. One voice was much lower than the other.

There was a shuffle of heavy footsteps overhead. I almost bolted for my room, thinking one of them was about to leave. Then the argument resumed. A silence, and their voices returned, quieter. Another silence, then shouting. Then a quiet that went on so long I decided they had made up and gone to bed.

I returned to my room. Just as I sat on the bed, wondering where I had put my Houston bar guide, there was a dim light from the hallway and the sound of feet descending the upper stairs. It was the blond man, leaving in such a hurry that I couldn't even get another glimpse of his face.

A few minutes later, the trapdoor opened again. The game was about to pay off.

I had been waiting all week for a good look at him, remembering his naked shoulders, his beautiful long black hair. The night was warm. I was horny. My cock was hard. It showed as a thick ridge in my jeans. My chest was covered with a thin sheen of sweat. I rose from the bed and stepped into the hallway just as Michael did.

His black hair was unbound and hung straight, parted in the middle. It was sleek and thick like combed silk.

He had one of those paradoxical faces that look more masculine with long hair than short. His eyes were dark brown, with long lashes and straight black eyebrows. He had a wide mouth and full lips that looked red and moist against his pale cheeks. He looked like he was barely into his early twenties. He had to be older than that, I thought, to own his own house.

His body was even better than I had thought. Huge, square-muscled shoulders. Hard, round biceps with a pale blue vein running down each arm. His pectorals rose slablike above his rib cage, sleek and hairless with nipples the size of half-dollars. His stomach was an expanse of gentle ridges that funneled down to narrow, muscle-flat hips. The twin arcs of his pelvis were as deep and defined as those of Michelangelo's *David*.

He was wearing nothing but a pair of white nylon briefs, so sheer that his big flaccid cock and balls nestled visibly inside. Below, his legs were fluid pillars of muscle, like white marble. In the light reflected from the bare wood, he seemed to shine with a pale amber glow.

He smiled faintly. "You must be the new guy." His voice sounded almost artificially deep.

"Yeah," I said, extending my arm. He caught my hand and we shook fingers-up, head-style, the way hippies and bikers used to. "I'm Bill Gray."

"Michael Black. Black and Gray, huh? That's cute." There was not a trace of humor in his voice.

Our hands stayed locked together as I looked into his deep

brown eyes. He lowered his gaze, taking in my body as I had taken in his.

Then he broke the handshake. "Be seeing you," he said, and walked to the bathroom. The long black hair fanned over his wide shoulders. His ass, small and round with muscle, seemed to shimmer inside the nylon briefs. I noticed for the first time just how large his legs were. My two hands wouldn't have met around his calves.

The next morning I asked Karen about the blond visitor. "Oh, that must have been Carl," she said. "He used to live here. In your room."

After that first meeting, I saw Michael only rarely and in passing. He seemed to keep odd hours, even odder than mine. He was never rude, but always distant.

I knew he was gay. The blond hunk Carl turned out to be a regular visitor, sometimes coming three or four times a week. Carl was so oblivious of me and the band around my left arm, I decided he had to be another top. I knew they liked rough sex. Very rough. I could hear them above me at night. Flesh striking flesh with a sweaty crack. Heavier blows—the distinct whoosh and snap of a belt or a whip. Knees knocking on the wooden floor as someone crawled back and forth, grunting.

I would have him, I told myself. I would make him do more than grunt.

No matter how often I went out, no matter how many other men I met, I found my fantasies returning to Michael. When I masturbated at night, he was the one I thought of. It was his pale skin and the long hair that set him apart, matched with his larger-than-life physique, the combination of sultry brown eyes and an innocent, nature-boy face. I wanted to own him, to possess him, to devour him.

It was a game, and I would win it. I would see his pretty face all slack and hungry, his brown eyes gazing up into mine while his thick red lips were stretched around my nine inches. I would hear him gag on it and groan. I would twist that deep grunting voice into a high-pitched whimper. I imagined him naked, erect, on his knees—arms twisted and bound behind his back, his big chest thrust up sleek and vulnerable, his long hair making him look like a conquered savage. I knew how to make those big flat nipples stand up red and swollen.

His ass had limitless possibilities. Every mark would show across the pale drum-tight flesh.

His hair would have its uses. To inflict pain, to bring hot tears to his eyes. To twist around his neck like a collar. To use as reins when I rode his face like a saddle, or mounted him like a steed. Later it might have a more important use—as a final act of humiliation, I would force him to shave it, stripping away his last shred of resistance, like Samson, chained and degraded. His naked skull would mark him as my slave for all the world to see.

I had gotten what I wanted from other men. I would get what I wanted from him. I had plans for Michael Black.

My chance came the next Sunday. I got up around noon, feeling lazy and relaxed, ready for anything. I slipped into a pair of jeans and went down to the kitchen.

The door to the back porch was open. Michael was sitting on the steps, looking at the garden. I stepped outside and sat beside him.

"Mind if I join you?"

"No." He glanced up at me, then looked back at the garden. He was wearing a pair of jeans that hugged him from crotch to calves like a glove, and a white tank top that looked a size too small around his shoulders but hung loosely below his pecs.

"You must work out a lot," I said.

"Couple of hours every day. And Lan-Tzu class three times a week." He glanced at my naked chest. "You too?"

I shrugged. "Not since I was in New York. I haven't found a gym here yet. You don't get much sun, though. Burn easy?"

"No," he said. "I'm just not crazy about sunlight. I'm basically a nocturnal animal." He picked up a joint and a book of matches from a lower step. He lit it, inhaled, and offered it to me wordlessly. I shook my head.

"Gave it up about a year ago, when it started doing strange trips on my head. Thanks, though."

"Too bad. Sharon grows some pretty mean weed in the garden." He exhaled through clenched teeth. "It helps me focus my power."

Whatever turns you on, I thought.

"You're not originally from Houston, are you?" I asked.

"No. Born in Utah. Then southern California."

"Why would you leave that for this?"

"Too much sun out there, for one thing." He smiled. "And work's easier here."

"Oh? I didn't think you worked."

"I work," he said coolly. I got the idea he didn't care to talk about it. But after another hit, he elaborated. "I supply special experiences for people who can pay. Experiences they can't get anywhere else. I like Houston because people here have lots of money and not much imagination. They ask for easy stuff and pay through the nose for it. Not like the Coast." He shook his head. "People there wanted heavy trips, really taxed my energy. And there are more of us out there. Here, I'm a rarity."

The joint was making him talkative. It was pretty murky, but I got the idea: he was a hustler. He had a very special appeal; the paying market might be small, but he had a corner on it. There must be plenty of rich hayseeds in Houston who'd pay to stick it to a muscular young longhair.

I decided to play dumb. "Shit man—you mean sex?"

He stared straight ahead, his jaw tight, and took another hit. "Sometimes. But I don't always charge for that. I enjoy myself too much." He gave me a Mona Lisa smile.

I smiled back. I'd never paid to screw a guy and I didn't intend to start, even with Michael.

We sat in silence until he finished the joint. He turned his face to mine. His brown eyes seemed to sparkle. His jaw slackened. A real stone puppy, I thought, ready to curl up in the palm of my hand. I slid my fingers over his thigh and onto his cock, rock hard and thick inside the tight denim.

"Wanna go upstairs?" I said.

He paused, staring at my face. I stared back and squeezed his cock until I got the answer I wanted.

"Sure."

I followed him inside and up the stairs. "My room," he said, as we emerged on the first landing. I followed him up through the trapdoor.

He made a circuit of the room, lighting candles until the chamber glowed with soft amber light. He pulled a cord that slid a cover over the tiny skylight, leaving only candlelight for illumination. It was high noon outside, but here it was midnight. He made another circuit of the room, pulling open the black velvet drapes. The four windows had been sealed over on the inside. In their place were full-length mirrors.

The deep darkness above, the dim light, the mirrors all around made it impossible to sense the true dimensions of the room. It seemed to expand into infinity, endlessly reflected in the opposing mirrors. I was in his private world now, a place outside of time and space.

The effect was very special, secretive, and hypnotic. And promising. Michael had imagination.

I walked to the middle of the room. I could feel my cock pulsing against my left leg. Michael finished his preparations and stood before me, his face quizzical, his hands at his sides.

"Take off your clothes," I said.

He looked at me for a moment, expressionless. Then he grabbed the bottom seam of his tank top and pulled it over his shoulders. Suddenly I knew who he reminded me of: Li'l Abner, the cartoon hillbilly who used to be in the Sunday comics when I was a kid—the exaggerated shoulders and chest, the wasp waist, the bulging thighs and calves.

"Yeah," I breathed. "Now your pants."

They were so tight he had to peel them off, turning them inside out. His balance never faltered as he bent over and lifted his feet. He was as graceful as a dancer.

He stood and slid his fingers under the waistband of the clinging briefs.

"Leave those on," I said quietly. I wanted to save the sight of his naked ass for later. His cock was hard, causing a bulge that pulled the waistband an inch from his flat belly.

I took my time, trying to stare him down. Michael never lowered his eyes. I could read no expression in them.

"Come here," I said. He walked to me slowly. It was breathtaking, just to watch him move. Even the simple act of walking he performed with animal grace, fluid and sexual.

He stopped a foot away, looming above me. I didn't like his face being above mine. It wouldn't be for long.

He raised his right hand to touch the leather band around my left bicep. "You have a beautiful body," he said softly. He brought his hands to my chest and combed his fingers through the thick mat of blond hair. "Like Carl," he whispered.

I grabbed his wrists and pushed his hands to my crotch. "Take it out."

He looked down as he unbuttoned my jeans, spread the flaps, and circled his fingers around the thick base of my cock. He had to use both hands to pull it out.

He held it tightly. I saw a strange smile on his downturned face. He weighed it in his hands.

"Yeah. Big and heavy. Just like Carl's."

"Then get on your knees and suck it. Just like you suck Carl's cock."

Michael knelt. In the mirrors to my left and right I saw his body, lean and sleek in profile. I watched the head of my cock slide between his lips and shuddered at the contact. In the mirror before me I saw his back-thrust ass inside the translucent briefs. I twisted the hair at the nape of his neck into a single cord and used it to hold his head in place.

His back was untouched. Maybe Carl didn't want to see that ivory perfection marred by welts. Michael would find out soon enough where the comparisons ended between Carl and me.

I yanked his head forward and gave a sudden thrust with my hips, trying to catch him off-guard. Start him off gagging. Get his saliva running. Make him take it my way from the very start.

But it slid down his throat without a hitch. I looked down at his upturned face. His eyes were shut; the long lashes flickered. His cheeks were drawn taut. His thick red lips circled the base of my shaft. His jaw was thrust sharply into my balls. His throat was distended, packed with a solid truncheon of flesh.

I fucked his face hard and deep, never pulling more than halfway out, watching his throat expand and contract as I pumped into him. The candlelight flashed on the trickles of spit that ran from the corners of his mouth onto his corded neck. I kept expecting him to protest and push me away, gasping for breath, but he seemed resigned to letting me fuck his face as long and as hard as I wanted.

I finally pulled his head back by a fistful of hair and emptied his throat with a jerk. Keep him cock-hungry, I thought. He leaned back, gasping. His mouth and chin were wet with spittle. His lips glistened in the firelight.

I rested my cockhead against his lower lip while he caught his breath. He swallowed hard and spoke in a murmur, moving his wet lips over the knob of my cockhead. "You must have some toys down in your room." He rolled his eyes up to mine.

"Yeah," I said. "In a wooden locker by my bed." I reached down to gently squeeze his right nipple. "Be a good boy and go fetch it."

While he was gone I stripped off my jeans. I flexed my upper body and looked at my reflection in the mirrors. Michael had said I had a fine body—a real compliment coming from a man with such an exceptional physique. And why not? I wasn't as tall as he was, or as broad; but I was thicker in the chest, more compact. The years I had spent working off the anxieties of New York through sweat and hard exercise had paid off, many times.

I liked the difference in our bodies. My deep tan and stark tan line against his pale flesh, the rich golden hair on my chest and limbs against his sleek nudity. The nine-inch column of flesh that stuck up from my crotch, and that hard round ass of his, waiting to be split wide open. I pumped my left arm and watched the bicep strain against the studded band.

Michael returned. He knelt and placed the long box at my feet.

"Go ahead," I told him. "Open it. If you see something you like—ask for it."

He lifted the lid and gazed down at the jumble of steel and leather. He noticed the dozen varieties of tit clamps. He picked up a chain-linked pair and stared at them.

"You're really into pain," he murmured naively. "You like to put these on other men's nipples. Twist them. Pull on them. A way to put pain in them. Make them whimper and beg."

"Uh huh," I said drily, answering his innocent act with a smirk. "You've got big tits. Probably take two clamps each."

Michael put the clamps back in the box. Afraid of them, I thought. Good.

He took out a pair of padded handcuffs. "To bind them. Put them at your mercy. So they can't strike back. So you can feel free to use them however you want."

"That's right." I spread my legs and stroked my cock with two fingers. It was throbbing at maximum erection, almost achingly hard.

He set the cuffs aside, on the floor, then took out my pride and joy. My riding crop, an intricately twined handle with a thin, two-foot tongue of stiff leather. It had been a gift from a not-very-shy trick in the Village. "It's yours, Bill," he had said, "if you'll use it on me." And I had. I was amazed Michael had the nerve to choose it.

"And you use this on their naked skin, as if they were animals." His tone was fascinated but detached, as if he were an observer, taking inventory. He really knew how to ask for it.

He looked up at me with those deep brown eyes. "Is that what you want to do with me, Bill? Cuff my hands behind my back, clamp my nipples? Make me crawl after your big cock, beat me, fuck my ass?"

His deep voice, low and soft, reverberated in my head. I felt the rush of a perfect moment. "That's right, Michael. Now hand me the crop."

He held it horizontal, offering it with both hands. I took it by the handle and ran the tongue through my fist. I touched the tip against his chest and gently tapped his nipple. Then I drew it up and cracked it across my thigh to make him flinch.

But he didn't flinch.

Instead his face seemed to harden, to become steady and purposeful.

He rose to his feet and stared down at me. Suddenly my whole left arm went limp, as if the nerves had been severed. The riding crop slipped from my hand. I didn't hear it hit the floor. I tried to look down and found that I couldn't take my eyes from his.

"Stay." His quiet voice boomed deeply in the silence.

And I stood, my body relaxed but paralyzed, as he walked to a casket across the room. I couldn't turn my head to watch him. I was forced to stare straight ahead into the mirror. It reflected the fear and astonishment frozen on my face.

Michael returned. Several lengths of thin chain were looped over his right forearm.

He slowly circled me, examining my naked body. I felt like an insect paralyzed in a spider's web, waiting to be eaten alive. But I didn't panic. My mind seemed to be slowing down, shifting into neutral, losing touch with reality. I should never had smoked that weed, I thought, then remembered I hadn't.

I tried to open my mouth to ask him what the hell he had done to me. But I couldn't speak. My jaw was frozen.

He had said he was into some sort of martial art. Paralysis with a touch? But he hadn't touched me. There was no way he could have drugged me.

He ran his hands over my body, exploring my back and arms, cupping my pecs and buns. He inserted his middle finger into my mouth to wet it and slid it gently up my ass. My mouth stayed open, as his finger had left it.

He stood beside me and spoke in my ear, keeping his long middle finger inside me, gently probing. He wet his other hand in my mouth and stroked my cock. I watched in the mirror— his lean profile, the rolling muscles in his stroking arm, my mouth left gaping open like an idiot's.

"I've been paid $25,000 for what I'm about to do to you, Bill." Stroking, probing. "But that was for a man who wanted it. Or thought he did. And he wasn't very attractive. You are, Bill. Big cock. Hard ass." He frowned at my chest. "All that hair is unfortunate. It hides your muscles. You'll look better after the hoop."

He slid his finger from my ass, gave my cock a hard squeeze and released it. He stood before me and slipped the chains from his forearm. There were two of them, one quite long, the other the length of a bracelet. They were made like dog chokers, with nooses and sliding rings to control the pressure.

He put the bigger chain over my head and pulled it tight around my neck. The metal was as cold as ice, unnaturally cold. The loose end hung between my pecs. Then he slid the smaller chain over my cock and balls, circled them tight and left the end dangling from the underside of my testicles.

He bent over and retrieved the padded handcuffs, twisted my arms behind my back and cuffed my wrists. He stood in front of me and smiled grimly.

"And now this," he said, "since symbols are so important to both of us." He unsnapped the leather band from my left arm. I felt as if my last protection had been stripped from me. He tried to fit it over his own left bicep, but the muscle was too big. Instead he slipped it over my right arm and snapped it tight.

He stepped aside so I could see myself in the mirror. Naked. Cock hard and circled with cold steel. Arms bound. Choker around my neck. Leather strap on the right, marking my subservience. I groaned inside, confused and helpless. In five minutes, against my will, he had completely reversed our roles. And I had no idea how he had done it.

Then, as fogged as my mind was, I noticed something. I couldn't be certain in the dim light, but the silver chains around my neck and cock seemed to glow faintly, circled by a ghostly blue light. As I watched, the blue aura grew stronger, until I saw it clearly in the glass, like wisps of phosphorescent blue mist around my neck and between my legs.

I was not afraid—not quite. Not yet. A numbness was seeping into my head, a comfortable sense of detachment.

Damn it, I thought, maybe he slipped me a drug of some kind. But I knew, somehow, that the chilly numbness wasn't in my head. It was radiating from those cold blue chains.

Michael returned. With both hands he held what looked like a hoop of glass tubing, two feet in diameter. The hoop glowed, like blue neon.

Silently he positioned the ring above my head and lowered it slowly to the floor. As it passed around my body it seemed to shed a cocoon of light behind. I saw myself in the mirror, encased in a cylinder of blue haze.

"Now we wait," Michael said, "to let the energy soak in." He cocked his head, looking me up and down as he groped himself inside his nylon briefs. His dark, handsome face went slack with lust—lips parted, eyes narrowed, sexed-up.

I felt the hair on my body stand up straight, as if charged with static electricity. Something weird was happening in the mirror. I saw a mass of suspended particles in the space between my body and the cocoon of blue light, too vague to make out in the mirror. I tried to look down. My neck was paralyzed. Michael saw me straining. He reached inside the light and pushed my face down.

My body was being stripped of its hair. The process was silent, painless, magic, I suppose. The short hairs detached themselves from my skin and drifted slowly through the light-suffused air, made contact with the field of circling blue light—and disappeared.

At first the air was choked with free-floating strands, silky yellow ones from my chest and arms and legs, kinky dark ones from my crotch. Then the migration grew sparser, until I saw the last curly strand unfurl from my left nipple, stand straight and pull free. It wafted gently like a weightless mote of dust, drew steadily toward the barrier of light, touched it—vanished.

I had been shaved once before, long ago. Before the muscles, before the armband, before the Harley. The job had taken hours, and left me with nicks around the base of my cock and around my tits. The master had not been pleased with the effect—he said it made me look too much like a boy instead

of a man. Since shaving had been my idea, not his, he had
punished me afterward with a razor strop.

My skin had been city-pale then, my body undeveloped. I
hadn't liked the look either; the hairlessness seemed to expose
every flaw. Now, gazing down at myself in the blue light, I was
mesmerized by the smooth planes of my chest, all tan flesh and
ridges of muscle, clearer than I had ever seen them before. My
nipples looked naked somehow, vulnerable. My cock, still as
hard as when I pulled it from Michael's throat, reared up big
and stiff from my denuded crotch, the tight chain around the
base fully exposed. There was no stubble. My body was as sleek
as Michael's.

"It'll grow back," he said. He grabbed the hair on my
head—thank god he had not taken that—and pulled my face
up.

It was as if I saw another man in the mirror. A hunky
blond slave, totally hairless, his mouth hanging open like a
dog's, his cock hard for his master.

Michael moved in front of me, blocking my reflection.

"You've got to trust me, Bill. Give in. You remember
how to give in. Cooperate, do your part, and you won't be
hurt. Understand?"

No, I didn't understand. Nothing made sense. All I knew
was that he had me in his power—literally, completely. *I've been
paid $25,000 for what I'm about to do to you. But that was for a
man who wanted it—or thought he did. . . .*

He slipped a finger through the steel ring at the end of
the chain that hung from my neck and pulled it toward him,
tightening the choker. He licked his other hand and put it on
my throat, kneading and exploring with slick fingers. The
choker pulled tighter. I felt my windpipe flatten.

"Don't be frightened," he whispered. How could I not be
frightened—he was strangling me. The chain pulled tighter and
tighter. My throat grew numb under his fingertips. I couldn't
breathe. My paralyzed body convulsed.

Then—I heard a rattling of metal and saw his right hand
pull away. The choker dangled free from his forefinger. I felt
myself being lifted up—a sensation of weightlessness and ver-

tigo—the room fell and whirled around me. I tried to scream with horror, and couldn't. I caught a glimpse of something in one of the mirrors—my body, stock-still within the blue light field—Michael standing aside—holding something in his hands—holding—my head—

I blacked out. Only for an instant, I think. Then I was looking up at Michael. He was holding my face between his hands. He sat in the thronelike chair, leaning back with his ass on the edge. My head was between his thighs.

His briefs were gone. His cock loomed above my face. Beyond, his flat-muscled stomach was bunched into tight folds of flesh beneath the sculpted domes of his pecs. His eyes were on mine. The look of his face frightened me—a look of contempt and total control.

"Stop twisting your face up, Bill. It makes you ugly. Cock, Bill. My cock. Look at it."

It hovered over me, white and thick. It was perfect, like the rest of his body. Alabaster white and enormously thick, tapered slightly at the base. The head was huge. The skin was pearly white and translucent, as smooth as glass, showing deep blue veins within. The circumcision ring was almost unnoticeable, the color of cream. The shaft looked as hard as marble, but spongy and fat, as if it were covered by a sheath of rubbery flesh. I could feel its heat on my face.

"My cock, Bill. Taste it." He rubbed my face all over his meat. I felt its fullness on my cheeks and nose. The big head pressed against each of my eyes in turn.

"Lick it. Lick my cock, Bill." I opened my mouth—able to move it now—and stuck out my tongue. He slid my drooling mouth over his meat, flattened my tongue against the bulging shaft, ran it over the beveled edge of his cockhead, allowed me to probe into the deep slit at the tip.

He pushed my face onto his shaft and filled my mouth with his cockhead. It came back to me, the old days, when this was what I craved from other men, the privilege of feeling their meat warm and solid in my mouth. I realized he was trying to pacify me—giving me something big to suck on to make me forget the shock of what had just happened—or what I imagined had happened.

I rolled my eyes up and drew on the massive beauty of his chest and arms the way my mouth was drawing on his massive cock. My throat had grown thick with saliva—I tried to swallow, found I couldn't, just as I couldn't speak—realized I wasn't even breathing. The accumulated spittle frothed around my lips and oozed over his shaft.

He pushed my face all the way onto his cock. There was a bruising pain as it entered my gullet, as if he were shoving a beer bottle down my throat. I retched and spattered his balls and thighs with spit. I was gagging, but not choking—how could I choke when my breathing had stopped?

His hips never moved. He forced my head up and down, driving my throat onto his shaft and pulling back till my lips caught on the ridge of the head.

He fucked my face that way, using it like a cored melon or a pillow, for what seemed like hours. He took it slow, pleasuring himself, as if he were alone in his room masturbating. In and out of my throat, with slow luxurious strokes. Then bursts of violence—pushing my face into his groin, flattening my nose against his steel-hard belly, grinding deep and hard, making my throat convulse and ripple around his shaft. Juices ran from my stuffed mouth until his lap was slick with spittle and precum.

My mind settled into a profound calm. I was aware, alert. But there was a sensation of timelessness, disembodiment. I was outside any normal dimension, as if, freed from breath, freed from my body, I was beyond panic or pain.

He coaxed me through clenched teeth, his voice low, his mammoth chest heaving so I knew he was close. "It feels good down your throat, doesn't it, Bill? My cock in your mouth. What you really wanted from me, what you need. To have your throat crammed with meat. You're a born cocksucker, Bill." He would get close that way—I could feel his cock spurting precum—then pull me off till I held only the head. Hold off, catch his breath. And start over again. Until my jaw hung open like a broken hinge. Until his surging tube of meat felt a part of me, and I couldn't tell where my throat ended and his thick shaft began.

He got close again. Pulled my mouth off his cock. Held my head up by a fist in my hair, his other fist around his cock. The shaft glistened in the candlelight beneath a thick glaze of spit. He stroked himself haltingly. His hips bucked gently. On the brink.

His eyes were almost closed. The pupils flashed like sparks between the long, dark lashes.

"I'm gonna come now, Bill. Yeah." He hissed with pleasure. "My cock is gonna shoot. You want it in your mouth? Sure you do. The big bad leather boy wants my come in his mouth. Then beg for it, Bill. Beg me to shoot it down your fucking throat."

I tried. My lips couldn't even shape the words. I flexed my jaw, twisted my tongue, and curled my lip like a spastic. There was no sound except the hollow gurgling of the mucus in my throat.

Michael cried out and pushed my face onto it, down to the base. It jerked in my throat like a startled snake. His fingers bit into the base of my skull like pincers. A wild animal roar filled the darkness. I instinctively tried to swallow as the pumping started. His come clogged my throat, backflushed into my mouth. It tasted bitter and strong.

He held me down on his pulsing meat for a long time. No need to pull out. I didn't need to come up for air.

I rolled my eyes up to look at his heaving chest, sheened with sweat, and his face, beautiful and composed except for sudden moments when his eyebrows drew together and he whimpered like a puppy having a bad dream. At those moments his cock would give a little jerk.

He pulled me off at last. My mouth and throat were so full of spittle and bitter semen that it ran like slag over my chin. Thick ropes of mucus were strung from my lips to his big soft cock.

He rested my head on his shoulder and held it there while he recovered. The seeping fluids ran from the corner of my mouth onto his chest and down to his crotch.

Straining my eyes to one side, I saw a reflection of my body in one of the mirrors, still frozen in the cocoon of light. Where my head should have been, there was only darkness. I felt a dizzy fear, but it was muted by the dim light, the unaccountable sensation of freedom, the memory of his cock. Vaguely, I knew fear would serve no purpose. My only hope was to trust him.

At last he opened his eyes. He saw that I was looking at my abandoned body.

"It's true," he said softly. "You're not crazy. It's no illusion. You're here, your body is there. It's one of the things I do." He took a deep breath. My head rose and fell on his chest like a cork on a wave.

"You can handle it, Bill. I knew when I first saw you. Despite the armband on the left. Despite the heavy come-on. You know how to give a man what he wants. How to give in, even if he's handing you pain, degrading your ego. Well, this is what *I* want, Bill. This is what turns me on. I'm going to do what I want with you. You've got no choice."

The room whirled around—weightlessness again—then settled. Michael was standing over me, his big cock slick and half-hard above my face. He had placed my head on the chair. I could smell steamy sweat, where his ass and thighs had rested on the wood.

"It will help," he said, "if you think of it as another man's body." He walked to the center of the room and circled the headless body immobilized there. I glanced around; the chair was set so that I couldn't catch a reflection of my face. But I saw my body reflected all around in the mirrors. There was no bloody stump where my head should be—only the smooth, natural depression inside my collarbone.

It was a beautiful body, I had to admit. I suppose anyone who has seen his body harden and fill out from hard work becomes a narcissist. Looking at my body in the dim light, studying the play of light and shadow across the sleek flesh, I felt a strange quiver of desire. It was crazy, something was wrong in my head that I could look at my body and feel such cool detachment. At the time, I didn't realize that. I was where Michael had put me, in some strange psychic zone.

That body turned me on. The hairlessness showed off my muscles, as Michael had said it would. Everything looked larger, fuller. Especially my pecs, big mounds of sleek muscle. The nipples, normally buried in swirls of hair, stood out from the taut flesh, looking exquisitely sensitive, begging to be touched. My cock and balls, hairless and chained, looked larger than life, but not commanding; exposed and vulnerable. *Do it.* I begged silently. *I want to see it crawl. I want it.*

Michael stooped and took hold of the glowing blue hoop on the floor. He did not pull it up and over my shoulders, but sideways, though my legs, as if the hoops were made of nothing but light.

"Yeah, another man's body," he crooned. "Hairless. Handcuffed. Nude." He flicked one of the erect nipples. The body flinched. He circled around. "Fantastic ass. I like the way the tan line frames those cheeks." He slid a fingertip over the crack. I saw my buttocks tighten—and felt it—in a way—far off. A ghost sensation, the way an amputee might feel a lost limb. Like being in two places at once.

He stood beside the handcuffed body and looked in my eyes. He grabbed one of the hairless nipples between his finger and thumb and pulled downward until the captive body was forced to bend sharply at the waist.

"A slave's body, Bill. A big hunky stud in handcuffs. How shall we use him? We can do anything we want. Things you haven't dreamed of."

Michael took two tit clamps from the box on the floor. I groaned inside when I saw them. Alligator clamps with powerful springs, the ones I used only on my most advanced and jaded partners, and then only as a test or a punishment. Michael approached my body. It stood relaxed, unseeing, unsuspecting. He squeezed my pecs and kneaded my nipples, until I saw my stomach draw taut and my chest rise in silent offering.

Michael smiled. He place one open clamp over my right nipple and let it snap shut.

Far away, I could feel the sharp teeth penetrate my flesh.

I saw my body jerk wildly, tugging at the handcuffs, trying to retreat. But Michael slipped a finger into the chain dangling from my balls and held my body in check. He watched my chest spasm and writhe, touched his fingers to the knotted muscles in my arms and belly. Then he attached the second clamp.

My body twisted so violently the cock chain snapped from Michael's knuckle. I watched the body stumble to its knees, scramble up and stagger blindly into one of the mirrors, crazy with pain.

Michael picked up the riding crop and walked with long slow strides to the crouching, trembling body. He raised the leather high above his head and slashed it across my shoulders.

My body jerked, spun, rolled away—staggered to its feet, tripped over my pants on the floor, rose desperately, ran blindly into a wall—turned and took a defensive stance, hiding its stinging shoulders against the wall. Tits clamped and cock hard. I couldn't understand that, the way my cock stayed so stiff the whole time—not yet.

Michael followed slowly. He looked at the crop. Looked at my chest, muscles in high relief, tense with pain. He touched the crop to my cock. My body flinched. Michael squeezed his hard-on. Then he raised the crop and slashed it backhanded across my stomach.

I saw my body double over and run, reeling with pain and confusion, trying to escape. Michael followed it patiently around the room, taking his time, stroking his thick white cock and wielding the crop. Like a hunter, exhausting his trapped game. Playing with me.

At last the pain-wracked body collapsed kneeling in the center of the room. Shoulders against the floor, heaving—ass thrust in the air.

Michael stood over the broken body. He slowly masturbated as he beat my ass with the crop, blow after blow, until the pale buns were red and blistered.

Michael discarded the crop, grabbed my body by the clamps and forced it to stand. In the reflections I could see every mark—the long red stripes across my shoulders, the back of my legs, my stomach. My cock—a slave's cock, rock hard after the beating, veins pulsing, dribbling from the tip. I suddenly knew why—the body craved it, but so did my head, watching, crazy with excitement at the spectacle. Two places at once. Masochistic victim and sadistic observer of my own humiliation, wanting more.

Michael played with the clamps—twisted, pulled the hard flat muscles into sharp peaks, watched my body twitch and heave. He pulled the clamps off, one at a time, and tossed them away. He caressed my body, watching the skin writhe when his fingertips brushed over the tender stripes.

He cocked his head and flashed me a cryptic smile. "Good slave body. Takes it well. Ready for whatever's next. Shall I fuck it?"

He rubbed his hard cock against mine. "Sure. Give him what he wants. But do it *my* way."

He hooked his finger through the dangling cock choker and pulled it taut. Tighter and tighter. The chain sank into the gathered flesh, my cock bulged until I thought the skin would burst. I knew what was about to happen, and my mind plummeted deeper into the numb stupor that was its only protection.

Michael licked his free hand. His saliva seemed to glow with blue light. He worked his wet fingers mysteriously around my cock and balls. I saw his lips move, as if he were whispering inaudibly. The thin chain flashed with blue flame—

Then the chain slipped through. He dropped it quickly and raised his hand to lift the genitals free. He held the nine-inch shaft by the testicles in his right hand. In its place there was a smooth hairless swelling of flesh between my legs.

Again I tried to scream, though I knew it was hopeless. "I said, don't twist your face up like that," he growled. He swung the disembodied cock and slapped me across the face with it. My eyes welled with tears, making the candlelit room swim and sparkle.

My mind was sinking. I longed for unconsciousness. But his voice pulled me back.

"It'll stay hard," he said. He was rubbing thick lubricant over my cock. There was a dim sensation of pleasure somewhere below me. "All the energy of the spell holding you is focused in your cock, like a powerful conductor. But I have a warning for you. When you come—when your cock ejaculates—you'll break the spell. You'll remain in whatever condition you're in at that instant. So unless you want to stay in three pieces, you'd better hold off." He smiled and slid my cock through his fist. "Of course, you won't have much control."

He returned to my body and struck it with the cock, wielding it like a blackjack. The body jumped like a startled animal.

He dug the nails of his left hand into my right nipple and pulled the body, headless, sexless, up onto tiptoes. He stepped forward and rubbed his cockhead against the denuded stump where my cock had been. My body responded instantly—thighs parted, hips rocking back and forth. The body rubbed its groin against the blunt tip of Michael's cock.

He bent at the knees, lowering his cock and breaking the contact. My body followed blindly. The hairless groin sank down and searched for Michael's cock, found it, rubbed itself on the silky knob. Humping, like a bitch in heat.

Michael folded smoothly to his knees and settled his ass on his ankles, his hard cock pointing up like a missile. The handcuffed body spread its knees and squatted deeply, craving more contact.

Michael licked his middle finger and rubbed it against the sleek spot between my legs. My body squatted, swayed back and forth, barely kept its balance. Once again, I sensed what was about to happen. The unbelievable. The unthinkable.

There was no sign of an opening in the place where my genitals had been. Just a bald swelling, like the ball of a shoulder. But as I watched, Michael slowly, gradually buried his finger in the flesh. He began to slide it in and out. My body begged for more.

He turned his head and shot me a quick glance. His face was slack, lips parted, eyes flashing with triumph. As if to say, see what I can make you into? See how badly you want it?

As he finger-fucked me, he reached around with his right

hand and began to push the disembodied cock—my cock—into my squatting ass. All nine inches, all the way to the balls in one steady shove. He pressed his palm over the crack to hold it in.

My hips squirmed on his finger, pushed back onto my cock. Michael removed the finger and my groin tried to follow, ready to abandon the cock up its ass for more of his hand. Again, I could see no opening there.

But when he grabbed my tit to pull my body forward and down, his cockhead slipped inside. And my body squatted deeper, desperate for it, until Michael's thick shaft was completely swallowed.

Michael gasped and rolled his big shoulders with pleasure. Closed his eyes and hissed inaudible obscenities. Or incantations.

And my body—the body he had handcuffed, beaten, clamped—decapitated, emasculated—subjected to something unspeakable and inhuman—it rode his fat cock and screwed back onto the shaft he held up its ass. Mindless but hungry. More a whore than a slave. More animal than human. A creature of dark magic. His creation.

I was thankful that body had no head. It gave me a way to fool myself. To say that it wasn't me.

There was a sudden ghost sensation, more vivid than the others—a flash—as if I felt my cockhead rubbing against his, deep inside my bowels. It jolted me, like two charged wires touching. I felt feverish. The lights dimmed.

For a long time my consciousness came and went. My eyes would flicker open, glimpse grappling bodies, hear Michael's sex-charged groans. Scenes in the mirrors: Michael's beautiful ass, fucking wildly, my legs wrapped tight around his hips—Michael on his back on the bed, my body on its knees above him, fucking itself on his cock while he pulled on my tits—my body, shoulders on the bed, Michael standing between my drawn-back legs fucking with long strokes while he used my hard cock like a truncheon across my stomach and chest—

After a long blackness, I felt Michael slapping me awake. I opened my eyes and saw a cock before my face. But not

Michael's cock. A bigger, coarser instrument, knotted with thick veins and streaked with rectal mucus. My throat filled with fresh saliva. I opened my mouth—

—then realized it was *my* cock held before me. I closed my mouth, recoiling from the insanity of it.

"Go ahead." I heard Michael's voice above me. "It's not as pretty as mine, but it'll give you what you need. Go ahead. What's wrong? Don't wanna taste shit? Come on, you've made plenty of guys suck it after you've screwed 'em. Besides, it's your shit, man."

I looked hard at the cock. I had seen it in mirrors of course, even in photographs. But now I saw it as my slaves had. Huge and pulsing, inches from my lips. And I knew why men had groveled for it. Knew the power that made them crave it. I opened my mouth and moaned silently.

Michael laughed and shoved it down my throat. Rammed it in and out, the way I would have. I discovered how it felt— exactly how it felt. I remembered the riding-crop trick in New York—the sweltering afternoon with the six-pack when I tied his face to my crotch and kept my cock down his throat for hours—coming, pissing, coming, pissing. Now I knew why four hours hadn't been enough for that cocksucker.

I felt pleasure in my cock as I sucked. Almost like sixty-nining, sucking and being sucked. Two places at once.

I squeezed my throat around the huge dick, milking it, savoring the pleasure I was giving and receiving. Then Michael spoke.

"Remember, Bill. When it shoots, the spell breaks. And if that happens while you're still in pieces—there's nothing I can do to put you together again." He kept sliding it in and out of my throat.

My blood froze. I stopped the undulations in my throat.

"Come on, Bill." His voice was low and evil. "Your cock's close. Been close for hours. The balls are way up in the sack. Come on," he teased, ramming it hard and fast, "make it come. Work your throat like a good cocksucker. Don't you wanna know how it feels when you shoot in some guy's mouth? Must be good—I bet they always come back for more. Don't you wanna taste your own come?"

I looked up at him and pleaded with my eyes. He kept sliding the big dong in and out—I felt it expand, the way I always do when I'm on the verge—

I clamped my teeth down on it, hard, to stop the stroking. Michael laughed. "Okay. I believe you." He whipped the spit-streaked plunger from my throat and tossed it on the floor. I heard it land with a heavy thud and felt ghost pain in my balls.

He picked up my head and carried it to the center of the room. My body was lying on its side on the floor, exhausted. Michael squatted, placed my head on my shoulders, wet his fingers with glowing blue saliva and stroked the connection. I felt warmth flow from my neck to my chest, my hips, my legs. Thank god, whole again—almost.

I spent a few minutes coughing and swallowing convulsively, clearing the juices that clogged my throat. Michael undid the handcuffs and pulled me to my feet. My legs were shaky, there was pain everywhere. But it was wonderful to feel anything beneath my neck.

Michael stretched and yawned. "Shit, I'm beat," he said. "Been fucking you for hours, baby." He pinched one of my nipples, making me throw my head back in pain. "Came in you twice while you were out. Once in your ass, and once—well, you saw. Think I'll take a shower and hop right in bed."

"But—" I looked at my cock on the floor and quickly looked away.

"Oh, yeah," Michael said. "That. Go ahead and take it. It's yours."

My chest knotted with horror. "Please," I whispered.

"What did you say? I couldn't hear you."

I lowered my eyes—caught a glimpse of the bare flesh between my thighs—shut my eyes tight.

"Oh please, Michael. Let me have it back. Oh please, for god's sake—"

I felt a heavy slap across my face and knew it wasn't his

hand. His voice was deep and unctuous above me. "That's no way to beg."

I kept my eyes shut.

"Get on your knees and beg with your mouth."

I knelt and took his soft meat between my lips. My face was wet with tears.

"Make me come again, Bill. It won't be easy. Three times is usually my limit. Show me how good you are. Show me how good you suck cock. Make me come, and I'll let you have it back. That is—if you don't shoot first." I heard and felt the slick crackle of flesh on flesh above my head. He was holding my hard cock and stroking it.

I sucked and tried to think of nothing but his cock. Slowly, slowly it hardened, until the beer-bottle thickness gorged my throat. It wasn't so easy this time. I choked, gagged, felt my gorge rise—but I never let go. I forced my throat onto him over and over, strangling myself.

"Better than your cock, isn't it, Bill?"

Yes, he was right. His cock, so thick, so flawless, it *was* better.

He began to moan and twist. He was close. I was going to make it.

Then he pulled out. Held my face off, fought off his orgasm. "Not yet," he whispered, "not yet."

He tortured me that way. I brought him close over and over, sucking desperately, using every trick I could remember. Then he would pull out and make me start over, all the while working my cock.

"Think about it," he crooned. "What happens if I make you shoot first. You'll be what you are now, forever. Might not be so bad." He reached down and stroked a finger over my sexless groin. I felt an incredible flash of pleasure, unearthly. I jerked back and whimpered around his shaft.

"You'd be my slave, Bill. *Really* my slave. You've been playing that game for years, but this is real. I'd own you—or own your cock, which is the same thing. You'd be mine. You could never show yourself to another man like that. Think about it. Have to come crawling to me for sex. Maybe I'd be

in the mood. Maybe not. And you've seen the kind of games I
like to play."

With that nightmare in my head, I gave him my last ounce
of energy. Worshiped him like the primal force he was. Sucked
and sucked and *sucked*—

—and finally heard his roar above me. Felt his meat stiffen
and pump. Tasted bitter semen—and at the same instant, my
own hips began to jerk. I was coming, in response to him. *Too
late*—

I felt his hands on my crotch—blue fire—

And when it was over, I was whole again. Michael pulled
his shaft from my throat with a pop and collapsed onto his
throne, chest heaving. He looked worn out and happy. I was
too drained even to hate him. Too exhausted to stand. He
forced me to lick my cum from the floor. Made me kiss his
feet.

I looked up at him. After long minutes I caught my breath.
The numbness seeped out of my head. Even as wrecked as I
was, I had to know how.

"Michael, what you did—what you do . . . I don't know
what it's called, I don't even know if it has a name . . . but
what . . . what—"

"Something you're born with," he said. "There are others.
I've met three in my lifetime, heard of more. We keep our
distance from each other. Don't get ideas about learning it.
I've studied, learned the ancient laws, found new ways to focus
my power. But either you have it—and you know it—or you
don't. I knew that you didn't when I first saw you. The tan is
a giveaway. You like sunlight far too much. I can't teach it. I
can only share it."

He pushed his big toe into my mouth. "So if you ever
want it again, you know where to come. You'd be crazy to ask
for it, though. I like danger. The possibilities—the games—are
endless. Sooner or later . . ."

He pulled his toe from my mouth and pushed my face to
the floor with his foot. "Now get out. I'm tired of you."

I staggered naked to my room. It was dark outside. I
looked at the clock. I had spent eight hours in his room. I

closed the door and crawled into bed. I saw the leather strap
on my right arm. I wanted to put it back on my left, but I was
afraid he would know somehow.

I heard Michael in the hallway, then in the shower. He
was singing happily, basso profundo, as I dropped off to sleep.

Sunday morning I woke up sore and stiff. My ass ached and
there was a lingering fire in my groin. The marks he had put
all over my body stung beneath the sheet. My nipples were
raw. My arms ached. My jaw ached.

I stared at the ceiling and thought about the night before.
Perversely, my cock began to harden.

There was a knock at the door. I stiffened with fear. "Who
is it?"

"Sharon."

"Oh." I pulled the sheet up to hide my chest. "Come in."

She entered with a tray of food. "Michael said you were
under the weather today. I thought I'd bring you something to
eat."

"Thanks. Just set it on the dresser. I'll eat it later."

"Okay. You do look pale," she said maternally. Then she
looked puzzled and frowned. She was looking at my armband,
on the right now. Or was it my hairless arms?

"Well," she said, "I'll check on you later. Call if you need
anything."

I ate the poached eggs and toast, drank the soup. I noticed
that my pants and my wooden locker were by the bed. Michael
must have returned them. I cringed to think that he had been
in the room while I slept.

I tiptoed to the bathroom to put ointment on my welts
and take a long, painful crap. It felt like I was shitting my guts
out. There was blood, but not enough to worry me. Then I
returned to my room and slept like a dead man till dusk.

Later in the evening I went to the bathroom again—dry
heaving this time. As I was leaving I heard someone in the
hallway. I couldn't bear to see Michael again. I switched off
the bathroom light, cracked the door and looked out.

It was Michael's blond friend, Carl. The regular visitor

who used to live in my room. Who wouldn't make eye contact with me. Whose pants seemed to have no bulge at the crotch. He was wearing a tank top. His tanned arms and chest were smooth and hairless.

I went back to my room and tried to stay there. But I had to know.

I crept up the stairs to the trapdoor. Heart pounding, I opened it a few inches, turned my head sideways and peered in.

Michael was seated in his throne. He was wearing only his white tank top, stretched tight across his pecs and loose over his flat stomach. His half-hard cock rested like a club on the chair between his thighs.

The blond was kneeling naked before Michael, his back to me.

"Not tonight, Carl. I'm bushed."

"Please, Michael, I need it. Now. So bad. It's been so long." He was rubbing his hands between his legs shamelessly.

"I said, *not tonight*." Michael's voice was hard.

The blond leaned forward and licked Michael's cock with long strokes. He was sobbing.

"Oh, all right." Michael pushed him aside and walked to the dresser, his pale, fat cock swaying. He opened a drawer and took out something wrapped in blue silk. "Just a simple fuck tonight." he said. "Nothing fancy."

He returned to the kneeling blond and unwrapped the object. It looked like a big, stiff dildo. I knew it was not.

"Stand up and face me, stupid."

Carl stood and turned. I could see between his legs now. I saw the smooth, sexless flesh there.

I closed the trapdoor, ever so slowly. The blood pounded in my head like thunder.

That night, under cover of darkness, I moved my things out of the house on Beauchamp Street and went to a motel. Occasionally I have felt an urge to see Michael again—a glimpse of his broad shoulders, from a safe distance, would do. But I have never returned.

STEVEN SAYLOR
WRITING AS AARON TRAVIS

GETTING

TIMCHENKO

"HEY—LET'S GET TIMCHENKO!" GARY SHOUTED.

I shook my head.

"Come on, Kevin. It's been months since we gave the old Cossack a little hell." He gave me his melting grin and jabbed me in the ribs with his beer can. "For old time's sake."

I flinched. Smiled. Shook my head again.

It was graduation night. After the speeches and hand-shakes, Gary and I traded our robes for T-shirts and jeans and headed out for a final cruise. We were driving down Main Street in Gary's pickup with the radio turned up full blast, starting on our second six-pack. The windows were down. Above the rush of wind and Dolly Parton on the radio, Gary was shouting again, about getting Timchenko. I just kept shaking my head.

Main Street turned into the highway, and we left the town behind. Amethyst is just a dot on a map of Texas; you can drive straight through and hardly notice. Gary turned onto the dirt road where we usually traded handjobs, and I felt a

tightness in my pants. Five minutes later we were parked alongside the barbed-wire fence, beneath an ancient oak.

He left the radio on but turned the volume down. The green
light filled the cab with a murky underwater glow. Outside there
was a full moon blanketing the scrubby mesquites and cactus
with silver. Just beyond the fence were a few stragglers from a
herd of cattle, settled on the grass like a shadowy outcropping
of rock. My cock was stiff inside my jeans.

"You sure you don't want to get Timchenko tonight?"

"Aw, Gary." My head was fuzzy from the beer, and I
could feel his heat, the heat I always felt alone with Gary.

"Hey, tell you what. You pull one last trick on Timchenko
with me tonight, and I'll let you give me a blow-job."

My ears burned. I looked him in the eye and forced a
laugh. "What the hell makes you think I'd want to do that?"

Gary shrugged and grinned. "Just a hunch." He reached
for my hand and put it on his crotch. "Come on, Kevin. Don't
you wanna do it just once, 'fore you leave town?"

He undid his fly, working around my fingers. Another
second and it sprang free, filling my hand, standing up straight
from his lap, pale and hard in the radio light like a phallus
carved from soft green marble. I leaned over without a thought
and took him in my mouth.

I was awkward, unable to take it all. I used both hands
to stroke the base and slid down in the seat until I was practically flat, one knee against the floorboard and my face in his
lap. I hunched my crotch against the edge of the seat. Above
me Gary closed his eyes and rolled his neck, breathing deeply,
green light glowing soft against the muscles of his throat, his
jaw and cheekbones gilded with moonlight. His cock was warm
and smooth in my mouth.

Toward the end my jaw grew tired, unused to the strain.
I finished him with my hands, lathering his cock with spit and
staring in fascination. He shuddered and jerked in my fist. I
covered his cock with my lips and his semen erupted musky
and slick against the roof of my mouth. I swallowed in time
with the clenching of my cock as I shot in my pants.

When it was over, Gary slipped his cock back into his

jeans. He caught his breath and then laughed, reached over to grab my shoulder and shook it. "All right!" he said. I thought he was talking about the blow-job, and smiled a little sheepishly. But Gary had only one thing on his mind. "Now we get Timchenko."

There was a little all-night convenience store at the truckstop. Gary ran inside and came back clutching a small paper sack. He pitched it into my lap and we wheeled out of the parking lot, burning rubber. The sack was unexpectedly heavy. I looked inside. It was a two-pound package of sugar.

We poured every bit of it into the gas tank of Timchenko's Volvo. Or rather, Gary poured while I watched, one eye nervously on the screen door of the Timchenkos' back porch. Gary was making too much noise, giggling, dropping the cap of the gas tank, and pitching it onto the hood. I saw a light go on in the house and grabbed his shoulder.

Gary saw it too. He quickly screwed the cap into place and crumpled the empty sack in his fist. We turned and started running. The pickup was parked up the street and around a corner. In the stillness I heard the screen door open, but by then we were safely out of sight beyond the next house.

We jumped into the cab, slamming the doors behind us. Gary revved the engine and peeled out. But instead of heading in the opposite direction, he drove right past Timchenko's house.

Timchenko was standing in the driveway beside the Volvo, wearing his round glasses and a terry-cloth bathrobe and holding a flashlight. As we roared by, he pinned the beam directly on us. The light blinded me; I knew he'd seen me, but I ducked anyway. Gary just let out a whoop and waved his arm out the window, yelling something at Timchenko that I couldn't quite catch.

For years before that night, our persecution of Mr. Timchenko had been unrelenting. It was perverse and unaccountable. We had no reason to torment fusty Timchenko, with his round head and round glasses and his strange stilted accent. But boys, as my father would wisely say, will be boys.

Gary was Timchenko's chief tormentor. Gary was my idol. He was all hard sinew and smooth charm—tall, wiry, and compact, with wavy black hair and a lazy grin, the kind of kid who could talk his way out of any fix.

My parents never understood the connection; what could Gary and I possibly have in common? My father was on the town council, my mother ran the P.T.A. Gary's mom was an alcoholic and his dad was a fix-it man on welfare. I was teacher's pet from as far back as I could remember. Gary made lousy grades and never came out for anything, not even athletics, though his body seemed made for competition. Everybody knew he was no good. Everybody liked him. Especially me.

There was nothing much to do in Amethyst on a weekend night except cruise the streets. In four years we covered every back road in the county, listening to the radio and guzzling beer while we ran up enough mileage to drive to Patagonia and back. The handjobs were his idea—Gary always led, I followed. For him they were simple relief. For me they were something else. Holding his big cock in my hand, squeezing it, watching it shoot into the handkerchief he'd be holding capped over the head, those were moments I waited for and cherished.

Getting Timchenko was also Gary's idea.

The Timchenkos lived in the house next to mine. They had no children. Timchenko repaired clocks in a dark, dusty little shop off the courthouse square. He was a short, stocky man with a moustache, barrel-chested and prematurely balding. People said his name was Russian. His frail, thin wife spoke hardly any English at all. There were only two churches in town, Baptist and Methodist, and the Timchenkos went to neither. Gary said they were Russian Orthodoxs.

In every way, Timchenko was an easy target. Ladies on their way to church might shake their heads to see the pecan tree in Timchenko's front yard draped with toilet paper, dissolved into mush after a heavy dew. They might comment, "What a shame," before driving on; but a shame is only that, someone else's problem, and the Timchenkos were such *strange* people, after all.

Gary often slept over at my house on Friday nights. After

dark we would slip over to Timchenko's place. In the morning we would skulk upstairs and peer out the attic window, waiting for him to step outside. The toilet paper was a favorite routine, but Timchenko's little Volvo made an even choicer target. Doggerel written in lipstick across the windshield. The distributor cap unplugged. The air in all four tires let out. Timchenko would stalk out to his driveway, throw his hands in the air and curse in Russian, then patiently begin to repair the damage.

Up in our secret watching place, Gary and I would roll against each other, laughing. The closeness of his body and the excitement in his eyes would start the blood pounding between my legs; and later in the day, with Gary gone and my parents out, I would lie alone and naked on my bed. Across the honeysuckle patch that separated my bedroom window from the Timchenko's living room, I would hear the whir of Mrs. Timchenko's sewing machine as I masturbated for hours, remembering Gary's cock in my hand and imagining it in my mouth.

Timchenko had a garden in his backyard. Once he planted a rosebush. On a Friday morning I noticed that the buds had opened all at once, blood red and heavy with scent. Mrs. Timchenko had been in the hospital all week—the first stay of several. Timchenko drove her home late that night. In the morning he was up bright and early to show her his achievement. He led her carefully down the back-porch steps, talking in Russian. Then there was abrupt silence, except for the sound of bees nuzzling the honeysuckle. The rose bush was naked, a spray of thorny stems with every blossom clipped and stolen.

Gary and I watched from the attic window, surrounded by red petals. Timchenko must have heard us—two boys laughing behind and high above him, muffled by distance and panes of glass. His wife continued to stare at the rosebush, but Timchenko slowly turned his head and looked over his shoulder. Gary jerked out of sight, laughing harder than ever and poking my ribs to make me do the same, but I knocked his hand away, snagged on Timchenko's stare. There was not a single emotion to be read on his face. It was Timchenko who looked away first. He put his arm around his wife's shoulder and led her back into the house.

After that, my interest in tormenting Timchenko cooled. Gary kept after me to help him "get" Timchenko again. I refused, and Gary sulked. The handjobs grew less frequent, and I had the feeling that Gary was punishing me. By senior year I was too busy to bother with pranks, anyway—lining up a summer job, trying to get accepted to college. Perhaps I was finally beginning to grow up, and to outgrow Gary.

But on graduation night, Gary seduced me, quite literally, into that final assault. It was not without an aftermath.

The morning after graduation night, I woke with a blinding hangover and a raging hard-on. I had been dreaming all night, restless dreams of Gary's hard pale cock, into which Mr. Timchenko and his flashlight kept intruding. I was sitting in my robe in the kitchen, listlessly watching my mother fix pancakes, when there was a knock at the door.

Somehow I thought it was Gary. I jumped up, head pounding, and walked to the living room, but my father had already opened the door. I froze. It was Mr. Timchenko, shifting nervously from foot to foot.

I hurried back to the kitchen. After a long moment my father followed. I flinched. He was talking hurriedly—but not to me, to my mother. "Timchenko's wife is sick again. He needs to get her to the hospital, but there's something wrong with his car. I'm taking them."

"The hospital again?" My mother whipped the batter in the bowl crooked under her arm. "I hope it's not too serious." She shook her head. "They have more trouble with that car."

For the rest of the day, a hangover was the only excuse I needed for the misery I felt.

Later that afternoon, a tow truck arrived for the Volvo. Timchenko must have known what had happened, but he never told my father. His wife was still in the hospital when I left for my summer job in Houston a few days later.

Over the next two years, I didn't get back to Amethyst very often. When I did, I always called Gary; we'd take a cruise down the drag for old time's sake, but we didn't have much to talk about. He was working at a garage and thinking about getting married. He never asked for another blow-job. He never even mentioned Timchenko. Perhaps he was growing up, too.

It was spring break of my sophomore year when I finally saw Timchenko again. I had noticed small signs of decay in the once-tidy house next door—peeling paint, missing shingles, the garden dormant and cluttered with debris. I was helping my mother dry dishes when I asked her if someone else had moved into the Timchenkos' house.

"Oh no, he's still over there. Of course he's all alone now. Mrs. Timchenko died—you knew that, didn't you? Oh, it must have been sometime after Christmas. A brain tumor, all this time. We never see him. Never seems to step outside the house."

I only nodded, and let her change the subject.

That night I dreamed of Mr. Timchenko. I woke up in darkness, trying to recall the details, but the dream left only a sad, disquieting residue. I noticed a faint light through my bedroom window. A lamp was on in Timchenko's living room, and his silhouette, in glasses and terry-cloth robe, paced back and forth behind the thin lacy drapes.

I woke feeling strangely content. My mother spent the morning baking. After lunch she went shopping. As soon as I was alone, I walked over to Timchenko's house. As an excuse I took with me a box of my mother's cookies.

Timchenko answered the door wearing his robe and a pair of slippers. His jaw was covered with stubble.

"Mr. Timchenko—Kevin Landrum. From next door."

He nodded. "Oh yes, I know."

I was ready for suspicion or anger, but the resignation was so heavy on his face that no other emotion showed through. I suddenly regretted coming; but I pushed ahead. "My mom baked some cookies. She thought you might like some." I held up the box. "Could I come in for a minute?"

He seemed uncertain, then nodded. He apologized for the clutter—clothes strewn about, empty glasses on the coffee table, a plate and fork balanced on the arm of an easy chair. The place was filled with clocks, ancient and new, clucking softly like a brood of hens. I looked about the room, at dusty trinkets arrayed on shelves and an icon of a saint above the mantel-piece, at the deserted sewing machine, an old back model with the word *Singer* embossed in a script long out of date.

"What's this?" I said, walking to a tarnished urn displayed on a small serving table.

"Oh, don't touch it—it's very old, very fragile, from my great-grandfather's time. It's called a samovar. . . ."

That was enough to break the ice. He slowly grew more animated as he showed me his things. I listened at first with genuine interest, but gradually grew more distracted, realizing I had no idea how to tell him whatever it was I had come to say.

I studied him in glances. His hands, thick-wristed with short fingers, handling each object he touched with a nimble-ness that surprised me—a clockmaker's hands. His face, round and plain, with a strong nose and mouth and deep brown eyes, unassuming and masculine. The smooth skin of his balding forehead. His short, plump calves, covered with wiry black hair. The stout mass of his body concealed beneath the robe. I noticed a picture in a silver frame set atop the television set, of Timchenko and his wife as newlyweds, and was startled at the young man I saw there, wearing the same round glasses but not yet old enough to have a mustache, his hair full, black, and wavy, like Gary's hair.

Timchenko offered tea and went to the kitchen, leaving me alone in the room surrounded by a sad nostalgia that was not my own. When he returned, we sat side by side on the sofa. When he handed me the cup our hands briefly touched; after I had drunk it down and felt the warmth spread through me, I laid my hand on his thigh. He flinched a bit and gave me a look like a child.

Having got that far, I touched his arm, and was surprised to find it round and hard beneath the natty cloth, then the back of his broad neck. He closed his eyes and sighed, allowing me to knead the knotted muscles. Beneath the plumpness that covered his body, Timchenko was unexpectedly solid.

For long afterward, I wondered at the ease of that seduction. I was only twenty, after all, and who at twenty understands the simple appeal of their flesh, whatever the sex? Timchenko responded. I could give him nothing tangible to make up for what I had done; all the words I could think of seemed weak and flimsy. I offered the only recompense I could give.

I did it on my knees, framed between the warmth of his thighs. I held his sturdy calves at first, then ran my hands upward over his hairy trunklike legs and onto his hips, then farther up to grip the stocky width of his torso. Timchenko's cock, like his body, was broad, thick, and plump; unlike Gary's, I could hold the whole of it securely in my throat.

I took my time. Timchenko melted into the sofa. His head lay on his shoulder, eyes closed, lips parted. At first his hands rested limp on the cushions; eventually he reached up to touch my shoulders and stroke my hair and the sides of my face. He seemed to be dreaming, fondling my face in his sleep.

My cock was stiff in my pants. I didn't touch it. I concentrated instead on Timchenko's pleasure, performing a strange alchemy at the place where I held him inside me, changing bitter into sweet. It was an act of penance, not love, but somehow it felt the same. Timchenko stiffened on the sofa, clutching my shoulders and making a strange mewling sound in his throat, and when he came in my mouth the transformation was complete.

He lay inert and passive on the sofa with his eyes closed and a faint smile on his lips. I studied him for a long moment—his body cradled deep in the cushions, his chest slowly rising and falling, his cock drooping moist and satisfied between his thighs. I finally stood. Timchenko opened his eyes and pulled himself up from the sofa, covering himself with the robe.

At the door he shrugged sheepishly and asked if he could hold me for a moment. His clockmaker hands were clumsy as he squeezed me hard against his chest. When he stepped back, I saw tears in his eyes. He was staring over my shoulder at the framed photograph on the television set.

I suddenly felt small and presumptuous; but when he

smiled weakly and reached up with the corner of his robe to wipe his eyes, I felt an affection for him that was simple and uncluttered and quite genuine, despite the fact that I knew it would quickly fade, like the soft, hazy residue of a dream.

"Thank your mother for the cookies," he said, smiling crookedly. I nodded and left.

PART THREE

WOMEN AND

GAY MEN'S

EROTICA

The gay experience has captured the imagination of other writers besides gay men. Whether it's the ideal of androgyny that some think gay men embody, or the appeal of the freedom from sexual roles and restrictions that gay men seem to represent, or an exploration of bisexuality (or even omnisexuality) that women think they might experience with gay men, we have been the topic of many women's writings.

Pat Califia is a lesbian who has been a central part of gay men's publishing for years. If her contributions had been limited to writing the ever-popular "Advocate Advisor" column in the *Advocate,* her place would be secure. She's done much more than that, including a stint as editor of *Advocate Men,* one of the premier gay erotic magazines. While Califia's pornography has been mainly focused on lesbian sex (*Doc and Fluff,* etc.), she's also written many stories that have been published in the gay male press, ones that are especially popular when she's explored and blurred the lines between homosexuality and bisexuality.

Anne Rice seems to work at destroying the lines between types of sexuality completely. She became a gay icon with the publication of her first book, *Interview with the Vampire* (New York: Knopf, 1976). Her rich gothic tale of a world hidden from view, into which members were initiated by an act as passionate as sex, was seen as a metaphor for gay life as a whole. Rice pursued many other avenues of writing while she continued her vampire lore, using acknowledged pseudonyms to separate the various types. Her explicit historical pornography (*The Claiming of Sleeping Beauty,* etc.) was published under the name A. N. Roquelaure; more contemporary erotic work was presented as Anne Rampling's. One of the most popular Rampling novels was *Exit to Eden,* the story of a private and extravagant S&M club on an island in the Caribbean. In the novel, her major male character, Elliott, has volunteered for a term as a sex slave to the members, fulfilling his own deepest erotic urges. In the final manuscript, the plot involving Elliott's love for the female head of The Club meant that two incredibly explicit and erotic chapters describing his homosexual adventures with the men on the island had to be held back. They're published here for the first time.

BELONGING

"BARTENDER!" JERRY SHOUTED, LOUD ENOUGH TO be heard over the raucous country music and the buzz of a very drunk Saturday-night crowd. He was a handsome kid, but spoiled-looking. In his mid-twenties, he still wore the brooding expression of an adolescent who perpetually feels fucked over and misunderstood. His clothes were cheap synthetics, too flashy for what they had cost him, and they made him seem oddly sleazy for somebody so young: James Dean playing the part of a bookie or a gigolo. He slammed his glass on the counter, not once, but three times, and the startled, portly man at the sink in the middle of the bar hurried over to him, wiping his hands on his apron.

The barkeep was too harassed to notice the details of his obnoxious customer's personal appearance. His tastes ran to plump redheads with balconylike bosoms. But there was somebody else in the bar whose preferred sexual quarry was young men whose expectations far exceeded their willingness to exert themselves. He had tracked Jerry to this noisy lair, and he was enjoying the opportunity to observe that sulky mouth and to laugh silently to himself about the rude and ridiculous things that inevitably came out of it. Much better for a mouth like that to be taught silence. Hidden within the sozzled crowd, this hunter stroked the tool he used to gag his attractive-but-lazy prey. It was in good working order.

"Yeah?" the bartender said, none too friendly. The loud-mouth was bobbing and weaving, scowling at the mirror behind the bar, obviously close to losing it.

That bitch Caroline, Jerry thought, the fucking bitch. She won't let me in, and she won't answer my phone calls. How can I get to her? If I could *talk* to her I'd make her understand. It's that guy I saw at her place, I know it, it's *him,* I'll bet he's with her right now and they're screwing their brains out. Shit! What makes her think she can do this to me, the whore? "Scotch and soda," he blared. "On the double."

"Forget it! The only thing I'm serving you is a cup of coffee. Finish what you got and go home."

There was no arguing with that grim, jowly face. Jerry picked up what was left of his drink and jostled his way through the crowd to the other side of the bar. There was a place by the pinball machine where he could lean against the wall. It took him two tries to light a cigarette. "Fuck, I must be high," he thought and tried to focus his eyes on the tip of his nose. Ouch. Yes. I am definitely getting drunk in this here shit-kickers' bar. He'd met Caroline in a much classier joint than this.

I must have looked like a fool, he thought, barging around, describing that cunt to everybody. Took me forever to figure out she'd stood me up. Then this woman said, "Be quiet. Sit down and help me finish this champagne." Caroline never said "please" or "thank you" or asked a question, she just told you what to do and you did it, but he couldn't say she was rude, just very sure of herself. *Way* too sure of herself. She was wearing a severely tailored, dark wool suit, and he would have sworn she was wearing a man's shirt and tie if not for the pearly stickpin that held the length of silk in place. Her short, black hair was expensively styled. He remembered thinking, I sure got lucky, this one's old enough to know what women want and rich enough to pay the price.

Drunk as he was, it finally occurred to him that one of the men over by the pool table was not part of the quiet, businesslike game—a handsome bastard with a big, hooked nose and a black beard that made him look grim as hell. He wasn't dressed very nice for a weekend, just faded jeans and a T-shirt, one of those wide garrison belts that cops wear, and a black leather jacket. His hands were so big, you could hardly see the beer can he gripped.

Jerry's bitter reverie recovered from this brief interruption, and flowed on, well rehearsed. All I did was drop by one Friday night. Is that a crime, huh? If a guy's been making it pretty regular with a broad for a couple of weeks, you figure he can drop by without getting arrested, right? Especially if he brings something along, I mean it isn't like I went over there empty-handed, for Chrissake, I *had* a six-pack.

The guy by the pool table turned toward him, hooked his thumb far back between his legs and scratched his balls. He had a contemptuous look on his face, a look that said, "Kiss my ass."

When I rang her bell she didn't even use the intercom to ask who it was, just hit the buzzer and let me in. The front door to her loft wasn't locked. I walked right into her living room. And there's this dude stretched out in the armchair, watching porno movies on the color TV! Boy, was I mad. Anybody else would have slugged her.

Now the big man crossed his arms on his chest and pushed his hips forward a little. By some accident or some genius of self-arrangement, the length of his cock was a visible tube down the inner seam of one leg of his jeans. Then he made it jump. Jerry began to lose the thread of his aggrieved monologue. His mouth was awfully dry. He took a sip from his glass and adjusted the waistband of his slacks. It had been a long time since he'd gotten any. Weeks.

Ever since she'd thrown him out, in fact. She had wheeled around, white-faced, and said, "You were not asked to be here." Step by step she had backed him into the foyer, not seeming to hear him as he demanded angrily who that man was, what was going on, until finally he shouted, "Goddamnit, I need to know that you belong to me!"

Her face broke into the biggest smile. "Don't worry," she said softly. "I know exactly what you need. And I'm going to make sure you get it." Beguiled by that sweet face and the sweeter promise, he had let her put him out and gone his way, confused but expecting to hear from her any day, to collect his reward for being so patient and understanding.

"Instead, all I get is a goddamn runaround," he told his warm, flat drink.

Thumbs hooked in his pockets, the dark man stroked himself discreetly, fingertips fanning out on his buttoned fly. His eyes flicked toward the back of the bar, then back to Jerry, with a questioning (but still hostile) stare. Here was a promise of satisfaction that would not be withdrawn at the last minute. Queers just couldn't get enough of a real man's dick, Jerry thought. But it was funny, he could usually spot faggots, and this guy was such a bad-ass, he looked like a truck driver or even a biker, maybe. I look more like a queer than he does, he thought, smoothing back the short sides of his hair and checking that the long top of his d.a. was still combed back, perfectly greased and in place. But that wasn't too funny, and the injustice of it, the implied accusation, made him determined to follow through with the cruise. Shit, he'd never come here again anyway, he just stopped here because it was close to her house and he needed a drink after being turned away from her door again. So he headed toward the john, giving a look over his shoulder to see if the other guy had noticed. Wouldn't the girls here just curl up and die if they knew what went on in the men's room?

The bathrooms were on opposite sides of a small hall. Jerry kicked open the door that said "Men" and inhaled the familiar, raunchy aroma. After two or three breaths you didn't notice the smell anymore. He kinda missed it. There were urinals along one wall, and some stalls. He really did need to pee. Let the fag come in the door while he had his cock out already; it would probably be a real treat for him. No reason why he,

Jerry, should be the only one to get any fun out of it. Not that he was going to reciprocate or anything. He wasn't in high school anymore, for godsake.

Yeah, he really needed to piss, all right, but as he took his cock out, the familiar touch made it semirigid. His hand traveled up and down a couple of times in a lazy J./O. gesture. Nothing was getting out of his bladder now. It almost hurt, being caught between two pleasures, anticipating both of them, not really able to enjoy either one.

Then somebody else kicked the door open, but this was different—it sounded like storm troopers. He turned, startled, and let go of his pants. They slipped down over his ass. The guy in the leather jacket was coming at him with a great big knife! Who did this mad fucker think he was, Rambo? He stumbled back, almost tripped on his pants, but the guy stepped on the loose end of a trouser leg, and Jerry pulled his feet free. His loafers went flying. Then a hand like a bear trap fastened on his shirtfront. "Hold still, boy," growled the mantrapper in his ear. The knife went between his shirt and his chest, and Jerry pulled away, frantic to keep that cold edge away from his suddenly hot skin. Ten inches of steel severed his shirt with one yank. He tried to get away, but was caught by the seat of his shorts—and those, too, were neatly severed and ripped off his body. He had long since lost his erection, and a sudden spurt of urine wet the rags that had been his underwear. He was completely naked. But before he could scream, a fistful of the shorts was stuffed in his mouth, and the knife was under his chin. One of his arms was bent and twisted behind his back, high enough to make him dance on tiptoe. "Spit that out and I'll cut your throat," the man said, and Jerry believed him.

He was turned around (amazing how quickly pain could make him obey) and quick-marched down the short, dark hallway (jeez, they ought to mop that floor), into an unlit parking lot, where gravel hurt his feet, up to a black van with oversized tires, a CB antenna, and customized flames curling around the windows and wheel wells. The man let go of his arm (but the sharp edge of steel kept his chin up), and released the side door of the van. Then the knife was gone, and he was shoved facedown onto the floor. "Put your hands between your ankles, fuck-face," his captor snarled, and he complied, even though it put his ass up in the air. There was a straight steel bar with four manacles on it—two big ones on the outside, two little ones on the inside—and his feet and wrists were put in the appropriate holes and the ratchets snapped shut.

"We got a long drive ahead of us," sneered the stranger. "This oughta take your mind off it." Something pointed and greasy intruded between the cheeks of Jerry's ass, and made him cry out. The cry loosened his bowels enough for the plug to lodge home, deep inside. Then it started to buzz. It must have a battery. This startled him so much he barely noticed the van had started rolling. Oh, fuck, this was the worst. He had never imagined anything like this ever happening to him. God, he had never been so scared or unhappy—until he realized the vibrating butt-plug was giving him an erection. At that, he cried. He hadn't cried since the first time he went to camp. The other guys had made him get out of his sleeping bag to join in a circle jerk. He was the last one in the tent to come, so he had to eat his own load in front of everybody.

He kept crying until his untouched, unloved cock pulsed and he shot all over his own chest and belly. It was humiliating to come that way, all alone, being made to come by an object he had no control over, worse even than jacking off after a date with some cock-teasing bitch who let him spend his money on her and then wouldn't put out. The only good part of it was that the contractions of his orgasms pushed the nasty rubber plug out of his ass. The cum dried slowly, itching, shrinking, pulling his nipples in and making them hard.

They had stopped moving. The door of the van slid open, revealing a garage. The kidnapper clapped new irons on his wrists and ankles, then released him from the bar. As he was yanked out of the van, his tortured shoulder and neck muscles cramped, and so did his calves. He screamed and almost fell. But the man just picked him up, threw him over his shoulder, unlocked a door, carried him down a flight of stairs, and thrust him into a small cell. What kind of maniac has a real jail cell, with real iron bars and a door that locks, in his basement? The

intense physical pain and the sudden conviction that he was
going to be killed made Jerry break away from the hand that
steadied him. He began to shriek and stumble around the cell.
If his hands had not been manacled behind his back, he would
have beat on the bars. He tried to kick over the cot. It was
bolted to the floor.

"Good way to work the cramps out," said the stranger,
and stepped out of the cell, turned a key, and left him alone
with nothing but a single lightbulb (situated outside the cell,
and protected with a strong wire cage) for company.

The rampage—such as it was—petered out pretty fast. In
such a small space, with nothing to turn over or bust up—in
fact, there was nothing in his environment that Jerry could have
a significant effect upon—it did not relieve his feelings. He
gave up and huddled on the cot for a while, but it was chilly
in the cell, so he got up and began to pace, trying to keep
warm.

He thought briefly of suicide. But how? There was no
mirror to break. He had no belt, no shoelaces—not even a
button to swallow! There were no sheets on the cot—just a thin
mattress with a cover he could not tear with his fingers. There
wasn't even a toilet to drown in! The only methods available
(strangling himself with his chains, perhaps, or banging his
head on the floor) would have required a force of character he
simply did not possess.

His prowling led to only one major discovery—a drain in
one corner of the cell. So he could piss without fouling his own
nest. Good. But as soon as he had relieved this major discomfort, he became aware of two others—hunger and thirst. These
torments kept him on his feet until he was so tired he fell onto
the cot and slept.

He woke up terribly cold, stiff, with a bad headache and
an even worse taste in his mouth. He heard steps. The flight
of stairs down to the basement was fairly long, and the man
coming down them was taking his time. Instead of just waiting,
he took a piss, but his urine was so concentrated that it burned.
What was this guy going to do, watch him die slowly of de-
hydration? When he saw the big man standing outside his cell,

one hand on his belt buckle, the other on a canteen slung over his shoulder, all the resentment turned into relief. Here, finally, was something new, some alternative to the boredom of his own companionship.

"Thirsty?"

"You know I am!"

"Want a drink, do you?"

"Yes!"

"Then ask for it with some manners, boy, and call me 'Sir.'"

"Wh . . . wh . . . I . . . I will not!"

The dark brown eyes, under brows so bushy they met in the middle of the forehead, regarded him without a trace of impatience or anger. But there was also no compassion or remorse in that gaze. "Don't be stupid," he was told. "I got you locked up tighter than the president's rear end. There's no food and water in that cell. If you want any it has to come from me. So you just call me 'Sir' like a good boy and count yourself lucky I don't make you call me God. Because your life is in the palm of my hand."

"I . . . can't . . ."

The cap of the canteen was slowly unscrewed. It was tilted. Precious water was about to be poured, wasted, onto the floor—

"Please! Sir! Let me have some water, Sir."

The cap was put back on the canteen, and the man moved menacingly toward the bars of his cell.

"But I said it, I said it, please, let me drink!"

"Oh, you'll get something to swallow, all right. Get down on your knees."

This was tricky to manage on a concrete floor, with no help from his hands, but he did it without hurting himself. His face was inches from the bars when a piece of sex-meat as dark as his captor's sun- and wind-burned face flopped into view and hit him on the cheek. He cringed. It was so much bigger than his own, and it wasn't clipped. The long foreskin, gathered at the tip of the cockhead in a soft pucker, made it seem even more alien. His captor skinned his dick, slowly, and Jerry felt gooseflesh go up his neck.

"This is the first thing I'm gonna feed you," the big man said. "Before anything else goes into your mouth, this does. That's how you earn your groceries. You better get used to it now because around here we eat three times a day. C'mon, boy, say, 'Thank you, Sir,' and kiss it."

Jerry's gorge rose, and he tried to back away, but his tender knees and short chains made him slow on the floor, and a callused paw darted through the bars, found his throat and squeezed it exactly the way it had squeezed a can of beer in the cowboy bar, so long ago.

"Whatsa matter, gorgeous?" (Squeeze, squeeze.) "You couldn't take your eyes off my basket in that breeder bar." (Stroke, squeeze.) "What did you think I was taking you back to that toilet for?" (Extrahard grip, the edge of the hand felt like iron.) "You probably thought I was going to suck on *your* ding-dong, didn't ya, huh?" (A stroke hard enough to make him choke a little, a softer stroke.) "We just never know how things are going to turn out, do we?" (Both hands were around his neck, twisting in opposite directions.) "The universe just chews us up and spits us out." (Both hands, jacking off his throat.) "But you ain't going to spit *this* out." (Blunt, strong thumbs pressing in at the joints of his jaw, forced into the muscle until he cried with pain, and the cockhead slid between his lips and left a salty smear across his mouth. The taste of it, at least, was familiar, just like his own.)

For one split second, the smartest part of him whispered, "Suck it! You can't help it anymore than you can help kneeling on the floor or being cold and thirsty." But then pride and stupidity intervened (as was their habit) and he bit down on the deliciously resilient knob that was lodged in the hollow of his cheek. As soon as he had done it, he realized his mistake. It's the kind of thing you'd better do all the way or not at all. He had not anticipated how hard it would be to hurt another man's dick. His own ached with sympathy.

The cell door slammed open and suddenly he had more company than he dreamed would fit in such a small place—mad company, bad company. In two shakes of a dog's tail (or my tail, he thought bitterly), he was facedown on the cot. His ankle chain had been padlocked to the frame at the foot of the narrow bed, and it did not give him enough room to roll over. "You damn fool punk," the stranger said wearily, and took off his belt.

Every single blow hurt worse than the last. Not only was this man energetic and strong, but his strokes fell on a rather limited area—Jerry's butt and thighs. The broad, long garrison came down so hard it felt like a solid object rather than a flexible piece of leather. Jerry very quickly realized that sucking cock was not nearly as bad as this. Each blow had him rapidly revising his opinion of the relative merits of the two experiences—giving head and getting beaten—until he thought he'd rather deep-throat this man than go to heaven, if only it would stop the beating. The worst part of it was that he seemed to be saying all of this out loud, with a lot of "Sirs" and "please" and "I'll do anything you say" thrown in for good measure.

Still, it didn't stop until he had lost his breath and couldn't plead for mercy or call himself any more bad names. When it did stop, he was astonished by how little time had really elapsed. The Master (he had somehow become that in the dialogue that had accompanied the belting) was not even winded. Jerry looked at the man and his belt and his arm with new respect. When he was unchained he knelt by the side of the cot. "Thank you, Sir," he said and kissed the cock that was put to his dry lips. Then he opened his mouth. The hands were on his throat again, squeezing, and every time they eased their grip, the Master's cock went down his throat another inch. It was difficult but not awful. He arched his thighs and came up to get more of the rod. Just opening his mouth was not enough. He had to provide friction, traction. But it was hard to suck it and keep his teeth out of the way.

Above him, the Master was hissing, and one big fist was twisted in his forelock, practically banging his forehead against the muscular stomach, hard now with excitement and need. When his Master came, it was like having a hose down his throat that someone had suddenly turned on. It jerked as if it wanted to escape and sprayed hot thick stuff down his gullet.

Somewhere, far away, another hose spurted sticky stuff over his thigh.

When he came to and realized he had come himself, once again without being touched, the fragile equilibrium he had achieved as a result of being beaten vanished, and he retched. The Master watched him crawl to the drain and attempt to be sick.

"Don't feel bad, shithead," he said, not unkindly. "You ain't the first piece of so-called trade I busted down to cocksucker. Knock that off and come rinse your mouth out."

The boy (as he was coming to think of himself) was not too far-gone to recognize common sense. He abandoned the stinking drain and crawled over to his Master, who shoved his big leg between Jerry's thighs and told him gruffly to lean against it. The first swallow of water was tipped delicately into his mouth. It was still cold and smelled deliciously of the metal canteen and its wet wool cover. After that, the water was poured from up higher, so he had to abandon the prop of his Master's thigh and open his mouth under it, like a dog drinking from a faucet.

Standing over the shackled body he had just possessed, the Master said, "You got a lot of vanity, and it's all misplaced, boy. Whyncha try t'be proud of something you really can do— like let a big, fat dick tickle your tonsils? You're really good at that."

Then he was left alone and was glad because he was tired. The room was not so cold now. He slept. When he woke up, he realized he must have slept very deeply because he had not heard footsteps coming down the stairs. It was the smell of soup that woke him. There was a big bowl of it on the floor, in one of those fancy dog dishes that are weighted so they can't be tipped over. "That's smart," he thought. "I won't get it all over the floor." It was not until he was halfway through bolting down the wonderful stuff that he realized how low he had to be to think there was anything admirable or practical about eating from a dog bowl. But that didn't keep him from licking both the bowl and as much of his face as his tongue could reach, clean.

Then he realized he had a spectator. The Master wiped his face with a bandanna taken from his back pocket. "Good boy," he said. "You ready for another lesson?" Jerry was dubious. But the belt was safe in its loops, buckled, and no other weapons were in the Master's hands. "Maybe, Sir," he said. Sir laughed. "You don't have much choice, do you, boy?" "I don't have any choice, Sir," he said ruefully, as he was once more stretched stomach down on his cot and the ankle chain used to padlock him to it.

"Want some more water, boy?" He looked at the source of the offer. The Master had hung a bright red bag from the cell door and was offering him the nozzle. "Come on, it's clean, nothing but water," said the Master, and let a jet of it hit him in the face. Anything to delay the insertion of that nozzle where he knew it was meant to (and would) go. He opened his mouth and accepted a few swallows. Then the bag was taken off the door and his Master stuck his big cock into it. There was the unmistakable sound of somebody taking a healthy piss. "The enema du jour is prepared fresh daily," said the Master, and hung the bag back up. Jerry managed a weak smile.

"Before we do this," the Master said, "I think you ought to know that I'm not going to stop until I have exactly what I want from you." He lit a match on the sole of his boot, then slowly turned a big cigar in the flame. The cell was soon full of fragrant tobacco fumes. "We're being all cutesy right now but as soon as I do anything serious you're going to fight me again. I don't mind because I know I'll win. But it will make this easier on you if you know you're going to lose. Have you got any questions?"

"What are you going to do to me, Sir?"

"You're going to do anything I tell you to do and before much longer I won't have to tell you, you'll *know* what I want. But before we can reach that stage, I want to know everything about your sordid and misspent, snot-nosed youth. We're going to flush the past right out of you, starting now."

The nozzle was greased and inserted. "Just be glad it ain't my cigar—or something bigger," the Master chuckled. Then he wiggled some of the plastic tubing into his ass. Jerry squirmed.

"Come t'think of it, you kinda like getting things shoved up your ass, don't you, pisspot? In fact, you creamed all over the floor of my van, didn't you? Now how do you suppose a straight boy learned how to do a trick like that, huh?"

There was a long, deadly silence. Jerry tentatively pulled on the ankle chain, but the pain was awful and the padlock was not going to pop open on his say-so. He would not answer the question. Not even to save himself a beating.

The Master sighed. "I think you ought to see some of my home movies," he said softly. From his cot, Jerry watched him leave the cell and click off the lights. There was the sound of another button being hit, a motor revving up—and film flashed on the back wall of the cell. The picture was large and grainy and so close he could barely see it, but the subject was so familiar that he didn't really need to watch it.

No wonder Caroline had always insisted on balling in her living room, on that big sofa. He was such a chump he never thought it was odd that she wouldn't take him into her bedroom. He just thought she couldn't wait to get some, had to have it the minute they walked in the door. She must have had a hidden camera set up in there, filming the whole thing. And, of course, the Master was the man he had accidentally discovered in her apartment.

She had Jerry on her lap. She was spanking him. How had she ever talked him into that? He had done something to make her call him a "bad boy"—oh, yeah, he wouldn't go down on her—and she had teased his prick enough to get him over her lap. (She had also had him by the balls, and had let him know—giggling—that she would hurt them if he did not do as she said.) Now she was putting a plug up his ass, rolling him over onto his back and poising herself over his erect cock, sinking down on it, holding his hands up over his head, playing with his nipples. The film had no sound, but he could remember the dialogue. "Who's fucking who now, little boy, huh? Who's fucking you? Can't you feel it up your ass? When I sit on your cock it moves it around. I've turned on the vibrator, it's going to make you come, it's my cock that's going to make you come."

The Master released the clamp on the enema tube, and water started to flow into him. He was allowed to use a bedpan, then made to bend over for another dose of water-and-piss, all in the ghastly flickering light of these movies, made of the stuff of shame. He had been so stupid then. He had excused everything she did to him on the grounds that she was a horny, older woman who was so hot for him, she couldn't help but go overboard expressing her lust. Now he saw the truth. Caroline had picked him up, initiated him into a series of demeaning and subservient acts (the film showed her shoe in his face, the long and dangerous heel going in and out of his mouth), and he had not resisted or protested. In fact, it was the best sex he had ever had.

Another session on the bedpan, more water. He was fascinated by the sight of her putting clips on his nipples, clips that were connected by a chain. Now she was tying his cock up. The long ends of the leather laces were brought up and secured to the tit clamps. And the harder she pulled, the harder he got. The Master's hands fastened on his teats, hauled on them—rougher, more comforting than Caroline's sharp nails. He was lying on his back on the cot now. He didn't know if he was still watching the movie or just replaying memories in his mind. Clamps (identical to those in the film) were fastened on his nipples. He felt leather lace being wound around his cock and balls. The inevitable duplication—lace tied around chain, both pulled until he came up off the bed, hard between the legs, his balls swollen to bursting point, aching for more pain if it meant more sex, more stimulation for his cock, more intense release. Release from that woman, that awful, wicked, vengeful woman who had gone to so much trouble to get him into permanent trouble.

Damn her, damn her, he brought his knees up as his Master climbed onto the foot of the bed. He was wearing leather chaps, a leather jacket; nothing else. As the Master bent over Jerry to unlock his wrist chains, the boy kissed his chest, rubbed his face into the coarse fur, grateful for the lack of perfume, the presence of hard muscle instead of soft breasts. He barely noticed the weight that rested on his well-clamped tits as the Master reached for the head of the bed and refastened his hands to it, so they were no longer pinned underneath his body. He was too busy sucking on those nipples, nipples that were not in pain; it was his job to give them pleasure while his own suffered. It was his vocation.

The laces kept his cock out of the way as a hand full of lubricant spread him, speared him, went where the nozzle and warm water and piss had prepared a way. He was clean inside and smooth, open to the touch, but always clinging, providing a snug fit for the fingers that stroked him, longing to retain them and love them and keep them inside, where they gave him so much pleasure that he gasped, choked on his desire as the fingers were withdrawn. Restlessly, he moved his slippery ass so the ring of muscle lodged against the head of the cock that was being pointed at it, and absorbed it. The whole length of the thing inside him throbbed. This was not a piece of plastic, it was flesh, man flesh, like his own only free, free to use him. (And once again it was his task, his calling, to pleasure a part of his Master while his own, equivalent part was hurting.) There was a little pain around his opening, a feeling of something resisting then being broken, and he wanted it to be broken so he could experience everything fully, without resistance, without pride, meet thrust with thrust and groan into the same mouth that covered his and groaned.

"Fuck me, Sir, please, fuck me harder," he begged and got his wish. He could not come because of the binding around his cock, and he was glad, because he wanted to be a vessel, receive; he had fucked everything up, made a mess of it all, couldn't control or manage or direct things; it was better to get fucked, to be controlled, to be shown how his body responded automatically to this touch, this stroke, this degree of dilation and penetration and be rubbed here inside, there, the feelings kept changing and growing, how could he feel so much and still feel more and not explode or be damaged or destroyed?

His torso was imprisoned between arms that bulged with the strain of holding up a big man's body during a full-out fuck. He turned his head and kissed the arms, licked them, tried to get his fettered hands down far enough to caress them. "Tell me," Sir gritted, "what a little shit you are."

There was no time for a full confession. He knew Sir would extract all the details: The faggots he enticed and then rolled (and what really happened between him and the men he did not rob). The jobs he had botched with petty thievery or laziness. The women who had treated him with almost as much contempt as he felt for them. The physique magazines and where he hid them and what he did in the stores where he bought them. For now it was enough to just say, "I *am* a piece of shit, this is all I'm good for, I have to have your cock in me, please, please, please, Sir, please."

The cock went in and in again, meeting no resistance, but the lining of his ass had been roughened somewhat, giving the fuck a new texture, a slight edge. "I belong to you!" he cried, and with a sharp jerk, the Master released the cock-laces and let the slave's jism spill between them. "I belong to you!" Jerry continued to cry, even after his cock ran dry. After all, his Master's tool was still at work, and that was the only thing that mattered. A wolf's grin split the Master's black beard. Caroline had kept her promise—with a little help from her big brother.

The projector ran out of film and the loose end of celluloid flapped like a scarecrow in the wind, but the two of them never noticed they were fucking in the pure white light of an empty screen.

ELLIOTT:

THE GARDEN

AND THE BAR

I SUPPOSE I HAD THOUGHT THOSE CROWDED TER-
races facing the sea comprised the whole club, that now we
should be sheltered by the sprawling branches of the trees from
adoring eyes.

But again, Martin's words came back. "It is large beyond
your imagining," and I bowed my head, panting with the others, my body moist from the run, only half believing what I
saw: the garden stretching out endlessly, linen-draped luncheon
tables everywhere crowded with elegantly dressed men and
women, naked slaves in attendance with trays of food and wine.

Scores moved back and forth from the buffet tables, under
the lacy limbs of the pepper trees, laughing, talking in small
clusters, and of course there was still the crowd on the terraces
of the main building gazing down on the throng below.

But it wasn't just the size of the gardens, or their crowds.
It was the odd way that the crowd resembled any other, the
flash of sunglasses and jewelry on tanned arms and throats, the
sun exploding in mirrored glasses, the chink of silver on china,

men and women in dark tans and Beverly Hills chic, lunching
as if it were perfectly normal for naked slaves to attend them,
it happened everywhere, and of course there was the usual
gathering of some fifty naked and trembling newcomers with
their hearts in their mouths at the gates.

It was as devastating to see backs turned, faces in earnest
conversation, as it was to see bold stares and smiles.

But again, everything happened very fast.

The mass of slaves were writhing with movement, men
and women trying to huddle together, and the handlers surrounding us, apparently waiting only for us to catch our breath
before we were ordered to follow the path.

A strong, red-haired slave broke into the lead when ordered, and another followed, whipped by the handlers who
seemed now an altogether different lot.

These men, young and well built, were dressed all in white
leather, tight pants, vests, and even held white leather straps.

They seemed made to go with the pastel tablecloths, the
huge flowered hats worn by the women, the white or khaki
shorts and stiffly pressed bush jackets of the men.

I braced myself for the sight of a woman handler but there
was none, though there were plenty of women scattered all
through the garden, and everywhere I looked, I saw short skirts,
exquisitely shaped legs, bright sandal high heels.

I knew there would be women trainers of course, the real
masters and mistresses here, who worked for and with the club
members. And my mind flashed back compulsively to the few
women trainers I'd known under Martin's regime, those "fem-
inine" bedrooms, the eeriest and most drenching experiences
of the secret life. . . .

But we were being run too fast now to see much of anything, plunging under the green shade of the trees as we followed a path through the great mass of tables, the conversation
seeming to roar in my ears.

The grass, soft as it was, scratched at the balls of my feet.
But I was dazed by the lush growth on all sides, the jasmine
and roses everywhere, and the birds I glimpsed in gold cages,
giant Macaw parrots, snow-white cockatoos.

Paradise, I thought, and I was a pleasure slave in it. Well, I had asked for it, hadn't I? To be used and enjoyed like the food being eaten, the wine being poured. It was surrounding me just as surely as if I had slipped into some unexpurgated history of decadence, and found myself being driven into the garden of a powerful Persian lord. And though there were limits here that made the cruelty of other times unreal, the vision of this place was so overpowering that all limits seemed unimportant. It was devouring, and I was staggered, lost.

My earlier avowals haunted me.

But the mere physical spectacle of the place was becoming something of a blur. One of the handlers, a young dark-haired boy with powerful arms for his small frame, was lashing me repeatedly and the more he whipped me for nothing the angrier I became. My cock stayed hard, too hard, for all the energy the run took from me, but I made my face a mask.

I would give nothing, no response to him, I thought, but at the same time I was afraid I couldn't keep it up.

The blows were beginning to cause real discomfort, that creeping, swelling warmth that excites and weakens at the same time.

And never before had my legs been whipped so much before the rear was punished, and I wasn't used to the soreness all over, the blows coming on without rhythm so that dignity was hard.

The slaves around me pressed to the middle of the path to escape the straps, but I refused to do this, letting the blows fall.

The red-haired slave kept ahead of me, and I could see that same stubbornness in him. His body was in beautiful condition, and the sight of the strap scoring him suddenly incited me worse than anything else.

The path twisted and turned through the garden. I realized we weren't being driven to one spot. We were being shown off. A tiny psychic explosion went off in my brain. There wasn't any escape from this. It was happening.

Heads turned when we passed, members, guests—whatever they were—pointing, commenting. And as the young dark-haired handler sought me out again for a hail of whacks with the strap I became furious, forcing myself ahead, away from the strap, which was a mistake. He was in hot pursuit, smacking at my ankles. He caught me twice on the soles of my feet.

On some level, my reason said, "It's his job to do this, and what's the difference? You're here to be reduced to nothing, to surrender your will." But I couldn't concentrate on this.

And I realized I was losing some vital perspective, and with that realization came a heightened sexual torment, one of those torrential feelings of nakedness and exposure that can wash over me at any moment as if the experience with all its terrors had just begun.

I fell back into the herd, but he stuck with me. I wondered what I had done to deserve such love. I sensed if I cried out, winced, he might be satisfied, but I wouldn't, no matter how much the belt hurt.

But the scene around us was changing. We were driven past crowded swimming pools with vast flagstone terraces, past the high mesh fences of the croquet courts.

The walls closed in as we were driven through a grove of high ferns and weeping willows, and glancing up I saw men and women leaning over railings above to observe.

I was sore now, a mass of tingling aches, and each new sight stunned me gently, nudging me forward as surely as the handler's belt.

But as we moved back into the thick of the tables again, I saw one of the many guests motioning to the handler and pointing to me. I was being pulled out.

I thought I had seen this happen earlier to one of the other slaves but I wasn't sure.

In any event, I was yanked off the path and to a halt, and it was my relentless young handler with the dark hair who had hold of me, and though he pulled me roughly I didn't remove my hands from the back of my neck. I didn't break form.

My body felt swollen and hot. Another wash of self-consciousness. Cock jutting out, and my hair snagged in my face.

"On all fours with your legs straight," said the handler

with a surprisingly calm voice. No anger in it after all those blows, just the job being done expertly, and not the abominable luck of this position.

I find it infinitely worse than being on hands and knees, because the head is thrown so far down and the rear end is elevated and all the more easy to violate or merely to see. And as soon as my hands hit the grass and the handler smacked me, I felt myself choking on discomfort and fear. Another point of renewal. It was as if the flogging with the belt had just begun.

Shoes surrounded me, yellow patent leather around naked toes, high cork clogs with pink straps, moccasins, and the inevitable boots, and the conversation was rising like impenetrable smoke. I was forced forward in this awkward position toward a collection of men and women about a table and heard a loud, almost raucous babble of foreign speech.

My feet were kicked wide apart. My neck was whipped with the belt, so I lowered my head.

And as I looked at a particularly beautiful pair of brown boots before me, one voice distinguished itself, crisp, and coming very rapidly in an Arabic tongue, and I heard a woman give a deep soft laugh.

I wanted to run. I don't mean I really thought to do it. I would never had gotten away, but I was terrified that I would lose control and bolt. My chest was heaving and I saw my own hard cock again, and suddenly the immensity and the closeness of everything was too much. I was moaning against my will.

The handler slipped his hand around my thigh, forcing my legs wider, and I was ordered by him in cool polite English to run in a small circle in place.

I found myself scrambling awkwardly, my calves and thighs taut and aching from this position, and the foreign voices rose and fell in obvious commentary, and then again, there was that soft laugh.

The belt cracked me and I must have stiffened indignantly because there was immediate responsive laughter again and I felt a hand stroking my head. I was facing the table. The man in the smart brown boots reached out and clasped my chin. He pulled my head toward him and lifted my face.

I was almost dizzy. I was absolutely lost. I could see all the dark olive-skinned faces for an instant—the woman with her eyes shaded by two perfectly round black lenses, the man smiling as he held me, a young man taking a long draw on his black cheroot—before I obediently dropped my eyes. A stylish bunch, none of them older than me, my equals out there in the unreal world, the man who held my chin leaning forward and asking questions in French of the handler: when could I be examined, when could appointments to use me be made? And the handler answering in French that I was a postulant and that it could only be done later tonight.

I knew my upturned face was blood red. My body was trembling with the violent inner struggle to keep still, to forget that my legs were spread apart, my backside up, my scrotum, penis, exposed.

And even as this sense of exposure deepened, this sense of being immersed without name or other identity in what was happening here, I heard the moan grow louder and without choosing it, I struggled desperately, madly, to free my chin from the hand that pushed my face up.

Bad. Really bad. Breaking form. I gained control again but it was too late. There were loud scornful noises at the table, like those of elders scolding an impertinent child, and I heard the angry outburst of the handler as the strap came down. Another handler materialized immediately and caught up both my ankles, bringing them together high in the air.

I was thrown forward on my outstretched hands.

And as my legs were swung roughly to one side, the handler lifted my face again.

"So we have a proud young buck who thinks he's too good to show his face to his masters and mistresses," he said. The handler holding my ankles propelled me forward. "Kiss those shoes, all of them, and do it well and do it quick."

Okay. Do it, no matter what this feels like. This is just the beginning. I pressed my lips repeatedly to the leather, scrambling on quickly to one pair of boots after another, the belt coming down on my backside all the harder, as laughter and conversation roared all around. I was stroked, scolded, ridiculed, and pitied, not as a handsome and expensive slave but as a dog who'd displeased.

And yet my cock never faltered, registering every humiliating pinch.

But abruptly my ankles were released, and I was told to crawl on my hands and knees, with my chin lifted, the handler's voice angry now, impatient—"You need a good lesson!"—as hard cracks of the strap drove me on.

Impossible to analyze this. I tried to tell myself, "What difference does it make? They'll punish you, humiliate you, do what they want with you." But it made all the difference in the world. I'd blundered already, goddamnit, I'd already failed.

All around were the noisy little luncheon circles, the thick grass scratching my knees and open palms. Someone gave me a naked-handed spank as I went by: someone reached for my chin and stroked it upward, pinching my cheek.

I tried to show perfect submission, perfect willingness. But tears were threatening, actual tears. What had it taken before this to bring tears? But forget all that. Forget it for two years.

The thought of the other slaves being commended on their control, being displayed with flawless poise and compliance, filled me with a staggering anxiety. Again, I thought, what does it matter? But it did matter. I wanted to be perfect within this decorous and devouring system. That was the whole point, to obey.

Ahead I saw the little herd of fifty postulants, and prayed desperately that I'd be allowed to join them again.

But in a moment, my little blunder of "pride and insolence" was reported to the trainer-in-charge. The trainer took a shock of my hair and lifted my face.

"Proud slave," he said, fixing me steadily with his cold black eyes. He held something before my eyes and I saw it was a broad grease pen. He bent over me and quite suddenly I felt the jab of the pen into the sore flesh of my backside as he said "proud slave" again, obviously writing the same words.

I was gasping, unable to wipe the picture of it out of my mind. I moved forward, chin high as ordered, driven round in a circle around the little herd of obedient ones, the belt flailing as before. And twice we made the little journey. I was frantic. There was no way to show contrition, no way to correct the error. To be a slave meant to be mute, powerless, to be caught in a momentum beyond one's own control.

I thought of Martin in San Francisco and how disappointed he would have been at this little failure, this botched beginning at The Club of all clubs, how he would have seen it as a reflection upon himself.

But I was allowed to rest for a second. The trainer conferred with the handler and told him to take me to the bar.

"Give his obedience a good testing," he said.

And numbly I watched the others being driven away before I was made to crawl as before ahead of the whipping strap.

The bar was just that, a dimly lighted sanctum of chrome and glass and tufted black leather, opening off the garden where a great many men crowded together at the proverbial brass rail.

The memory of all the bars I'd ever known, and the flirtations in them, and the pickups, and the tension of sensual expectation, charged the atmosphere as I was forced inside on my hands and knees. I wasn't fantasizing over a drink at a table, I was *in* the fantasy, locked into some purely degrading role.

For a moment I couldn't see as I was led across the sawdust floor. The light of the garden had been too bright. And then it materialized before me, faces in the dim silvery glow, video screens flashing pale blue and red, the ebony billiard table with its severe Art Nouveau carvings surrounded by its shifting figures, the crack of the ivories, the unmistakable smell of hard liquor mingling with the cooled air, the smell of the beer.

I saw the flash of muscled arms, white shirts and tight pants in the shadows, caught the faint fragrance of expensive male cologne. A trace of music pulsed from some hidden source, and as I was whipped along the floor, I heard a ripple of laughter as someone read aloud the words written on my rump, and I carried myself with a remembered notion of dignity that was growing more fragile and illusory all the time.

I was being shown to the men, driven to turn and move back toward the door again, and, trembling all over, I did exactly as I was told. One of the tall figures above me snapped his fingers and leaned back on his elbows as I paused.

A soft, almost gentle voice told me in English to kneel up. I complied, trying not to see those nearest me, my hands sliding behind my neck. I was pushed forward until I was staring right at the man's broad leather belt.

"Unzip my pants," he said in that same gentle manner, "and not with your hands either, proud slave."

I had expected much worse that this. I was shaking badly as I obeyed. I glanced only very quickly and furtively at the new master. I saw the gold watch on his wrist, the dark hair of his chest above his open white shirt, something like a smile on his face. Maybe forty, I thought, no more, and something mingled in the face like affection and contempt.

A swimming sense of the whole bar came over me, the men watching, the low throb of the music and the conversation, the undiluted male atmosphere that made a catch in my throat.

I got the small metal zipper in my teeth and at once the bulging cock freed itself from a nest of moist, black, glossy pubic hair. Strong clean smell of a man.

The sight and the smell maddened me. My own organ moved almost convulsively, so I had to tense my hips.

I struggled for command, but I was shaken by the master reaching forward with his lowered hand. My balls were still thrust forward and bound to my cock by the little leather strap put around them on the ship. And he stroked the tight skin now with his nails, pulled at it, and then yanked me forward by my cock. I couldn't keep quiet.

He laughed softly, rubbing my head hard with the flat of his hand, and running his thumb down my cheek. The lump in my throat was rising again, thickening, almost suffocating me. And I could feel my eyes glazing over and the bar melting into a blur.

But he was offering me his own cock now, and brushing my hair back from my forehead with his open hand, he murmured a sort of wordless command under his breath.

At once I had the cock in my mouth.

It pulled me out of the chaos into which I was slipping. Its heat, its thickness against my lips and the roof of my mouth made the hunger between my legs into a knife.

It doubled as I sucked on it, stroking it with my teeth, tightening my teeth around the very tip of it and then going down on it until I could feel and smell that soft, wet pubic hair.

I drew back the full length of it and then plunged into a steady rhythm, my own hips pumping helplessly, and quite suddenly I felt the handler's strap.

Only I don't think it was the handler because the blows were worse. And as they cut across my backside, they came with the rhythm of my sucking and my thrusts.

It was almost unendurable, the pleasure of that thick, swollen organ and the humiliating, stinging pain of the strap. It brought me back to the bar and my place in it, while the cock connected me to the pure pleasure, and wrenched between the two I was able to forget the garden, the earlier failure, to think only of giving pleasure, the thing I came here to do, and when I thought of the other men watching me, the pleasure shot to a high pitch, going on and on as I locked my arms around the master's hips. The pain throbbed all through me even in my temples at the very moment that the cock shot its sour salty fluids in my mouth.

For a moment it seemed I would come, my cock spurting into the air. I clung to the man, licking the cock even as he withdrew it, and the noise of the place pulsed through me like a light.

The master laid his hand on my forehead again and I was told to look up as he drew back. My desire was so heated and desperate that I couldn't focus well. Yet I saw his flushed face again in the dim light, black eyes dazed and almost dreamy, thick graying hair at the temples, and a thin smile on his lips.

He held up a small object in his hands.

"Well, don't you know what this is?" he asked as if he expected something. He had the tone of one talking to a child. And I heard the handler explain I was only a "Bad Postulant," and the man very patiently held the object closer so that I saw it was a small cylinder made of shining metal, and he withdrew from it now several large bills that he returned to it once I had seen, and snapping his fingers told me to turn around.

"You're very good for a postulant," he said.

I think I guessed what was to happen, the little ritual, and I swallowed hard. I turned on my hands and knees, and the handler told me "up," so that I was standing on all fours again, my rear exposed, and I shuddered, expecting his touch.

The sounds of the bar melted away. I felt that metal cylinder pushed into my backside and then driven in deep with a sharp shove. I didn't dare wince or move, that intimate touch infinitely more annihilating than the thrust of a cock. And to be made to stand still for it gave me the most pervasive feeling of subservience. I almost moaned. I felt the man's hand conferring one last demeaning pat, and then a hard pinch and I was pushed gently on.

The handler had already found another man for me, and I was being cracked hard to make me hurry to the end of the bar, the cylinder inside me shifting as if it were alive.

This man was taller, leaner than the other, and when I saw the length of the cock I almost drew back. It hit the roof of my mouth, driving hard as I tried to close my lips on it, a low laughter erupting around me, and the man took hold of my head and started to drive the cock at his own rhythm, his full weight pushing against me with each stroke.

I don't know how many men I gave pleasure to before it was finished. Probably six. Four of them "tipped" me, as the handler explained it, and each time I felt that odd terror when I was made to turn around and offer my backside for the little cylinder.

I say odd because it was nothing like the fear of humiliation when I was finally driven back out onto the lawn.

It was fear connected to passivity. On the lawn I felt a war of feelings, and my tears almost came.

I'd felt sheltered in the bar, by the darkness, and lost in the pleasure-giving.

But now we were back in the throng, my backside humiliatingly red, scarred with the lettering "Proud Slave," and the handler seemed more determined than ever to have my chin held high and to make me move as fast as I could.

The desire had become a dull pain in my organ and in my head. I saw the cocks in flashes before my eyes. I could still taste them and their fluids. In my rectum I could feel those little cylinders and had to tighten my muscles not to expel them, even in fear that I might not be able to hold them in.

But with relief I realized we had left the crowded garden. I was being whipped alone down a narrow ribbon of grass that ran along the side of a vine-covered wall, told to move fast, and in the silence the strap sounded very loud. I felt a new vulnerability to be so alone with this handler and the sound of his calm authoritative voice.

Finally no one was in sight.

"Stop," he said, "and squat."

I did it, feeling the cylinders poking at my sphincter. I couldn't hold them.

"Now drop that load, all of it," he said. And with a sudden groan, I started pushing the "tips" out. My face was blazing as I felt them slip one by one on the grass. And I hated the son of a bitch in a confusing, intimate way, not for his obvious little theft (he pocketed them immediately), but for the shiver of feeling that came with the expulsion of each cylinder and the way that he smacked me again immediately with the belt.

ANNE RICE

ELLIOTT:

BELOW

STAIRS

WHAT WAS HAPPENING TO THE OBEDIENT ONES? What was it like being chosen, led away to some private room for examination? Could Lisa choose more than one?

Maybe my mind kept going back to it to avoid what was really happening. Dangling by my ankles, the strap playing on me whenever the handler chose, I was jogged and pulled through a dizzying labyrinth of rooms and pathways and corridors, elevators and ramps, watching as the various slaves were packed off to their punishments, whipped on hands and knees into the vast tiled kitchen with its stainless-steel sinks and counters, thrashed through the haystrewn stables, and into the laundry with its sweet smells of freshly pressed linen and scented soaps.

A flock of fancy uniformed maids received the frantic Gregory, chasing him before them with their brooms.

But finally we were below stairs, in a vast basement room full of buckets and mops and the pungent smell of cleansing chemicals.

And to a handful of young and rather cheerful male servants I was unceremoniously delivered, an amusing enough surprise it seemed, as they looked up from their card games. I was set down on all fours on the white tile before them and told to bow my head so they might see the writing on my back. They looked trim as hospital orderlies in their smart-belted white cotton coats as they went back to their cardplaying.

There were others in the basement, men coming and going, and even some naked male slaves, and though these men seemed slightly rougher than the handlers above they had about them the same air of refinement I'd seen everywhere at The Club. They weren't really coarse men, just sort of ordinary. Excellent builds, routine faces.

"Come here, Elliott," said the one who appeared the oldest, snapping his fingers and then tugging my hair as I neared the table where he shoved me hard to show me that I was meant to turn around. He gave a low whistle as he inspected my sore legs and rump.

"Have they ever been to work already on you," he said almost casually, then to one of the others he made some small comment on the card game. There was something so plainly humiliating about all this that no one at Martin's house could have ever rigged it. I heard the splat of the cards on the table and felt the tip of his boot in my anus. He pushed me forward. "And is it ever going to be sorer than that by twelve o'clock tonight."

There was a round of laughter.

"Look at those muscles," said one of the others. "We're going to make good use of them, Elliott. Ever done any hard work in your life?"

"No, master," I said before I realized it. Not a very clever answer. There was more laughter.

"Well, you're going to work here, young man, and I'll tell you something else too, a postulant who gets himself this duty on his first day comes back to see us often as time goes on."

"That's cause we're so charming!" said one of the others.

"You'll get to be a regular," said a third one, with a rather low, almost velvety voice. "Come over here and let me have a look at you."

The mercy of it was I could keep my head down. Same exquisite boots that the others wore; it was the uniform of the place undoubtedly, classy boots. Even the maids must have had them. And the black-wash pants were tapered, and the coats made of heavy cotton, almost as heavy as khaki. The hand that pinched my butt now was rough. I must have given some little movement because I received an immediate hard spank. Rough as a paddle.

"See those bucket handles, Elliott?" said the deep-voiced one. "Know why the handles are coated with soft material? That's to protect your pretty teeth. And you'll find some brushes over there with soft leather handles. You'll learn to scrub with your teeth, and wipe with your teeth, and maybe a few other things with your teeth." More laughter. The card game continues with a new shuffle and deal.

"Kneel up, let me see that cock."

I didn't take time to think. And heard the immediate mockery, pretended shock. "Oooooh, that's beautiful, Elliott, I'll bet that feels good, doesn't it!" And the dreaded slap to the cock, and then another.

I flinched, unable to help it, keeping my eyes focused on the tile floor.

"And look at the rest of that equipment, it must weigh ten pounds."

The hand slipped under my bound testicles. It was almost too much. I knew my cock was dancing, carrying my hips forward with it. And for two days, I had to put up with this. I couldn't make it, not that long. I'd go down on the floor, rubbing it against the floor. I couldn't think about that.

But I was shoved back down on my knees.

"All right, all right, let's outfit you for the job," said the older man, sliding his chair back with a scraping noise on the tile.

Again the snap of the fingers and the command, "Heel." No one had ever given me that command! But I knew what it meant and I followed fast.

He stopped. "Is that how you obey when I say 'heel'?" he demanded. And that big hand slammed my rear almost pushing me forward. "When I give you any command, to come, go, heel, you move! Now let me see you trot."

I tried to comply.

"I said trot!" The hand again smacking my rump and then grabbing hold of it hard. I let out a little whistle of pain between my teeth. Two days.

"Trot means lift those knees and hands off the floor. It means sprightly. Didn't anyone ever teach you that? You're at The Club, young man, you're one of four thousand slaves at The Club, and whether you clean the lavatories, or give My Lady her silver handmirror in your teeth, you move!"

At once I trotted forward, struggling to give the desired effect. My face must have been purple, but the psychic miracle was working again: I *had* to please. To please; it was all I focused on. Anger coming from them would have been too much.

"Halt, now heel." I scrambled, trotted to obey, twisting about to kneel at his right, and immediately there came a mocking applause from the others.

"Good boy, Elliott." And, "That cock knows its master's voice when it hears it."

"All right," said the elder moving forward to a row of metal lockers. "Now kneel up, and let me see your hands go where they should. All right, good."

He had removed a leather leash with a thick collar on the end of it, but much too small for my neck. And in a moment I knew what it was for as he snapped open the old strap on my cock, and put on the little collar pushing my balls even further forward than before. The scratching of the new leather, his hand on the balls almost drove me crazy. A bit of liquid seeped from the tip of my penis. I felt it bubble up over the crown.

"Oh, you behave yourself, young man," he said in mock outrage as he buckled the strap. Straightening up, he gave the leash a jerk and I struggled to follow him on my knees, the pressure of the strap stroking and tormenting my cock much worse than the other, so that a loud gasp came out of me before I could stop.

He didn't notice or care.

"Now, you take the handle of this leash in your teeth," he said giving it to me, "and that's where I'm to find it whenever I want it, you understand?" he said.

He was about to say more as he shoved the leather into my mouth, but something had caught his eye. I could see a light flashing up on the wall.

"You see that, young man? You're to watch for that. And whenever you see one of those lights flash, you're to trot out from wherever you are and come to one of us with that leash handle in your mouth. That's the signal that the lavatory in question needs attention, and we're going to it right now. And we don't clean the private bathrooms, young man, not the nice little ones with the carrara marble and the coordinated colors opening off the quiet little bedroom suites. We clean the public lavatories of The Club on every floor. As you're about to see for yourself."

The leash handle was yanked from me again, and I was pulled forward but mercifully I was allowed on all fours, running in the trot after the man as he strode down the carpeted hall. Other uniformed servants passed us, with mops and buckets or stacks of towels, and other scurrying punished slaves.

I had a close look at one of the others in the service elevator as we went up, a stocky young man heeling anxiously beside a young orderly, not daring apparently to glance at me, his backside striped in pink with a map of with welts.

"Remember what I told you, Elliott?" said the man who was leading me. "About bad little boys who start out with us coming back again and again? Take a good look at Andre. He's been with The Club for years, but every month or two he's back with us for a nice long visit."

This seemed to increase the slave's tension, and when the door opened he scrambled out behind the orderly without having to be told.

A strip of very rich champagne-colored carpet stretched before us when we left the elevator.

We must have been four floors up, and immediately I heard the soft free-flowing chatter of a crowd. How big was the place? I couldn't imagine. But the size was its own source of subjugation. I felt lost. We were passing enameled doors with brass numbers. Then I saw out of the corner of my eye a huge salon full of sunlight and cigarette smoke, potted palms and other tropical plants rising here and there over the heads of the crowd.

I glimpsed on the edge of the room two model-perfect women, wraithlike giants with skillfully lacquered hair in haute couture gowns speaking to one another in nasal French rapidly. No eyes moved toward us as we hurried past, as invisible it seemed as servants always are, and we were very quickly inside a blue-tiled lavatory, with some twenty marble stalls. It looked clean enough for surgery. But my new master unlocked a cabinet and threw down a small broom expertly made for me to use with my mouth as he had told me before.

"Be sure to keep that leash handle in your mouth too; sweep hard and fast," he said. "Start at the far end, and I want the floor spotless right now."

I started sweeping at once, the movement of my head causing it to ache, but nothing in the world was going to cause me to displease these men, to get this punishment increased, and as my master saw to towels and soap, I swept the entire room, finally gathering the bits of paper and dirt into his dust pan and getting a kind pat on the head.

The doors opened and two men in midconversation moved past us, one of them pausing at a basin to carefully wash his hands. They gave us not so much as a glance as my master locked the cabinet and snapped his fingers, whispering the word "Trot" as he gestured to the door.

The halls were streaming with guests now. Gleaming patent-leather shoes brushed close to me, the flash of red toenails under nude stockings, white sandals, the inevitable boots. But I kept my head down, following as fast as I could the tug of the leash, my heart racing from the relentless pace. A woman's chiffon dress brushed my hip, but there wasn't the slightest evidence anyone took notice. I didn't know whether it was worse than being scowled at, mocked.

The next lavatory had to be scrubbed.

The mixture of chemicals was mild enough so that it didn't burn my eyes as I moved the scrubber back and forth with my teeth. But my neck ached, and the master, apparently seeing me slow down, gave me that rough hand again.

"You want a good old-fashioned spanking, Elliott?" he laughed almost genially as I tried to work faster. "They tell me my hand's the best paddle in The Club." He swatted me again with so much force that I dropped the brush, struggling to get hold of it.

"Did I hear a little whimper, young man?" He had thrown down a handful of white towels.

Not from me, you didn't, I felt like saying, but it might have been a lie.

"Now put that brush back in the bucket and wipe that floor dry. You can use your hands and use them well. And in the future when I point to a floor and the bucket, you'll know what to do, and if you don't, you go over my knee."

My head was swimming when I finished. Some crucial change was taking place in my mind, the exertion breaking down the barriers, and a primitive titillating fear taking the place of thought. I scrambled to put away the bucket and drop the towels down the linen chute.

"That's not what I call fast, beautiful, now move through that door!" And that hand came down again almost sweeping me out into the corridor.

I was only saved from it by the crowds in the corridor, and the press in the elevator, and I knew it.

As soon as we reached the cellar room, I was told I was going to "get it."

"Might as well get down to business right now."

The others were still playing cards and didn't look up from their game, and those at other tables went on as before, slaves obediently at their feet.

I was pulled along roughly to the wall, the leash was

stripped off me, and I winced as I saw a long-handled wooden paddle being taken down from a hook.

"You ready for your spanking?" he demanded.

I started to answer, but my voice evaporated. My pulse was pounding. I'd been lashed all day, but I hadn't been really spanked. Careless blows with the belt, angry blows, blows full of annoyance, driving blows. That was one thing, but at the thought of the utter humiliation of a real spanking, my cock felt ready to explode.

And it was these men, these priceless specimens of ordinary masculinity, servants of The Club, not some elegantly turned out guest above ordering me thrown over a padded chair in his suite for the "honor." It was to be a hard brutal job below stairs.

I knew I was going to lose all control. A picture of that beautiful trainer flashed into my mind. What would it be like, being punished by her, really humiliated by her? I couldn't think. But I was reaching out to her in my mind as if she were a lifesaver. Did I want that instead of this?

But the man had seated himself near the card table this time. And he was beckoning to me and slapping his heavy thigh. It was like some nightmare memory from early childhood, maybe of something that had never actually happened to me, but had always been threatened, glimpsed happening to others. It was being inside one of those crude cartoons I'd secretly pored over as a boy, in which some naked-bottomed little delinquent was paddled over a knee as the tears flew out from his squinted eyes. I wouldn't stand it—it was too sublime—I'd lose all control.

"I should spank you right through the cellar," he said under his breath, grabbing a chock of my hair and pulling me toward him. "I should spank you right through the furnace room, and the storage rooms, and make you repeat their names to me, and find your way back to them under command. But we have a long night ahead of us and I'm already tired."

"No, give it to him right there," said one of the men at the table, the one with the velvety voice. "I haven't really *heard* that young boy yet."

At a distant table somebody called for action, saying it had been too long since one of these spoiled brats really got it, and the master pulled me up.

"Over my lap, young man, and you're to keep that cock back out of the way."

I bent over his lap as I was told, my bowed head toward the other cardplayers, who egged the master on as before. The paddle needed a workout. And "I'd whip these other beauties," said one of the others at another table, "but they've been whipped full sore."

I lay still, unable to understand what I was feeling, how the dread alchemized into paralysis, trying to keep my cock away from his leg. I felt his left hand on the small of my back. I kept my head low down, and it felt good to be able to cover at least my neck.

I was shaking as violently as I had all day when with a loud smack he began. A groan came out of me immediately. And the second time it came again. I couldn't keep it back.

The third and fourth wallops were so hard I couldn't keep quiet. I was going to lose this battle and it was nothing but a little sport for the broom-and-mop crowd. I tried to clamp my mouth shut.

But he cut loose as though he would make me cry out or wear himself out and it seemed his paddle was bouncing off my rump and I was rocking across his lap. One of the men let out a whistle. I heard some one clap his hands. "Give it to him, Tony. Whip that boy."

I tried to think of Martin in San Francisco; we were in the House in San Francisco, this wasn't happening. Only trouble, it was.

My butt was on fire. The spanking pounded on. One of the men had come over to watch. "Look at that boy dance," he said. "You're too quiet, Elliott, too reserved, let that ass move!"

I gave a low openmouthed cry just as I vowed I wouldn't, each crack of the wooden paddle an explosion of pain that shook my whole frame. I could hear my cries now, I couldn't stop them, I was choking on them, but still I held back the tears.

The paddle smacked at my thighs. It cracked hard on my rear again. It rested flat and still for a moment pressing on the burning flesh before it shattered me into a loud guttural moan that almost sounded like a plea. Again the men laughed, one of them clapping his hands. And as the blows came faster and faster I could hear nothing but my own openmouthed moans, coming so rapidly they were one long cry.

"Atta boy, atta boy," my master was saying. "Just what the master ordered, and now we're going to hear that polite, gentlemanly voice again, saying 'Thank you, master.' "

"Thank you, master," I cried out to a general round of laughter.

"Again? Again?"

"Thank you, master, thank you, master, thank you, master." I was trying to say it, not cry it, but I couldn't control it, and I realized my body was rocking, undulating completely beyond my control. I felt my penis like a great throbbing shaft jutting from between my legs, and I was gasping "Thank you, master!" over and over as if it were a plea.

Suddenly I realized my eyes were filled with tears. I couldn't see the floor below me, and my voice had grown thick and quivering, "Thank you, master" coming in choking noises. I could not believe my failure, I couldn't believe it, and yet I had lost everything, letting go of the words "Thank you, master," the paddle slamming me over and over again.

Roughly I was thrust off the master's lap onto my knees. "Trot!" I heard the loud command, but it was coming from a younger man, the one who'd risen from the table, and I felt the paddle crack me with new vigor. "And I'll take a little 'Thank you, master,' with it loud and clear."

I rushed forward, my tears almost blinding me, the paddle right behind me, smacking me forward, as I cried out "Thank you, master," and the boots beside me kept easy pace.

Applause came from a table as we passed it.

"Pick up those knees, young man, trot!" someone called out. And another, "Move it, young man," as desperately I tried to obey. I had come to the end of the room, and I was turned and spanked hard back along its length, my backside steaming with pain, and suddenly the words I was crying died again into wide openmouthed cries that were almost gasped.

"Bring him here," said one of the men at the first table, "and give me that paddle, I want to have a go at those thighs."

I was thrust over his right knee, head dangling, and I felt the paddle wallop my legs as he promised in a riff of blows until I was passed to another who shouted:

"Kneel up!" that dreaded command as he pushed my face high with the palm of his hand. Tears were washing down my face. It was excruciating to show it. My hips were knocked forward by the paddle, my cock quivering. I couldn't brace my hips hard enough and there was laughter all around.

One of the men was standing before me unzipping his pants. "Keep it up," he said to the other, and as the paddle kept smacking, he drew my head toward his erect cock. My mouth opened for it, my hands still locked obediently to the back of my neck. And as he held my shoulders firmly, he drove it back and forth through my lips.

It was delicious, it was the reward, the prize, the brass ring, having it, but even my noises weren't stilled by it but went on muffled by the cock.

When the hot sperm shot into me, I swallowed greedily but even then I was crying, and now my head was forced down into the warmth of another man's crotch. I was ready for the cock, but there was another man behind me for whom I was being prepared, and the paddle had stopped.

My rear throbbed with its own humiliating rhythm, and I felt the flesh being pulled roughly and the nudge at my anus which meant the man was about to go in. I pressed my lips to the crotch in front of me, and the thrust came hard and dry.

My own cock tugged me mercilessly forward. And suddenly I felt a hand on it, hot, silky fingers batting at it that made me give a long groaning sound.

They opened, slapped at the length of it, smacking the tip over and over and then clamped on the tip hard, stroking roughly, and I came in a riotous explosion, my hips convulsing, the cock in my mouth and the one in my backside jetting with equal force.

It went on and on in sharp throbs, my moan rising and falling and then one at a time they pulled themselves free and I lay down, butt back, on my heels, head to the floor.

"Oh, that felt good," the man behind me whispered, "that tight little asshole. Good."

I was as exhausted as I'd ever been, as utterly spent.

For a long moment, I was let to breathe, and then I felt a little humiliating spank of the paddle and a hand before me pointed to a long wooden table against the wall.

I moved to it, the paddle coaxing me just a little, and I was shoved up to lay my chest on the table, my legs spread out behind me. And when I heard the zipper, and felt his hands spreading my butt I moved my hips to receive the new cock.

PART FOUR

THE SEXUAL

UNDERGROUND

Even the world of gay pornography has an underground. A vibrant world of small presses, most of them author-owned, keeps the cutting edge of gay erotica sharp.

Larry Townsend originally published many of his novels with Greenleaf Classics, one of the original gay pornographic houses in this country, and with the famed Olympia Press in Paris, which published erotica in English that was often smuggled into the United States. When those avenues didn't hold up well enough, the companies sort of slipped away more than folded, and Townsend decided to publish his own work. That led him to discover many other leather-S&M writers who weren't getting into print. He expanded his small press to include anthologies of other writers. The books are marketed through a newsletter that not only lists his literary offerings, but also keeps readers up-to-date on his travels, especially those that involve his other favorite hobby, opera.

Gordon Hoban was an actor in the Mark Taper Forum's Los Angeles production of *A Meeting by the River,* written by

Christopher Isherwood and Don Bacardy when he first thought
of becoming a writer himself. He credits Isherwood's example
as his impetus. Hoban moved into scriptwriting first, authoring
a couple episodes of the television hit "The Paper Chase" and
working later on Twentieth Century Fox development projects
for the movies. On the sly he was writing pornography as Tom
Hardy. As he saw his script work being more and more dictated by committee, he realized that the porn was the source
of his greatest satisfaction and that much of that satisfaction
came from his ability to control the writing.

He escaped to an isolated valley in Hawaii where he lived
for the first several years under a tarp and walked for miles to
a pay phone with a pocket full of change whenever he wanted
to contact the rest of the world. The sacrifice enabled him to
start Omnium Publishing, with which he's published his stage
plays, as well as his erotic novels.

LARRY TOWNSEND

FROM

RUN, LITTLE

LEATHER BOY

HOW I CAME TO BE INVOLVED IN ALL THIS TROUBLE, and why I should have developed a taste for black-leather S&M sex at all, is a puzzle that neither my friends nor family—nor, God forbid, my father—have ever been able to understand. Still, it happened, and while I have time available to me I would like to tell how. Perhaps this will help answer my own question: Why?

Yet where do I start? Does it all devolve to that moment of my sexual awakening, or do the roots extend backward in time as per the sage opinions of our professional mind-gougers? And were my desires truly unnatural? After all, they took shape within my mind and spirit without my commanding them. For me, any other course would have been unnatural. Nor can I point to any specific incident of my prepubescent years to explain how the seed was planted.

I was the product of a wartime romance. My father, a terribly busy, terribly stuffy corporation president in my earliest recollections, had been an army officer stationed in England during World War II. While there he met my mother, who was the daughter of a socially prominent, equally proper family. They were as well matched economically and socially as any American and any Englishwoman can ever be. They were married shortly after VE Day, and I was the result of their union— born in New York a year or so after the end of hostilities.

I attended a number of the "better" private schools, where I never seemed to fit very well. I was unhappy with them, and they with me. I did, finally, manage to graduate from one, mostly because I resolved to toe the mark rather than chance being shunted off to still another of these tradition-hobbled institutions for the incorrigible well-to-do. After this came college, and with it a certain self-realization. This, I suppose, formed the first step in my progression toward infamy—this, and the image I retained of that night with my unnamed seducer in the front seat of that car. I had a few experiences after that, all of a similar nature, though never with quite so attractive a man, and never with one in leather. Yet, strangely, even then, the memory of those leather pants held a significance. I felt this, but did not possess the insight to name or explain it.

Later, during my freshman and sophomore years, there were a couple of brief flings in the beds of occasional night wanderers I met in a park near the campus. But there was never a real, obsessive yearning until the first semester of my junior year. It was then that I became so attracted to our second-string quarterback that I made the mistake of trying out for the football team. At five-foot ten, 150 pounds, I was not heavy enough for the line. Nor was I skilled enough to find a place in the backfield. After a few practice sessions at which I really tried—tried much more conscientiously than I ever had at anything else in all my life—the coach took pity on me.

"Look, Wayne," he began with his typically tactful kindness, "you're useful as teats on a boar hog out there, so why don'cha give it up?"

"I've *got* to make the team," I told him.

"Well, you're not *gonna* make the team," he replied flatly, "so before ya bust yer pretty face, quit!" With that, he turned away to shout at another of his charges who had committed some terrible act of incompetence.

The long and short of it was, I did not make the football team; but I did manage to make my second-string quarterback. This happened very easily and naturally in the equipment shed at the far end of the playing field. It was a warm day, and he was dressed in just a pair of athletic trunks and tennis shoes. The sight of his deeply tanned, symmetric body compelled me to follow him, though there was no denying my full knowledge of my intentions right from the start. Chuck, to further justify my attention, was built a little like Steve Reeves around the time he won the Mr. America title. He also had the same kind of dark, curly hair. While his face might not have been quite as pretty . . . well, I think the general impression has been conveyed.

I bolted from my room and down the stairs, almost falling the length of the second flight in my haste to reach the ground. Once outside, however, I slowed my pace and sauntered in the direction of the field. Technically, the equipment was available on weekends to anyone who wished to sign it out. Despite this encouragement by the administration, there were seldom any takers. No one was out this afternoon except a couple of neighborhood kids, trying to operate one of those gasoline model airplanes that flies on the end of a long wire.

Chuck was inside the shed by the time I got there. I could hear him clumping about as he counted the various bins of equipment. "Need any help?" I asked. I stood in the doorway, not able to see very clearly into the darker interior. I knew, though, that the sunlight was making a halo in back of my head, emphasizing the blond hair and silhouetting the slender outline of my body. While no competition for the muscular magnificence of someone like Chuck, I was solid and well-defined as a result of swimming and gymnastics. My face was also a fortunate attribute. I had noticed Chuck's appreciative glances in the past, always when he thought I wouldn't notice.

"Hi," he answered casually. "No, not much to do. I counted the stuff when it came in Friday."

I edged into the shed, purposely bumping the door with

my foot to make it swing partially closed. Chuck did not seem
to pay any attention. "Kinda dull afternoon," I muttered.

"Yeah."

"They usually are, though," I added.

"Yeah," returned Chuck. He leaned his upper torso deep
inside a bin, exposing the fleshy roundness of his ass.

I sidled up next to him, allowing my hip to just graze his
rump as I continued to feign an interest in what he was doing.
When I touched him he jumped, which assured me of his being
attuned to my attentions. When he straightened up he did not
move away, but stood facing me, our bodies so close we each
tended to lean back a bit; otherwise we would almost have been
kissing. As it was, our groins were less than two inches apart
and the protrusion of his was no less pronounced than that of
my own.

With a boldness born of youth and inexperience—at least
limited experience—I placed my hand about his swollen
mound. Chuck's blue, unblinking eyes stared into my face. I
could not interpret what little expression he showed other than
to assume his permitting me to fondle him was an indication
of acceptance. Finally, still without moving, he cleared his
throat. "Are you a cocksucker?" he asked bluntly.

"I'd suck yours," I replied.

"Be my guest," said Chuck, and with a quick thrust of
both hands across those narrow hips he dropped the trunks so
that they fell about his ankles. The massive shaft that sprang
free from his hairy groin was all the invitation I needed. However, the situation was unique in my experience to that point.
Without meaning to be immodest, I was very blond and was
certainly not considered unattractive. In all my previous contacts the relationship had either been mutual or the exact reverse of what was happening between Chuck and me.

Still, the idea of kneeling in front of this magnificent living
sculpture and taking that demanding cock between my lips was
fraught with exciting elements. I felt the myriad compulsions
of one seeking subjugation—perhaps degradation, though at
this stage of emotional development the significance escaped
me. Regardless, I slipped slowly to my knees and placed my

hand about his responsive bolt. Like the rest of him, this pulsing cyclops was large and comprised of bulging sinew. The thick, gnarled veins were driven against his satin skin in a display of might that sapped any power of resistance. And, of course, I had not come here out of desire to resist.

My lips enclosed the wide, heart-shaped cockhead. My tongue flicked in taunting caress against the tip where droplets continued to form, rewarding my touch with their slightly salty nectar. Chuck's big hands moved from his hips to rest against the back of my head. I felt their powerful pressure ease me forward, more completely onto that impossible hardness. In just the few moments since my initial contact his huge distension had gained another modicum of rigidity, and now exerted a terrible upward pressure. It felt almost as if he were trying to lift me from the floor. Suddenly, from the edge of my vision, I saw his bulging biceps flex still harder and I was driven fully onto his cock.

"Eat it, cocksucker!" he growled.

The abrupt impalement almost made me retch. I coughed up quantities of phlegm to coat and increase the slickness of his unwieldy column. This was not at all as I had planned it, but the very subservience of the position was contributing to my own arousal. I could feel the oozing discharge in my groin as I gulped and strangled on the hard-driven ram.

Chuck was far from gentle. He held my head exactly where he wanted it as he began a regular, desperate thrusting with his hips to assure my taking him the precise depth and speed he desired. That this caused his beet-red sex to choke me until tears were running down my face only seemed to excite his passions. He was grunting and moaning, called me "queer" and "cocksucker." He ordered me to "Take it! Take it!" as he slammed his groin against my lips and refused to lessen one iota the pressure against the nape of my neck.

As I struggled to fulfill the demands of his naked lust, I fumbled to open my pants, finally managing to extract my own cock and fondle it while I was forced to accommodate the tearing bulk of this—my first, though undeclared master. I suppose the rudimentary roles did occur to me, even then.

Certainly the overemphasized positions of dominance-submission were unmistakable. Though he was actually hurting me, and the entire posture was uncomfortable, it was still the most exciting situation I had ever been in—more so even than my initiation by the young man in the leather pants. Over the years, I had wondered at the pleasure he and his successors had taken when they pressed their faces to my crotch in unreciprocated servitude. Now I knew!

There was also the element of danger, doing it in the fieldhouse without even bothering to lock the door. Before me stood this naked giant with his total display of unbridled power, driving his manhood into me as if he were, indeed, a master possessing his helot. I was trembling with my own sense of spiraling arousal. I had to let go of myself or I would have climaxed long before Chuck had reached the peak of lusty possession. Glancing up, I could see the shimmering layer of sweat that coated his body. Through the cloth of my T-shirt I felt the moisture seeping onto me from his hard, quivering thighs.

I was soaring by then, completely overwhelmed by the roughly masculine power. My jaw ached and my knees were already raw from their contact with the uneven surface of the flooring. None of this mattered. I was accomplishing the satisfaction of needs I did not yet fully understand. I knew only that I was taking this monstrous cock, and it was exciting me almost to an unassisted climax. Then Chuck tensed against me while a series of pulsing discharges coursed the length of his iron. When I felt the channel expand against my lower lip I seized my own rod, and almost as soon as I touched it there was a boiling response in my balls. Chuck bolted into me and I shot my sperm in furious cascades across the gray, splintery floor.

Only when his prick was softening did he finally let go. I was weak, gasping for breath as I sat on my heels and looked up at him. He smiled, though not in a strictly friendly sense. Rather, his china-blue eyes seemed hard, boring into me with an expression of near contempt. "You liked that, huh?" he asked gruffly.

I nodded. "Yes," I whispered.

He stooped, pulling his trunks back around his hips and adjusting the still-swollen sex within his jockstrap. "Come around next Sunday," he said flatly. "And . . . bring some grease," he added.

During the following weeks, I continued to obey Chuck's instructions, meeting him every Sunday afternoon in the field-house and offering my body in any way he wished to use it. Never once did he reciprocate—never touched me except to brace his hands against my ass when he fucked me. Other than this, nothing—not even allowing his fingers to graze my cock or placing his arms around me. It was a completely one-sided relationship, with the affirmation of our respective roles reiterated and solidified in each subsequent meeting.

It was causing a very strange set of responses in me. Like an addict, I could no more think of passing up these sessions than halting my respiration. The need to meet Chuck and to debase myself in whatever way he demanded was a compulsion over which I had no control. Still, the unfairness rankled, and several times during the succeeding weeks I resolved to stay away. But the closer it came to Sunday, the more desperately I looked forward to what I knew would happen in that field-house. I would think of it in class and find myself struggling to suppress an unwanted display of arousal. It became so bad that I took to wearing a jockstrap under my shorts, but I was still embarrassed by an inability to control myself.

Worse than this, the singular thought was dominating everything I did. Raw desire competed with a feeling of revulsion—both over my lack of ability to refuse him, and later a self-defeating cycle of self-condemnation over the fact that I felt I had to condemn myself. Confused? Words can hardly express it! I toyed with the idea that I might have loved him, but I decided that was not the case. It was lust, pure and simple; it was the worship of a living idol, and I was helpless to control my impulsive craving.

GORDON HOBAN

"MALORY'S BIG BROTHER" FROM THE GREEN HOTEL STORIES

MALORY PROPPED HIMSELF UP ON HIS ELBOWS, watching the smooth rippling of the river as it swept past the low bank on which he lay. Though he was eighteen, there was an oddly nebulous quality about him, a sense of still being unformed, that made him seem years younger. Some might have remarked on it as stupidity but others would have noted it as a state of innocence, a tabula rasa, ready for the imprint of adventure.

He was a beautiful boy, far more beautiful than he realized. His hair was thick and fine and straight, golden like corn silk, tumbling over his ears and around his face. Fine strands of it fell over his forehead in the breeze. He blinked his eyes, bluer than the river ever thought of being, and shook his head. The movement of the water was hypnotic, lulling him into a pleasantly passive state.

The sun felt warm on his face. He looked around. He was alone. He often slipped away to this deserted spot to daydream and escape from his duties on the farm. Not that he wasn't conscientious. He always did what was required of him, but he noticed that if he was able to finish his duties quickly his father or his older brother would just as quickly find something else for him to do if he were in sight. . . . So from time to time, he would escape to this place.

He liked the way the sun felt on his skin. He wanted to feel more of it. He undid the buttons of his shirt and let it fall open. His skin was as smooth and flawless as pale pink china. The muscles of his chest and abdomen were hard with the natural definition of constant farm work. As the warm breeze moved across the glowing skin, his nipples tightened into firm pinkish-tan cones. He looked down at himself and touched the tips, wondering at the tingling sensations that radiated out from the nubbins.

At the juncture of his legs he could feel the swelling tautness of himself, growing big and hard down there. He moved one hand to his crotch and rested it on the warm thickness. His pink lips fell open as his breath came faster. He looked around again. There was no one in sight. All was still. Only the soft rustle of trees, swaying in the wind, and the sounds of birds competed with the soothing murmur of the river.

He shrugged his shirt off over his shoulders and let it fall to the thick grass. Then his hands went to the waistband of his jeans. He undid the button there and worked the buttons of his fly open, spreading the flaps over the bulging whiteness of his undershorts. He rested one hand lightly on the mound and sighed. Quickly he reached down and undid his shoestrings, kicking off his worn tennis shoes and pulling off his socks. He hooked his thumbs in his shorts and jeans, skinned them both off together, and settled his bare butt on the grass. It felt so good being naked outdoors.

He rested back on his elbows again, let his thighs flop

apart, and studied his prick. It jerked in rhythm with the beating of his heart as it swelled thicker, standing up and swaying back and forth, like the grass in the breeze. The shaft was creamy pale and smooth, with a tracing of pink running up the underside of it from the puckered sac of his large nuts to the ruddier knob flaring out from the pulled-back collar of foreskin. The delicate knob was moist and glistening in the sun.

At first he did nothing but look at himself, enjoying the simple pleasure of exposure. Then he began to touch himself, exploring the terrain of his body in a state of wonder, fresh with astonishment at the constant newness of this kind of pleasure. He shivered as his fingers touched his tits, and then moved down the gentle but definite indentations of his firm belly, tickling at the golden hairs around the base of his thick column. Then he moved past the stalk, teasing himself with restraint, as he cupped his balls in his hands, enjoying their fullness before he moved his fingers down behind them, tracing the delicate cleft of his ass, gently probing the tiny pucker there. He closed his eyes and pushed harder, grunting softly at the warm tremblings that shot through his thighs. Soon he would move his fingers back to the thick cock itself, wrapping them around its pulsing thickness, squeezing it to make the good feeling grow.

A loud crackling in the underbrush jarred his concentration. He jerked his head around to see Cal, his older brother, approaching through the trees.

"What are you doing?" the older man called.

"Nothing," Malory gasped, rolling over quickly.

Cal was the last person Malory expected to see. He had thought his older brother had gone into town to take advantage of his wife's absence while visiting her mother to do some "catting around" as Cal put it. He was several years older than Malory and as unlike his blond brother as it was possible to be. He was dark and stocky, his hard belly already showing signs of his beer drinking.

"What the fuck you laying out here bare-ass naked for?" Cal demanded, stomping through the long grass until his heavy work boots were practically on top of Malory. Malory was speechless as he stared at the thick soles of the boots inches from his head. "What's the matter. Cat got your tongue?" the burly man persisted.

"Uh, no. Cat ain't got my tongue," Malory stammered finally, raising his head to look up at his big brother standing over him. The older man's eyes looked wide and excited. Malory could feel the heat of them on his bare flesh as Cal stared down at his ass.

"What are you doing?" Cal asked again, his rough voice sounding thicker, huskier.

"Uh, I was swimming," Malory said.

Cal's wide eyes moved over him some more. "You don't look very wet to me," he grunted.

"Uh, I didn't go in yet. I was just going to go in."

"Huh," Cal grunted.

Malory didn't know what that meant. All he knew was that it was making him feel real funny the way his older brother was standing over him, looking all over his nakedness like a cat fixing to pounce. He didn't know what to do. He couldn't get up to put his clothes on without giving Cal an eyeful of his throbber, which was now harder than ever, pressed between his belly and the tickling grass. And on top of that he had said he was going to go swimming. It would look funny if he got dressed right away without doing it so he just lay there and said the first thing he could think of that sounded halfway reasonable.

"Yeah, I was fixing to go in swimming, but the sun feels so good, I think I'll just lay here and catch me a few winks before I go in."

"Huh," Cal grunted again.

Malory laid his head down on his arms and closed his eyes so he wouldn't have to see the way his brother was looking at him.

"I got to take a piss," Cal muttered above him.

"I ain't stopping you," Malory replied, trying to keep his voice brotherly casual.

"Huh," Cal grunted again.

Malory waited for the sound of his brother's boots moving away to take his piss. All of a sudden warm water splattered down his back.

"Hey, what are you doing?" he hollered, rolling over to see his brother pissing on him, standing over him with his big hose hanging out of his open jeans, shooting a thick spurting stream of golden piss all over him. "Hey, stop it. You're pissing on me. Stop it."

The stream sprayed up his chest and cut off his words in a gulp as Cal caught him in his open mouth with a rushing shot and then momentarily blinded him with a splatter in his eyes so he couldn't even see. Coughing and sputtering, he pulled himself to his knees as the stream trickled to a stop. Malory choked with anger and shame as he wiped the piss out of his eyes.

"What the heck are you doing? What are you pissing on me for? I'm going to tell Pa on you," he cried as he wiped his eyes and shook his wet hair out of his face. He started to get to his feet.

"Stay there!" Cal snarled at him.

"I ain't," Malory retorted and got a smack on the side of his head that made his ears ring.

"Stay there," Cal repeated.

Malory stared up at his brother standing over him. His big dick was still hanging out of his fly. A drop of moisture glistened at the head of it. Malory didn't want to look at that. He forced his gaze up higher, to his brother's face, and saw more of that wild look in his eyes.

"You look good down there," Cal grunted.

"Well, I ain't staying down here," Malory said, starting once more to rise. Cal gave him a smack on the other side of the head. Malory sank back to his knees, suddenly feeling weak and powerless.

"That's better. Do what I say."

Malory was afraid to say anything. He knelt there, feeling piss trickle down him and disturbingly aware of the throbbing hardness at his crotch that showed no signs of going down.

Indeed the head of it was bouncing back against his belly with every breath he took.

"Got yourself a big one, don't you. Must run in the family," Cal chuckled. "Not as big as mine though," the older man added. "Take a look at this."

Malory did as he was told—as much to avoid another blow to the head as out of curiosity, he tried to tell himself, as he focused on that big, hanging dick. Cal wrapped his fingers around it and began to pull at it, toying with it, teasing it to a rapidly enlarging state until it was soaring out over Malory's upturned face, a darker, larger version of Malory's own dick.

"Pretty big, huh?" Cal grunted.

It sure looked that way from Malory's point of view, big and stiff and moist. Cal's hand worked over it, slow and steady, until it was rock hard. Malory couldn't take his eyes off it. He kept staring at it as Cal hunkered down, squatting with his heavy thighs spread wide on either side of the naked blond, imprisoning him between their solid bulk. Cal's eyes got even wilder-looking as he moved his free hand to his brother's body, touching the smooth skin of his chest, touching the tip of one tit, touching it almost gently at first.

"Like a girl's," he murmured. "Pretty as a girl's."

Malory groaned at the touch of his brother's callused finger, shuddering at the weak, warm feeling that rushed through him. "What are you doing to me?" he gasped.

"Shut up," Cal grunted, gathering the tender tip between his thumb and forefinger and squeezing it.

"Please, don't," Malory begged. "Stop."

"Shut up or I'll slam you another one."

Malory bit his lower lip, trying hard to control himself, trying hard to keep the whimper that was bursting up in his chest from escaping. The feeling was intense in his tit as Cal squeezed at it harder, pulling it out from his chest, twisting it around and then doing the same to the other one until they were both sticking out from his chest like little drums, and his chest was heaving up and down with his heavy breathing.

"You like that, don't you?" Cal said, his voice sounding so different Malory hardly recognized it. "You like having your little pussy tits squeezed and worked over by your big brother, don't you?"

"No, I don't," Malory gasped. "No. It hurts. Please. Stop it."

"Why? You want to do something else? Is that why you want me to stop? Cause you can hardly wait to get on to something else?" As he mumbled he moved up on his haunches, working his hand faster over his jutting pecker, shifting his feet, moving himself closer to his kneeling brother, getting that drippy cockhead closer.

"No," Malory pleaded. "I don't like it. Stop. Let me go. Please, Cal."

Cal moved his hand from his dick to Malory's other tit, holding on to both of them as he straightened up a little to bring his crotch more on a level with Malory's flushed face. He kept pulling on them, using them to force Malory close so that the head of his throbbing dick bounced against Malory's nose, leaving a damp spot on the tip of it. Malory jerked back but Cal dug his nails into his tits, holding him tight, prodding his rammer against Malory's lips.

"You got pretty lips, such pretty lips. Pretty as your little tits. I want you to put those pretty little lips on my dick. Give my dick a pretty little kiss," Cal murmured huskily.

Malory pulled back against the pain in his nipples, clamping his mouth shut, turning his head away from that big smelly rod. Cal's hand left his nipples, clamping around the back of his head as the big man stepped one foot over his shoulder, spreading his legs and holding Malory in the fork of them.

"Suck it, you little fucker. Get that mouth open and suck it," Cal ordered, grabbing Malory's hair and jamming his face against his hard dick, rubbing it around so Malory, even with his eyes shut, could see inside his head that pulsing thickness and the soft hairiness tickling sweatily at his cheeks.

He pushed at Cal's muscular thighs, trying to force him back. Cal stumbled, stamping one boot down on Malory's ankle behind him. Malory groaned and fell backward, twisting his legs painfully under him as Cal dropped down with him, on top of him, setting his crotch down hard on Malory's face.

"Oh damn, oh damn," Cal hollered above him.

Something wet and thick and sticky pumped out over Malory's face, dripping everywhere, down his cheeks, into his nose, making him sputter and choke as the flood continued, running into his hair, down into his ears as he was drowned in Cal's hot flow.

"Oh, man," Cal sighed. "Oh man, I couldn't hold back. Just rubbing around on you gets me so hot, I couldn't hold it."

The hot, hairy pressure of his genitals lifted as he rose shakily to his feet. Malory lay there, feeling the wet stickiness dripping off his face.

"You're a fucking mess," he heard Cal snicker.

He opened his eyes to see his big brother standing astride him, shaking his now floppy dick, flipping the last few dribbles down on Malory's naked body.

"You should have took it in your mouth, like I said, asshole. Not so messy that way." He smirked as he gave his dick one last shake and tucked it back in his jeans. "Next time you'll take it in your mouth, asshole, or I'll punch your teeth out."

Cal laughed as he walked away. Malory closed his eyes, but he could hear that laughing for a long time as he lay there, wet with piss and sticky with jism, and his prick throbbing hard up against his belly.

IN THE

MAINSTREAM

The power of the pornographic has become obvious even to those gay writers whose work has come to be accepted in the mainstream. When Edmund White writes his novels, it's obvious that he would have to explore his characters' sexuality in order to maintain their high level of authenticity and verve. The two selections from his work here are fine examples of his willingness to do just that.

Alan Hollinghurst's *The Swimming Pool-Library* swept the best-seller lists in the United Kingdom and the United States. The book's intensely specific sexual content didn't seem to put off the critics or the readers. *The Swimming Pool-Library* has a special place in English-language literature because it is probably the last book about gay sexuality that was written before the impact of AIDS hit. Since then, all attempts at writing about sexuality by dating the action in pre-epidemic times, a favorite ploy among secondary authors, have seemed artificial and avoiding. Hollinghurst's lustful writing is almost nostalgic now.

This selection takes place in a pornographic movie theater, the Brutus Cinema. Many novelists have used the pornographic institutions to explicate their characters and to give them a place in time and social context. Another author who uses the location of a dirty-movie theater in his work is David Leavitt, who has one of his main characters in *The Lost Language of the Cranes* talk about how important pornographic movies were to his development as a gay man:

> "I started going to the Bijou and other porn theatres when I was thirty," he said. "Boy, was I scared the first time I went—but also excited. Because what those men were doing on that screen—that was what I wanted to do, what I'd always wanted to do. And they did it so naturally, so willingly. They weren't shy or scared. They weren't worrying about whether it was wrong. It's strange, but those porn films were kind of healing for me. Everyone thinks pornography is alienating, and I guess it is, but for a man who's as scared as I was—well, it was telling me what I felt wasn't so wrong, and that I wasn't alone in feeling it. They were saying, Don't push it out of your mind. Revel in it. Celebrate it." He smiled. "The way those men made love," he said, "there was rebellion in their eyes. That meant something to me, Philip, it really did. So I got braver."

EDMUND WHITE

FROM

A BOY'S

OWN STORY

"TIME FOR BED, YOUNG FELLA," MY FATHER SAID AT last.

Downstairs I undressed by the colored light of the glass-brick bar and, wearing just a T-shirt and jockey shorts, hurried into the dark dormitory and slipped into my cot. Nights on the lake are cold even in July; the bed had two thick blankets on it that had been aired outside that day and smelled of pine needles. I listened to the grown-ups; the metal vents conducted sound better than heat. Their conversation, which had seemed so lively and sincere when I had witnessed it, now sounded stilted and halting. Lots of fake laughter. Silences became longer and longer. At last everyone said good night and headed upstairs. Another five minutes of moaning pipes, flushing toilets, and padding feet. Then long murmured consultations in bed by each couple. Then silence.

"You still awake?" Kevin called from his bed.

"Yes," I said. I couldn't see him in the dark but I could

tell his cot was at the other end of the room; Peter was audibly asleep on the cot between.

"How old are you?" Kevin asked.

"Fifteen. And you?"

"Twelve. You ever done it with girls?"

"Sure," I said. I knew I could always tell him about the black prostitute I'd visited. "You?"

"Naw. Not yet." Pause. "I hear you gotta warm 'em up."

"That's correct."

"How do you do it?"

I had read a marriage manual. "Well, you turn the lights down and kiss a long time first."

"With your clothes on?"

"Of course. Then you take off her top and play with her breasts. But very gently. Don't get too rough—they don't like that."

"Does she play with your boner?"

"Not usually. An older, experienced woman might."

"You been with an older woman?"

"Once."

"They get kinda saggy, don't they?"

"My friend was beautiful," I said, offended on behalf of the imaginary lady.

"Is it real wet and slippery in there? Some guy told me it was like wet liver in a milk bottle."

"Only if the romantic foreplay has gone on long enough."

"How long's enough?"

"An hour."

The silence was thoughtful, as though it were an eyelash beating against a pillowcase.

"The guys back home? Guys in my neighborhood?"

"Yes?" I said.

"We all cornholed each other. You ever do that?"

"Sure."

"What?"

"I said sure."

"Guess you've outgrown that by now."

"Well, yeah, but since there aren't any girls around . . ."

I felt as a scientist must when he knows he's about to bring off the experiment of his career: outwardly calm, inwardly jubilant, already braced for disappointment. "We could try it now." Pause. "If you want to." As soon as the words were out of my mouth I felt he wouldn't come to my bed; he had found something wrong with me, he thought I was a sissy, I should have said "Right" instead of "That's correct."

"Got any stuff?" he asked.

"What?"

"You know. Like Vaseline?"

"No, but we don't need it. Spit will"—I started to say "do," but men say "work"—"work." My penis was hard but still bent painfully down in the jockey shorts; I released it and placed the head under the taut elastic wasitband.

"Naw, you gotta have Vaseline." I might be knowledgeable about real sex, but apparently Kevin was to be the expert when it came to cornholing.

"Well, let's try spit."

"I don't know. Okay." His voice was small and his mouth sounded dry.

I watched him come toward me. He, too, had jockey shorts on, which appeared to glow. Though barechested now, he'd worn a T-shirt all through Little League season that had left his torso and upper arms pale; his ghost shirt excited me, because it reminded me he was captain of his team.

We pulled off our shorts. I opened my arms to Kevin and closed my eyes. He said, "It's colder than a witch's tit." I lay on my side facing him and he slipped in beside me. His breath smelled of milk. His hands and feet were cold. I kept my lower arm scrunched under me, but with the upper one I nervously patted his back. His back and chest and legs were silky and hairless, though I could see a tuft of eiderdown under his arm, which he'd lifted to pay me back in reciprocation. A thin layer of baby fat still formed a pad under his skin. Beneath the fat I could feel the hard, rounded muscles. He reached down under the sheet to touch my penis, and I touched his.

"Ever put them together in your hand?" he asked.

"No," I said. "Show me."

"You spit on your hand first, get it real wet. See? Then you—scoot closer, up a bit—you put them together like this. It feels neat."

"Yes," I said. "Neat."

Since I knew he wouldn't let me kiss him, I put my head beside his and pressed my lips silently to his neck. His neck was smooth and long and thin, too thin for the size of his head; in this way, too, he still resembled a child. In the rising heat of our bodies I caught a slight whiff of his odor, not pungent like a grown-up's but faintly acrid, the smell of scallions in the rain.

"Who's first?" he asked.

"Cornholing?"

"I think we need some stuff. It won't work without stuff."

"I'll go first," I said. Although I put lots of spit on him and me, he still said it hurt. I'd get about half an inch in and he'd say, "Take it out! Quick!" He was lying on his side with his back to me, but I could still look over and see him wince in profile. "Jesus," he said. "It's like a knife all through me." The pain subsided and with the bravery of an Eagle Scout he said, "Okay. Try it again. But take it easy and promise you'll pull out when I say so."

This time I went in a millimeter at a time, waiting between each advance. I could feel his muscles relaxing.

"Is it in?" he asked.

"Yep."

"All the way in?"

"Almost. There. It's all in."

"Really?" He reached back for my crotch to make sure. "Yeah, it is," he said. "Feel good?"

"Terrific."

"Okay," he instructed, "go in and out, but slow, okay?"

"Sure."

I tried a few short thrusts and asked if I was hurting him. He shook his head.

He bent his knees up toward his chest and I flowed around him. Whereas face-to-face I had felt timid and unable to get enough of his body against enough of mine, now I was glued to him and he didn't object—it was understood that this was my turn and I could do what I liked. I tunneled my lower arm under him and folded it across his chest; his ribs were unexpectedly small and countable, and now that he'd completely relaxed I could get deeper and deeper into him. That such a tough, muscled little guy, whose words were so flat and eyes without depth or humor, could be so richly taken—oh, he felt good. But the sensation he was giving it was a secret gift, shameful and pungent, one he didn't dare acknowledge. In the Chris-Craft I'd been afraid of him. He had been the usual intimidating winner, beyond excitement—but here he was, pushing this tendoned, shifting pleasure back into me, the fine hair on his neck damp with sweat just above the hollows the sculptor had pressed with his thumbs into the clay. His tan hand was resting on his white hip. The ends of his lashes were pulsing just beyond the line of his full cheek.

"Does it feel good?" he asked. "Want it tighter?" he asked, as a shoe salesman might.

"No, it's fine."

"See, I can make it tighter," and indeed he could. His eagerness to please me reminded me that I needn't have worried, that in his own eyes he was just a kid and I a high school guy who'd done it with girls and one older lady and everything. Most of the time I had dreamed of an English lord who'd kidnap me and take me away forever; someone who'd save me and whom I'd rule. But now it seemed that Kevin and I didn't need anyone older, we could run away together, I would be our protector. We were already sleeping in a field under a sheet of breezes and taking turns feeding on each other's bodies, wet from the dew.

"I'm getting close," I said. "Want me to pull out?"

"Go ahead," he said. "Fill 'er up."

"Okay. Here goes. Oh, God. Jesus!" I couldn't help kissing his cheek.

"Your beard hurts," he said. "You shave every day?"

"Every other. You?"

"Not yet. But the fuzz is gettin' dark. Some guy told me

EDMUND WHITE

FROM THE

BEAUTIFUL

ROOM IS EMPTY

WHEN I RETURNED TO SCHOOL I STARTED CRUISING all the time, all the time. Every free moment between classes I was in the student union or the third-floor toilet in Main Hall. I'd sit for hours in a stall, dropping cigarettes into the bowl, studying a book on Chinese social structure or Buddhist art, awaiting an interesting customer, like one of those gypsy fortune-tellers who prospect clients in storefronts where they also live. Their mixture of homely paraphernalia and mystical apparatus (TV beside crystal ball) might serve as an analogy to my blend of scholarship and sex.

I was obsessed. Hour after hour I'd sit there, inhaling the smells other people made, listening to their sounds, studying the graffiti scribbled all over the thick marble partitions in Main Hall or the metal ones in the union.

Someone comes in, heavy brown cordovans before the urinal, worn-down heels and scuff marks on the leather—neglects himself, can't be gay. I can hear his urine splatter but I can't see its flow. I wait for it to stop—the crucial moment, for if he stays on, then I'll stand in my stall, peek through the crack, soundlessly unbolt my door as an invitation. Now, in this indeterminate second, I can put one head after another on his unseen shoulders, invent for him one scenario after another. I get hard in anticipation, stiff before the void of my own imagination.

Nothing. His calves flex slightly as he buttons up (heavy weight to lift) and then he's gone. One of the toilets two stalls down drips and I picture the mad anesthesiologist mixing poison, drop by drop, into the sedative.

Time and again I'd focus on this stranger on the other side of the door, will him into wanting me, impart to him perverse demands, blond hair, full lips, only to see him through the crack in the door: the middle-aged janitor with hairy ears. But then, just as I was ready to cash in my chips, someone else sat beside me, dropped his pants to the floor in a puddle, revealing strong tan calves above crisp, white, ribbed athletic socks. A silence like a storm cloud gathered over the room, blocking out the hall noises. He tapped his foot slightly; I tapped mine. Then two taps, matched by two of mine. Three and three.

And without further prelude, he sank to his knees shoving his brown thighs and white groin under the partition, and I also knelt to feast on his erection, inhaling the clean smell of soap, my hands exploring the lichee-size testicles, then traveling up smooth skin. I'd dreamed about this moment so long that now I wanted to freeze the frame.

In my anthropology class I was learning that although man was started off as an animal subject to natural selection, he had soon begun to evolve in a direction determined purely by culture. Human beings stood upright to free their hands, they needed their hands to hold tools, the tool-and-weapon-wielding parts of their brains developed to accommodate their newly prehensile grasp, language was enabled by tool-wielding—but now, if culture were yanked out from under us, we'd be destroyed, like one of those cartoon cats who scamper off a branch and tread thin air until sudden awareness makes them plummet.

Here, under my gaze, was this creature, half-natural but half-invented by himself. The tan line suggested poolside swimsuit, frosted glass, sunglasses—everything as symbolic as the life pictured by advertisements. But the hickory-hard straining of this cock upward spelled animal—a straight line of ascent inflating slightly as the balls rose and tightened for blast-off, a thrust that propelled life upward. The cleanness, however, the feathery lightness of the blond hairs, the neatness of the circumcision were all preppy, while the heavy hamstrings (and now the jets of semen filling my mouth) were primate.

For an instant I stayed attached to him, though here I was on a dirty tile floor on hands and knees before a stranger I'd seen only from the waist down but whom I remember to this day because he'd presented himself so fearlessly, because his body, at least the half of it I knew, seemed ideal, and because his desire was so strong it was as expressive as words or deeds, the things that normally define individuals.

Then he was gone. His exit was so hasty I couldn't see him, just a flash of blond hair and white shirt collar through the narrow vertical slit of my sentry box. I waited patiently for someone else.

I was alone with my sexuality, since none of these men spoke to me, nor did I even know their faces, much less their names. Their most intimate tender parts were thrust under the partitions, like meals for prisoners, but if I poked my head under the partition and glanced up at them, they'd hide their faces with their hands as a movie star wards off a flash. I'd rush from one toilet to another between classes. Sometimes all four stalls in Main Hall or all eight in the union would be occupied, full house. I'd wait for someone to emerge, but if no one did I would realize I was spoiling their fun and leave. Perhaps my presence was interrupting an orgy that would resume the second I left and even now eight doors concealed eight erect penises.

Someone with a convict's patience had drilled a dime-size hole in one of the marble slabs in Main Hall. I'd sit on the toilet, suddenly remember the hole was here, between this stall and the next, look up and see a black pupil, glossy, quivering.

If the eye persisted in its liquid restlessness, at once thoroughly anonymous and shockingly vulnerable, I'd look back toward this live camera, this unseen seer. I stood up to explore my erection. I posed a bit self-consciously, turning halfway toward my audience while still keeping my feet forward in the usual position so as not to arouse suspicion in anyone outside glancing at the floor.

His lashes squeezed shut for a second as he blinked. The effect through the judas was of a carnivorous plant swallowing a black, trembling life. The soul and intelligence usually attributed to the eyes had been annulled by this extreme close-up: nothing left by motility. "The quick," I thought, as in the phrase, "The quick and the dead."

Then I exploded, he flushed and shot out of his booth, the door to the hall sighed shut behind him, and I was alone with the faintly blue light filtering down through overhead frosted glass onto white porcelain and with the sound of the leaking toilet and a paw full of come, which I licked clean and swallowed like a savage or a cat. If I'd had the courage, I would have advised my anthropology class that primitive man believes in the conservation of energy through the recycling of bodily fluids.

ALAN HOLLINGHURST

"THE BRUTUS

CINEMA"

FROM THE

SWIMMING

POOL-LIBRARY

THE BRUTUS CINEMA OCCUPIED THE BASEMENT OF one of those Soho houses which, above ground-floor level, maintain their beautiful Caroline fenestration, and seemed a kind of emblem of gay life (the *piano nobile* elegant above the squalid, jolly *sous-sol*) in the far-off spring of 1983. One entered from the street by pushing back the dirty red curtain in the doorway beside an unlettered shop window, painted over white but with a stencil of Michelangelo's David stuck in the middle. This tussle with the curtain—one never knew whether to shoulder it aside to the right or the left, and often tangled with another punter coming out—seemed a symbolic act, done in the sight of passers-by, and always gave me a little jab of pride.

Inside was a small front room, the walls bearing porn-mags on racks, and the glossy boxes of videos for sale; and there were advertisements for clubs and cures. In a locked case by the counter leather underwear was displayed, with cock-rings, face masks, chains, and the whole gamut of dildoes from pubertal pink fingers to mighty black jobs, two feet long and as thick as a fist.

As I entered, the spotty Glaswegian attendant was getting stuck into a helping of fish and chips, and the room stank of grease and vinegar. I idled for a minute and flicked through some mags. These were really dog-eared browsers, thumbed through time and again by those rent-boys who had the blessing of the management and waited there for pick-ups; curiously incredible stations of sexual intercourse, whose moving versions, or something similar, could be seen downstairs. I looked at the theatrical expressions of ecstasy without interest. The attendant had a small television behind the counter which was a monitor for the films being shown in the cinema; but as there was no one else in the shop he had broken the endless circuit of video sex and was watching a real TV programme instead. He sat there stuffing chips and oozing batter-covered sections of flaky white cod into his mouth, his short-sighted attention rapt by the screen, as if he had been a teenaged boy getting his first sight of a porn film. I sidled along and looked over his shoulder; it was a nature programme, and contained some virtuoso footage shot inside a termite colony. First we saw the long, questing snout of the ant-eater outside, and then its brutal, razor-sharp claws cutting their way in. Back inside, perched by a fibre-optic miracle was a junction of tunnels which looked like the triforium of some Gaudi church, we saw the freakishly extensile tongue of the anteater come flicking towards us, cleaning the fleeing termites off the wall.

It was one of the most astonishing pieces of film I had ever seen, and I felt a thrill at the violent intrusion as well as dismay at the smashing of something so strange and intricate; I was disappointed when the attendant, realising I was there and perhaps in need of encouragement, tapped a button and transformed the picture into the relative banality of American college boys sticking their cocks up each other's assholes.

'Cinema, sir?' he said. 'We've got some really hot-core hard films. . . .' His heart wasn't in it so I paid him my fiver and left him to the wonderful world of nature.

I went down the stairs, lit by one gloomy red-painted bulb. The cinema itself was a small cellar room, the squalor of which was only fully apparent at the desolating moment in the early hours when the show ended for the night and the lights were suddenly switched on, revealing the bare, damp-stained walls, the rubbish on the floor, and the remaining audience, either asleep or doing things best covered by darkness. It had perhaps ten tiers of seats, salvaged from the refurbishment of some bona fide picture house: some lacked arms, which helped patrons get to know each other, and one lacked a seat, and was the repeated cause of embarrassment to diffident people, blinded by the dark, who chose it as the first empty place to hand and sat down heavily on the floor instead.

I had not been there for months and was struck again by its character: pushing open the door I felt it weigh on sight, smell, and hearing. The smell was smoke and sweat, a stale male odour tartishly overlaid with a cheap lemon-scented air-freshener like a taxi and dusted from time to time with a trace of Trouble for Men. The sound was the laid-back aphrodisiac pop music which, as the films had no sound-track, played continuously and repetitively to enhance the mood and cover the quieter noises made by the customers. The look of the place changed in the first minute or so, as I waited just inside the door for my eyes to accustom themselves to the near dark. The only light came from the small screen, and from a dim yellow 'Fire Exit' sign. I had once taken this exit, which led to a fetid back staircase with a locked door at the top. Smoke thickened the air and hung in the projector's beam.

It was important to sit near the back, where it was darker and more went on, but also essential to avoid the attention of truly gruesome people. Slightly encumbered with my bag I moved into a row empty except for a heavy businessman at the far end. It was not a very good house, so I settled down to watch and wait. Occasionally cigarettes were lit and the men shifted in their seats and looked around; the mood faltered between tension and lethargy.

The college boys were followed by a brief, gloomy fragment of film involving older, moustachioed types, one of them virtually bald. This broke off suddenly, and without preamble another film, very cheery and outdoors, was under way. As always with these films, though I relished the gross abundance of their later episodes, it was the introductory scenes, buoyant with expectation, the men on the street or the beach, killing time, pumping iron, still awaiting the transformation our fantasy would demand of them, that I found the most touching.

Now, for instance, we were in a farmyard. A golden-haired boy in old blue jeans and a white vest was leaning in the sun against a barn door, one foot raised behind him. A close-up admired him frowning against the sun, a straw jerking between his lips. Slowly we traveled down, lingering where his hand brushed across his nipples which showed hard through his vest, lingering again at his loose but promising crotch. On the other side of the yard, a second boy, also blond, was shifting bags of fertilizer. We watched his shirtless muscular torso straining as he lifted the bags on to his shoulder, traced the sweat running down his neck and back, got a load of his chunky denim-clad ass as he bent over. The eyes of the two boys met; one close-up and then another suggested curiosity and lust. In what seemed to be very slightly slow motion the shirtless boy ambled across to the other. They stood close together, both extremely beautiful, perhaps eighteen or nineteen years of age. Their lips moved, they spoke and smiled, but as the film had no sound-track, and we heard only the cinema's throbbing, washing music, they communicated in a dreamlike silence, or as if watched from out of earshot through binoculars. The picture was irradiated with sunlight and, being fractionally out of focus, blurred the boys' smooth outlines into a blond nimbus. The one in the vest appeared to put a question to the other, they turned aside and were swallowed up into the darkness of the barn.

Where did they get them from, I wondered, these boys more wonderful than almost everything one came across in real life? And I remembered reading somewhere that a Californian talent-spotter had photographic records of three thousand or more of them ranging back over twenty or thirty years and that a youngster, after a session in the studio, mooching through the files, had found pictures of his own father, posed long before.

In the meantime there were other arrivals at the cinema, though it was difficult to make them out; while the sunlit introduction had brightened up the room and cast its aura over the scattered audience in the forward rows, the sex scenes within the barn were enacted in comparative gloom, allowing the viewers a secretive darkness. I tugged my half-hard cock out through my fly and stroked it casually.

One new entrant tottered to the deserted front row, which in this tiny space was only a few feet from the screen. There was a rustle of papers, and I could see him in silhouette remove his coat, fold it neatly and place it on the seat next to that in which he then sat down. The rustling recurred intermittently, and I guessed he must be a man I'd seen at the Brutus the very first time I went there, a spry little chap of sixty-five or so who, like a schoolgirl taken to a romantic U picture, sat entranced by the movies and worked his way through a bag of boiled sweets as the action unfolded. A fiver from his pension, perhaps, and 30p for the humbugs, might be set aside weekly for this little outing. How he must look forward to it! His was a complete and innocent absorption in the fantasy world on screen. Could he look back to a time when he had behaved like these glowing, thoughtless teenagers, who were now locked together sucking on each other's cocks in the hay? Or was this the image of a new society we had made, where every desire could find its gratification?

The old man was happy with his cough-drops, but I wanted some other oral pleasure (the Winchester slang 'suction', meaning sweets, I realised was the comprehensive term). Not, however, from the person who came scouting up to the rear rows now, one of the plump, bespectacled Chinese youths who, with day-return businessmen and quite distinguished Oxbridge dons, made a haunt of places like this, hopping hopefully from row to row, so persistent that they were inevitably, from time to time, successful.

The man on the end of the row had to shift, and I realised I was to be the next recipient of Eastern approaches. The boy sat down next to me, and though I carried on looking at the screen and laid my hand across my cock, I was aware that he was staring at me intently to try and make out my face in the darkness, and I felt his breath on my cheek. Then there was the pressure of his shoulder against mine. I gathered myself emphatically, and leant across into the empty place on the other side. He sprawled rather, with his legs wide apart, one of them straying into my space and pressing against my thigh.

'Leave off, will you,' I whispered, thinking that a matter-of-fact request would do the trick. At the same time I crossed my legs, squashing my balls uncomfortably, to emphasise that I was not available. The sack-lifting boy was now sliding his finger up the other one's ass, spitting on his big, blunt cock and preparing for the inevitable penetration. As he pressed its head against the boy's glistening sphincter, which virtually filled the screen in lurid close-up, I felt an arm go along the back of the seat and a moment later a hand descend unfalteringly on my dick. I didn't move, but sensing the power that speech had in this cryptic gathering, I said loudly and firmly: 'If you come anywhere near me again I'll break your neck.' A couple of people looked round, there was an 'Ooooh' from the other side of the room, spoken in a uniquely homosexual tone of bored outrage, the tentacles withdrew, and after a few moments, compatible perhaps with some fantastic notion of the preservation of dignity, the advancer retreated, earning a curse from the man at the end of the row, who was forced to get up again, attempting to conceal his erection as he did so.

Exhilarated by my control of the situation, I spread myself again; the boy duly came over the other's face, and very pretty it looked, the blobs and strings of spunk smeared over his eyelids, nose, and thick half-opened lips. Then, abruptly, it was another film. Half a dozen boys entered a locker-room, and at just the same moment the door from the stairs opened and something came in that looked, in the deep shadow, as if it might be nice. It was a sporty-looking boy with, evidently, a bag. He was not sure what to do, so I bent my telepathic powers on him. The poor creature struggled for a moment . . . but it was hopeless. He stumbled up towards the back, groped past the businessman (I heard him say 'Sorry') and sat a seat away from me, putting his bag on the seat between us.

I let a little time elapse and distinctly heard him swallow, as if in lust and amazement, as the boys stripped off and, before we knew where we were, one of them was jacking off in the shower. Something made me certain that it was the first time he had been to a place like this, and I remembered how enchanting it is to see one's first porn-film. 'Christ! They're really doing it,' I recalled saying to myself, quite impressed by the way the actors seemed genuinely to be having sex for the pleasure of it, and by the blatant innocence of it all.

I then proceeded by a succession of distinct and inexorable moves, shifting into the place between us and at the same time pushing his bag along the floor to where I had been sitting. I sensed some anxiety about this, but he carried on looking at the screen. Next I slid my arm along the back of his seat, and as he remained immobile I made it as clear as I could in the dark that I had my cock out and was playing with it. Then I leant over him more, and ran my hand over his chest. His heart was racing, and I felt all the tension in his fixed posture between excitement and fear, and knew that I could take control of him. He had on a kind of bomber jacket, and under that a shirt. I let my hand linger at his waist, and admired his hard, ridged stomach, slipping my fingers between his shirt buttons, and running my hand up over his smooth skin. He had beautiful, muscular tits, with small frosted nipples, quite hairless. My left hand gently rubbed the base of his thick neck; he seemed to have almost a crew-cut and the back of his head was softly bristly. I leant close to him and drooled my tongue up his jaw and into his ear.

At this he could no longer remain impassive. He turned towards me with a gulp, and I felt his finger tips shyly slide onto my knee and shortly after touch my cock. 'Oh no,' I think he said under his breath, as he tried to get his hand around it, and then jerked it tentatively a few times. I continued stroking the back of his neck, thinking it might relax him, but he kept on feeling my dick in a very polite sort of way, so I brought pressure to bear and pushed his head firmly down into my lap. He had to struggle around to get his stocky form into the new position, encumbered by the padded arm between our seats; but once there he took the crown of my cock into his mouth and with me moving his head puppet-like up and down, sucked it after a fashion.

This was all very good and with my hangover I felt it with electric intensity. But I was aware of his reluctance, and let him stop. He was inexpert, and though he was excited, needed help. We sat back for a while, my hand all the time on his shoulder. I loved the nerve with which I'd done all this, and like most random sex it gave me the feeling I could achieve anything I wanted if I were only determined enough. There was now a fairly complicated set-up on screen, with all six boys doing something interesting, and one of them I realized was Kip Parker, a famous tousle-headed blond teen star. I ran my hand between my new friend's legs and felt his cock kicking against the tightish cotton of his slacks. He helped me take it out, a short, punchy little number, which I went down on and polished off almost at once. God, he must have been ready. After a shocked recuperation he felt for his bag and went out without a word.

I'd had a growing suspicion throughout this sordid but charming little episode, which rose to a near certainty as he opened the door and was caught in a slightly brighter light, that the boy was Phil from the Corry. He had smelt of sweat rather than talcum powder and there was a light stubble on his jaw, so I concluded that if it were Phil he was on his way to rather than from the Club, as I knew he was fastidiously clean, and that he always shaved in the evening before having a shower. I was tempted to follow him at once, to make sure, but I realised it would be easy enough to tell from seeing him later; and besides, a very well-hung kid, who'd already been showing an interest in our activities, moved in to occupy the boy's former seat, and brought me off epically during the next film, an unthinkably tawdry picture which all took place in a kitchen.

FIRST

PERSON,

NONFICTION

Since so much of the importance of gay men's writing about sexuality is reportage of what happens and what goes on, of course it's not limited to fiction. The essay has become a vital vehicle for writers wanting to discuss their sexuality.

Andrew Holleran has written many novels and short stories, but he also has a claim on being one of the foremost gay essayists. His column in *Christopher Street* magazine regularly explores the world in which he lives, both the small town that is his home and other nearby spots in northern Florida, as well as New York, where he used to reside. "Mmmmpfgh" is an excellent example of Holleran's use of his skill to document the sexual exploits of his time.

Scott O'Hara is a highly unusual porn star. He's been featured in many pornographic films and often participates in live sex shows at such venues as New York's annual, notorious Black Party. But O'Hara isn't willing to be a passive sexual object; he often writes about his experiences, making himself the ultimate observer-participant.

John Wagenhauser is a new writer who has been able to capture the feel and emotions of gay sex life for the post-AIDS generation. No longer able to enter into a world that has no sexual limitations, not when the entry fee could be a life-threatening disease, the young men of Wagenhauser's generation are out discovering wholly new sexual options. His essay here, on attending a jack-off club, shows that, no matter how much has been lost, there is still erotic passion to be found in gay men's lives today.

ANDREW HOLLERAN

"MMMMPFGH"

PEOPLE DESPERATE FOR SEX ALWAYS HAVE A LOOK—
in the dunes that line the gay beach south of Jacksonville, Florida, at least. They arrive fully dressed, for one thing, not in
bathing suits. There's no pretext of swimming. They park the
car, get out, and walk across the highway to a path that runs
the length of the dunes; a path that is intersected by other paths
leading back to grottoes—patches of white sand between the
thick growth of palmettos, sabal palms, and wild vines that
cover the dunes themselves. At the intersection of the main
paths and the little paths leading back into what amounts to
rooms amid the shrubbery, people stand. Sometimes they are
swimmers who have walked up as part of a long day at the
beach. Mostly they are people whose facial expressions are so
distinctive—the fully dressed, having driven here for just one
thing: to eat penis.

The people who come to the beach *not* to swim come
mostly at the end of the day—after work, with all the pressure
and hypocrisy the workplace may entail—and when they take

a position on the dunes, fully clothed, their purpose plain, they have a guarded, dolorous, unhappy expression. ("The look of lust," wrote Nabokov, "is gloomy.") Otherwise I'd say they were ashamed, or angry at having come here, at needing a penis. There is nothing cheerful about driving all this way to have sex; it's more like a desperate act. The beach is so beautiful I like to think it clears everyone's head, and soothes the soul, whether they have sex or not. But this is probably naive. (I, for instance, go to the baths after leaving the beach, which takes the pressure off; since I don't have to get laid, I can swim.) There is no mistaking the expression on the faces, the desperation, the need, the element of gloom attached to being willing to spend a couple of hours waiting in the dunes for some little bit of human contact.

Yet these figures also present a romantic picture—standing on top of a dune, staring out to sea, the wind blowing their shirts or hair back, like the French Lieutenant's Woman. They too are waiting for a French lieutenant, or at any rate, some version of him—as patient as hunters hoping for a flock of ducks, or eagles trying to perceive the movement of wildlife below.

Or, if not on top of the highest dunes, you come upon them when you take your own walk along the path, like Keats's Autumn sitting disheveled on the granary floor, in crevices you never knew were there—sometimes having sex. One never knows whether people having sex want an audience or are offended by it—just as you never know whether they come here wanting to eat a penis or have theirs eaten—and so I keep going, rather than spoil the scene. But one generally sees the whole spectrum of behavior—from the orgiastic to the shy. Once, while in the surf, I saw a man jerking himself off in full view, facing the ocean, on the crest of a dune, as he looked back over his shoulder at something I could not see—presumably other people having sex in one of those "rooms" in the shrubbery. I rushed up from the ocean to see myself, but before I could reach the top of the dune, I saw him spurt his sperm into the wind off the sea. Another day, I saw a man knitting in a crevice between two dunes, on a little canvas chair he'd set up at the entrance to a grotto—the beach equivalent of the man at the baths lying in his room with the door open as he reads a copy of *Time*.

Looking for sex takes such a long time—even, or especially, when one is desperate to have it. People spend hours in those dunes walking up and down, back and forth, or gazing out to sea for what seems like eternities, and often they seem to leave without having made any contact whatsoever. Then, as you are leaving the parking lot, a small car will drive furiously down the dirt road and come to a stop at the edge of the tidal estuary behind the beach, on the other side of the A-1-A: a fat young man who stops his car to stare at the sunset. (There is a play called *Sunsets* about just this moment, this need, in fact, by Cal Yeomans; though the play takes place, I suspect, on the west coast of Florida, it's the same here.) I would find it difficult to vent my frustration by staring at a swamp at sunset in splendid isolation. As it is, I can't imagine going home after the beach—the long, rural drive, the loneliness when I get there—and the only reason I can drive off calmly, unlike the youth who nearly drove his car right into the swamp, is that I know I can keep cruising at the baths. The beach and the baths are connected by thirty minutes on a fairly empty expressway—at the hour I use it—heading west into the setting sun. I traverse the thirty miles in a state of incandescent lust. All is hope, all is anticipation, all is possibility; I'm going to the baths, invigorated by and covered still in the salt sea. To do just one by itself would diminish the experience—together, they're thrilling. Yet what is astonishing, when I get there, is that the same endless failure to connect one observes so often at the beach—among people who obviously want to connect very badly—appears at the baths too.

There the paths along the dunes are a series of hallways; there the rooms among the shrubbery, real rooms—but there, the same need collides with the same inhibitions, reservations, distaste, discouragement. As Cynthia Serrano wrote in the *Native* about the paucity of sex among her lesbian friends: "Everybody wants to do it, but not with each other." At the beach, and the baths, one often sees the same people, over and over

again—waiting, themselves, for someone new to drop in. Then
the competition starts. (And now there's something new; when
you leave the baths around ten or eleven, there are now people
sitting in cars in the parking lot, cruising—knowing, perhaps,
the stalemate, the gridlock, that occurs inside, wanting to save
the eight or twelve dollars, finding it easier to connect in the
parking lot than the steam room.) They might be right. Down
here, parking lots are what the sidewalk is in New York—a
place free of the conventions and formality gays create even in
places they supposedly patronize to escape society's conventions and formalities (baths and bars).

Stalking the dunes, walking the halls, has always seemed
to me a crucial part of deciding whom to have sex with—it is,
after all, a process of selection. Eventually, if you're lucky, desire "crystallizes" on the body and face of someone else; at
least, that's how Stendhal explained love. Crystallizing means
only X will do. I try to crystallize at the baths; it's such a long
drive home if I don't. One Friday after leaving the beach, desire precipitated on three: a well-built blond in his thirties with
golden chest hair and a ruddy tan; a young person with dark,
neatly combed hair, sad beautiful blue eyes, a sprinkling of
black hair across his white chest, and a bottom half twice as
thick at the top; and a clone—a man in his late twenties, early
thirties, with bushy brown hair, a thick moustache (moustaches
have become such a rarity, they now seem all the more dear,
suddenly), an aquiline nose, a black-haired, deeply tanned body
with a skinny chest, long gangling arms, lean shoulders, and
the whole rangy boy-body one can imagine swinging through
trees. He also had, in view when he came out of the steam
room, a large, fat penis and seemed, moreover, the only person
truly electrified, eager, impatient to connect.

The blond man with the curly hair ended up pairing off
with a chubby black man; half an hour later, they were out on
their own again, looking for more. The young person with the
sad blue eyes who had looked at me on coming in refused to
meet my eyes again. The perfect clone went to his room, lay on
his bunk, opened the door, and lowered the lights. Ageing is so
insecure a state, one asks questions—about having sex with

a clone—one never did ten years ago. Like, if I go into the room, will he turn me down? I admired him so much I couldn't bear the humiliation and disappointment of that. So I pretended to have no interest as I walked by his open door. Eventually the door closed; who got the part, I don't know. Meanwhile the rest—unable to connect—walked round and round. "I think everyone's shy," said a very plump blond youth with glasses who sat down beside me on a bench in an alcove and provided human friendship. (The friendship everyone who goes out cruising needs.) "Really?" I said. "Yes," he said. "I know someone who came here once and didn't speak to anyone for two hours." "Try a whole night," I said, feeling more and more isolated, thinking I'd have to reread *The Confessions of Danny Slocum*. When you want sex very badly, it often becomes harder, not easier, to find. That is, sometimes your lust is so intense, so incandescent—or your haircut so right—you don't want to lay your eggs at the feet of just anyone. I couldn't decide if I wasn't doing it because I had too much, or too little, self-esteem at the moment. *It takes a certain security,* I realized suddenly, *to debase oneself.* To kneel, to worship at the altar of another man's masculinity, or beauty. A security one has in much greater supply when young than one does when age begins to seed its self-doubts. That complex negotiation between two men—two men who, of course, are not supposed to feel this way about each other—is something one can find very difficult. I was so attracted to the clone, however, that even if I couldn't bring myself to enter his room, I was willing to wait while he had sex with other people. I walked past his room again. I heard voices. Then the light was turned on. The verbal exchange following the act. Lights up, the show is over, time to part. (This was why I hadn't gone into the room, too.) I went back to the bench. Ten minutes later, the clone walked by—at a faster pace than before, holding his towel closed, not even knotted, cruising now with the determination of someone who has just had sex. Someone who has just had sex at the baths usually wants to have it again, right away. The first trick breaks the ice, melts the inhibitions, bestows confidence, makes one lubricious. (Which is why, mired in thought, I told myself that having sex would solve all my problems.) Instead, I continued to plotz on the bench, watching now a very handsome mulatto with a perfect body but an unfriendly face walk past, wondering if he would end up with the clone. (A thought that was torture.) It came down to figuring out the plot and situation of a silent movie without subtitles. What did the clone want, really? His body was tan all over, which meant he sunbathed nude, which meant he was either a circuit-queen vain about his dick (if you've got it, flaunt it), or that he was a sensuous person—that rare thing, a nice guy who loved the pleasures of the body, the beach, the weather on his skin. I couldn't tell which. At the baths, one hasn't much to go on. You have three seconds to say yes, and only once do you get asked. It was late, I was tired, and embarrassed at this point by my drawn-out search, the tedious tramping around the halls; at a certain point, the people condemned to the same frustration cannot even stand the sight of one another—everyone's ashamed of his own failure. When I walked by the clone's corner room, the door was closed again.

The music being played on the second floor was loud— the sort of raucous, jagged rock someone must think is sexy, but is not. But as I passed the door, I heard a sound, an odd sound, that of a baby that has just been fed a bottle he then gags on, a murmur of pleasure suddenly cut off when the mouth that has finally wrapped itself around the thing it has been searching for so long suddenly realizes it is too full, the throat cannot ingest what presses against it. The sound that everyone in these places would love to make. So lovely a sound, I left the baths, drove home, and in a state of infantile desire, did what babies cannot do: turned the clone into this column. And typed the letters that all those people in the dunes would love to pronounce, that lie beneath the surface of all cruising: *Mmmmpfgh.*

THINKING OFF

YEAH, SO I CAN SUCK MYSELF. IT'S CERTAINLY NO big deal to me; I've been doing it since I started jacking off. But it's always been a big attraction to other guys—and women, too, come to think of it. Not that I play around with them very much, but when the opportunity arises, it can be fun. Doesn't really feel any different—just a little softer, less muscular. But where was I? Sucking myself off, while everyone else gasps in amazement, right.

All through my teen years, along with standard jack-off techniques in the bathroom, I'd suck myself off now and then, just to see if I could still do it. I think the most public I ever got about sex in those days was going into the woods to jack off—I'm sure I never showed anyone what I could do. I guess I thought everyone did it, it wasn't as though anyone ever told me not to, or taught me how—it just came naturally. Speaking of which, I had been jacking off (and self-sucking) for nearly a year when I first had a real gushing climax—and it wasn't even in my mouth. I ate it though—couldn't wait to see what cum tasted like. I wasn't disappointed. And next time, I made a point of shooting off in my mouth. Eventually, the novelty wore off; but I've always believed that direct from the dick is the only way to eat cum.

That doesn't take into account, though, the changes that took place in my sex habits a few years back. It's got to put a new perspective on things when you realize that what you're drinking—however much you've grown to like it—may be a deadly dose. I'm not sure I believe that swallowing cum is an avenue of transmission; I know too many men, alive and healthy, who've spent their whole fucking lives behind glory holes. And yes, I do envy them that. Because I'm not sure— and when there's doubt, uncertainty, fantasy blossoms, but real sex goes out the window.

So my own cum means as much to me now as it did back in those days when it was the only supply I had; and I don't give it up for just anyone. Has to be someone I care a lot about—or at least am real turned on to. Or a good audience.

Yeah, that's really the best. I can enjoy sex one-on-one, but what clicks my trigger is having an audience . . . dozens of men with their eyes glued to me up there on stage, teasing them, easing off my clothes, working it up . . . seducing them, no matter how willing they are . . . sweating, beating, rubbing, licking . . . my dickhead, my pits, my sweaty arms, chest, fingers fresh from playing with my butthole, even my fuckin' toes . . . scooping up precum, rubbing my face with it . . . it's the smells of sex that are present onstage: sweat & cum & ass & feet & spit & rubber . . . yeah, I sometimes use rubbers to cum off in onstage: it still holds the fantasy, straight boy tryin' to get a piece at a drive-in movie, my dad poppin' it to the new next-door neighbor on her couch while I peep, fascinated, through the door . . . reality is no place for the stage, and vice versa. Give me fantasy!—and I get *down* in my fantasies when I'm up there showin' it off. Let it all loose . . . sex with women, kids, dogs, horses; killing sex . . . hanging, castration, fucking to death . . . hey, it's *fantasy,* for Christ's consumptive sake! And if you can't go wherever you want to in *fantasy,* then you're one sorry uptight motherfucker! And one of my favorites, real tried & true standby: I slip & fall on the stage, after I've been up there teasing these men for fifteen or twenty minutes, getting them all hot; before I can get up, half a dozen men from the audience, inflamed beyond reason by my prick-teasing attitude, grab me & hold me down while, one by one, the entire audience takes turns fucking me, right in the spotlights. I eventually give up struggling—no use. By the time they've finished it's dawn, I'm slicked down with cum, and when the last of them disappears, all I can do is roll over and beat out that long-suppressed load that's been building in my balls all night. . . .

Once again—fantasy, okay? I've *been* raped; it wasn't fun. Two big black dudes (oh God, do we have to go into this? Is it catering to racial stereotypes and prejudices to describe simple *reality?)* who offered me a ride home—what did I know, I was seventeen, quite green behind the ears—took me to a park and raped me—or tried; neither one could really get it in me, they were both too high or scared and I was tight as a virgin, which I wasn't too far from being. They settled for beating me up, taking my clothes, and leaving me semiconscious on the street in a neighborhood I'd never seen before—and even at the time, I almost couldn't help laughing. I mean, what did they get out of it? I at least got a very dramatic story to tell . . . and it did nothing to diminish my strong rape fantasies.

And that's the real wonder of fantasy: it's *not* real. You don't have to worry about it getting carried away—it will do exactly what you want, and no more. You needn't deal with it in the morning if you're not a morning person. (I am: I'm more likely to jack off when waking than any other time. A fresh beginning & all that. Daylight streaming in—it makes me feel very sexy.) There are no consequences, physical or otherwise. One of my more persistent fantasies involves a Doberman pinscher, and if I'm not mistaken, what I have in mind could get me arrested in all fifty states, if practiced. *(Why* is an utter mystery to me. I suspect the dog would enjoy fucking me, and I don't contemplate involving a third party—so who is injured? . . . but I digress.) I've never acted on this fantasy; the furthest I've gotten is encouraging an eager puppy (owned by a willing coconspirator) to lick me all over, which proved mildly titillating, and pleased the dog no end. The dog even qualified as a juvenile—proving that there is no age limit on enjoying sex. I suspect that I won't get any closer to realizing this particular fantasy anytime soon because of the dawning realization of the vast difference between fantasy and reality. Perhaps I'm losing my sense of adventure, but I no longer feel the need to experience every sensation the world has to offer. Some of them are better left to the imagination.

Which brings us to the most telling criticism of modern video erotica: the directors don't seem to understand the erotic strength of *suggestion*. They all want to bludgeon us with fifteen fucking minutes of nonstop fucking—to prove, presumably, that the participants in fact fucked for at least fifteen minutes. Thank you, I'm capable of imagining that, probably more vividly than the performers are capable of showing it.

The point here, I think, is that even if I trained a dog to fuck me—and I suspect it takes more patience than I could devote to the project—it probably would not live up to my expectations. I'm sure that, given time, I could grow fond of a dog's technique, but I doubt that it feels the same as a man fucking me. And I doubt that I could get a rubber on the dog . . . but as long as it remains untried, it will continue to be prime fantasy material.

And this is really the greatest part of being on stage: at least for the moment, I *am* these men's fantasies. I become more than just myself; I open myself up to all possible interpretations, I am anything they want me to be. It's the only time in life when I get to be more than one person; it's the only time I can forget the person I think myself to be. That husk doesn't matter now, the frenzy of imagination takes over, *they* are in control—and as often as not they don't even realize it, don't see that by beating their meat they are guiding me, molding me, exciting me, in much the same way they think I'm doing for them; they *will* me to bend over and slurp on my cockhead one more time, and I do it, smearing precum on my face—lip gloss, I call it. Without that collective energy, out there forcing me, mentally raping me, telling me in a hundred silent voices just what they'd like to do to me, surrounding me and crushing me in sexual bondage—without all that I would truly be alone on a very large stage. I have performed that way: to men who, I was sure, couldn't care less what I was doing—it's a frightening experience. I need men who are alive, who *want* something from me, who are willing to give for it. I wonder if they know what they're giving: support, enthusiasm, sexuality. An audience is at least as important to the performer as vice versa. . . . Actor? No, I don't act, I perform. "Player" if you must. "Entertainer"—I hope so, because I'm certainly entertained. Fantasy is my business, and it's a business I love. Satisfying men: now *there's* a profession worth a lifetime of pursuit.

JOHN WAGENHAUSER

SAFE SEX

WITHOUT

CONDOMS

ODYSSEUS, AN EARLY EXPERIMENTER IN SAFE SEX, FELL into it in this way: he was torn between his longing to hear the song of the Sirens and his fear. Sailors were regularly lured to their deaths by that tantalizing call. Yet Odysseus *had* to experience it, he would not shut his ears. But neither was he keen on suicide.

He found a way.

Desire, above all, desire. But desire is death, the experts urged. "So what else is new?" our hero wondered. Above all, he valued desire. "Tie me onto the mast." And they did, and he heard the Sirens singing, while his muscles ached against the ropes, and he tugged and pulled in a fury of desire but was restrained. Afterward, he said, "That was the best I ever had it. I came without even touching myself—I *couldn't* touch myself. I bit my lip." (And there was blood clotted there yet.) "I never wanted it so bad. Every inch of my skin was reaching out for them. When I get home I'm gonna have Penelope tie me down. . . ."

■   ■   ■

I remember in the early years of the AIDS crisis, desire and death and fear, all mingled together. You could feel it, palpable, everywhere in the gay community. To be afraid of our desire—we thought we'd escaped that, and now we were being called back. We who had once been afraid of going to hell, and had come out of that night, now we were afraid to die. For sex, all for sex. And the same primal responses roll into place. Old demons come to birth again: He was walking down the street when he saw him, eyes smiling encouragement, jeans sitting on his hips like a blanket folded heavy on the arm of a chair—one brush from an elbow would knock them off. Knock them off, these things on his warm brown skin, knock them off and lay bare that abdomen like a sapling stretching over the stream, that belly like a goblet, those thighs. . . .

But no, the response was fear. "I walked past," he told me with a shrug. "And then, you know, I turned around to get another look. But all of a sudden, I felt afraid. It was *here*," and he pointed to his belly. "I could feel it *here*, the fear."

Eros and Thanatos, sex and death, inextricably linked. ("So what else is new?")

Fear lacerates. It's a two-edged blade, without a handle. How to hold it, that's the problem, how to find a third alternative between total paralysis and complete denial of very real danger. We have to walk a tightrope, and balance is never easy to acquire. But creating the impossible third alternatives that we needed—that weren't offered to us by this narrow world— this is our history; this is what we've always done, this is how we came out in the first place.

One must be careful how one follows desire. ("So what else is new?") We resisted desires to plunge from precipices, laugh during funerals, and put our hands on the bodies of strangers in the subway. Desire, never a sure and trustworthy guide in and of itself, is indispensable for all that. We must not feel that it suddenly became a betrayer. (It always was. Odysseus knew, long ago.) It is not a deposed god. It never really had divinity, but it was a path to life and therefore the Godhead, and still is.

■ ■ ■

I met this guy, James. James held onto me, kissed me, his lips trembling so much you could tell his mouth was his primary sexual organ: he liked nothing better than to kiss and to bite and lick, but this was early on in the crisis, and everyone was afraid of saliva even. So when he kissed me on the mouth, he kept his lips closed, like a movie star in the fifties. He sucked my jaw, and licked me behind the ear, and came all over my stomach. . . . but kissing my mouth he kept his lips shut firm, although his eyes—open—pleaded, begged, implored desire. Tied to our masts, never has a closed-mouth, movie-star kiss been so hot, rarely has desire stood up so firm as when his eyes were begging me, and his lips were closed.

James hated condoms, but they're not at all necessary for safe sex. We used to jerk each other off while he sucked my fingers, while I bit his nipples, while his eyes locked on mine and begged and drank—such hungry eyes he had.

He used K-Y. Water soluble, it dries quickly when exposed to air, becomes sticky, a hindrance. So he kept a crystal bowl of water next to his bed, and all night his hand would dabble in the water, softly splashing, then come back to me, cool at first but once again slippery, succulent as the fruit with which goblins tempt virginity. As the alchemist knows, the antidote can be a dose of the poison itself.

And it is not desire we are to fear. It is not even sex, as the foot fetishist knows, so long as he sticks single-mindedly to his fetish: to feet, and shoes, and nylon stockings. He laughs when he hears that the preachers are saying that God's wrath is poured out on perverts. Happy pervert, he who the more purely perverted he remains, the less he has to fear.

Before anyone was aware of the human immunodeficiency virus, J.O. clubs existed, an odd sexual specialty, a bunch of queer perverts practicing safe sex before being compelled to by AIDS. Some members have expressed resentment toward the new flood of men interested in J.O. "They just want to join because of AIDS. But they don't really know what it's all about. I was into it long before AIDS."

■ ■ ■

Longing for the night, invitation folded in my pocket, I go to the bathroom five or six times to look at it. (I can't unfold it at my desk because of the drawing of two guys with very large cocks and nipples as huge as thumbs.) *Eight o'clock. Get there by eight-thirty, when we lock the doors. $10. Bring a friend, or cum alone.* My heart is turgid, heavy in fear and anticipation. I've never been to the baths, I have no experience in group sex. Now I'm going to a J.O. club. It feels like the first night I went into a gay bar, fear and anticipation. The flip side of Eros: fear. The flip side of Thanatos: anticipation. Also like the first night, when finally I knew I wouldn't go to hell for this, tonight I know I won't have unsafe sex. They have rules, masts we all ask one another to tie us to.

These are the rules:

LIPS ABOVE THE HIPS
ON ME, NOT IN ME

Rent (or borrow) someone's loft, or maybe a theater space. Buy beer and soda (in six-ounce cans; people have a habit of leaving them around unfinished). Stock up on lubricant and paper towels, artfully scattered around the room in convenient locations. Agonize over the tapes for the stereo. Trade free admissions and tips for half an evening's service on clothes check, bartending, and cleanup.

Right inside the door hand each person a hanger and position a lot of chairs nearby so they don't have to hobble around taking off their pants. There are always some bags to check, but never shoes. The floor gets sticky, so everyone keeps their socks and sneakers on. An anomaly, this room of near-naked men and dicks sticking out of jockey shorts, all clodding around in their sneakers. And they can keep their clothes tickets in their socks, too.

Most guys wear jockey-style briefs, with a few jockstraps scattered throughout. Here and there someone is naked (except for the sneakers), but on the whole there is some unspoken need to start the evening just slightly dressed in some way (which makes keeping track of your shorts a problem).

The fashion changes, evolves according to rules that escape me. One night, Calvin Klein's candy-striped briefs are in, and everyone's wearing them. Suddenly, a month later, there's a switch to those boxer briefs, half boxers and half jockeys; the familiar white cotton knit tracing the leg, duplicating the skin, all the way to midthigh. How did they know? What faint breath of the zeitgeist am I not attuned to?

One guy, short and stocky, muscular, with an arrogant look on his face, struts around in a bright yellow bathing suit— marvelously, spectacularly ill-fitting, so tight around his high round ass that the seams pull, showing white threads. Its height reaches to only just above the cheeks, where the very top of the crack between flows out to the dimples of his lower back, and the front is so low, so inadequate, that the bulk within pulls the material away from his stomach, revealing the tangle of pubic hair just above the root of his cock.

These parties always seem to take forever to get started. Everyone stands around in their underwear talking and laughing and drinking beer, catching up with friends. By now I'm an old timer, and still I never know what to say to anyone. I listen to their conversations, wondering what it is they find to say. But it's just conversation. It starts to get crowded. I like squeezing through the room, you can feel the heat come off their skin as you pass. Even when your shoulders don't touch, and your arm doesn't brush his back, still your body heat and his caress each other, like spirits intermingling. As it gets more crowded, passing through means more contact, a breast against an upper arm, a polite and gentle hand on the small of my back, a friendly pause of palm on warm cotton-clad asscheek. In conversation, someone playfully tugs at the elastic waist of my jockeys, as someone else, passing by, rubs the lump in his shorts against my buttocks.

I talk to Peter, lanky, thin, looking shy and out of place at a J.O. party—but I remember his earlier performances. He stands in his tan bikini, one arm across his chest, covering his nipples like Venus, the other clutching a can of beer. I haven't seen him in almost a year, not since he found True Love. His lover doesn't like him coming here, but lately there's a platonic third they discuss all too frequently, and Peter says, "I needed to do something real dirty again and put it in perspective."

I shake my head understandingly, not understanding—does he want me to tell him to get out of the relationship, or to tell him that they'll pull through? He seems too depressed for sex; will he have a good time? I start to run my fingernail along the rim of elastic where it crosses his abdomen, awed I realize by the presence of one I thought out of reach and affirming the chaste path. He takes another swig, and then in acknowledgment places the icy can against my nipple.

Around the fringes, there are the grumblers: "When are they going to get started?" "I have to get up in the morning." "What do they think they're *here* for?" I have sometimes taken things in hand and been the first to begin. But when the space is not open, when there are other rooms, enclosed recesses, you never know who started it, you just realize it's going on already. The guys who organize these things, they try to break up the space, even if they have to hang up sheets. People come to a sex party, and they're all walking around in their underwear or naked—hard-ons hanging out, banging around—but they still need there to be another place, the place where you "do it," the sex room. So just as in a nonsex party, where everyone crowds the kitchen, no matter how small, everyone eventually winds up packed into whatever "secluded" area there is—as though there were a possibility for seclusion or privacy here. But it's okay, I like the press of sweaty bodies.

The camaraderie is what chiefly strikes me—after, of course, the unbridled lust. (Sorry, make that "bridled lust," tied to its mast.) It's not a cruisy atmosphere as such, much friendlier. Eyes everywhere that crinkle and shine a welcome. Men still check you out, look you up and down, they're interested or they're not. But the overwhelming impersonalization of it, the absolutely uncompromised lack of commitment—not even necessarily for five minutes—adds a humaneness. The barter here is too ephemeral, so no one spends all night weighing, "Is this *the man* I want to commit my night to?" If you pause to give someone a hand in his endeavors, explore a pectoral or lat, you're still free to move on a moment later or remain for half the party. The bumblebee lands briefly on the clover flower and is gone.

(How frivolous, how fickle can you get? But the poison is the antidote.)

Saving that first orgasm for someone fantastic, someone spectacular—of course. Why come with just anybody? Yet there will be more orgasms tonight. And even when I'm popped out, no more cream in the pot, I like to wander around, linger a bit, flop my dick here and there, even if I can't get it up right now. That intercoital downtime can be as amusingly recreational as anything life offers. Or get away from the "sex room," wander over toward the bar, talk to someone you haven't noticed yet, or someone you've been stroking, or wishing you were stroking. Having just jerked off in a crowd can be quite an icebreaker.

This guy with dark curly hair—this Michelangelo-sculpted beauty, leaning against the wall, fingering the outline of his penis in his old frayed briefs—is teasing the blond with the overdeveloped chest (a rib cage that doesn't fit correctly over his stomach). I smile at something I overhear, and he says something in his friend's ear, nodding toward me. "Oh yeah," he answers, laughing at a private joke, stepping back to include me in a circle of three. "I was saying, 'I like your chest,' " says Michelangelo. I know he's flattering me, quite sure I don't have a chest that anyone's ever remarked on before. I answer, "I like your . . ."—what? he's marvelous—"everything." I blew it and laugh, embarrassed, but he laughs with me, and starts to touch my pectoral; he seems sincere about it. His name is Ray. I put my hand on his slim ass, a swimmer's ass. The blond, Jimmie, reaches forward, slides his hand along my other pectoral, down my stomach, across my swelling crotch. Ray familiarly jerks Jimmie's Calvin Kleins down to midthigh. I reach over and circle his balls and the base of his cock with my fingers, while I lean my other shoulder into Ray, who starts to kiss me, but with eyes open and intent across the room. He breaks away to say in Jimmie's ear, "Now he's ditched the tall one, he's trying to horn in on the Young Lovers."

"He," I learn, is Ray's lover. Whenever I see Ray, that night or at the next party, he always knows exactly where his lover is, what he's doing, and to whom. With grim irony, he reports to Jimmie, to me. "Which one is he?" I ask. "What's he wearing?" (I think I liked the idea of a rival.) The blue boxer shorts. The escapades of the blue boxer shorts on which Ray dryly comments never seem to me either out of place or strikingly praiseworthy. But Ray slides between exasperation and awe.

There's an acrid smell in the room, beer and fresh sweat and lubricant in plastic jars.

Groups form, a threesome or foursome here and there, or a cluster around a central core, bees vibrating on a comb. These clusters form and break continually all night: someone who everyone's been keeping track of out of the corner of their eye greases up and starts whanging—everyone wants to watch, to touch, to be a part of it (and to glean what attention for themselves they can get out of being near the center). So long as the core doesn't dissuade outside participation, the accumulation can grow like coral.

And guys laugh as they pause, looking around, and someone knows what they mean and hands them the lube from where it lay hidden behind a cluster of brown and black and pink flesh.

Then there are the exclusive *pairs*—two guys who'd rather focus on each other, no inviting eyes wandering the room, no movement, no impulse for anyone but each other. You'd think they didn't know they were in an orgy. This magic works here too. And if someone is insensitive or blind enough to approach and offer assistance, his hand is gently deflected (a move that can happen anywhere in the party, even in the most indiscriminating groups), but other than that, his existence is ignored. (But being ignored—beware—is not confined to exclusive pairings.)

But groups are my favorite. Four or more guys, in a circle, laughing, grunting, fingers locked in armpits, touching faces, reaching forward to stroke bellies—dicks moving to the rhythm of their own hand or another's—arms around one another, body weight leaning thigh into thigh, a palm weighing testes. Who's touching me? Oh, him. Hi, man. It's okay if someone joins in, even if he isn't your type, even if you wouldn't pick him out of any crowd. What's it hurt, the touch of an imperfect stranger, one more hand on your dick tonight?

And it gets awful hot (blandly, I refer to the temperature), especially in summer, with a furnace heat that under other circumstances makes me cringe from direct contact. It astounds me, how much some guys sweat, how slippery their skin gets, this juice from inside their own bodies drenching them like a swim in a salty sea—it runs off their chest, sprinkles the floor. When they shake their heads, in laughter, in ecstasy, or just to clear vision, drops fly, splashing my face.

I worm my way into a mass of bodies, toward this black guy I was talking to earlier, Paul, who's standing behind a white man with an impossibly long, skinny penis, wearing nothing but sandals and a leather string around his neck. Paul's arms are wrapped around his torso, fingertips tugging at the nipples. Their skin smacks as Paul's body makes a wet seal on his back and separates. Paul's dick is firm between the white thighs, sliding under the balls. The other guy, his hair pasted to his forehead, doesn't see me, doesn't even see the guy in front of him, working his cock. His eyes stare into some other vision, his focus perhaps the thrust between his legs. But Paul smiles at me, nodding, and I run my hand along his skin, following the sweat that flows down his dripping chest (the lube from my hand makes a stark white smear against his black skin and nipple, outlining and accentuating the muscle, like perfect lighting), down abdomen, oiling his lunging buttocks. He releases a hand, grips my balls—too tightly—I wince—he grabs my cock out of my hand, pulling me against him, against the two of them, their wet skin slapping against me from shin to knee. (With my leg I can feel Paul's white jockey shorts, taut from knee to knee, and soaked in sweat.) Paul lets go of my dick, puts his arm around my shoulder, clenching me tightly to them both with his bicep. My dick lodges in the crack where his hip slides against the thigh and buttock of the other; to catch my balance, I drape my arm around the white guy's waist, across his stomach. I try to catch his eye, but he remains oblivious. Paul kisses me and starts nibbling my lip—I'm distracted—the white guy has begun to shudder, heaving his body back and forth—his eyes relinquish whatever vision held them and roll up under the lids. . . .

It is, in large groups, necessary to communicate your orgasm widely. Everyone likes to share. "Come on man, yeah—shoot it—shoot—SHOOT!" A stinging slap on the ass is welcomed by some. So moan especially loud when you're close, something that comes from the back of the throat, the base of your gut, something that sounds like pain.

Things are slowing down. A lot of guys have left, a few groups of diehards remain among the crumpled paper towels and cans of beer that litter the floor, the chairs.

I wonder if I got so much attention tonight because I've been working out lately. But *have* I been working out all that much? Are my tits all that fantastic? Or is it more the look on my face, hungry but without desperation?

Recognition here can be as shallow and pointless as anyplace. Or, let the need on your face cross the line into "needy," and you'll be as ignored and invisible as anywhere. My caveat, as always, is, you may find a lover here, just so long as you're not looking for one. That seems to be one of the pacts Eros has made with mankind.

Some guys are getting dressed and talking, one of them that white guy with the leather string around his neck, the one who ignored me as I pressed against him and Paul. I find myself surprised as he jokes with his friends and giggles, and I think, "Well, he can smile, huh?" Just like a normal person, approachable, amicable. As I slide behind him to put my clothes ticket on the counter, he sees me, he remembers and smiles and rubs my back. I'm in heaven now: I've made a friend for life, a buddy. I'll look for him next time, but I already know he'll either remember me then or not.

PART SEVEN

POST-AIDS,

POST-

POLITICAL

As the gay world has evolved, its erotic imagination has expanded to include new possibilities and new realities. Certainly the most pressing facts of gay life in the past ten years have been AIDS and the political response to it. The threat to gay sexuality that's been posed by the right wing, often by using AIDS as a tool, has led many artists and publishers to rush to the defense of sexual expression. One of the strongest expressions of alarm has come from *Thing,* a Chicago-based publication that published a special sex issue in the summer of 1990 as a challenge to the danger its editors saw. Here's the introduction to that issue:

WARNING

Some material in this section contains graphic depictions of homosexual sexual activity. The fact that this needs a warning is a manifestation of society's ability to dictate arbitrary "standards". Who knows, a store owner might get arrested selling this to a person under eighteen.

Or perhaps *Thing* will wind up on some list at the FBI (if it's not there already!).

The fact that sexual art is under such heavy scrutiny as it is in 1990 provokes the exploration of sexuality in art, if only to assert the right of its existence. The works presented herein are a strong statement of self acceptance in the face of a "Big Brother" ready to control our desires and destinies.

In the real world, people have sex. Some with members of their own sex, others with members of the opposite. Some with both. So, what's the big deal? Isn't art supposed to be about life? The systemic devaluation of homosexual life is appalling. Gay and lesbian tax dollars and votes are separated from any representation of our rights simply because of the gender of people we choose to have sex with. Are we not members of the same "community" whose standards define obscenity? We must assert the worth of ourselves and our sexuality, and our right to full representation in the political process.

By its very nature, sex is a private thing. But by addressing it publicly, we can challenge the agenda of those who would not have us doing it in private, either.

STAND UP FOR YOUR LOVE RIGHTS

Barry Lowe, an Australian playwright, is one writer who's determined to continue to address the importance of sex in our lives. His story here represents the many writers who have used nostalgia to rekindle their sexual ardor. The character standing in the middle of a contemporary jack-off club uses a childhood incident to get himself in the mood in the middle of an exercise dictated by medical reality.

Much of gay pornography has been written with little or no overt political context. There was certainly racism in many of the simplistic tomes that portrayed black men as nothing but the passive sexual pawns of white actors. Now black gay writers are creating their own erotic images. W. Delon Strode is one. "The Reality of a Dream" is a strong evocation of the sexual power that one black man can have for another.

John Wagenhauser's "The Group" provides a powerful political context for his characters. With membership in activist organizations such as Act-Up now a common experience for many gay men, the presence of politically radical personalities in fiction is a continuation of the pornographer's drive to make his work authentic in all the details.

If Barry Lowe worked with nostalgia to face the limitations of AIDS, Stephen Greco works with dynamite in his story "Good with Words." Confronting the horrors of AIDS with a potential sexual horror, Greco also uses his story to challenge the limitations put on writing by a society living in total fear of its own lust.

BARRY LOWE

SOGGY

BISCUIT

JUST AS STEVEN WAS WRAPPING THE MILK ARROW-root biscuit in the waxed paper his mother always used for his school lunch, Graham lunged.

"If you don't want that biscuit, I'll have it," he said as his hands closed around nothing but air.

Steven wasn't about to be deprived of such a prize possession. Not on sports day. "You're always bloody hungry, Graham. Get your mother to give you more sandwiches," Steven grizzled, hiding the biscuit at the bottom of his Globite schoolcase underneath his spotted white sandshoes and his white shorts.

"You're actually going to sport this afternoon?" Tarli stared incredulous. Going to sport was unheard of in their circle. They were the sissies, the campers, as they were mocked by the more athletic members of the school. Now Steven was thinking of going to sports afternoon instead of sitting in the claustrophobic classroom of bookworms, high academic achievers and general teenage misfits with that guardian of the chron-

ically nonathletic, Miss Smith. She'd seen so many forged notes,
supposedly from parents concerned that their son not be forced
to play contact sport, that Steven's weekly "Please excuse Steven from sport this afternoon on account of he's suffering from
asthma" amused her only inasmuch as he'd obviously looked
up the correct spelling of the disease from which he was supposedly suffering. Most of the others didn't even bother with
this degree of subterfuge, although their disabilities made for
more entertaining reading.

Simon was dismissive of Steven's efforts to join those more
athletically inclined. "Steven's heard they play soggy biscuit in
the dressing sheds after soccer."

"So that's why the milk arrowroot?" Tarli twigged.

"What's soggy biscuit?" Graham asked. The others had
always considered him the most dim-witted, not because of a
lack of intelligence—if anything he had too much but didn't
turn it to something that would prove useful, something like
thinking about subjects other than math and French and chemistry. Graham was an achiever.

Not that he wasn't interested in the boys at school. But
he was a one-boy boy. Always had been. Always would be, the
others guessed. He'd set his heart a little less highly than the
others, on one of the friendlier and less perfectly handsome
and, therefore in Graham's eyes at least, one of the more at-
tainable prefects. While Steven and Tarli aimed highest, for the
school captain, handsome in a boyish, open sort of way, and
the school vice captain whose dark Mediterranean looks hid
that smoldering sexuality that suggested he'd beat the shit out
of you if you so much as approached him.

But Steven had heard that both of them were open to a
little game of soggy biscuit if the mood was right and it usually
was after Wednesday afternoon sport, away from the spotlight
and the inquisitive stares of the teachers. They had reputations
to uphold. Not like Michael Crowe who used to flash his dick
in the toilet at lunchtime if anybody asked. Steven and Tarli
had seen it once and they hadn't even been excited enough to
touch, like some of the younger members of the school had.

Michael's father was some big wheel in the infant television industry. Or so Michael told Steven one day when he invited him to his house. Steven declined, not so much because he didn't want to go—the idea of touching Michael's dick when no one else was around had its appeal—but because he knew his father wouldn't let him go. Michael's reputation was legendary, even outside the school. Why, one year he hitched to Melbourne for the running of the Cup. He'd take his clothes off in the train and flash his dick at the schoolgirls from the school over the railway line. Michael was like some doomed exotic creature that was performing for its very life.

"Graham!" Tarli said with an edge of put-down in his voice. "Haven't you heard of soggy biscuit?"

"Even I've heard of soggy biscuit." Simon felt superior for one of the few times in his school career. "But don't they normally play it with a Sao biscuit?"

"Mum was all out of Saos," Steven said. "This milk arrowroot was the closest she had. Anyway I don't much like Saos."

"So tell me, what's soggy biscuit?" Graham was persistent. It was his most endearing, and his most irritating, quality.

"Well," said Tarli taking a deep breath and speaking as if to a child. "You put the biscuit, usually a Sao," he glanced quickly at Steven, "but a milk arrowroot will do, you put the biscuit on the ground . . ."

"Doesn't it get all dirty?"

"Graham, do you want to know what soggy biscuit is or not?"

"Yes."

"Then shut up and let me finish."

"And don't sulk," Steven added when he saw Graham pout at being told what to do.

"You put the biscuit on the ground," Tarli continued. "And then everybody stands around it in a circle. And then they all sort of pull themselves."

"What?"

"They pull themselves off over the biscuit," Tarli repeated impatiently and also a little embarrassedly.

"Why?"

Steven jumped to Tarli's aid. "The idea is that you get your dick out of your shorts and pull yourself off over the biscuit. . . ."

"But it must be hard to aim at such a small target." Graham was being pedantic again.

"It doesn't matter if some of it misses, just so long as some of it gets on the biscuit," Steven ploughed on.

"Surely a slice of bread would be better," Graham said with all the practicality of the innocent. "Or a pancake."

"Graham, you don't understand," Simon was exasperated.

"You're right. Why would grown boys want to stand around a biscuit and pull themselves off?"

"For a start," Tarli said, "you get to see everyone else's dick."

"For seconds," Simon added, "you get to pull yourself in public."

"I wish you'd use the proper word," Graham interrupted. "Masturbate sounds much nicer."

"Been at the dictionary again, Graham?" Tarli could scarcely conceal his contempt.

"So what's so exciting about masturbating on a stupid old biscuit? I'd much rather do it while I'm looking at my muscle magazines."

"Ah, but the purpose of soggy biscuit," Steve was asserting himself again, "is that the last person to cum," he paused for effect, "has to eat the biscuit."

Graham's mouth opened in disgust. He didn't believe Steven's explanation. "That would make you sick!"

"No it doesn't. At least I've never heard of anyone being sick from it."

"And they do this in the dressing sheds after soccer?"

"Every Wednesday."

"I don't believe you."

"Have you ever done it before?"

Tarli looked at Steven as if to warn him off.

"Well . . ."

"You haven't?" Simon asked in surprise.

"Not with anyone from school," Steven admitted reluctantly.

"Tarli! You and Steven?"

"We had to practice our technique somehow," Tarli sounded defensive.

"Why wasn't I invited?" Simon wailed.

"Because your mother doesn't let you eat sweet biscuits," Steven said.

"I can bring my own Sao next time." Simon was miffed. Unlike the others in the group he'd set his sights a little more realistically. Not the school captain, vice captain, not even one of the prefects. He'd set his heart on Steven. They'd mucked about in a childish sort of way at Steven's place one night when his parents were out but Steven's lunge for his crotch was so unexpected and, Simon suspected, done more in fun than lust, that nothing had come of it.

Simon had visions of living with Steven after school although they'd never talked about it. In fact, none of them ever talked about leaving home. They'd just never thought about it.

"They eat the biscuit?" Graham was obviously in awe of the outcome of the schoolboy game. "Why would you want to eat it? I don't understand."

"It's the punishment," Simon said. "For losing."

"So the aim is to cum as quickly as possible so you don't have to be the one to eat the biscuit? The soggy biscuit?"

"Now you're getting it."

Graham's mind was now working on the mechanics of the operation. "So how quickly can you do it?"

"I haven't timed myself, why?"

"Well you don't want to be too slow about it otherwise you'll be the one who has to eat it."

"So?" Steve was being practical.

"You don't want to eat the biscuit?"

Steven nodded his head "yes" as Graham attempted to take in what he was hearing. "But think of the germs. You'll end up in hospital."

"I don't expect you to understand, Graham."

"And, quite frankly, I don't."

"Have you been practicing?" Tarli asked.

"I've found out a method of pulling my dick where it's not so sensitive," and Steven began to demonstrate.

"You know I hear Michael Crowe has a hole in the pocket of his shorts so he can play with himself while he's waiting for the ball," Simon said then giggled at his unintentional joke.

"I don't think I could show my penis in public," Graham said.

"Is that why you use the cubicle when you go to pee?" Tarli laughed.

"Simon gets a stiffy in the showers after PE," Steven said.

"I do not!"

"You do so, I've seen you."

"Well, you shouldn't be looking."

"A dressing shed full of stiffies." Tarli was in heaven just thinking of it.

The hooter sounded, calling them to their respective afternoon lines. Tarli and Simon went reluctantly to Miss Smith's sports-evaders' line, jealous at Steven's pluck, while Graham had already forgotten the lunch-hour conversation and had his nose buried in a book of poetry that would occupy his afternoon productively. Simon and Tarli, on the other hand, would have their faces buried, too, in books but their imaginations would be with Steven and a dressing shed full of stiffies.

As it was, Steven's reality was nowhere near the success of Tarli's and Simon's combined fantasies. Not only had Steven forgotten the rules of soccer, he'd actually put his hands out to catch the ball when it had come toward him. It was an automatic reflex, he told his angry team members. And to his later mortification, Richard Beeby, the kid was so low on the school pecking order that even the sissies didn't talk to him, had also volunteered for sport that afternoon and had proved somewhat adept at kicking the ball at the right time and, even more galling, in the right direction. As Steven's stocks plummeted, so Richard's rose. He saw his chances of being invited to the soggy biscuit rapidly fading.

And all because of that Richard kid who they hadn't given

the time of day when he'd wanted to join their sissy ranks. They'd rather cruelly rejected him and he'd become a loner. . . .

His thoughts about Richard were rudely interrupted when he heard his name called and he turned back to the direction of play just in time for the ball to bounce off his forehead. It scrambled his brains and gave him a terrible headache but obviously he'd done something right because the other members of his team were shouting their approval and running toward him. It was only later that he'd discovered that his head butt of the ball had sent it flying in the direction of the opposition team's goal, enabling one of his more able teammates to sink it for the winning point.

While he was feted for his cool thinking and excellent head pass he thanked the gods that no one had seen it for what it was—an incredible fluke. Now he would be hero enough to get that much-sought-after soggy biscuit invite.

"Good head pass," Richard Beeby said to him quietly as they headed for the showers.

"You did pretty good for yourself, Richard," Steven said without malice now.

They'd come to an understanding but not a truce because in that instant of conversation Steven could sense that the major battle was to come. Richard Beeby was after that biscuit, too.

The showers were the buildup to what was to come. Everyone behaved like a yahoo—splashing water, flicking towels painfully at the groin area of others, making sarcastic comments about being a "camper" (they never got the terminology correct) if someone were caught looking at anyone's crotch for too long. The school captain and vice captain sailed through these shenanigans nonchalantly, confident in their position within the schoolboy hierarchy, reinforced by the rather large and hairy appendages that dangled between their legs. They were the envy of everyone.

Richard also seemed to be sailing through the welter of dicks with blithe disregard while Steven was finding it difficult to concentrate on what he was doing. A few of the rowdier elements in the showers had sprayed him and flicked at him

with their towels but he'd had no stomach for joining in. He
was afraid there would be no soggy biscuit that afternoon.

"How about a game of soggy biscuit to welcome the new
boys?" David, the school captain, said quietly. The dressing
area erupted in a chorus of agreement and Steven relaxed for
the first time that afternoon.

"So, anyone got a biscuit?" David continued. There was
a sudden look of distress which Steven took delight in because
he could suddenly produce his milk arrowroot and save the
day.

"What sort of biscuit do you need?" It was Richard Beeby
asking the question. Steven couldn't believe his ears.

"A Sao's best," David said. "Do you have one?"

"I think I do," Richard replied, searching through his
schoolbag, at last producing the desired object. At that moment
Steven had murder in his heart.

"Great!" David said taking the biscuit from him and placing it on the concrete floor. "We're never organized enough to
remember to bring one. Sometimes we have to play without
the biscuit."

Steven's mind boggled.

"Do you new boys know the rules?"

Both Steven and Richard said they sort of knew but would
he explain them? They both wanted to hear David explain the
details of the orgy that was about to take place and about which
they'd only heard rumors before.

The participants were already gathering around the sport-
ing arena as David outlined the very strict rules of the competition, stressing that if they were losing they could not pull
out and that they would be forced to eat the biscuit even if
they had to be held down to do so.

It was ironic, Steven noted in later life, that the proof of
virility at these games was the speed with which you could cum,
whereas later it would be how long you could hold off from
orgasm. But that was in the future. All Steven cared about now
was beating Richard Beeby to that coveted cum-splattered Sao.

The competition began informally. Some of the boys already had erections and were tugging them in as many fashions

as there were acne spots. As they were about to blow they would move toward the biscuit and deposit as much of the fluid as possible on the desired target. These were the boys to whom the event was merely a game; there was no redeeming erotic element at all. The second wave were those to whom the erotic element was palatable and they got off on the idea of displaying themselves in the all-male environment.

There was an unwritten rule that the school captain never lost. About midway through the game the frenzy of pulling stiffies would subside and the boys would give way as David made his way to the biscuit and deposited his load with a great deal of groaning and swearing. The others stood back in awe as the stream of cum arced in the air, hung there glistening for milliseconds and fell to be mingled and married with that already jellying on the forlorn Sao.

Steven and Richard had been regulating their strokes deliberately, Steven trying hard not to memorize the dimensions, colors, and techniques of those stiffies around him. He looked over at Richard, who was glassy-eyed, concentrating for all he was worth on the one possession he was determined to win. They were the only two remaining in the competition, the others having cum very quickly after David, lest they be left with what, to them, was the undesirable end product.

But Steven's mind was stuck in a groove like a scratched record. The pictures in his mind were on a loop, and he was playing over and over the magnificent spectacle of David's orgasm, an event so cataclysmic to his limited experience that before he could stop himself he, too, was depositing his load on top of David's.

He let out a low "Oh, no" as he realized he had lost the game. A triumphant Richard Beeby unloaded a matter of seconds later to the jeers and smutty comments of those who still had any interest in the game.

Those who had wandered away for a surreptitious cigarette now returned to watch the ultimate humiliation.

"You don't really expect me to eat that?" said Richard pointing to the jelly Sao on the floor.

"It's part of the rules," David said seriously. "If you don't we'll be forced to feed it to you."

"Go ahead and try," Richard said defiantly.

That was all they needed, and a roomful of naked male bodies grabbed him and held him while others, their dicks dangling all over his body, pushed the jelly Sao into what Steven thought was a remarkably unreluctant mouth. Richard caught Steven's expression and smiled. He'd won. Maybe no one else in the room, bar Steven, would have thought of it as a victory. But Richard did. And in his struggle with all those naked boys he was being touched. He was being talked about. He was being thought about. Steven mouthed the word "bastard" when he next caught Richard's eye.

The last of the biscuit disappeared down Richard's throat and he was thrown into the shower to wash off. The game was over. The sexual tension had been relieved. By the time Steven left the dressing sheds all the boys had disappeared. They hadn't waited for him. The next day he would be back to being a sissy again. He hadn't won the ultimate prize but he'd seen their stiffies and the way they used them. He had enough to fuel years of fantasies. He walked out of the dressing sheds, leaving Richard in the showers humming happily to himself.

That had been twenty-five years ago yet Steven found himself in a similar circle, jerking off with a group of men. They were anonymous men. Sure they had bigger cocks, better technique, and great bodies. It was one of the safe-sex circle-jerk clubs he had joined hoping to recreate those feelings from his schooldays in the early 1960s. But there had been no need to bring a biscuit. It was no longer safe to play soggy biscuit.

And in the dark anonymity of the steam bath he ached for those schooldays of lust and innocence.

W. DELON STRODE

THE REALITY

OF A

DREAM

AWAKENING WITH SUCH AN ABRUPTNESS, XAVIER found himself wondering where he was. His heart . . . it beat with such intensity. The air around him . . . so black and dark, so stifling and humid.

Perspiration caused the sheets to cling to him, not to mention something semihard beneath the sheets. He slowly began to realize that he was at home, in the bed, *alone!*

Leaning over to read the fluorescent numbers on the alarm clock, he read them in slow motion: 2:49 A.M.

Still trying to catch his breath, he sighed. "Just another fucking dream. There's no way I can get back to sleep after this hype." With one hand he reached for his robe and with the other hand, a cigarette. Realizing at this moment that the air-conditioner was on the blink again, he dismissed the notion of the robe and trudged innocently naked to the kitchen and opened the refrigerator.

"Aahh! That's better," he sighed as he turned up the pitcher allowing the ice-cold juice to run past his mouth, down his neck, across his chest, and down his throat. "I have got to fix this air-conditioner!" Returning the juice to the freezer and slamming the door, he took a drag of his Newport and headed for the nearest ashtray.

Upon reentering his bedroom and tossing on the robe previously thrown to the side, Xavier realized that in his bedroom the heat seemed to magnify. Turning on the lamp and sitting on the bed, Xavier peeked at the unit that at this moment wasn't even serving as reasonable decoration. As he bent knees to chest to check the extension cord, his dick fell away from his robe into the open as if it were attempting to demand attention. At the sight of this black, uncut, damn-near-seven-inch, semihard cock, he instantly remembered the reason he was awake at this very moment. As he repeatedly muttered, "What a motherfucking dream," vivid visions came to mind of the dream that moments before had been his only existence. "I'm tired of living in a world of dream," Xavier snapped as he pulled the extension cord from the wall. Pictures of the fine stud's ass that he had come so close to penetrating in his dream danced wildly about in his tortured mind. His dick began to grow, and as it grew, began to cry for release.

Forgetting all about the air-conditioner, Xavier took off his robe, reached behind the nightstand, grabbed the sample of K-Y lubricant, and lay back on the waterbed to take care of the ache in his loins.

With closed eyes, rapidly beating heart, and lubed dick, Xavier thought about the dream stud. He was chiseled to perfection, muscles rippling everywhere through the strains of the spandex biker's tops and shorts. The neon-blue shirt grasped his upper body as if to say, "Mine!" The shorts clung even tighter giving an almost transparent view of the muscular cheeks of an ass that screamed, "All yours!"

In most of his dreams, Xavier didn't recall many details of where and when. The dreams lasted no more than three or four minutes anyway; just long enough for him to get erotically upset and to awake possessing that feeling of incompleteness.

This particular dream, however, was different. The feeling that came over Xavier was one of complete awareness of every detail. He was at the park, sitting next to the water under a big weeping willow, feeding Ruffles to the ducks and squirrels. He had been running and was panting and breathing quite heavily. Suddenly there was another presence in the dream with him and he turned to investigate. *Boom!*

Not more than ten feet away was one hell of a dream stud! Standing at 6′1″ or taller the man was the epitome of Adonis. With his back toward Xavier, nothing but sheer, athletic muscles adorned his chocolate body. Screaming cheeks that begged for a warm pair of hands to caress them, a hot, wet tongue to bathe them, and a long, thick, uncut dick to fill them were poised for Xavier's enjoyment.

Suddenly, as if he felt the gazes that were being thrust upon him, the stud turned and returned Xavier's gaze with a piercingly beautiful pair of brown eyes. His hair was faded asymmetrically, his face smooth and clean shaven.

For what seemed like hours, their gazes at each other continued. Xavier began to let his eyes nonchalantly wander down the stranger's body. Nice, big, faintly hairy arms and legs; thick thighs; rippling stomach muscles; and "oh hell no . . ." Xavier thought as he looked finally at the stud's print. The guy was obviously wearing nothing but the skin beneath the spandex shorts as the very thick circumcised print of a huge dick showed itself most clearly.

"Hello." The stranger finally spoke.

"What's up?" Xavier responded. After seeing this guy give such a magnificent profile, Xavier didn't want to move, for his own dick had begun to grow considerably.

"Nice, huh?" the stud asked.

Not knowing if he were referring to himself, the weather, or to what, Xavier responded with a safely toned, "Yes, very." As he threw the last of the chips into the water for the ducks, Xavier stood and stretched, giving the stranger equal opportunity to check out his physique. And it was obvious that the first thing noticed was this humongous, thick dick that seemed to reach halfway down the thigh. It, too, was straining against a pair of biker shorts and the print exposed left nothing to the imagination.

Obviously moved by what he saw, the stranger decided to take the seat by the water that Xavier had relinquished. For the first time, Xavier noticed that he was breathing rather heavily. "Been running?"

"Yeah," was the answer, "every day for at least two hours."

What do I say next, Xavier thought as he simultaneously spoke, "You look like you might spend a lot of time at the gym as well."

"Three times a week is all I can spare for the gym, but I run every day, rain or shine. And you?" the stud asked gazing at Xavier's print. "Seems as if your muscle has seen quite a few workouts." At that, Xavier was at a loss for words. It was obvious that this guy was wanting a response. Statements like that are just not made nonchalantly without hopes of something more than a verbal response.

"Oh, it's been a while," Xavier said as he ran his hand across the length of his dick.

"Wanna work out with me?" the stranger asked. Before Xavier could answer, the stranger had stood and begun to take off his shorts. Ass turned toward Xavier, he reached behind, pulled at Xavier's dick and said, "Work me out, please!"

It was at that moment that Xavier woke up. He couldn't determine whether it was the fever the dream stud had given him or the fever from the malfunctioning air-conditioner that awoke him.

Trying desperately to add the proper ending to the dream as he jacked his black meat back and forth and faster and faster, Xavier just gave up and decided to save this load for another session.

Going to the washroom to clean up, he decided to try the switch on the fuse box and see if that would kick the air back on. It worked. He smoked another cigarette, brushed his teeth, and crawled his naked flesh back into bed.

JOHN WAGENHAUSER
WRITING AS WOLFGANG

THE

GROUP

I CAN'T SAY WHAT CITY WE'RE IN. WE JUST CALL
ourselves "the group." We're anarchists, revolutionaries—
strictly underground.

We're a bug up the system's ass. They call us terrorists,
but we don't believe in violence against people. We're into
subversion: vandalism, trashing computer systems, stealing
stuff—even just graffiti—anything to fuck up the system, and
remind them that we're here, and that they're worthless, hyp-
ocritical, and stupid. Getting away with it—that's all that mat-
ters. Break the rules and get away with it and come back with
something bigger, bolder, harder, more dangerous.

Because everything this society stands for is fucked up.
Like Arthur says, we gotta reject everything society stands for.

There are seven of us, five guys and two women. We don't
have a leader, we're totally democratic. But Arthur—that's not
really his name of course—he's not officially leader or anything,
but he's the best, the ultimate—he doesn't know any limits.
He's like, the total anarchist. And he's always at the center of

everything we do. We don't have any leaders, but whatever Arthur says, whatever he dares us to do, that's usually what we do.

Arthur doesn't look like much. He's medium height, and he keeps his brown hair cut short. A lot of his clothes come from thrift stores. Arthur believes the first duty of a revolutionary is to survive. For that you need protective camouflage. It's dangerous to be conspicuous.

But when he opens his mouth, you have to listen. He's caustic, aware, always questioning everything. You start admiring his mind, but then you notice the way he moves. He's never clumsy, never hurries, but he's always right where he should be. He's like an animal, at home in his own body.

You could say I was pretty hot for Arthur—not that I dreamed of ever letting anyone know. I was ashamed of all these gay feelings I had. Being gay, that was too wimpy. I joined the group because I wanted to give myself self-confidence. Not be shy and timid all the time, but bust the world's ass.

So it killed me that Arthur always called me "the kid," and then everyone else did, too. And I felt like a total kid too, a stupid dork kid, wanting him all the time—except, like, when we were breaking into some place—then I felt so high, so powerful. We'd be so exhilarated, we'd grab each other and hug. Arthur would say, "You done great kid," and hug me so I could smell his curly hair. I only wound up wanting him more than ever.

We were all sitting around one night, talking about what to do next—Arthur, Kurt, John, Scott, Janice, Red, and me—the whole group. We started jawing about this and that, and Arthur was being real quiet, which always makes us keep an eye on him, because it means he's thinking, and when he opens his mouth, it changes the group, it brings in a new climate, a new direction. Kurt hates this, and I could see him getting jumpy. You see, because no one ever said Arthur was in charge or anything, it just happened, but Kurt wishes it was him. You can tell he likes to run things. He's short but real stocky, real muscular, blond and handsome and all. And always taking his shirt off and showing his muscles and his skin. When he walks, he swings his shoulders around real wide, a short guy with big shoulders and a compact, hard ass, and it bothers him that everyone listens to Arthur all the time. We'll do what Kurt wants sometimes, but only if Arthur agrees. No one else in the group notices it, this supersubtle tension between them, but often I see their eyes meet for a split second—and I know that they know.

Well, this one night, I was watching Kurt. He could hardly sit still, because he knew Arthur was going to say something, we could all feel it.

But none of us expected what he said. He lifted up his head, and he moved his eyes around the room, looking at each one of us—looking into *each* one of us—and he said:

"We ought to have an orgy."

Immediately, I felt a lump in my throat—and in my pants. I'd give anything to see these guys naked, watching them pumping into a woman. But I was terrified too. I felt naked at the threat of having these desires pulled out into the open. This was the one secret I had from the group.

So I don't know if I was more relieved or disappointed when I heard everyone else's reaction.

"We don't have enough women," John said, and you could tell he wished we did. He's a big guy, tall and beefy up top. A handsome guy, with a profile that always made me wonder whether it was true what they say, that a big nose means you have a big dick. John's was prominent and solid and thick, and I'd often caught myself staring at his crotch to try to get a hint.

Red snarled, "Laying on my back while you guys pull the train ain't exactly my idea of a good time."

"Yeah," said Janice. "You're not gonna queue up for a joyride on *my* belly. Fuck that shit!"

Scott laughed and said, "I guess we need a pussy recruitment drive."

Kurt didn't say anything. He was gauging the group, watching Arthur, wondering what was next.

Arthur shook his head. "You are one piss-ass bunch of anarchists," he said. "You say, 'We break all the rules, we're not afraid to do anything.' But when it comes time to prove it, you all tiptoe away."

Nobody dared to move a muscle, but everybody knew what he meant—they must have.

With a smirk on his face, Arthur got up, opened a bag he had brought, and dumped a pile of about fifty rubbers on the floor—rubbers and lubricant and shit. Then, still smirking, he walked across the room—right toward me. Outside, I was frozen; inside, my heart was banging away at about one hundred miles an hour. He walked right up to me, and in front of everyone he put his fingertips under my chin, lifted my face up to him—his open mouth hit my lips, his tongue, hot and slimy, slid into my mouth. His cheeks against my face were like sandpaper. I closed my eyes and kissed him back. I pushed my tongue into his mouth too. He pulled me up by the shoulders so I was standing and pulled me into his chest.

I put my hands on his ass—I was too embarrassed—moved them up to his waist. I had my eyes clamped shut, terrified. I could feel all of them watching us. When I opened my eyes for a second, I could see his black eyes glittering at me; Arthur never closed his eyes, he watched everything.

He was grinding his hips into my crotch. It was then that I realized I was as hard as a rock, all cramped up into a ball inside my shorts, and he was hard too; I could feel a knot in his jeans, that he rubbed up, down, around the lump in mine.

He pulled away from my face, leaning back from me, thrusting his hips against mine. I could feel his hands—I kept my eyes shut tight, my mouth open. I was trembling, knowing that his black eyes were still on me, that they were all watching us. He put his hands on my chest and rubbed them up and down and up and down to my pants. He grabbed the waistband, flicked it open with this thumb—my breath was stopped, my eyes shut tight, I was floating in space, floating in blackness with my heart booming in my ears and his hands tugging my zipper down, tugging my pants down off my hips, down my thighs. Sweat poured down my sides, my mouth dry. Somewhere there was a room with the lights on and the group watching Arthur grab the elastic of my underwear, wrenching it down—then a burst of light as my dick bobbed out, straight and hard, and I opened my eyes in the bright room, meeting his sparkling black eyes under his curly hair and saw there was sweat on his forehead too. He nodded at me, smiling, as he pulled down his zipper and reached in, bending over so he could get it out, pulled out his cock, and held it in his hand—long and deep red, hard like a tensed muscle.

He held it tight in his hand, stroking it, and grabbed mine with his other hand, pulled on it roughly, pulling me forward, so that I put my hands on his waist to keep my balance. He kissed me again, lightly, pulling my dick, barely kissing me, his open eyes smiling encouragement. With Arthur's eyes on me, smiling like that, it didn't matter what the others thought.

He put his hands on my neck, my shoulder, pressing down gently, furrowing his brows into a question, a request. I knew what he wanted. I could feel my dick bouncing against his, hot as a poker, could feel the hot flesh of his cock and the roughness of his jeans.

What did it matter what the others thought? I wanted to do what he wanted. I lowered myself onto my knees. It was hard with my pants around my calves, but I got down on the floor, and stared at that rod sticking out of the dark slit in his pants. I opened my lips and took the head into my mouth. It was slimy on the end, with a salty flavor. I could smell sweat and—Arthur. He leaned forward, and I let about half the shaft slide into my mouth, until it hit the roof of my mouth, then I pulled back, then I let it slide in again.

Arthur grunted. He started tugging at my T-shirt, pulling it up. I had to let him out of my mouth as he pulled it off—I was grateful to feel the cool air hit my sweaty back and sides.

I took him in my mouth again, pressing my lips against his cock, licking the bottom with my tongue. I slid my head over his hard dick again and again, until I started to choke from it hitting the back of my throat. I sat back and looked up at him, sheepish. He grinned and shrugged, like, "Couldn't do better myself." He took off his shirt while I licked my tongue around the head of his dick, tasting the salty warmth again, getting ready to try to take it all in my mouth. "Yeah," he said.

He threw his shirt behind me and opened his belt. I helped him tug his jeans down around his ankles, then ran my hands up his hairy legs—what great big balls he had, swinging in front of my face, below that red stick! I took it in my mouth again, let it slide back, back, until I almost choked, then slid it out, and in again.

"What do you think this is, a show?" he said, loud to the rest of the group. He put his hands on my jaw and pulled out of my mouth.

"Yeah, Janice and Red have the right idea." He started to kick out of his shoes, his jeans. The women were sitting next to each other now, their arms around each other, kissing.

Scott had a big smile on his face, rubbing himself up and down the front of his pants, turning his head from me and Arthur to where the women were groping each other. John was sitting next to him on the couch, dumbfounded; Kurt was watchful.

"This is a participatory democracy, damnit," Arthur said, and everyone laughed, Scott the loudest, and he yanked open his pants, pulling his hard cock out of his jockeys.

Naked, Arthur strode over to the couch where Scott was now wanking himself, sitting closer to John. He put his hand on John's shoulder. "Come on, John, let's get this show on the road. Go down on him." Coaxing. "Go ahead." Half playful, half pleading. John laughed, embarrassed, good-natured. Under Arthur's eyes, he put out his big hand, like a clumsy paw, and circled Scott's rod. "Well, kiss him at least," Arthur said. Scott scuttled over closer to John and started kissing his mouth. Short, embarrassed kisses, like he was just trying it out, surprised that it felt okay. Arthur, leaning over them, started fumbling with John's pants. When he got his cock free, I almost gasped. I was right: it was immense! It looked like it must be ten inches, a great marble column of meat, already hard.

As I sat there pulling my pants off, out of the corner of my eye I saw Kurt stand up. Slowly, methodically, he unbuttoned his shirt. I realized his feet were already bare. He was watching Scott and John kissing and pulling each other's joints, while Arthur hovered over them and pulled off their clothes. I wanted Arthur to come back to me, I wanted him to leave them alone and let me take his dick in my mouth again.

Now Scott lowered himself onto the floor and, leaning over John's massive thighs, he opened his mouth wide and engulfed the head of his cock. John fell back and grinned, an unbelieving look on his face, glancing up at Arthur and over at the women. They were half naked too, and Janice had her face buried in Red's lap. I had the feeling they'd done this before.

On the other side of the room, Kurt was standing in his white jockeys, surveying it all, and rubbing the front of his crotch. Honey tan and blond, his body was covered with a light fur of golden hair. Exact muscles outlined his chest, with little red quarter-sized nipples in the center of each pectoral. His stomach was hard and rippled, his flanks smooth and muscular. The soft, warm, white cotton jockeys wrapped around his perfect hard butt.

"Come on, Scott," Arthur was saying. "The kid did better than that. He wasn't afraid to choke a little." Suddenly something white flew across the room. Kurt had thrown his jockeys at Arthur's feet. Everyone looked at the shorts, then at Kurt— he stood naked, his dick jutting out from its warm brownish-yellow nest. The air stopped moving in the room. He and Arthur must have stared at each other for a full minute, Kurt's one hand open at his side while he massaged his thick golden dick with his other.

Slowly, Kurt walked across the room to Arthur. Arthur stepped forward. Their eyes were locked on one another. Everybody was watching them, like they suddenly realized that something they didn't know was at stake was being resolved. Kurt walked right up to Arthur, looking up into his eyes— Kurt could make being looked up at feel dangerous—and carefully, deliberately, put his hand on Arthur's shoulder. I swallowed. Arthur nodded, his black curls bobbing. "Fuck me," he whispered.

I could hear Scott sharply inhale and realized we'd all stopped breathing. Kurt smiled—half snarled, almost. With Kurt's hand on his shoulder, Arthur squatted, knelt, then sat on the floor in the middle of all the condoms. He picked one up, handed it up to Kurt.

Nobody was moving. Only I noticed Scott slowly stroking his dick, watching. Looking down now at Arthur, Kurt unpeeled the rubber, unrolled it along his golden rod, then knelt between Arthur's legs. Arthur leaned back on his elbows, moving his legs farther apart to accommodate Kurt between them. All the while their eyes never broke, but held the line between them, as Kurt spread lubricant along his shaft.

"You want it?"

"Yeah."

"Say you want it. Arthur—say you want it."

"Fuck me, Kurt. I want you to fuck me."

"Say you want my dick up your ass."

Arthur lay back, flat on the floor, and threw his hands out behind his head. "I want your dick up my ass, Kurt"—a harsh whisper—"I've done everything in the world but murder, blow my dog, and take it up the ass. I don't think I'll ever suck off a dog, but now I want a dick up my ass." He lifted a leg and hooked his ankle on Kurt's neck. "And I want you to do it, Kurt. I want you to be the first."

Kurt put his hands under Arthur's thighs, spreading him out, and looked at his asshole. I couldn't believe what I was seeing as Kurt leaned forward with his hand on his cock, aiming it into Arthur. Arthur's eyes on the ceiling waited. I watched them wince—open wide in surprise. Kurt hissed through his teeth, pushing in. Arthur gasped—held his breath—moaned in the back of his throat. His fists were locked tight behind his head, his arms tensed so hard they looked like anchor cables. His whole body was rigid as Kurt slid back out and then, with his toes in the rug, started to push forward—

Arthur's hands came around quickly, landing one on Kurt's shoulder, one on his butt. "*Oooh,* man—go *slow*. Oh, Kurt. *God*—this takes dedication. Being a homosexual ain't sissy stuff."

On the couch, John laughed, a nervous laugh. He sounded like I felt. Like he was staring so hard, he could feel Kurt's thing shoving into his own butthole. John's cock was standing up rock hard like a tower.

"Easy is for wimps, Arthur," Kurt said, clenching his teeth and ramming home.

Arthur closed his eyes—tight—and nodded. His hands fell off of Kurt's back. They gripped into fists so tight the veins bulged. He pressed his knuckles against the floor hard enough to lift himself high, while Kurt plunged in, working back and forth like a piston looking for revenge.

We all sat, listening to them breathe and grunt, watching beads of sweat appear first on Arthur's face, then on Kurt's, until they started to drip down off his hair.

But Arthur never asked Kurt to slow down again.

Kurt even tried to get him to, or maybe he wanted to relent. He said, "How is it Arthur? Is this too hard for you?"

"No—*uhn*. Hard . . . as you want . . . as you . . . want it, Kurt . . ."

And again: "Hard . . ."

So Kurt kept slamming into him until he started going, "Ah . . . Ah . . ." and then we knew it was almost over. It seemed like it took forever. Kurt dug into the rug and lifted Arthur clear off the floor, from his legs to the middle of his back, going *"Unngh! Unngh!"* and screwing up his face so tight you'd think he was the one getting fucked.

When he pulled out, we all just sat there for a minute, transfixed in awe. It was like this sacred moment, having sat together and watched Arthur—*Arthur*—get fucked in the ass. There was this embarrassed, respectful air. Us, the group— ain't that a joke?

Arthur broke it. "Don't wait for me, guys 'n' gals. Keep the boat moving. I'll jump in in a minute."

The girls started kissing again, and Scott turned back to John and put his mouth over the top of that tower of meat. Kurt was beaming, glowing with victory where he knelt between Arthur's legs, pulling off the rubber. I sat there, wanting Arthur to turn to me, wanting to taste him again.

He rolled his head toward me. "I didn't forget ya, kid."

He swung his legs around Kurt's head, and tossed me a plastic-wrapped condom.

"Why don't you go where angels have trod?"

I was in shock. Did he really want me to? I almost didn't dare, but Arthur ripped open the condom, grabbed my still-hard dick, and started rolling it down. His hands felt so good on me, so warm, glopping the lubricant on. Then he put one greasy hand on my chest and leaned forward, kissing me. I closed my eyes and kissed him back, jabbing my tongue into his mouth. This time I grabbed his shoulders, his pecs—I let my hands run over him, feeling his back, his armpits, his biceps, his muscled thighs—really touching him at last. I rubbed my face against those sandpaper cheeks, pressing into his lips. As I kissed him, he pulled back, drawing me forward until he was lying on the rug and I was on top of him, our hard dicks pressing and rubbing between our bellies.

Arthur lifted his legs around me, around my butt, so I could get at his ass. I kneeled there, his thighs spread around me, his crack spread, revealing the little pucker of a hole, the hairs still curled wet and sticky from the gunk. Above it his balls, like golf balls caught tight in their sack of skin, and then his cock, hard across the belly, with the red knob on top.

I leaned forward, picking up his legs so his hole was higher, and positioned my dick right on it. I looked at his face. He looked a little grim, like he always did right before a job. But he forced a smile and nodded like he always did too: "This is gonna go great."

So I pushed the head in. I had never fucked a guy before. I couldn't believe how tight it was in there—in Arthur. He inhaled, real harsh, and the edges of his mouth trembled, but he held the smile.

I wanted to tell him I'd go easy for him, but after Kurt refused, I knew he'd act like I thought he couldn't take it. So I didn't say anything, just pushed in real slow, listening to his breathing, gauging when he was ready for another push.

Real slow and easy, back and forth, I eased my dick through his sphincter, until we were breathing together, Arthur and I—God! how beautiful he was!—and then I started picking up speed. Behind us, we could hear them slurping and sucking, and then John hollering, and I knew he was coming in Scott's mouth. But I was concentrating on Arthur, on filling his butt-hole with me.

And it felt great, knowing I had power to hurt Arthur, but taking him just to the edge and bringing him back. I was in control, my elbows under Arthur's knees, pumping into him, pumping *with* him, knowing that I was bringing him pleasure, that he was liking this. He was grunting with it, picking up his cock and holding it, and then dropping it before he made himself come.

Together we rocked faster and faster, me inside him, in-side Arthur—he was so beautiful, I needed to touch the little curls of hair around his nipples. . . .

And when I did, suddenly I was coming—I couldn't turn back—I picked him up—I thrust deeper into him—he grabbed his cock, giving it two hard strokes, and exploded with me, splashing and spurting hot white cream all over his chest while I shot into him, all the time going, *"Ah! aah! uhng!"*

We sat on the rug then watching Scott go wild. He'd just sucked off John, and now he was sitting on the floor, sucking on Kurt's rod, licking his balls, sniffing and slurping and tast-ing, all the while madly jerking on his cock. His fist was a blur. Kurt stood over him, leaning against John's knees, getting him-self serviced. When Scott started to come, he lifted his buttocks off the floor and rubbed his face into Kurt's dick and balls while hot white lava burst up into the air and cascaded down his fist again.

Kurt still wanted him to suck, but Scott was out of breath. Arthur walked on his knees over to them, smiling and laughing, squeezing Scott's balls and slapping his back. He pushed his tongue down Scott's throat, making out with him between John's legs, feeling with his hand along John's thigh to his spent balls and the great, top-heavy thick hose that lay there.

But I met his warm fingers on that hot sausage—I claimed it with my hand.

Fucking Arthur, I had a feeling of power I'd never felt before. But I knew what else I wanted. So I said, "Arthur, you had two rides already." I already had a condom in my hand, and I held it up for John. He grinned and reached up for it. *"Yeah,"* he said, and I felt his meat lurch and swell, like a python.

Arthur looked at me, puzzled, as he and Scott scooted out of John's legs, and I straddled his lap. I thought, *He didn't expect this from "the kid."*

My legs were slung over John's thighs, my asshole hanging out over empty space. He was smiling, and I started sucking on his tongue while I played with his cock and made it grow and expand and lengthen—and *lengthen!*—and harden, turning into that stone-hard tower that Scott couldn't get all the way in his mouth.

God! I never had anything up my ass before, and this was bigger than I thought a cock could be. I rolled the rubber down the shaft—it was a snug fit. I slathered lubricant all over it, and with his hand under me, John slopped it all over my butt and slid a finger in and out of my hole. That finger felt so good, thick on his massive hand, like a screwdriver handle—but it was a pencil compared to the pole between his legs.

Then he picked me up—he put his hands under my armpits and picked me up and lowered me onto his monolithic dong. I grabbed it in my hand and aimed for my hole. . . .

And sat on it like a barstool. There was no way it was going inside me. Especially not holding myself in that position, with my asshole clenched tight.

John put me down on the rug, made me lie flat, and gently had me roll over.

Lying on my stomach, I felt his hot weight over me, his cock heavy between my ass cheeks. Heavy and thick and hot, his cock moved back and forth while his tongue licked the back of my neck, my ear.

Hoarsely, he whispered: "I want to go inside you," and I felt every muscle in my body relax. I lay there then, with his breath on my neck and ear, his hamlike chest on my shoulder blades, his knees between mine, pushing them wider, and the head of his dick, heavy and hot, leaning against my butthole.

"Hmm," I nodded, and he pushed it in. . . .

It was like expensive vodka, so smooth going down, you don't feel it till it hits your belly.

Then—God, I felt torn in two. Like shitting a big load, only going in instead of coming out. But also—I was full of the biggest man I'd ever imagined, and John was breathing "Feels *good*" into my ear, just that: "Feels *good*," like he really meant it, like I'd never heard him mean anything before.

And I thought, *Yeah, it feels good. . . . I feel good,* and I let myself *be* my ass filled with John, filled to bursting. I just existed as an extension of my sphincter relaxed to its limits around John's cockhead.

And then, slowly, he started to slide back and forth, pushing it farther in and then pulling almost all the way out. It felt great and at the same time it was excruciating, yet it was *total*—total John, with his unbelievably humongous dick sliding into me, farther and farther, until I was taking the whole thing. This was the most *total* thing I've ever done—and I've trashed military installations.

And then there were knees in front of my face. Kurt was kneeling, and then he sat so that his balls almost touched the floor, banging my chin, his dick in my eye, silently demanding I blow him.

I opened my mouth and let Kurt slide in till he gagged me, while John slid up my ass. Above me, I heard Kurt sucking John's grunts out of his mouth. Trapped under John's weight, stuffing my mouth with Kurt till my nose pressed his scrub of golden bush, I sucked on that rod and opened my bowels for John, until he started moaning and thrusting like a steam engine, and I came with him, spurting into the rug, and pulling Kurt's dick all the way into my throat.

I didn't show up at the group for about a month. When I did, I wore a T-shirt that said "Silence = Death," and brought a boyfriend, this kamikaze I met at Act Up. Arthur didn't like us recruiting members for the group by bringing in lovers, but this guy had a plan to smuggle experimental AIDS drugs into the country, so I just ignored what Arthur might think. The guy fit right in.

Nobody called me "the kid," either.

Kurt didn't swagger as much as he used to. I know that when he fucked each one of us, or got us to suck him off (he'd already had both Janice and Red—but so had Arthur), he thought he'd be the big man all of a sudden.

But Arthur, who lay back and let everyone plow him, one at a time, everyone respected him more than ever. We were in awe. He is *the,* fucking, total, ultimate anarchist of all time.

And all I have to do is dare him, and he rolls over and lets me screw him whenever I want.

GOOD

WITH

WORDS

LAST NIGHT I DREAMED I WENT BACK TO THE MINE-shaft. I knew I had come home even before entering the unmarked door and climbing the flight of stairs to pay my $5. Outside, on the sidewalk—where I'd sometimes linger and survey the street action that was often hot enough to induce me to skip the bar entirely—I savored the exhaust that was being sucked out of the bar's downstairs suite by powerful, industrial fans. Beer, piss, poppers, leather, sweat—the smells blended into a perfume more reassuringly familiar than the Bal à Versailles I remember from my mother's dressing table.

The first beer at the upstairs bar was just a formality. I gulped it down and immediately asked the tattooed bartender for another, the second one to sip—a prop, really, to keep my hands occupied until something better came along. Inside, a typical evening was under way: someone in the sling, ingeniously concealing someone else's arm up to the elbow; onlookers rapt, then moving on casually, to survey some of the other attractions that were taking form in the shadows; assorted human undergrowth here and there, some of it inert and some gently undulating like deep-sea flora. On the platform toward the back, a tall, blond man was getting blown. I stood nearby for a while and watched—evaluating his musculature with a touch, scrutinizing his gestures for a flaw in that impeccable attitude, observing the degree to which his arched posture expressed a belief in this kind of recreation—then I turned and went downstairs.

I always spit in the back stairway, as a sort of a ritual of purification, I suppose. Below, things were steamier and I adjusted my fly accordingly. The piss room was packed, unnavigable with dense clumps of flesh around each tub and growing outward from the corners. So noting who was doing what, I passed along the edge of it all, slowly, as if in a dream—which it was, of course—though even when it wasn't, back when the Mineshaft was open, it all seemed to be. A wet dream; some kind of prenatal fantasy, dark and sheltered; bathed in the music the management knew was perfect for down there, slowish, hazy waves of taped sound that always struck me as exactly what music would sound like if heard from inside the womb; a dream engulfed, as the evening built to its climax, by the fluids—no, the tides—of life itself.

I walked past the posing niche and entered the club's farthest recess, the downstairs bar. There, on his knees, was Paul. Known more widely than seemed possible as The Human Urinal, Paul had installed himself in one of his favorite spots for the early part of an evening, a relatively open and well-lighted place that invited inspection but did not permit extended scenes. Paul moved around, you see. As an evening progressed he would migrate to increasingly more auspicious locations until, around dawn, you would probably find him in what was by then a hub of the Mineshaft's hardest-core action, the upstairs men's room, where he planted himself efficiently, mouth gaping, eyes glazed, between the two nonhuman fixtures.

How I admired that man and his dedication! What fun we would have in the old days, both here and with the straight boys at the Hellfire Club! Paul is immobile as I pass, but I see by his slowly shifting eyes that he knows I've arrived. And he's

glad: even in the dark I sense that his pupils have dilated a
fraction when he notices I'm carrying a can of beer. I raise it
slightly in his direction in a kind of toast. He understands. I
stop for a moment opposite him, the constant flow of men
between us. Then, because I feel I should follow through with
a sympathetic gesture, I bring the can to my lips while pissing,
almost incidentally, in my jeans.

I don't look down, of course, but I know that a dark patch
has appeared at the top of my right thigh. And I know that
Paul sees it, too—but since manners are everything in affairs
of the heart, we smile no acknowledgment. Burping unceremoniously, I move off toward the bar. . . .

I was intending to return to Paul after getting another
beer, but then I woke up. A garbage truck was roaring outside
my bedroom window and the dream was over.

Later that day I called my friend Albert, with whom I'd visited
the Mineshaft on occasion. When I mentioned my dream he
was unimpressed.

"Of course you're dreaming about the place, puss. It's
because you can't go there anymore. What other options *do* we
have nowadays for handling our genius, we who have dared to
build a world that allowed us to encounter it repeatedly?"

It was like Albert to use the word *genius* that way, with
overtones of "essential spirit," even "demon." Albert's good
with words, which he says is lucky. He's one of those people
who seems able to enjoy exchanging them during sex almost as
much as he did those fluids that are now forbidden. Albert
sighed, and added that we should be thankful to have glimpsed
"the golden age."

We discussed some of the old faces. It turns out that he'd
been talking to the real Paul, whom I hadn't run into for quite
some time. I was surprised to learn that my fastidious friend
actually once traded phone numbers with the Human Urinal
and recently has been indulging in a bit of phone J.O. with
him. It was "nothing kinky," Albert insisted. "We just chat
for hours like schoolgirls, about choking bodybuilder cops with

the severed penises of their teenage sons. What could be safer than that?"

I was happy to hear that Paul is still kicking. In fact, I was relieved, since it won't do to make assumptions anymore about people we used to see around. Yeah, Paul always maintained that he was exclusively oral, never anal, but the fact is that none of us is sure whether that or any particular limit is enough to guarantee someone's safety under present conditions. Wasn't one of Paul's favorite numbers, after all, to beg feverishly for "clap dick," and to revel in the disgust this elicited from many men who took him literally? I don't know— maybe the request was meant literally; since gonorrhea was so readily curable, it never seemed to matter much. It was strange, I know, but I realized when talking to Albert how fond of Paul's creative perversity I'd become, how much I missed his "genius" in a way that would be difficult to explain to someone who'd never experienced firsthand the catalytic charm of old-fashioned sex clubs.

I knew Paul slightly. Though not a chatty sort he would sometimes expose a portion of his outside persona to me, especially if a biographical detail or two could help add luster to a scene we were building. He was thirty-five, the only child of Polish immigrant parents who were now retired. He lived alone in a tenement on the Lower East Side and was involved with a man he called his lover, a man who also had a live-in girlfriend. All three—Paul, lover, girlfriend—were somehow involved in big real-estate deals and would often go jetting off for weekends in Europe or North Africa, though it was clear that Paul himself was not in the lucrative end of the business, since he spoke of having to take occasional jobs waiting on tables. Thin and darkly handsome, Paul was nonetheless at pains to downplay his appearance. I remember his pride when he arrived at the bar one night with a new haircut, a brutishly uneven head-shave that he said with a grin made him look "even more" like a survivor of Auschwitz.

I was a little apprehensive about seeing this man again. Sure, I had gradually come to understand his unspoken language and to sense how far his attraction to dangerous things really went. But the world has changed. Who knew what mischief he might be up to these days, what I might have to frown upon sternly, what I might even find myself somehow drawn into doing? Yet things have been *so* dry lately, I whined to Albert. Could it do any harm to just *talk?* Albert laughed as he gave me Paul's number.

Paul was napping when I rang. A ballet gala the night before had kept him out until breakfast and he confessed he was still in his tuxedo pants. After we brought each other up-to-date (and admitted indirectly that our health was fine) he said he'd be happy to get together again, "to see what develops." Nothing was said about conditions—more, I think, because neither of us wanted to queer an incipient liaison with ill-timed reality-talk. We set a time for later that day. Paul suggested a secluded men's room on a downtown university campus. That's a good sign, I thought—if he's fooling around with those finicky college boys, he can't be too heedless.

When I arrived at the men's room I found a scene already in progress that would have seemed innocuous enough four or five years ago, but now, in the era of AIDS, took on a faintly unsettling quality. Paul and someone else had positioned themselves not in a stall but right out in the open, and they were talking about death.

The other guy, a bearded man in his forties whom I'd not seen before, was dressed in a beat-up leather jacket, no shirt, and a pair of those drab, baggy chinos that janitors wear. Out of his fly was hanging a cock that must be described as substantial as much for its apparent weight and density as for its obvious size. Semisoft and just at the point of unwrinkling, the thing had a thick, meandering vein down the top that looked more like an exhaust pipe than a detail of human anatomy. He was lighting a cigarette when I entered and seemed unconcerned that his twosome had just become a threesome. And he was wearing a wedding ring. Paul was kneeling in front of the guy, his head hung low, dressed only in a yellow-stained T-shirt and a pair of pulled-down sweatpants. After a moment I saw that his legs had been bound behind him with a length of rope, which struck me as risky, since someone else always could just walk in unannounced. His hands were tied, too, though in front of him, so he was able to reach and clumsily manipulate his cock. The room reeked of pine cleanser.

I'd entered during a short lull—or maybe they'd been waiting for me. Instantly I found myself shedding the everyday state of mind that allows us to do things like hold jobs and get through city traffic and assuming a more intuitive, timeless disposition that's much better suited to the consumption of pleasure. Respectfully I approached. Understanding that this wasn't the time for a kiss and introduction, I grunted for them to continue.

"I want it, okay?" Paul said. It was that low, trancelike monotone I remember.

"Yeah? You like this fucker?" The other guy handled himself appreciatively.

"Uh huh. I need it. Put it in my mouth?"

A pause. The other guy farted.

"Why do you need it?" he asked.

Paul did something obscene with his tongue.

Seeing that this was indeed going to work, I took out my own cock and began to pull on it. Already it felt pleasantly *intrusive*, like a complication worth solving. I couldn't have said exactly why, but there was something palpably right about our little scene, something perhaps reflected in subtle linguistic details like the register of Paul's voice and the rhythm of the other guy's responses, as well as in grosser ones like choice of vocabulary and subject matter. I know from experience that arranging these things is far from easy, and even after this preliminary exchange I understood perfectly why Paul had wanted me to meet this guy. The scene heated up rapidly.

"I live for that dick," said Paul, his gaze fixed on it.

"Then tell me about it, man. Let me hear it."

Paul's drone became more animated.

"Please, let me have your dick. Slip it into my head."

Then he looked up at the guy's face.

"I'll take your load, okay? Let me suck it out of you. I don't care if I get sick."

I guess that was what they both wanted to hear. The other guy narrowed his eyes.

"I don't give a fuck about you, cocksucker—I just wanna get off. You gonna eat my come?"

Paul nodded: "Anything."

Both were pumping faster.

"Okay, let me feel that pussy mouth on my meat. I'll feed you my fucking load and get out of this shithole."

"If I get sick . . .," Paul began.

"So you get sick," was the reply. "I guess you die, man."

And at that moment—or one like it, since I was too deeply engaged by all this bad-boy stuff to remember more than the drift of the dialogue—the three of us shot. I think we'd all been close for a while and we shot powerfully—me, off to the side, near the radiator; Paul, onto the floor in front of him, grazing my foot; the other guy, past Paul's shoulder and onto the wall and paper-towel dispenser. It took only a couple of minutes for us to button up, undo Paul and perform a thorough wordless cleanup. Then our guest silently signaled his farewell, pulling Paul toward him and grazing him on the cheek with an affectionate peck.

After he left I raised an eyebrow.

"I know," Paul said. "Sweet man."

"Who is he?" I asked.

"Just a man," was the answer.

As I stood drying my hands, I couldn't help thinking how dismal a conclusion a stranger would have drawn simply by reading a transcript of our encounter. And even if he'd been there himself, would a *Times* reporter or health-department official have understood how loving it all was? Or how safe? Paul and his friend must have agreed fairly explicitly, though in their own language, to stay within certain limits. They wanted to raise a little hell, anyway.

I winked at myself in the mirror. Well, boys, I thought, we did it.

Hearing that word "die" during sex did leave me feeling a little clammy, though. I've lost so many friends. So has Albert, I know, yet afterward he made light of my reservations.

"Isn't the best way to honor their memory to care for ourselves and the friends we've got left," he asked. "It sounds to me like the three of you were eminently careful. If you'd only invited me."

But using death in that way. It felt so . . . odd.

"Look," Albert explained, "is it really so different from the old days, when we used to talk about things like getting worked over by a gang of Nazi motorcycle Satanists? Death by gang rape is hardly more attractive than death from AIDS. Sex is theater, darling, even now. And words are only words, even if they do bring the big, bad world into the bedroom where we can play at controlling it."

When I equivocated, he grew stern.

"Stephen, if you can't tell the difference between talking about something and the thing itself, then you belong in a cave drawing bison on the wall."

I thought of that remark sometime later, when I attended a play at which I was seated two rows away from someone who was so stirred up by an onstage murder that he began talking violently back to the actors. . . .

CONTRIBUTORS

*"CLAY CALDWELL" is only one of the pen names of an author who, among other incidents in a checkered literary career, once wrote dialogue for Disney comic books—"but never for The Mouse," he insists. "Impossible to work with!" Beginning in the late 1960s he authored scores of pioneering porn paperbacks under a variety of pen names for imprints like Greenleaf, Pleasure Reader, and Surree, including *Lights Out, Little Hustler* by Lance Lester, *One in Every Closet* by Rod Hammer, and the Clay Caldwell classics *S&M Truckers, Pledge-Slave* and *Humpin' Hayloft Cousins*. Some of his other pen names include Lance La Fong, Thumper Johnson, and David E. Griffon. He now divides his time between running a small farm in southern California, volunteering at his local public library, and producing new stories under the Caldwell pen name.

*Quotation marks indicate a pseudonym.

PAT CALIFIA's erotic fiction includes lesbian, heterosexual, and gay male characters. Her book publications include short fiction *(Macho Sluts)* and a novel *(Doc and Fluff)*. For ten years, she's written "The Advisor" column for the *Advocate*. She has edited *Advocate MEN* and other erotic magazines. Very few things surprise her.

LARS EIGHNER is the author of *Bayou Boy and Other Stories* and *Lavender Blue: How to Write and Sell Gay Men's Erotica*. He has written for various skin magazines, as well as for *The Guide* and *The Advocate*. He is currently engaged in writing a memoir, *Travels with Lizbeth*, with reflections on homelessness, hitchhiking, the bonds between a man and his dog, scripting porn videos, and scavenging a living by dumpster diving; excerpts have appeared in *The Threepenny Review*.

STEPHEN GRECO is a senior editor of *Interview* magazine.

GORDON HOBAN grew up in Minnesota, lived in Los Angeles and New York City, and now resides in a not-as-remote-as-it-used-to-be wilderness valley in Hawaii. He was always an avid reader, but as he entered puberty he realized that nobody in the fiction he got from the library seemed to be thinking about sex as much as he did. He wrote scraps of stories about soldiers and sailors and prisoners to fill the gap. He left Minnesota to go to Hollywood. He wrote erotic work, at first using his pen name, Tom Hardy. The boyhood scraps grew into stories and finally books, including the best-selling *Adventures of a High School Hunk* and the play *Mainland*.

ANDREW HOLLERAN is the author of the novels *Dancer from the Dance* and *Nights in Aruba,* and of a book of essays, *Ground Zero*.

ALAN HOLLINGHURST was born in 1954. He read English at Magdalen College, Oxford, and subsequently taught there and at University College in London. He is now deputy editor of the *Times Literary Supplement*.

MICHAEL LASSELL is the author of two books of poetry: *Poems for Lost and Un-lost Boys*, the winner of the 1985 Amelia Chapbook competition, and *Decade Dance*, the winner of a Lambda Literary Award.

His poetry has been published widely in literary journals from *Fag Rag* to the *Kansas Quarterly* and in such anthologies as *Gay and Lesbian Poetry in Our Time, Poets for Life: 76 Poets Respond to AIDS,* and *High Risk.* His fiction was included in *Men on Men 3* and *Indivisible;* he also contributed to *Hometowns: Gay Men Write about Where They Belong.* He lives in New York City, where he is writing a novel.

BARRY LOWE is an Australian playwright who has had many of his plays produced in that country, most with a gay theme. He was the editor of *Campaign* magazine from 1981 to 1987. His short stories have been published in *Westerly, GLP, Now 9pm, Cargo, Campaign,* and others. He also wrote the notorious "Lowe-Life" column in the *Sydney Star* in the early eighties, which gave a humorous look to his and his lover's sex life.

ROBIN METCALFE abandoned a career as a sleeping-car porter for Canadian National Railways in 1985. Since then he has earned his livelihood writing art criticism and gay porn. He has edited several periodicals, including a gay and lesbian regional journal, a literary annual, and a crafts magazine. Over the years he has been Halifax, Nova Scotia's Official Homosexual, a two-time coverboy for the *Body Politic,* and a founding member of the Bad Boys Club. He likes to take his shirt off when he dances.

SCOTT O'HARA is a well-known porn star; his credits include *California Blue, Below the Belt,* and *Oversized Load.* He was raised on a farm in Oregon and aged in San Francisco. He has found perfect peace on a farm in Cazenovia, Wisconsin, and is working on reintegrating Spunk into his writing and his character. He has published in the *James White Review, Advocate MEN, Drummer, Opera in America, RFD,* and *Gay Community News.*

ANNE RICE was born in New Orleans, where she now lives with her husband, the poet Stan Rice, and their son, Christopher.

LEIGH RUTLEDGE is the author of *Gay Decades* and several other books. His stories and essays have been widely published in the gay press.

"D.V. SADERO," a former lifeguard and newspaper reporter, makes his living as a private investigator in San Francisco. He writes erotic fiction in his spare time. Much of his material comes from personal experience and the rest from asking half-drunk men in bars, "What's the weirdest sex you've ever had?"

STEVEN SAYLOR, under the pen name Aaron Travis, is the author of *Slaves of the Empire* and the former editor of *Drummer* magazine. Saylor's fiction and essays have appeared in the *San Francisco Bay Guardian*, *The Magazine of Fantasy and Science Fiction*, and the anthology *Hometowns: Gay Men Write about Where They Belong*. His current big project is a series of historical novels about ancient Rome, beginning with the mystery *Roman Blood*, about Cicero's first murder trial.

SAMUEL M. STEWARD received his Ph.D. in literature from Ohio State University. After an academic career including positions at Loyola and DePaul Universities and contributing to the *World Book* encyclopedia, he decided he would rather be a tattoo artist. He set up shop in Chicago as Phil Sparrow. He had written two well-received novels in his youth, but had left writing behind even earlier than he abandoned academia. Steward invented the pen name Phil Andros and went about creating the body of work that has inspired modern gay writers. He also went on to write mystery novels under his own name; the mysteries feature Gertrude Stein and Alice B. Toklas, with whom Steward had been close friends. He is still writing, now living in Berkeley, California.

W. DELON STRODE was born in McMinnville, Tennessee, near Nashville. He moved to Chicago in 1989 to pursue his dreams of becoming a journalist and found himself, within a year, a contributing editor of *Thing*, Chicago's underground 'zine of art, literature, and music.

LARRY TOWNSEND lives in Los Angeles with his lover of twenty-eight years. Since publishing *The Leatherman's Handbook* in 1972, he has continued to contribute a steady stream of leather/S&M novels, short stories, and articles. His most recent work is a suspense novel, *Masters' Counterpoint*.

JOHN WAGENHAUSER has at various times been a computer programmer, born-again Christian, and member of Act-Up. He has published in *Diseased Pariah News, Mandate, Out/Look,* the *Advocate's Fresh Men, Reactor,* and has been a regular contributor to *Body Positive.* He grew up on Long Island, spent the eighties in Manhattan, and currently lives with his lover of twelve years in San Francisco, where he continues to work on his novel, *Lives of the Saints.*

EDMUND WHITE teaches creative writing at Brown University. He is working on a biography of Jean Genet. He is the editor of the *Faber Anthology of Gay Short Fiction.*

T. R. WITOMSKI used to write for a truly amazing range of scurrilous magazines. Moving up in the world, he now, as the owner of Katsam Productions in Toms River, New Jersey, sells a truly amazing range of scurrilous videos. He is the author of *Kvetch* and—get this— writes regularly for *Operascene* magazine. He enjoys remarking rudely about those scumbags at Burroughs Wellcome. His performance as Fricka in the 1992 Bayreuth Festival production of *Der Ring des Nibelungen* is sure to cause a sensation.

ROY F. WOOD died of complications due to AIDS in 1986. His published works include *Reckless Rednecks: Gay Tales of a Changing South, Seth,* and numerous stories in *Drummer, First Hand, Mandate,* and many other magazines. His science-fiction novel *The Long Exile,* two mystery novels, and another volume of short stories will be forthcoming over the next several years. A longtime resident of Athens, Georgia, much of his writing dealt with the lives of gay men in rural America with rare sensitivity and understanding.

334

THE BIG GAY BOOK
A MAN'S SURVIVAL GUIDE FOR THE 90s

BY JOHN PRESTON

Here is an indispensable guide to finding goods, services, organizations, and everything else essential to a rich and exciting life. From information about the best places for gay men to live, to AIDS and health services, to fun facts about ordering hard-to-find videos or joining a gay band, editor John Preston has provided a wealth of specific, up-to-date information about where to find everything for and about gay men in the United States and Canada today.

"A handy resource for anyone interested in the gay movement today ... Comprehensive, concise and literate."
—URVASHI VAID, Executive Director, National Gay and Lesbian Task Force

Plume Softcover Edition: $14.95 U.S., $19.99 Canada (0-452-26621-1)

Buy them at your local bookstore or use this convenient coupon for ordering.